12x (8/10)12/11

D0198110

PRAISE FOR

THE
GYPSY MAN

"Robert Bausch's new novel has all the makings of a good blue-grass song; men in trouble with the law, lonesome women, hard times, tattered dreams.... Riveting."
— *The New York Times Book Review*

"Being inside the minds of these characters is an experience so intimate that this becomes one of those rare books that not only sees you through unbearable losses, it almost blinds you with love."
— *O, The Oprah Magazine*

"Affecting. Moves smoothly and unpredictably. Bausch [writes] with consummate style."
— *The Washington Post Book World*

"Bausch...has that rare ability to see past the obvious in the human condition and has an even rarer ability to put that vision on the page.... That he does so with such caring for his characters and attention to his story is a testament to his skills as a novelist and his heart as a human being."
— *The Denver Post*

CARMEL VALLEY LIBRARY
3919 TOWNSGATE DRIVE
SAN DIEGO, CA 92130

DEC 2 6 2008

"Reaches chilling moments of real pity and real terror as tragedy stalks up the mountain to Crawford."
— *The Washington Times*

"Striking... An exceptional novel." — *Library Journal*

"A small Virginia mountain community in the late 1950s is the setting for this vivid and heartrending tale of dreadful accidents, fear, guilt, heroism and redemption by the author of *A Hole in the Earth*... A thrilling read." — *Publishers Weekly*

"Powerful and pervasive and riveting right up to the surprising end. A truly memorable tale of horror and hope." — *Booklist*

CARMEL VALLEY LIBRARY
9 EL CAMINITO
CARMEL VALLEY, CA

DEC 2 0 2020

THE
GYPSY MAN

THE
GYPSY MAN

ROBERT BAUSCH

SAN DIEGO PUBLIC LIBRARY
CARMEL VALLEY BRANCH

A HARVEST BOOK · HARCOURT, INC.

Orlando Austin New York San Diego Toronto London

3 1336 08027 0912

Copyright © 2002 by Robert Bausch

All rights reserved. No part of this publication may be reproduced or
transmitted in any form or by any means, electronic or mechanical,
including photocopy, recording, or any information storage and retrieval
system, without permission in writing from the publisher.

Requests for permission to make copies of any part of the work
should be mailed to the following address: Permissions Department,
Harcourt, Inc., 6277 Sea Harbor Drive, Orlando, Florida 32887-6777.

www.HarcourtBooks.com

Library of Congress Cataloging-in-Publication Data
Bausch, Robert.
The gypsy man/Robert Bausch.—1st ed.
p.   cm.
ISBN 0-15-100172-3
ISBN 0-15-602873-5 (pbk.)
1. Mothers and daughters—Fiction. 2. Prisoners' families— Fiction.
3. Prisoners' spouses—Fiction. 4. Prisoners—Fiction.
5. Virginia—Fiction.   I. Title.
PS3552.A847 G97 2002
813'.54—dc21   2002005649

SAN DIEGO PUBLIC LIBRARY
CARMEL VALLEY BRANCH

Text set in Minion
Designed by Cathy Riggs

Printed in the United States of America

First Harvest edition 2003
A C E G I K J H F D B

To Betty and Skip Franzen,
who always know where the sunlight is,
and never curse the rain...

I am grateful to Sara Mason Miller, colleague and friend, who told me of the legend long ago; to Don Frantz for the best twelve years of my teaching life and for finding the stone; to Walt Bode who knows the truth of it, always and usually before I do; to Bill Miller, at George Mason University and to the creative writing faculty there, for support and faith I had no right to expect; and finally, again as always, I am grateful to Denny, who allows me the time to write by taking care of everything else . . .

Come away, O human child!
To the waters and the wild
With a faery, hand in hand,
For the world's more full of weeping than you
    can understand.

—FROM "THE STOLEN CHILD" BY W. B. YEATS

THE
GYPSY MAN

BOOK 1

PENNY

At the top of this mountain, where clouds are neighbors, you can see everything clear—close up or miles and miles away. The air is colder somehow and don't get hazy too often. From the back porch of my cabin I can see the white stone all the way across the yard. Maybe it's always been there, but it never meant so much until now. It was just a stone for a long time. Yesterday, my little girl found lettering on it.

I didn't mind it when it was just a white stone. It looked like a small piece of paper, sticking up out of the brown dirt. I remember one time I pointed it out to John and I said, "Look, it's like the mountain has a broke bone sticking out of it."

And John says, "What's that my daddy's always saying? 'Ain't no Bone ever broke. We bend. We don't break.'" He smiled, give a short laugh. You see that was John's last name: Bone. He used to be my husband.

I always liked to sit next to him in the evening and just talk. That day I leaned my head on his shoulder and just concentrated on the smell of him, on the curve of his arm. I don't remember if I knew already he was going.

"Seems funny for my daddy to be saying that, don't it?" he says.

John's father was a drunkard. And still is. Nothing else. He's under the care of a bottle.

I said, "You worried about him again?"

"Worrying about a thing don't change it," he says. "But if there ever was a broke Bone, he's it."

We was married only a few months when John got taken off. It seems like just yesterday. But it was a long time ago. And even though he said that about no Bone ever being broke and all, I wonder sometimes what's happened to him. I never see him, never talk to him. But John was about as solid as anyone I've ever known. It took me a year or two to speak of him in the past tense. Tory don't even remember him, and she's six going on seven. He ain't dead or nothing, but he may as well be. Plain as day.

I try not to think about John, but I see the light of him in Tory's eyes. The way she flashes scorn or pity, or when she laughs or teases me, or gets stubborn and can't say nothing but no—it's John in her eyes.

But like I said, John is gone. When they took him away he says, "I'm dead to you, and you got to be dead to me."

"I can't," I said. I wasn't crying, but it took all I had. I couldn't resist his will, too. "I can't think of you dead when I know you're alive."

"I ain't alive," he says. "I ain't alive again, honey, for twenty years."

"I'll wait then," I said.

"No," he says. "You ain't."

He wanted me to divorce him, but I wouldn't do it. I said, "Why let the state in on that, too?"

"In on what?"

"On our vows. Our betrothment."

Now I was being stubborn. Tory just a baby in my arms, and the state takes John away from me, for twenty years. He spends all his days and nights at a place called Richard Bland. It's a prison, in case you don't know. I ain't seen him in almost six years. I miss him sometimes, but not nearly as bad as I did in the beginning. You might think I'm only saying that, but it's true.

He's going to be there another fourteen years, so I don't see no point in pining over him. It is sad, though, because he was really innocent. Oh, he done what he done, but he didn't mean to. It was just an accident. But he got charged with manslaughter, anyway, and now my daughter is fatherless, as I was.

My father died in the war. Got killed in France, I'm told, although it might've been anywhere over there, as far as I know. I was eleven years old. When I was fifteen, I met John, and by the time I was seventeen I married him and give birth to Tory.

We been together, just her and me and my aunt Clare, since they took John away. We done all right, I guess. Clare runs the store and cooks for us—and sometimes I cook. I'm teaching Tory to cook a little bit, and she helps me with the wash, sometimes. On Saturdays I work in the Goodyear Tire and Auto Store. Just a clerk, you know, but sometimes I help with the ciphering and keeping the books and all. Mr. Henderson, the manager of the store, says one day he might send me to school to learn secretarial work. Or maybe even manager's school. Goodyear's got a program, he says. I don't know about being a manager, though. It's enough chasing Tory around.

We do all right. Clare says I got a big insurance check when my daddy died, and we're spending it in small pieces. "I pay us a little bit out of it every month or so," she says. "You'll still have most of that money when I'm dead and gone." It's supposed to be fifty thousand dollars. I ain't never seen the account but I know what the policy said. It's in a trust fund. And Clare makes a little at the store, and I bring home my checks from the Goodyear Company. It ain't like we're starving or nothing, but sometimes I wish Clare wanted more. More than just another man to run around with.

She's gone off again.

I was sitting out in the backyard after dinner last night when Tory found the lettering on the stone.

I asked her how she found it, and she says, "I seen it."

"But how?" I said.

She shrugged. "I don't know."

"Was you digging around it?"

"A little."

"And ain't I told you not to go digging in the mud around that stone and getting your hands dirty?"

She come up the steps and sat down next to me. "Look at my hands," she says. She held them out flat in front of me.

"Turn them over," I said. "Let me see your nails."

She clasped her hands together and put them between her knees. "My nails are fine," she says.

"Let me see."

"No."

"Well, you'll just have to wash them again before you go to bed."

"I ain't."

"We'll just see."

After a while, even with Tory sitting next to me and chattering about the stone, I felt kind of lonely and sad. It seemed like the air I inhaled could spread out anywhere in my body, and make me cold and afraid at the same time. I can't explain it. I wanted a car to come. Somebody I knew to get out and visit for a spell. Maybe a car with my aunt Clare in it. She's been gone this time for almost three weeks. Even for her, that's a long time without letting me know where she is, or when she might come back. Course, I don't blame her for wanting to get away from Crawford.

Crawford ain't much of a town—no bigger than a city park, even though it does have a sawmill, a post office, a fire station, and, of course, the brand-new Goodyear Tire and Auto Store where I work. I don't just work there, though. I always help my aunt Clare in her little grocery store. She's owned and operated that store all her life. I think she got it from her father. I don't know for sure. People say the store run a lot more smoothly before the war, and when Clare was younger and had the help of my father. Now, it runs when I'm there and when Clare feels like it.

Crawford's got a school, too. It's not a real school—it's a big house. Mr. Gault, the mayor, lives there with Myra, his wife, and does the town's business in a white room off his den. He's got a lot of flowers and tall, green umbrella plants and ferns in there for some reason—it looks like a funeral parlor most of the time. I like the smell in there, though. The school is in his basement. He's got five small rooms down there, with maps, blackboards, tables and chairs, like you'd see in any school. Tory goes there now, just like I did until a few years ago. Mr. Gault is the principal and his wife, Myra, teaches classes, too. And there always used to be another woman or two that he called the "faculty," but lately it's just him and his wife. Gault was my only teacher most of the time.

People might get the impression that this here's a lazy place, but it ain't. People work even whenever they don't feel like it and always if they can find work to do. We got no factories or department stores or auto dealers—although the tire store sometimes sells a used car or two if it becomes available. All we got is the mill and that don't provide near the work it used to. It's almost finished, too, I guess. My aunt Clare's tiny market does okay because folks don't like to drive down the mountain if they don't have to. She keeps bread and milk and butter and cheese and a few vegetables and such. Now and then she has dried meats or cured ham. I live with her across the way from the store and up the hill just before you get to the old Crawford place. Aunt Clare took in my daddy and me when my mother died, and we just stayed there until he went off to war. My mother died before I had any kind of memory of her, so I guess you could say that Clare's been like a mother to me, although it really don't feel like any such thing. Especially now, since she's gone off and disappeared again.

The old Crawford place used to be huge—and rich folks lived there. Like I said, that's how the town come to be called Crawford. People was always going up there looking for buried treasure or family valuables, digging up every square inch of the place just about. Or trying to. It's mostly rock up there, with just little dirt and moss growing over it. Ain't hardly nothing left of the place now. And Crawford itself? Nowadays, it ain't nothing but small farms in this part of Virginia. Small, poor farms. This ain't like the foothills. It's a mountain, high and rocky. You could stand on our front porch and shoot a .22 shell into West Virginia. If anybody could play the piano in that state, you could hear it. It snows three times more here than in Washington, D.C., which is where I come from. My father brought me here, and then when the war come he went off and died.

I guess Clare will come back, but I wonder sometimes what will happen if one day she don't. I mean, would the store and the cabin belong to me?

To be honest, I really don't want it.

I want Clare to come back. I shouldn't worry about her. She drinks a lot sometimes, and runs around with truckers and all. Just she never done it without telling me she was going to. "I'm going to be with this fella," she'll say. "I'll be seeing you soon." The longest she ever stayed away was two weeks. That was when I was in my last year at Gault's school, and she was beginning to notice that a lot of people she known and run with was getting old. That's what she said. "All my friends are getting old, honey." Like it wasn't happening to her. She's still a beautiful woman. She keeps her hair dyed jet-black, and lets it fall down her shoulders like I do. She don't look so young no more, but when she puts makeup on you might think she was a movie star. In the winter she was always fanning herself, complaining of the heat—even in the morning when the cabin had frost on the windows. The last time she disappeared, she was gone only three days, but I worried about her then, too, and she *told* me she was going.

I wouldn't worry this time except for two things. One is, she's been gone for almost a month now. I guess it was the end of July when she never come up the hill from the market, and I looked out the window and noticed she'd closed the door and put the CLOSED sign up. The second thing is Tory found that lettering on the stone in the back corner of the yard. When she told me about it, I was playing hide-and-seek with her in the twilight, you know, just having fun (we hide together—ain't nobody looking for us), when she turned to me and says, "Don't you want to know what the lettering says?"

"What lettering?"

She got down on her knees and brushed dirt and grass away from it.

"What you got there, Tory?"

"Lookit," she says. "Writing." She's right smart for six, and she wears jeans like me, but she is very serious for her age. She touched the stone. "It's so white."

"Come on now," I said. "Don't get yourself dirty."

She started digging around the edges of it.

"Don't be digging holes now," I said. "Look at your fingernails."

"I don't care about my fingernails," she says.

"Well, I do."

"Look," she says. "See the writing?"

"Get away from that old stone," I said. "I don't care what the writing says."

Sure enough, she had uncovered enough of the surface of the stone that I could see the letters I N M. Plain as day.

Tory got up and brushed her hands on her shorts. She got this look on her face, like she remembered something awful.

"What's the matter," I said. "Tory?"

She was looking at the stone, but then she turned her face to me and says, "Is this a gravestone?"

"I don't know," I said. "What if it is?" I couldn't tell if she was playing or if something really bothered her. I watched her face for a while, but she just stopped looking back at me. She studied the stone, then started picking around the edges of it again. She dug part of the dirt out of the way and she started pulling at it. It didn't move a single stitch. She may as well have been pulling the corner of a buried building.

"Come on, honey," I said. "Let's go on inside. It'll be dark soon."

"I can dig it up," she says. She pulled at it some more.

"Whatever that is, it's too big to dig up."

"Why can't I try?"

I leaned over and grabbed the sleeve of her T-shirt. "Up, girl. Up out of there."

She stamped her foot when she was upright. Then she folded her arms across the front of her, tucked her chin real close to her chest, and said, "Okay, then I'm just a tree."

She's always doing that. That's when I see the flash of her daddy's eyes and know even if I *was* his widow, I'd really still have a part of him. Sometimes when she gets mad at me, she just claims to be some solid thing that can't be moved. Or she'll say she's a small, fragile thing that will break if you touch it. One time she told me she was an egg. Sat in the kitchen chair, curled up with her arms wrapped around her knees, and didn't say nothing for one and a half hours. Swear to God. When I realized she was serious, I went in the bedroom and had myself a peaceful nap and thanked God for stubborn children. Eventually she moved, I asked her what happened, and she says, "I hatched." We both had a good laugh over that one. Then she had so much energy, you'd of thought I give her a whole bottle of Geritol, so I had to pay for my nap.

When she become a tree, I said, "You're going to have to be a tree inside," but she wouldn't speak to me or move.

"Come on, honey," I said. "The sun's starting to set. It's going to get awful chilly."

I waited there for a spell, then reached for her. She backed away. "You can't be a tree in a house," she says.

"You can be a child, though." I smacked her lightly on the behind, and she run to the back porch and up the steps. But she didn't go inside. She stood there looking sad. "It's still light out, Mommy."

I come up the steps in front of her. "Go on," I said. "Inside."

"It's still light out," she says. "The summer's almost over." I hated the sound of her voice when she whined like that.

"I can't stop that from happening," I said. "It's going to end no matter what we do tonight."

"It's still light out," she says again. I swear, sometimes her voice echoes in my sinuses.

"Quit whining," I said.

She folded her arms. She didn't have to announce that she was a tree again. I went in the house and come back out with a book and one of the folding chairs from the kitchen. "Well," I said. "I'm just going to make myself comfortable under the spreading branches of this here tree."

"I just want to stay out a little longer," she whimpered. I didn't actually hear those words, but I knew where the record was stuck.

I set the chair right in front of her and set down with my back to her. "Mmmm," I said. "It's so cool under this tree."

It was quiet for a spell. I pretended to read the book. Then she laughed. I stood up and she grabbed my legs and pretty soon I was laughing, too. We've always had fun like that, even when we're mad at each other. I sat down on the steps, pulled her down next to me. "We'll set here a spell," I said. I held onto her until it was almost dark, and she forgot about the stone.

But I didn't. I dreamed about it all night—dreams I can't even remember now. I just know it was there, in my sleep, floating around like something white under water.

Tory, though, she loves just setting on the porch with me, when the sun's about to sink behind the trees. We done it almost every night this past summer, so tonight, we go out there and sit down again, and she looks up at me and frowns.

"I ain't talking about that stone," I say.

She just stares at me, pouting.

"What?" I say.

"Tell me about Daddy."

She's always asking me about him. And I'm always trying not to lie to her. "Your daddy ain't here," I say.

"Why not?"

"He just ain't."

"Where is he?"

"He's someplace else." I look over at the stone again, the white tip jutting out of the dark earth in the shadow of the tree. With the sun dropping down between the peaks, the stone looks like it has its own light to give.

"Is he in jail?"

I search her serious eyes. "Who told you that?"

"Jail's someplace else, ain't it?"

"Who told you he was in jail?"

"Mr. Gault."

"He wouldn't do that," I say. "I asked him not to do that."

"I heard him talking," Tory says. "He didn't say it to me."

She looks out over the trees to the valley. The sun's weak evening light throws strange shadows against the far slopes and hillsides across from us. It's going to get much cooler soon. Tory has the most perfect skin and a lovely round little face. Her nose is small and tilted up slightly, like her daddy's nose. But her mouth is what stands out. A long, straight line from one cheek to the other when she's just thinking, and it looks like that's all there is, but then you see the lips, just as long and straight and almost white—like she put on lipstick or something. When she smiles her eyes change shape, and you just feel her happiness in your heart.

"Your daddy is in a place called Richard Bland," I tell her.

"What's that?"

"It's a place where men go when they're in trouble."

"Jail?"

"It's a correctional facility," I say. "Can you say that?"

She doesn't answer.

"Say it," I insist.

She looks at me briefly, frowning. Then she says, "I don't want to."

"Well, that's where he is. That's where he'll be until you're full grown. So you may as well forget about him. That's what I done."

A dark frown crosses her face.

"That's what he told me to do."

She won't meet my eyes. After a while she says, "Correxshin fussily."

"Facility," I say.

"Fussilty."

"That's close enough."

"Correxshin fussilty."

"You may as well call it a jail, hon. Everybody else does."

We sit there for a while, watching the sun weaken. Then she says, "Why can't we see him?"

"Because it would make him miserable."

"Don't he like us?"

"That ain't it." I put my arm around her, pull her against me. "You know what it's like when you're real hungry and Aunt Clare makes you them brownies you love?"

"Yeah."

"And you know how it feels when she says you can't have one until supper? When she lets you look at them, but you can't have none?"

"It ain't fair," she says.

"That's right, at least it don't seem fair. And don't you hate it?"

"I sure do."

"Well, that's what it's like when your daddy sees me and can't really touch me. How he feels when he sees you and can't hold you in his arms. You see?"

"Does he like the way we smell?"

"What?"

"I love the way the brownies smell," she says.

I laugh and squeeze her a bit. I kiss the top of her head, breathe in the fragrance of her hair, loving her, thinking of my man all the way down there in Richard Bland.

"It ain't fair," I say. "You know, honey?"

She leans over my legs and puts her head in my lap.

"It really ain't fair," I say.

JOHN BONE

It's getting to be fall again. I can smell it in the air that leaks in through the thatched screen and bars on the window. I share the cell with a man named Parchman, who sleeps now in the bunk next to me. I sit up, staring out at the moon, which almost sparkles in the clear, cool sky. The light seems to emanate from there, like the moon is its own source of energy.

Time don't mean a thing in here. A day can seem like a man's whole life: you get born in the morning, and by midday you feel like you've grown up. By nightfall, you're an old man, exhausted and waiting for death.

When I first came here, I believed I deserved it. Now, after six years, I am beginning to think maybe no man deserves to live like this. It don't matter what you know—what's going on in your mind. You fill up with ideas and thoughts and things you'd like to say; things you've noticed or suddenly felt; memories that come back to you like sudden pains—like blood vessels bursting in your skull—and there ain't a person you can talk to. You just have to swallow everything, everything you think and feel. Just the idea of maybe getting out of here early—of walking out the front gate a free man—makes the whole carnival in your head almost too loud to bear.

I might write it all down someday. Who knows? I spend so much time just being silent, maybe a pen and some paper would let me empty out a little bit. But I could never write anything down in here. You've got to keep that stuff somewhere, and in here, ain't nothing your own. You can't let nobody in this place know what you're thinking, or what's happening inside. You live day after day, pretending to feel nothing. The only thing you let the others see is silence and rage.

Hell, most of the men in this place haven't laughed in my sight since I came here.

Parchman turns over and looks at me. "What the hell you doing?"

"I can't sleep," I say. "I'm staring at the moon."

He says nothing, but he lays there with his eyes open. He looks like a pale corpse. The moonlight casts shadows of the bars all around us. The whole gray cell looks like something that ought to be dripping water, and the bars make shadow stripes on the barren walls. It is quiet, except for the low murmur of a thousand men snoring. They sound a little bit like the crickets and cicadas at night—except it's a lower sort of whirring and buzzing.

Parchman says, "Well, I guess I can't sleep neither."

He is a short, balding man—round faced and kind of puffy around the middle. He isn't but thirty or so, though he seems older for the stubble that's always on his chin and jaw. He's from Norton, Virginia. A town not too far south of Crawford. He was a coal miner who couldn't find any other kind of work when the mines closed down, so he went into business for himself: robbing gas stations and grocery stores with another ex-miner called Peach.

A few weeks ago, Peach escaped. I was there, and I could've run, too, but I didn't. No, what I did, I saved a man's life.

We were out on the road gang, up near Charlottesville. Way up in the mountains along Route 30. Parchman ran, too—but they caught him the very next day. Peach got away. And now I think Parchman wishes he hadn't run. He only has two years left on his sentence—but that will sure change now. He's in trouble and he knows it.

Parchman has been in the same cell with me almost the whole time since I came to Richard Bland. It was in the first year of my sentence that the warden decided to double up in some cells. Like most of them, my cell was designed for one man, but they put two cots in it, and ever since then it has been the two of us. He's not really a bad fellow, if people leave him alone; if he's not forced to defend himself all the time. When I sit on my cot and he sits on his and faces me, we ain't but two feet or so apart. I can smell his breath. We might sit like that for hours and say nothing, and then sometimes he wants to talk.

"I'm a robber," he told me once. "Pure and simple." We were sitting on our bunks waiting to be counted before being taken down to supper. This was a few months before Peach escaped. Suddenly Parchman started talking. "Yep," he said. "Me and Peach robbed a lot of places. But that ain't the half of it where Peach is concerned."

I said nothing. We'd just come in after working all day on the road gang, and I was sitting back on my cot, up against the wall, trying to cool off.

"You wouldn't believe what I seen Peach do."

"That so?"

"No, sir. It ain't the least."

We were facing each other, but since I was scooted back on the cot, he had to lean forward a bit to whisper to me. All real conversations in a prison have to be whispered. Everything you do—and I mean *everything*—is witnessed by somebody. Peach had just been made a trustee a few days before we had this conversation, and I think it bothered Parchman some. He didn't like it. "A trustee," he said. "Can you believe it?"

"I don't know nothing about it," I said.

"I seen him kill a man," Parchman said.

"Really."

"He don't even think about it."

I was quiet. He looked over his shoulder, then leaned a little closer to me. "Ain't that what you done?"

"What?"

"Ain't it that you killed a man?"

"Who told you that?"

He straightened up a bit. "You did."

"No, I didn't."

"You said you was in here for manslaughter."

I forgot I'd said that. It was in one of our earlier talks. "Okay," I said.

"You did say that."

"Okay," I said again.

"I seen it done, but I never done it myself."

"It wasn't no man," I said.

He looked at me.

17

I put my knees up in front of me and leaned my head back against the wall.

"What was it?" he said finally.

"What was what?"

"That you killed."

Now I met his serious eyes. He really wanted to know. "I killed a Negro girl," I said. It felt just as bad to say that as it ever did. I knew it would never go away—the feeling that I had altered the basic structure of earth and time; something elemental and true, like hot and cold, or up and down, now had to include the simple cold, undisputable and unrevisable fact that I had killed a young girl.

"I don't like saying it, even to myself," I said. "I can't change it. And I *hate* that I can't change it."

He got real quiet. Then I said, "I don't want nobody else in this place to know about it, neither. You got that?"

"Sure," he said.

"I mean it."

"Absolutely," he said. "Why would I tell folks?"

"I don't know about that. I just know I won't take it kindly if you tell anybody."

"I won't."

"It's my business."

He was quiet for a minute, then he said, "Can I tell them that you committed manslaughter?"

I just stared into his eyes, and he waited there for me to answer. "Go ahead," I said. "If you have to tell them anything."

This seemed to please him. He was the only person—the only "inmate"—in that place I ever talked to, and I guess that was why I told him. He's not too smart, but he leaves me alone, except for those times when he wants to talk, so I am glad he's in here with me. It could have been Peach or one of the Shivs or Queers.

The Shivs will kill you for a cigarette, or if you aren't ready to let them play games with you. Sometimes the games are sexual, but I've heard they'll get just as much pleasure out of cutting little designs in your ass, or on the top of your shoulders, just to see how the scars come out. You feed those guys anything they want to avoid the knife. They're in for life, and they don't really care what happens to them or nobody else. They make shivs out of the carved and sharpened ends of spoons, forks, butter knives, or even bedsprings. They can stick a shiv up under your sternum, tickle the bottom tip of your heart, and with a cut no larger than a small fingernail, drain the blood out of it and kill you in a few seconds or less. Parchman says you'll be dead before your bones hit the floor.

The Queers just want sex, and they aren't afraid to let folks know it. If you're not careful, they'll be going at you. They come on to you when you're awake, and if you say no, I've been told, some of them will try you when you're sleeping. "They're like Santa Claus," Parchman said once. Then he sang the verse, "They know you when you're sleeping, they know you while you wake, they know if you've been bad or good, so be good for goodness' sake." The Queers don't often get violent, but they're sometimes pathetic, and frequently they're the ones most tortured by the shivs.

Parchman is slow, and backward, and he doesn't smell so good all the time, but he's normal. At least he's normal.

A FEW DAYS before Peach escaped, me and Parchman were in the mess hall and Peach came over and sat down next to me. I'd seen him out on the road gang many times over the years, had sometimes met his gaze during one of the shakedowns or head counts, but we almost never talked. When he sat down, Parchman said, "Hey Peach."

But Peach didn't even look at him. He leaned over my tin plate, then looked at me. "Well," he said. "We're from the same part of the country." His voice was high and soft. Almost a woman's voice. But his eyes were cruel, hard little black beads under gray-brown eyebrows. His face was square, and his front teeth stuck out a bit too far, but he looked like a crude version of Clark Gable. He was shorter than me, but not by much. He was a lot taller than Parchman, but he didn't look tall. He was stocky, built powerfully, so his arms had a lot of room for artwork. He had tattoos up and down both arms. They were odd-looking paintings of birds' wings and colored snakes that wound around each forearm and disappeared in the sleeve of his prison uniform. "Yes, sir," he said. "Me and you come from the same part of the country."

I didn't answer him.

"You from Crawford, ain't you?"

I was chewing a biscuit that I'd dipped in potato soup, but I nodded. When I looked at him, he smiled. He said he wanted to congratulate me for my crime. It made me sick, but I didn't say nothing. I kept eating.

Peach said, "You killed a nigger, right?"

Parchman looked at me, then away.

"Parchman tell you that?" I said.

He slapped me on the back. "A good killing if you ask me. I don't know how a man can go to prison just for that."

Jewell, a black prisoner, raised his head and looked at me. He was sitting in the segregated section of the Mess Hall, but he could hear me. I didn't know what to say. I stared at my food.

Parchman said, "I never did tell nobody." He almost whispered it.

"I'll be a son of a bitch," Peach said. "You ain't ashamed of it, are you?"

I said very clearly, "Yes. I am."

Jewell was still looking at me. I met his eyes and said, "Why don't you just go back to what you were doing?"

"You studying some shit?" Jewell said. "You looking for trouble, white boy?"

Parchman said, "We're all gonna be in trouble if you don't pipe down."

The Negro didn't say nothing, but he picked up his bowl and started sipping out of it. I turned to Peach. "And why don't you leave me the fuck alone?"

Peach squeezed the back of my neck. "Well, that's a hell of a thing to say, ain't it?"

Parchman said, "He don't mean nothing by it, do you, John?"

No one said nothing. Peach kept squeezing the back of my neck, his grip getting tighter and tighter. He stared at the side of my face.

"He's just trying to have his supper, ain't that right?" Parchman said.

One of the guards came over to the table. "Put your hands where they belong, Peach."

Peach put his hands down in his lap. He kept staring at the side of my face, and I kept on eating. The guard, a man named McCarthy, stood there for a while. I looked at him and nodded a kind of thank-you. He nodded and moved off to the side wall.

I liked McCarthy, and so did most of the other prisoners. He always kept things peaceful, and he didn't feel the need to use his club. On the road, he never even carried a rifle half the time. He knew how to handle men without cruelty. He was the only guard in that place that I trusted.

"Well," Peach said. "Well, well, well."

I didn't say nothing, and I didn't look at him.

"I used to go looking for treasure up at that old Crawford place," he said. "Used to dig around up there."

I took a sip from the soup.

"Never found nothing though."

"Nobody else ever did neither," I said.

Peach turned to me. "You ever been up to the old Craw-ford place?"

I sipped my soup.

"You know, that great plantation that used to sit on top of the mountain? It's hard digging in them rocks up there."

"I been there," I said.

"You didn't ever find nothing, did you?"

"Like what?"

"Money. Jewelry. Whatever." His voice was so high it was eerie. He sounded like a spirit might sound if it could talk.

"There ain't nothing up there," I said.

"We sure tried to find what we could," he said. "Ain't never found a thing but old bricks and a lot of rotten wood."

"Used to be a icebox up there and a ringer washer," I said. "Maybe you could use that."

"You trying to be funny? Ain't that right?" His tone did not change, but he was looking at me now with those seedlike eyes. "Ain't that right?"

"I ain't trying to be nothing," I said.

He looked at Parchman. "He's a funny guy," he said, point-ing at me as though I wasn't there. "A real comedian."

"He's just trying to eat," Parchman said.

"He ought to go on Milton Berle," Peach said. He turned back to me. "You ought to be on TV."

I looked at him.

"Yeah, you been there. You been up to the Crawford place," Peach said.

"They didn't leave no valuables," I said. "And there ain't no buried treasure."

Peach leaned over to Parchman and said, "Did Bone here tell you about the Gypsy Man?"

"The what?" Parchman looked at me.

22

"The Gypsy Man," Peach said.

I said, "It ain't nothing," to Parchman. Then I turned to Peach. "I'm trying to eat here."

"Well, well, well," he said. "It's a shame when a man can't get the peace and quiet he needs to eat."

"What about the Gypsy Man?" Parchman said.

"He's a gobbler," Peach said. "He devours children and dogs and cats. A real live mountain ghost."

I shook my head. Parchman was looking at me, wide-eyed.

"Nobody knows about it," I said. "Most folks never seen him."

"Lot of people in Crawford believe it," Peach said.

"You believe in ghosts?" I said to Parchman.

He nodded.

"That's what it is. Some folks say it's a ghost."

"You believe in it?" Parchman said.

"I don't know," I said. "Sometimes I do, and sometimes I don't."

That satisfied him. Peach sat there for a while, looking at both of us. Then he said, "You know, I don't take it kindly."

"Don't take what kindly?" Parchman said.

I said nothing.

Parchman was quiet, too, now. I sipped the soup, tried to ignore the strong taste of lard and onion in the broth. There were tiny, sandy bits of potato in the soup, as always.

Peach said, "I don't remember seeing you up that way."

"Yeah, well."

"Maybe you was just a little fella."

"Maybe."

"I didn't pay no attention to the young'uns when I was there. I was too interested in the ladies."

Parchman seemed to take a deep breath.

"I left to go down to Norton and work the mines," Peach said. "Maybe you was just a baby then. It was a long time ago."

I was finished with my soup. I ate what little bread was left, then I just sat there, staring at the empty bowl.

NOW THE BRIGHT moon disappears for a moment, then reclaims the window. It looks as if a shadow passes in front of it—a huge flying thing. Parchman sits up on his cot and says, "What was that?"

"What?"

"Did something cross in front of the moon?"

"A cloud passed," I say. "It was going pretty fast."

He is very still for a while, then he says, "You want to talk?"

I haven't said much to him since Peach escaped, but I don't want to keep to myself no more on this night. "What about?" I say.

"I don't know." In the moonlight, his eyes look almost ghostly. "I wish I didn't run the other day."

"You were only gone two days."

"Yeah. But..." He falls silent, thinking.

"But what?"

"I wish I didn't run."

I look out at the moon. It's quiet for a spell, then I say, "It's getting to be fall."

He's still quiet. I hear him breathing.

"Another year," I say. "My seventh fall in this place."

"Yeah."

It's quiet again for a little while, then he says, "Why you think the state troopers wanted my shoes?"

"They wanted your shoes?"

"Yeah. They took them away from me when they caught me."

"I thought you turned yourself in," I say.

"I tried to, but they acted like they caught me. I mean, they made a big deal of it. And then they took my shoes. Why you suppose they done that?"

I shake my head. "I don't know."

"You ain't pissed off 'cause I run?"

"No."

"I didn't mean to. I was by myself for a while. Then I run into Peach."

"You did?"

"You think they'll catch him, too?"

"I expect they will."

"He's really a bad man," Parchman says. "I know what I'm talking about."

"I know where I'd go if I got out," I say.

"Where?"

"I'd go back to Crawford, pick up my wife and little girl, and head for California."

"I wonder if Peach will go back to Crawford?"

"Why would he do that?"

"It was his hometown one time."

"He ain't the type to be thinking about a hometown," I say. I want to feel exactly that way, but I don't. I can't get the idea of Crawford out of my mind.

"You know," Parchman says, "the warden told him you was from Crawford. Maybe he told him about—you know." His voice is solemn, almost sad.

"About what?"

He shrugs. "You know."

"No, I don't."

His eyes look like a dog's eyes, begging for food. "Maybe it was the warden told him what you done—you know. That you killed a nigger."

"Oh," I say. "Forget about it. I know you didn't tell him."

"I didn't."

"Anyway. That was a long time ago."

"I didn't tell him nothing."

"I never thought you did."

He's quiet again, for a while. The moon disappears behind another cloud, only this time it stays gone for a while and I can't see him no more.

"Why'd you kill a girl?" he says.

"It was an accident."

"Oh."

"No. It really was. I didn't mean to."

"Seems wrong to be in jail for it then, don't it?"

I shrug, but I have nothing to say. I hear water dripping somewhere. Sometimes, in the distance, I'll hear a train whistle, and it seems to burn its way into my blood like something electric and hot. I can't explain it. I actually feel a kind of burning pain in my chest, right under the skin, a feeling of loss and terrible sadness tinged with fear that seems to give off heat. At times like that I can't sit still.

The only person in the world I might've tried to describe all this to is Penny. And I *hate* her now. I hate her memory—the sight of her face in my dreams. It feels like real hatred. So whenever I recognize it, whenever I discover my hatred, I am filled with a kind of disgust and loathing for myself. At times like that I can't stand to haul bone, sinew, and flesh through the damp, empty days in the shadow of these walls. I breathe and shift from place to place, from hour to hour, no more than an animal, and terribly ashamed that I'm feeding this animal and giving it water. I just want to die for the guilt because I love Penny so much.

Parchman says something I don't hear.

"What?" I say.

"It ain't going to be fun without a little sleep."

"What?"

"Being on the road gang again tomorrow."

"I don't mind it. I'd rather be doing something than staring at these walls."

"It's still going to be hot tomorrow."

I look at the moon, moving again away from clouds and flooding the cell. "Nah," I say. "Feel the breezes coming through that window. They're dry."

"So?"

"It won't be so hot tomorrow."

"I hope so."

"I'm going to sleep," I say. I turn and lay down on the bunk. He sits there staring at me. In the moonlight, he looks almost like my father the last time he visited me here. I close my eyes and try not to see or remember anything.

A long time seems to pass, then Parchman says, "You know what, Bone?"

"What?"

"I think I'm in a lot of trouble."

"Nah. You were only gone two days."

"Why'd they want my shoes?"

"So you won't run again, I guess."

"They didn't take nobody else's shoes."

"Well," I say. I want him to stop. I want to sleep.

"You know what else, Bone?" he says.

"What?"

"I bet you get out early now."

I don't say nothing.

"You saved a man's life, so you kind of give one back, you know what I mean? It ain't like you could give back the life you took, but you did give back a life."

I try to let my mind go empty.

"Know what I wish? I wish you really could give back a person's life," he says.

Still, I am silent, my eyes closed.

27

"You *sort* of done that. That ought to count for something."

"Yeah," I say. "You'd think so." But I don't want to think so. I don't want to think about it at all. The idea grows so big in my head it intensifies everything—all memory and grief and desire. And loss. I keep my eyes closed as tightly as possible and try to picture Penny's face. I envision her holding our baby, and I wonder what my little girl knows about me. I have never seen her beyond the first few days of her life. I have only dreamed of her and tried to picture her from what my father tells me. I refuse to look at pictures of her or Penny. What has Penny told Tory about her father? I don't think I deserve it, but I sure would love to rise from the dead for just a little while and hold the members of my small family in my arms—just so I can apologize to them and beg them to forgive me.

If I could just do that; only that.

MORGAN

I'm old enough to remember the Crawford family. Or what was left of them. They're supposed to have settled this mountain. Back before there even *was* a United States. I guess it was thirty years ago or more when Wilbur—the last of them—disappeared in the woods behind the house up yonder. If that's what happened to him. Nobody really knows. Up by Miss Clare's store though, and down the road to the left, there's a driveway all covered with brambles and honeysuckle. That's the entrance to the old Crawford place. Up that road is what's left of it. I don't think there's nothing left anybody could carry away. Just a big chimney standing there like a stone monument.

Used to be a beautiful place, though. White as a dogwood blossom. Almost as big as the state capitol building in Richmond. When I was a boy, Wilbur was probably close to fifty and his mommy and daddy got wore down just having to live with him. You want to know why?

Now, I'm going to tell you something about the Gypsy Man. Because that's what we all called him. Wilbur Crawford, I mean.

Wilbur had a purple birthmark. Run from his hairline all the way down to his chin and covered most of the right half of his face. I seen it. All of us kids was afraid of him. He didn't look like a finished man. You know what I mean? Like maybe under everybody's skin is a purple layer, and if you peel the skin back, we'd all look like that.

And he was just sort of crazy, you know? Some folks get that way. There ain't no explanation. Maybe the good Lord just forgets some portion of a man's brain, and when he gets a certain age, he starts missing it. I don't know. But Wilbur never become anything but craziness and trouble. Not law trouble. His parents seen to that. But still, trouble. He lived in that big house with his folks, and whenever he felt energetic and like he needed some distraction, he'd go set a fire someplace. He'd set one in the woods behind the house, or even to one of the fence lines, or to a stand of trees, or almost anything. He didn't burn no barns nor houses, but still, he liked fires.

No kidding. When I was a kid, we'd hear the fire bell go off, and the fire truck chugging up that hill, and everybody'd say, "There goes Wilbur again."

I don't know if he ever went to school, or when he first started playing with matches, but he was pretty famous by the time I left home for the first time. I guess I went to work down in Lebanon Church right before the first big war. I was twenty or so. And Wilbur was about my father's age at the time. Early fifties maybe. His folks stopped coming to town sometime around then. They used to walk down the hill and stroll over to the lookout, and just set there watching the sun go behind the mountain for miles and miles. Hell, even back then the sight was worth seeing. Used to be a gazebo there, a place to sit down in the evening shade. The Crawfords would spend their evenings over there. It once belonged to them—I think it was their family that built the gazebo—and the old lady just didn't want to let a summer evening pass without sitting in the shade of the old cedar pilings that by that time was already beginning to rot. God knows what they talked about or what they might of been thinking. They was getting pretty old by that time. Must of been tough just considering the day soon when they'd be gone and wondering who would call the fire department.

Anyway, I went to work down in Lebanon Church and didn't hear too much about the Crawfords until that year we got into World War I. I guess it was around Christmas in 1917. Old lady Crawford died, and three months after that, the old man joined her. The usual stories went around about him having a broken heart and all, but to tell the truth, they was both so old and worn down it's a wonder they didn't settle up on the same day.

Then it was just Wilbur. Everybody in town just called him Gypsy.

I know why they called him that. It had nothing to do with his lineage or the fact that he was a pyromaniac. Nothing to do with that birthmark neither.

My daddy told me this story, so I trust it's true.

When Wilbur was a year old, his momma put him out on her front porch. In the sunlight. Like a pie cooling in a window. But you know, she put him there so he'd be warm and maybe fall asleep. This was late in the spring, when the sun is warm but the air ain't. You know what I mean? Up here, we've had thunder snowstorms. She only left him there a minute. She said she went back in the house to get a comb to brush her hair, but when she come back out, he was gone. There ain't no sign of him.

My father said this mountain echoed for days with Mrs. Crawford's screams. They say people can come up this mountain in the spring, and get down on their knees by any rock or stone and place an ear against the side of it and they'll hear her voice still. Just like the sound in a seashell, there's Mrs. Crawford when she was a very young woman, wailing over her lost child.

Her hair turned white in the first year after that, and her husband spent all his time on the road, searching for the boy. He had every cop in the state looking. He was so gaunt with grief, my daddy said his face looked like a skull with eyes and a thin layer of yellow-brown paper stretched over it.

They had nothing to do in that house. All that land, and money, and nothing to do but think about their lost child. It goes without saying they'd never consider having another one. Mrs. Crawford's hair actually turned white.

They never found him. At least not when they was consciously looking. One day, three years later, Mrs. Crawford stepped out the front door and found Wilbur, just a settin' there on the porch like he'd never been taken away. He had on blue coveralls, a nice blue-and-white shirt, and a note pinned to the pocket of his pants that said, "The boy is able. Thanks a lot." I swear that's what it said. "Thanks a lot."

Wilbur was almost five years old when the Gypsies returned him. They took good care of him, too. Up until he started making fires, he was the most well-behaved and quiet boy in Crawford. If it wasn't for the purple birthmark, you'd of thought he was a model child. At least that's what my daddy said.

Of course, by the time I known him he was this huge, purple-and-white man who wore blue coveralls and who just about everybody said chased little kids. Whenever we seen him we'd run until we thought we'd die from lack of air. He must a hated everybody in Crawford, including his mommy and daddy. Even though I was fully grown, and living on my own by the time he wandered off into the woods—if that's what he done—I was glad to hear he had disappeared again. That was the year I went to France. Way back during the First World War.

But you know what? He's been back here.

He's been back here.

JOHN BONE

I went to work in the mill after I married Penny. That's where I met Bobby Hale and George Pace. The two men I was with when I killed little Denise Walton.

Bobby and George and me started hanging around together. Bobby was tall—well over six feet, and he had thin, almost translucent blonde hair. George was about my height, but beefy and wide faced. When he smiled it looked like the top of his head could come off. They had both worked a few years in the mines down in Norton, and neither ever wanted to go back. They were single, young, and expecting to go to Korea before long.

"We've got to use all our good time," Bobby used to say. "Because we're headed for some pretty bad shit."

"I don't give a care," George would say. It was his favorite expression. "I don't give a care." They teased me about being so lucky. Already married and done with Korea. We'd go down to Lebanon Church and shoot pool or have a few beers. Penny didn't mind. She was pregnant with Tory, and she was taking it pretty easy to tell the truth. Being pregnant made her sick. All the time. She never wanted me to see her like that, so she'd tell me to go on and have a few laughs with my friends—wind down a bit after a hard day's work.

And I did work hard. I wanted to make a life for Penny and me and the baby. I was saving money. My father didn't work anymore, but he had insurance money from my mother's death, and he got regular checks from the army because of a bad wound he got in Italy during the war. You'd never notice it watching him walk, or work in the yard, but he had a degenerative hip, so the army agreed to pay him three hundred dollars a month, indefinitely. Until he died, I guess.

Life was simply perfect back then. That's how I looked at it. I'd come up the mountain after a few beers with Bobby and George, and I'd stop in to check on the old man. He'd sit me down at the kitchen table and want to laugh at all the old bad times when I'd find him passed out on the floor. It really was kind of funny to hear him talk about it. He never thought it was funny that Penny had to help him all those times, and he still seemed vaguely embarrassed in her company, but one night he told me he loved her as if she was one of his own.

"Just like my own daughter," he said.

I didn't say anything. We were sitting in the living room that night, and he was watching a baseball game between the Washington Senators and the New York Yankees. He loved both of those teams, and he never referred to them as the Senators or the Yanks. He always said the full name of each team. The Orioles or the Indians might be playing the Senators or the Yankees, but he'd always say it was the Washington Senators, or the New York Yankees. We were both sipping a jug he had set down on the couch between us. He had put a big bowl of pretzels on the coffee table. "I knew you were coming," he said. "How's Penny?"

"Sick," I said. "Again."

"It's too bad."

"She says being pregnant is an illness. A nine-month illness."

He laughed. "Yep," he said, "I sure do love that girl."

"Me, too."

He lifted the jug. "You hit the jackpot there."

I waited for the jug. When he handed it to me, he said, "She reminds me of your mother."

I took a long pull, then wiped my mouth.

"Go easy," he said. "Remember what you promised me."

I WAS ALWAYS "going easy." That's how I got in all the trouble.

We were riding in Bobby Hale's new red-and-white Ford Edsel. It was two years old when he bought it, but it was new to him. He still had temporary tags on it. "What'd you buy an Edsel for?" George asked.

"It was cheap and it runs good," Bobby said.

"Shit. The front end looks like a snout or something."

"You want me to drop you off somewheres along here?" Bobby said.

We were laughing. Bobby'd gotten a case of National Bohemian beer in tall bottles. We were going pretty fast up and down the winding roads between Crawford and Lebanon Church. We had nowhere to go. George was in the front seat with Bobby and I sat in the middle in the back. All the windows were down. I knew I should be with Penny, but Bobby wanted to celebrate, and we never got very far from Crawford. I knew I'd be going home soon. Bobby let George drive for a while and he sat in the passenger seat. They were drinking one beer after another and hurling the bottles out the window. I was already starting to feel the beer, and I didn't want to get drunk. I wanted to "go easy." But I didn't want to just sit back there and grin. I was always damping down the fun. That's what Bobby Hale used to say. I didn't want to be a drag on those boys and the celebration and all. Sometimes you just pretend with friends. So you're not up against them, too. You know what I mean? Anyway, I'd drink a few sips of a beer then throw it as far out the window as I could into the trees along the highway. They didn't know. As far as they could see, I was drinking the same as they were. I actually felt as if I was getting away with something and being good at the same time. That's what I wanted: to be good. To keep the promise I'd made to my father, and to come home to Penny clean and sober. She never worried about my drinking—or at least she never said anything about it. But I knew what must have been going through her mind whenever she saw me and my dad sharing a jug. I knew she wondered if I wasn't headed in the same direction. So I was being good. And the night air in the car, the cooler breezes under the trees, made me feel immortal and permanent. I was having this good life.

Then, just after dark, going around a tight curve on one of those mountain roads, I hurled a full bottle of beer out the window on the right side of the car. I wanted to get it far enough into the trees so Bobby and George wouldn't hear it hit, wouldn't know from the sound of it that it was full. But the car was moving fast, and the bottle clipped the top of the window, then flew a few feet out and hit Denise Walton in the back of the head. I still hear the sound it made in my dreams. I never saw her until the bottle hit. She was just a shadow that came into view just as the bottle hit the top of the window. I saw her fall, though.

It looked like something fell on her from above and crushed her face down in the road.

Bobby screamed, "Jesus."

"Stop the car," I yelled.

George slammed on the brakes and we lurched to a stop a few hundred feet up the road. The car raised a lot of dust in the gravel before it stopped. For a few seconds nobody said anything. The silence in the car seemed to increase—as if a lack of noise could somehow deepen and swallow everything. Bobby leaned out the window and looked behind us. "What was that?" he said. His voice was trembling. He still held a bottle in his hands. George was looking off behind me, through the back window. I opened the door and got out, and the others followed me. It was a moonless night, and in the darkness and all the dust raised by the car when it hit the gravel, I couldn't see anything. We stood there in the red lights of the Edsel, gazing back up the road. Except for the terrible racket of the tree frogs and crickets, we couldn't hear or see a thing. I started to walk back towards what I knew must be there. "It was a girl," I said.

"Nah," George said.

Bobby started to laugh, nervously. "Did you hit something?"

"You saw it," I said.

"Yeah. But did she get up?"

"Did who get up?" George said.

"How do you know it was a girl?" Bobby said.

"It was a girl," I said. "A little girl."

"What are you guys talking about?" George didn't quite believe anything had happened. "Come on," he said. "Quit fooling around."

"We hit a girl," I said.

"I didn't hit no girl," George said. He almost shouted it.

"I don't mean with the car."

"What the fuck?" George said.

The silence made our voices seem like shouts. It was only night, and darkness, as long as we didn't walk any further back up that road.

"Let's get out of here," Bobby said.

"I ain't running." I started walking back towards what I now could see looked like a small bundle of dark clothing next to the road. A long strip of it seemed to trail out on the ground toward us. The dust had settled enough that George and Bobby could see it as well.

"Oh, shit," Bobby said. "What's that?"

"Throw all that beer away," George said.

Bobby went back to the car and started throwing the rest of the beer into the trees. He was breathing heavy, and I think he may have been crying.

"Come on," I said to him. "Fuck that." I moved quickly now, not quite running because I wasn't in a hurry to see what it was, what I knew it was. But the thought ran through my mind that maybe she was just unconscious, maybe I could help her.

The long trail of clothing that was stretched out toward us wasn't clothing at all. It was blood.

And Denise Walton was dead when we got back to her and turned her over. They said she died before her face hit the pavement, but the blood around her eyes and nose, the look of surprise and fear on her face will never leave me.

It won't ever leave me.

GAULT

I have had ninth-grade students who already had children. Girls who got pregnant before they could conjugate the verb *to be*. I'm telling the truth. And every one of those children was capable of the most complex and exquisite mixture of joy and sorrow, hope and belief, fear and loathing. You only have to feel *for* another to be fully human, and most people—no matter how ignorant—are capable of that.

If they weren't, I wouldn't be a teacher.

Penny Bone was my student, and then I helped her enroll her girl in my school. I would describe Tory as a truly beautiful assortment of unruly behaviors wearing jeans and walking around the place as if she ordered it into being. I don't think she ever hears the word *no* at home. I'd wager a smart sum on that. She's intelligent enough, as her mother surely is. I've always believed Penny is too sharp to fall for talk about a Gypsy Man. She's above all that. At least I thought she was. She spends so much time chasing her little one around and working for her aunt Clare, I don't suppose she has time to worry about such things. But Clare wanders off again, stays away too long, and now it's the Gypsy Man who's come back to haunt us all. Of course, a woman in Penny's position does not have much opportunity for a lot of adult conversation. Maybe that's her problem. She'd have done well to sit in my classroom for a few more years.

To tell you the truth, my wife thinks she's a little off balance, what with her father getting killed in the war when she was so young, and having to go through her formative years living with Clare Richmond. That alone might make a person a little less conventional, to put it gently. In spite of her good looks, Clare is the sort of woman who, if she lived in the town she's named for, wouldn't be allowed out of doors. She has no allegiance whatsoever to *any* of the social graces. I'm not overstating a bit. If you exclude the things we all do in the bathroom, and the one or two hygienic activities human beings normally undertake in private, there is no discernible facade or pretense of which she is capable. If she feels like yawning, stretching, or asking you to please leave so she can go to sleep, she'll do it. She thinks that's being truthful. She doesn't know the difference between what she might be thinking and what people want to hear. And everybody knows she drinks too much.

She comes to the school some days to pick up Tory. She takes the little girl's hand and leads her on down the road, talking to her as if she understands everything, as if the child is a little adult. Clare talks about the bread she bought that day, or the price of cigarettes and how hard it is to keep some cigarettes on the shelves in her store. Tory acts like she understands everything the old girl says, but how could she? A little girl her age? I'd feel sorry for her, except I know Penny loves her so much, and I know she takes good care of her—even if she has no manners. She is always clean and her jeans don't have patches or holes. It must be hard on a young woman raising a little one all by herself.

Aunt Clare couldn't be much help.

I knew John Bone, Penny's husband, pretty well, too. He was a student in my school at one time. In fact, that's where he met Penny. His father lived a bit further up the mountain—up near Quincy. That was a little town with nothing more than a gas station and an apple stand just on the other side of the mountain, up the road from Crawford. Mrs. Bone died when John was only ten. She got stung by yellow jackets and turned out to be allergic to the venom. The story was that she fell down on top of the nest and the bees just kept stinging her, until she stopped breathing. She was only twenty-seven or so—a really young woman, and John was never the same after she was gone. Neither was his father, come to think of it. The old man started drinking a little more heavily and never really stopped. It was like he picked up a jug right after the funeral and just kept on pouring it down his throat, until after a while, the bottle seemed to swallow him. You know what I mean?

John, in spite of his father's continual drunkenness, seemed to regain himself, mostly. He was quiet and aloof—but he took care of his father pretty well. John had a rebellious streak, though. Some would tell you it was because of what happened to his mother, but who really knows such things? Some have said he was simply a defiant young man. That's the only way they could describe him, although he was never defiant just for its own sake. He could take authority if he thought it was right, or if he didn't see fault with it. The only thing was, he went his own way on most things, and sometimes when a young man does that it can look like defiance. He wasn't even afraid of

God. One time I told him I'd pray for him and his mom, and he looked at me, his head turned the way he always had it— just like a cat tilts its head when it hears a bird singing—and he said, "To hell with you and your God." Just like that. He was insulted that I mentioned God's name in the same breath with his mother. That's what he told me.

I said, "Don't you believe in God?"

And he said, "Maybe I do. If I did it'd be just so I can hate him. That's all."

Oh, he could be cynical—truly cynical. He could instantly and convincingly point out the absurdity of just about every-thing other people judge to be worthwhile; you'd never trust your own perceptions of the world if you listened to him long enough. He was a reader, believe it or not, so he knew more than most of the people around here, and you always had the feeling he was laughing at you behind your back; like he knew he was smarter, and he knew you knew it, too. He just had this way about him—he could look at you funny and transform what you cherished into something cheap and valueless. Not that he had a superior attitude or anything. And he *was* smart. He was one of my biggest disappointments, to tell you the truth. I never did get to him—encourage that bright mind of his.

John never believed over much in the Gypsy Man, I'll tell you. Or if he did, he never let on about it. I think he must have understood from the beginning that it was simply folklore, or at worst a kind of mythical story that some placed a bit too much faith in.

Don't you think it must be true that all mythical beings are a result of idle conversation and gossip that got out of hand and graduated to folklore? No doubt you will agree that igno-rance is not necessarily stupidity. Ignorance is just not know-ing, and not having a need or desire to know. We're all ignorant about something, and some of us are more or less ignorant about many things.

I've endeavored to educate children all my life because I think it is the most important thing human beings can do: pass on the old verities, tried and true, while engendering enough skepticism to provide for new discoveries, new truths. To my mind, there's nothing more improvident than an ignorant person, especially one who is smart. I know some children are smarter than others, but I've rarely worked with a truly stupid child—even after all these years on this mountain where provincial ignorance flourishes and gives forth a kind of charm that passes for country wisdom. I guess it's one of the true paradoxes of this world, and ought to be a revelation for some, that a person can know almost nothing, can carry bones, flesh, and sinew around, occupy space like a plant, and yet *feel* the same tangled emotions and fancies as the most enlightened intellect. If that's ironic, consider the irony for a second. If you examine it closely, you should come to see that it is not ironic at all, but rather tragic in the extreme. There's something tender, and even ennobling about that fact, isn't there? The world would be immeasurably diminished if the cave paintings turned out to be a great hoax; if primitive man really had no feelings to speak of, and ignorance really was empty and without the sorrow, the joy, the hopes, and fears—the truly sweet grandeur of a conscious, yet unwilling soul.

It wasn't long after Penny's father died when she and John met. John's mother had been dead for six or seven years by then, but they seemed to share something of that sort of grief. It produced something fathomless between them. They were inseparable right up until Penny's senior year, and then she turned up pregnant with Tory and that was that. They got married.

I thought they would be one of those worthy couples who love each other so completely they never seem to have had a life of their own before their marriage; one of those couples who go together in everything, through numberless days and weeks until one of them dies. They seemed that close, that attuned to each other's moods and habits. Everybody talked about the settling influence she had on him. He went to work at the mill, and for the first time since his mother died he behaved himself. Or at least he seemed to. None of us was prepared for what happened later.

Although I don't condone what he did, it was really kind of sad when he got himself in all that trouble. I mean, I don't think he was a murderer or anything like that. He didn't intend what happened. It was probably just what Penny said it was: an accident.

He pleaded guilty. He really was sorry it happened, so sorry in fact, that I think he accepted his sentence almost as if it were a judgment from above. It was just terrible luck. I mean really awful luck. That's all it was.

It could have happened to anybody.

PARCHMAN

I seen things. I been a witness to things nobody never dreamt of. I say to John, "You got to pay attention to me, here, because I seen things."

"Let me sleep," John says.

"Peach ain't straight in the head. And he done things... you wouldn't believe the things he done."

"Ain't we all," John says, but he ain't trying to be tough or nothing. He just says, "Ain't we all," like that, like it's kind of funny and sad at the same time, you know?

"I used to run with Peach," I say. "I know."

"Boys I run with all got off scot-free."

It's real quiet for a minute, then I say, "You was the only one got caught?"

"Nah, the other boys got caught, too. They got lighter sentences."

"Oh."

"Probably out by now."

"They grabbed me and Peach while it was happening, you know while he was beating up on that sailor. Once Peach gets going, it's hard to get his attention."

"Why you telling me this again?"

"I guess I don't know. Seems odd, don't it?"

"It does."

"Yes, sir. I guess it sure does."

"I'm trying to sleep. Ain't you worried about going out on the road with no sleep?"

"You remind me of my little brother, how about that?" I say.

He don't smile. He just looks at me hard. But he does look like my brother; it's the truth. Just like my little brother, Bobby.

"What if I ain't got no little brother," I say. "How 'bout that?"

He's still looking at me, wondering what I might be up to. "Lookee here," I say. "It don't matter why I'm telling you, I'm just telling you. If a person sees a drowning cat, he fetches it up out of the water, right?"

"You need to let me be, now," he says. "I'll worry my own way about Peach, too."

"If he goes back to Crawford, you'll worry, I'll bet."

He raises his head and takes a closer look at me for a second. Then he lays back down and stares at the ceiling. He's too quiet most of the time, his mind turning in there, and I can tell he ain't no dimwit.

"Suit yourself," I say.

"Just leave it," he says.

"I'm trying to do you a favor."

"I know you are."

"That's all."

"I understand about Peach," he says. "Men like that are all talk."

"Well, you don't know. You just don't know."

I lay down my own self, now. The moon's so goddamned bright, I don't see how I can keep my eyes closed. It almost hurts my eyes to look at it. I never could sleep with a light in my face. I say my prayers, ask the dear Lord to forgive all my sins and please let me sleep this night.

Hell, I pray for the same thing every night.

I don't know if there's a God or not, but it seems like there might be. I don't see how a thing as big as the world could of always been here. And what with mountains and lakes and rivers—with the sky sometimes when the clouds commence rolling over across the sun at dusk, and the light scatters a long way toward heaven, beams and rays of it across the sky—must be a God in there with all that some way.

PEACH IS MEAN. Plain and simple and that's all he ever was. Flat crazy and mean. Most of the time he don't even seem human. He can smile and laugh, tell a story or a joke, and you're thinking he ain't no more strange than nobody else, and then just like that you'll see him do something that makes your blood turn cold, and he'll do it with the same kind of smile as when a man says "mornin'." He don't get angry. He don't get loud. He just does things suddenly, like a machine somebody accidentally turned on. And then when the thing's done, he acts like he ain't done nothing at all. You got to see it to believe it.

So I just feel like I ought to warn John Bone. Even if John is fearless, that don't mean he can't be just as shattered as anything else that breaks. And human beings eventually break—even if they smile in the face of it. John stands upright. I can see that. He's a man, all right. He don't take no shit. But he ain't no match for Peach. Ain't nobody a match for a man like Peach. Most normal folks can't imagine it.

Once, a long time ago, John said, "It ain't fair what you got to go through all your life before it comes time to die."

"No," I said. "I know it ain't."

"So I don't expect it."

"Don't expect what?"

"Fairness."

"Oh," I said.

Then he said, "I had a wife. A little girl. Life taken me from them and put me here."

"It did?"

"Nothing I done," he said. "You understand? It was nothing I *intended.*"

"I guess I understand."

"It was a goddamned accident."

"Well, you was there, right?"

He almost laughed. He just looked at me, a bit of a smirk on his face, then he said, "Yeah. I was there. And now I ain't."

JOHN'S BEEN in this same cell with me for six years, and I still don't really know him very good. Once in a while, in the yard, Peach would say something to him—you know, rag him a bit about having the name Bone, or just because Peach didn't like nobody to act like ain't nothing bothers him. John Bone sometimes walks around like he don't mind being here. I know different because I'm in with him all day, but the others, they can't see it in the way he walks or what he says. Sometimes, he almost seems content. I know that ain't true.

John's got big hands and long arms and looks strong enough to handle Peach or anybody else in that prison. Except he don't have it in his eyes—you can look at him and know he

45

don't have it. He ain't going to kill nobody, and he ain't never killed nobody. At least not on purpose. When he first come here, his eyes looked almost like a woman's eyes or a small boy's eyes, still excited by things most of us don't pay no attention to no more: sunlight, breezes in the trees, and the way it smells in the woods after it rains.

For a while in the beginning there, I thought John would somehow rise up—you know, be above all the hard time in this place. But after a few months, then a year, and another year, the road gangs and the boredom did something to that little boy's look in his eyes, and something fixed and cold come into his expression.

One time, just after we come back from the mess hall, I said, "John, you all right?" and he looked at me, turned his head like a man half asleep, and looked into my eyes like he was trying to find something small that had gotten away from him. It was almost like he didn't remember me.

"John," I said. "You don't look so good."

"Leave me alone," he said.

He'd be quiet for weeks, sometimes. I'd talk to him, some nights, but I never got an answer, he almost never even answered me or seemed to know I was there. I just kept on talking to keep from losing my own mind. Once in a while he'd look at me, but only to shake his head like he was ashamed of something I said. Then he'd turn away. It looked like it would take too much energy to speak, and he didn't want to waste no energy. Then, in the weeks before Peach escaped, and even after, he started to talk a little more. Like he finally figured me out and understood that I didn't mean him no harm.

One day I was standing in line, waiting at the barbershop to get a haircut, and one of the guards, a fellow named Mac, come up to me.

"You know Peach?" he said.

"Yep."

46

"You were arrested with him, right?"

"All right," I said. "Without the bullshit, what do you want?" Mac was big and strong as an ox. But he was almost fifty, so his hair was gray, and his belly had commenced to roll over his belt. He wasn't a bad guard, as guards go. He'd shoot you in the back if you taken it in your mind to run—I mean he qualified on the range every month, just like the others. But you had the feeling you could trust him. He didn't do nothing mean just for the meanness, and when it was too hot on the road, he was the only one who'd take off his hat, wipe the sweat off his brow, and then tell the men, "Take a break and drink some water." None of the others give a tinker's damn if you was hot or how thirsty you was. Most of the men used to pray that Mac would be the fellow nearest them on the road, carrying a shotgun under his arm sometimes, sometimes with nothing at all, not even a club. They wanted him nearby because he kept the water barrel on the back of a pickup, and he made sure we never got too far from that truck. And if you got too thirsty, you could just ask him and he might stop and let you take a drink. He even give me a cigarette once, and I didn't even ask for it.

So I'm standing in line for the haircut, and he says to me, "How long you known Peach?"

"I worked with him down in the mines," I said. "A long time ago."

He didn't say nothing. Then I said, "Why you want to know?"

"What do you know about him?"

"I know a lot."

"Tell me."

"Why?"

He smiled a little bit. "Warden Buchanan was thinking of making him a trustee. So I was just wondering about him."

"A trustee," I said. "That would be just perfect." It was hard not to laugh.

47

"You think that would be a mistake, too?"

"How far you think you could throw a piano, if'n you could lift it?"

"That's what I thought."

"What about Bone?" I said.

"Buchanan don't like him much."

"Why?"

He didn't say nothing. He just adjusted the hat on his head and looked around.

"I mean he don't belong in here," I said.

Now he smiled a little and looked at me.

"No, really," I said. "I'll admit I probably belong here, and for sure Peach ought to be locked up. But that John Bone, he don't belong in here."

"What's it to you?"

"I don't know," I said. And I didn't know, except he reminded me of Bobby. But hell, I've picked up smaller men that looked like my brother and dunked them headfirst in a toilet, just to see how much change would spill out of their pockets. I spent my whole life taking care of myself and the hell with other folks. Something about John though. I reckon he was almost saintly at first. Like he was touched or moved by some kind of ghost, or maybe the Lord. I ain't a religious fanatic, but I got to admit, there must be something to it, since so many folks believe in it. Maybe there was a spirit of some kind in John. At first, anyway. He looked like a soul with flesh on it, white and innocent and willing to suffer no matter what. He come to us without fear. That's what it was. He looked everybody straight in the eye and seemed to welcome what he had to suffer.

Mac said, "He'll work the road gangs, just like anybody else."

"Well," I said. "If'n you made John a trustee, it would go better in here. That's all."

"It ain't much good for the guards in here," Mac said. "Being a trustee ain't a smoother ride. It just feels like it. Out on the road it gets just as hot for the fellows in uniform as it does for you boys in the yellow coveralls."

"Yeah, but you guys are just standing there. We're working in it."

He nodded, still looking at me with a kind of half smile. "You have a point there."

Cleaning the roadsides and such if'n you look at it the right way, it's hard work, but work anyway—all day so your mind stays busy and you don't go crazy staring at these goddamned cinder block walls. That's what John says about it. I don't know, though. I'd rather lay on my bunk than sweat in the hot sun.

JOHN DIDN'T know Peach like I did. I wasn't afraid of Peach, but I steered clear of him—I'm no fool. I ain't afraid of wasps nor bees neither, but when I find a nest, I go around it. Way around it.

When we got caught beating up that sailor, it took half a detachment of police to keep Peach pinned down long enough to cuff him. It ain't that he was strong. He *was* strong, but probably a lot of men have been stronger. It was that he went so unbelievably crazy; I mean animal wild, and it was impossible to get him to sit still long enough to put cuffs on him. They had to keep hitting him with clubs just to get him to calm down a tad. He was all bloody when it was over and he looked at me and said, "You ain't even scratched, you son of a bitch." And after that, he was thinking I ain't as good as he is because I surrendered without a fight. I said to John, "Peach was beat to a pulp and I wasn't touched. We both ended up here. What do you think? You think he was the smart one or me?"

One day about a year before we got arrested, Peach and me and a guy we used to run with, Rudy Bell, was sitting next to a blue stream in the mountains—somewhere near Elizabeth Furnace, way up in the Blue Ridge Mountains just the other side of the Virginia line, and a boy come on us. We was fishing for trout and drinking beer and just having a high old time. The nigger was short and young—with light brown hair, but dark black skin. It looked like he dyed his hair, but maybe not. He was toting a black bag, like a doctor's bag.

"Where you think you're going, boy?" Peach said to him.

"Up the road a piece," the nigger says.

"What you got there?"

"It's my bag."

Well, the boy couldn't a been more than nineteen or twenty or so, the way I figure it. He was wearing faded blue dungarees and a white T-shirt. His dark arms hung down out of the shirt, and the bag in his left hand was the same color as his skin.

"What's in the bag?" Peach said.

"Nothing, suh," the nigger says.

"You running away from home, boy?" Rudy said.

"No, suh. I ain't got no home to run from." The nigger smiled, just a small showing of white teeth. Then he started to walk on and Peach said, "Give it here."

"It ain't nothing in it," the nigger says, pulling back from him.

"Gimmee it," Peach said. He grabbed it out of the nigger's hand. The boy just stood there, looking at him. Peach opened the bag and turned it upside down. Some white shirts, a pair of blue dungarees, some worn-out old shoes, and a handful of tools spilled out on the ground. A small set of wrenches, some pliers, and a hammer. I think that was about it. Maybe a screwdriver, too.

"What you doing with these tools, boy?" Peach said.

I said, "Aww, leave him be."

Peach looked at me for a minute. Then he said, "What you doing with these?" to the nigger again.

"It's just some tools," he says. "I works when I can."

"You a mechanic?"

"Yes, suh."

"How old are you?"

The boy was embarrassed but proud, too, so he says nothing. He just stood there, looking at Peach.

Then Rudy caught a fish on his line and there was a commotion to get it in the bucket. Peach went over there and was fooling around with Rudy's fish, and the nigger picked up his things and put them back in the bag. He snapped the bag shut—it really was a sort of doctor's bag—and then started to mosey his way down the path under the trees. You could tell he was in a bit of a hurry though.

Peach come back up the bank and when he seen the nigger going down the path he run after him. "Come back here," he said.

The nigger started running.

No way Peach could catch up to him, so he just stopped and watched him running up the path. "I'll be goddamned," he said. He started laughing. "You see that nigger run?" He was howling he laughed so hard.

I thought that would be that, but later that night, when we was driving on up the road and heading for the Virginia line, we seen the nigger walking along the highway, carrying that bag, and Peach pulled the car over in front of him. The nigger stopped and looked like he studied running again, but Peach got out of the car and walked over to him, saying, "You go ahead and run again, you black son of a bitch. Go ahead and run again."

The nigger just stood there, holding the bag with both hands now, in front of him, like he wanted to protect himself with it.

Rudy got out of the other side of the car, and Peach said, "Let's go for a walk." He had the nigger by the arm. Rudy opened the trunk and took out a ax. "Come on," he said to me. "We're gonna have a little fun."

Now, I didn't want to have no part of it, but Peach looked at me funny when I said I was staying in the car, so I got out and followed them down into a ravine by the road. It was late in the afternoon by then, and the sun couldn't find its way down into that holler, so it was almost dark under the trees.

Rudy held the nigger by the arms, from behind, and Peach stood in front of them with the ax.

"What you think you're doing running away from me, boy?" he said.

"Now don't hurt him," Rudy said. "Hold still, boy. We ain't gonna hurt you if'n you just hold still."

"Don't you move a inch," Peach said. He held the ax in front of him, across his front, you know, like he just finished cutting a tree down or something.

The nigger, even if he wasn't twenty years old yet, only stared at him with those dark, angry eyes. He really was a magnificent fella, you know. I can tell you he wasn't no boy. He never even blinked. It was like he'd been there before, and seen it all before, and he felt what was going to happen, and he was just too proud to give them boys what they wanted. Of the four fellas standing in that ravine, he was the only man.

I didn't know what was going to happen. I thought Peach would get tired trying to scare him and he'd just rough him up a bit and send him on his way. Maybe take his bag or something like that.

But what he did—I still can't get it out of my mind. He had Rudy hold the boy's head forward, bending him over, you know. "Hold his head," he said. "Hold his goddamned head. Bend him over, and hold his head down." The boy didn't struggle much. He just leaned over, with Rudy behind him holding his head.

His hands covered the boy's ears. I don't think Rudy had any notion what was going to happen neither. He was laughing there for a while. In the beginning. He had both hands on the side of the boy's head, and leaned him forward, like he was trying to help him puke in a bucket or something, and then Peach stood off to the side and swung the ax and hit the boy with the sharp edge of it right in the middle the head. The top of his head. It made a sound like "chock." Like that. Like a flowerpot full of dirt when you drop it on a wood floor, you know? A hollow sound, but solid, too. It made me sick to my stomach, I ain't lyin'. And I could see the ax had gone into the boy's skull, but not very far. It was bleeding now, all over the place, but Peach pulled the ax out and swung it again, and it went "chock" like that again—really loud, and this time it went in much deeper. And you know the boy didn't even groan. Rudy was quiet, too, just holding him there. The boy's head dangled now, the opening where the ax come out shooting blood all over the ground. Some of it splashed on Rudy's pants and shoes.

Peach smiled. "Drop him, you asshole. He's bleeding all over you."

Rudy let go and the boy dropped to the ground, his face in the dirt, his head still shooting blood. Peach looked at me and said, "What's the matter with you?"

"I didn't think you'd do that," I said. Suddenly I was very sick, but I was pretty sure I better not throw up right then. I was taking big gulps of air to keep from gagging.

Peach leaned on the ax, smiling like he'd won something. "I sure made a fucking mess a his ass, didn't I?"

Rudy brushed his hands and then started wiping blood off his shoes. "Goddamned nigger sure had a lot of blood in him," he said. But he was pretty upset, too. I could tell. I thought he might get sick the way he looked at his hands and then his pants and shoes. "He sure had a lot of blood in him," he said again.

"Red blood, too," I said.

"What do you mean by that?" Peach said.

"Nothing."

Then Peach started laughing. He pointed at me. "Did you hear the sound Parchman made when I hit that son of a bitch the first time?" He was laughing so hard he couldn't stand up straight. "You squeaked," he said. "You sounded like a mouse getting squeezed." He was having trouble saying anything through the laughing.

I didn't know I made any sound at all, but I pretended to laugh, too. Peach still had the ax. Rudy was laughing, but I could see he wasn't happy about the blood. After a while, Peach wiped the ax off with one of the shirts in the black bag. Then he started up the ravine and back to the car, still laughing. Rudy took off his pants and wiped his shoes with them. "It's a god awful sticky mess," he said. Then he rooted through the bag looking for money. "It ain't nothing here."

"You going home like that?" I said. Then I turned away and puked into the bushes by the body.

It was real quiet.

Rudy said, "I got these here." He held up the pair of dungarees that was in the bag. He threw the bloody pants off into the leaves, then put the nigger's clean pants on. "Lookit," he said. "They fit like a glove."

"They look a little short to me," I said. I was shaking. I felt like my blood and all my guts was turning into something thick and cold and muddy. Everything narrowed in my eyes, so I felt like I was looking through two little round holes. A breeze sounded like a train to me.

"Come on," he said. "We better get out of here."

Peach was way up in front of us. I said, "Did you know he was going to do that?"

"Hell," he said, "I never know what Peach is gonna do."

"Goddamn," I said.

"What?"

"I don't know. Just *goddamn*."

Rudy didn't answer me. He was walking along, just as calmly as you please. When we started to scramble up the embankment, he said, "Watch out for poison ivy."

MORGAN

Don't work much anymore. Got a bad leg. Sometimes, it won't hold me up—just gives out like a rotten fence post. I'm lucky I don't fall down.

Used to work at the mill down toward Lebanon Church. Got to be foreman. Now I mostly sell firewood, cut down trees people don't want cluttering their yard, and so on. They're building whole neighborhoods down in Lebanon Church— lot of city folk coming up here to get away from noise and crime and one thing and another.

I get between fifty and a hundred dollars for a three-quarter-ton pickup load of firewood. It ain't even seasoned. I sell it to them by the rick or sometimes by the truckload. They don't complain. They wanted to get away from crime, but what I charge them for firewood is right close to it, wouldn't you say?

You want to know what's stirred up all this talk about the Gypsy Man? Penny's aunt Clare going off like that got it going, of course—Penny don't see nobody in that store she don't mention it to. So folks started talking about it again. It don't take much to get it going because this mountain's got a lost child. Folks go on remembering a thing like that, no matter how long ago it was. Things may quiet down for a spell, but then it starts up again. It never goes completely away. And once they start talking about a lost child, they start talking about Gypsy Crawford. It's just human nature.

So last Sunday, the Reverend Sloan mentions the boy in his sermon. Sloan is a quiet fellow, tall and sick looking. He don't say nothing in them sermons except things he reads from the good book, but he had something to say about the Landon boy last Sunday. "Let us pray," he said. "That the Lord give us to know what happened to little Terry Landon." I ain't saying somebody put the reverend up to it, but if it was somebody, I bet it'd be Sheriff Paxton. He don't want to quit on it neither. Even after all these years.

Anyway, Penny come down to see me. She asked me if I'd go up to her place and take a look at some writing she found on a stone in her backyard. I told her I'd be up there the next morning, and then in the afternoon that day, I was walking up the road toward Clare's place and just before I got up to the old girl's store, I seen something off to my right a little, by the side of the road. It's in the woods there, sort of in the path that winds down back toward town and the lookout. I walk over there, you know pretending I don't notice it at first, but I already know what it is. It's a pile of leaves and sticks settin' there. The leaves are piled up, wet and black, with a mixture of water, black oil, and maybe a little flour throwed in. They stick together pretty good, and they look just like a man a settin' there. The sticks like his arms, folded across the front of him. Ain't no clothing this time. I've seen clothing mixed in with the leaves before, but this time, it's only the leaves and sticks. The whole thing's a mess. It's starting to settle and rot, but it ain't been settin' there long.

I know what this thing is, see. It's a pattern. That's what. The Gypsies call this thing a pattern. The Gypsy Man left it there for me to see. He knew I would understand all about it.

I seen what must be going on. It's usually quiet around here. Folks just go about their business. They ask how you feeling. Say hello to one another at church maybe. We don't have no nigra families up here, and the ones we have further down the mountain, towards Lebanon Church, they stay clear of just about everybody. They don't want nothing, neither. Got their own school. Their own church. When they need something at the market, they wait their turn. Like everybody. We don't have no trouble up here. At least not anymore. It's the truth. Now the Crawfords settled this mountain way back in the beginning of Revolutionary times. That's what my daddy used to say. Old man Crawford brung his family up here and shaved the top of this mountain to build his house and feed the mill. I know for a fact that Crawford wasn't the old man's name, neither. That come later. His name was Crowfoot. He was a Indian. His momma was a full-blooded Cherokee Indian, and his daddy was a half-breed fur trapper. And he wasn't in no Revolutionary army, like some folks claim. He was in the militia. My daddy told me that was the story. That's what old man Crawford himself told my daddy when he was a little boy. Old man Crawford was the Gypsy Man's father, and the great grandson of the half-breed. But you can't find out a thing like that looking in books.

Folks can talk all they want about it. It's a free country. But now I seen a sign. I seen that pattern by the road. That's the Gypsy Man. I don't know what it means, but it may be the Gypsy Man's been waked up again, and he's on the prowl. It just makes it worse that Clare's turned up missing.

I like the peace on this mountain. In calm, it's a fine place to be. The air ain't nothing but pure sweetness to breathe. You always got breezes sifting their way through the leaves. But it can be a scary place, too.

I knew Penny's husband pretty good before he got sent down to the state prison. I believe he didn't mean what happened. I think he was innocent, but people around here all got opinions on it. That boy had a knack for getting in trouble, so it didn't surprise me none when trouble come looking for him. But he wasn't no murderer. Like most folks believe. He just had the worst luck of anybody I ever seen. Started when his momma died and just got worse. Except for when he married Penny. I guess you could say that was good luck.

Penny's about the prettiest woman on this mountain. Except maybe for her aunt Clare. Even after Penny had the little one, the weight she put on only made her look better. Most people don't notice how tall she is. Not that she don't stand up straight or nothing. She just looks petite, and normal, you know, like any young woman. But she's almost as tall as I am, and I'm five foot eleven and a half. Or I used to be before my leg started to give out. Maybe I lean a bit too much, now. Folks ask me how I feel, I tell them I feel seventy. When I'm seventy-one, I'll feel seventy-one. If I make it that far.

Penny's hair is bright and black, and I like the way she wears it long down the side of her face. She puts it in a clip or a barrette or whatnot and it hangs down behind her head when she walks. She's always wearing those tight jeans and flannel shirts. Sleeveless tops in the summer. Sometimes she wears light brown, knee-high boots. I like to watch her walk by. Not for any reason except she's young and pretty. She reminds me when I was young. I watch out for her when I can.

She's worried about her aunt Clare. I ain't said nothing to her about it, but to tell the truth, so am I. Clare's one of them women who gets into trouble, if you know what I mean. Last year a television actor come through here and she took up with him. He was looking for a place to film his next show—a mystery program or something. I never heard of him. Anyway, Clare took up with him, and pretty soon they're riding around here in his red Chevy convertible. Honking at everybody as they passed, waving beer cans high in the air. As if they was drinking to us on the pavement, those of us who ain't good enough to drive cars with cloth tops.

When he left he told her he'd send for her. Lord knows what other promises he made. But she never seen him again, except for on one of them daytime soap operas. He was a regular for a while on one of them. I don't remember.

For weeks after he was gone, we had to hear about it. How he'd be calling any day, and then she'd be gone, too. Once she stopped talking about him, we all knew what happened. I was kind of embarrassed for her.

Clare looks a lot like her brother: wide faced, full lips, with dull black hair. You know she dyes it. She was a real beauty when she was young, and even now she ain't that bad looking, but she's getting old and she knows it. A woman like that— you know, who don't take no shit from nobody—once they start to sag a bit and lose their youthful skin, they get to be pretty rough and trashy looking. She started letting her hair go. Putting on makeup a little too thick. Smoking more Lucky Strikes and talking in a voice that got deeper and deeper.

She turns up missing and for a few days you just think she took off with somebody for a little fun, that's all. She done it before enough times. When she first took up with the actor we didn't see her for a week or two before she started showing him off and putting herself on display with him.

But now she's been gone almost a month. So Penny's really worried this time. I didn't know what to say when she said she was afraid it was the Gypsy Man. I told her she shouldn't be thinking such things. But Clare wouldn't just disappear like that. Not for that long without saying nothing. And then I see the sign by the road, the pattern. I know we're in for another visit.

Not that I think Clare's come to no harm. At least I don't want to think that.

I tell you what. It's just possible that it ain't no Gypsy Man Penny needs to be worried about. No, sir. What Penny ought to worry about is in a bottle and takes on a very fine copper color when sunlight passes through it.

That's what I'm hoping anyway.

GAULT

Let me ask you something. How does Morgan Tiller know it was Gypsies who took Wilbur Crawford? I've heard the story told many times, and no one seems to know why in the hell it would be Gypsies that took the boy and not Arab nomads or Mongol raiders. Nobody knows why the boy was taken, either. All they know is it was Gypsies. How can you account for such a story?

To tell the truth, I'm not sure I even believe the boy was ever taken. By anybody. The Crawford family gave this town its name, so I suppose they would naturally be a part of its folklore—but I think that's all it is. The house itself, I was told, burned down shortly after the stock crash in 1929. That was thirty years ago. Wilbur was long gone by then, but people still say he burned it down. The Crawfords passed away the year Black Jack Pershing landed in France. Morgan Tiller was with Pershing, if you can believe what he tells everyone. That was the first year of what my parents called the Great War. I was born that year. When I was a little boy the saga of the Crawford family was one of the major topics of family conversation. My father said Wilbur attended his mother's funeral and then a few months later his father's. He dressed in a black suit. He cried like anybody would, prayed quietly over each grave. My father said he saw him placing flowers on his mother's grave. Then his father came over to him, whispered something in his ear. Daddy said Wilbur looked up, tears in his eyes, then hugged his father and sobbed on his shoulder. My mother told me she went over there the next day, with a potato-and-cheese casserole and a pitcher of milk. Mr. Crawford greeted her at the door.

"No," he said. "No ma'am. You don't need to be doing this for us."

"I want to," Mother said.

FlashScan System

City of San Diego Public Library
Carmel Valley Branch
* * * * * * * * * * * * * * * * * *

8/5/2010 2 46 18 PM
Title: VA uncataloged items
Item ID: touch-screen finishe
Date Due: 8/26/2010 23 59

1 item

Renew at www.sandiegolibrary.org
OR Call 619 236-5800 or 858 484-4440
and press 1 then 3 to RENEW
Your library card is needed
to renew borrowed items

printed by FlashScan System
www.tatcorp.com

FlashScan System

City of San Diego Public Library
Carmel Valley Branch
****

8/5/2010 2:46:18 PM
Title: VA uncataloged items
Item ID: touch-screen finishe
Date Due: 8/26/2010,23:59

1 item

Renew at www.sandiegolibrary.org
OR Call 619 236-5800 or 858 484-4440
and press 1 then 3 to RENEW.
Your library card is needed
to renew borrowed items.

"Well." He looked at his feet, moving the door ever so slowly. Mother said she was sure he'd close it if she didn't say something else. She put the dish in his hands, then held out the jug of milk.

"Take it," she said.

He put the plate down on a table by the door, then took the milk from her.

"Make sure Wilbur gets enough to eat," she said.

The old man smiled. "Well," he said. "He *is* a grown man."

Mother said she was embarrassed. "I know," she said. "But you both need taking care of."

"It's enough that you brought this here," Crawford said.

My father said Wilbur would visit the graves of his parents fairly often in the few weeks after they died. He'd walk down the hill from the old house carrying a small bouquet of yellow flowers and white daffodils in each hand.

He inherited everything—the house, the land, what was left of the Crawford money. But the house was already falling into disrepair, and the land was mostly what was left of the top side of the mountain. It wasn't good for much of anything, and it still isn't. It was too rocky, and the mill took most of the trees.

Then one day that year, my parents noticed they hadn't seen Wilbur in a long time. Some people got concerned. You tend to think of folks you know in a small town as though they're distant family, people you should tend to when they need it. So somebody went up there. My father was not among them, but he knew people who'd gone up to the house and he had a firsthand description of what they found. It was an empty house. Abandoned and dark, like a sunken ship. Curtains still adorned the windows, and lawn chairs were set up in a comfortable circle on the rear verandah. Mother said the state police and whoever was sheriff back then investigated the place. Some said the house groaned in the wind, what with so many people going through it. It was already beginning to rot in the cornices and railings. The place was just abandoned. Furniture, rugs, made beds, and an icebox full of wrapped food. There was an empty bowl on the kitchen table with mold growing thick in it. It was milk and cereal gone bad and thoroughly rotten.

Wilbur just vanished. But the state police said it was clear he wanted to vanish because there wasn't a stitch of his clothing in the place. His closets were empty. They didn't find a shoe. And everything was taken out of the vanities in the bathrooms. Wherever he was going, he took a suitcase and just about all of his money. The only mystery is where he went and why he didn't say anything to anybody. That's all.

Now, have you done the math on this? Think about it: if Wilbur *is* the Gypsy Man, he's more than eighty years old by now. So whatever unfortunate circumstances have haunted this little village, or might haunt it in the future, can't have too much to do with anything like a Gypsy Man. At least not *that* Gypsy Man. Wilbur Crawford would be just too old to be running up and down these hills and in and out of the woods on this mountain. I know Clare Richmond's run off again, and I know Penny's worried about her. She even came up here not long ago and asked if my wife, Myra, might not be able to keep an eye on Tory a little while until school starts. I presume it's so Penny can open the store and work in it awhile. She's got to need the money, and it can't be doing her or Clare any good that the store's been closed all this time. It was okay with Myra, though. She watches the little girl every now and then when Penny has to work at the tire store and her aunt Clare is keeping regular hours at her own little store. Myra and Tory get along just fine, thank you kindly.

But Penny shouldn't be worried over much about Clare. She's not missing, as much as she's gone, if you know what I mean.

After all, Clare *is* Clare.

What would the Gypsy Man want with her? I'd like to ask Penny that one myself.

MORGAN

Whats the matter?" I say. "Somebody chase you down here?"

Penny pulls the screen door open and steps inside. Breathing fast like a squirrel. I sit at the kitchen table, packing tobacco in my pipe. Can't decide if I should eat breakfast or not.

"I thought you was coming up, today," she says. "I waited all morning."

"It ain't much of the morning yet," I say.

"It's almost noon."

"Been looking for signs," I tell her. "I'll be up. What are you running from?"

"I was just running. I run down here. That's all."

"Something spook you?"

"No. I got to open the store. I don't have much time."

"You could of just called."

"You never answer the phone."

This makes me smile. "Well, sometimes I do."

"If you're standing right next to it."

"I don't get up and run just because a bell rings." I put the tobacco pouch in my back pocket, set the pipe in my mouth. "Where's the little one?"

"Myra's watching her. At the school. She's got to go back next week, anyway. Myra said she won't let her out of her sight."

"I guess Tory don't mind it."

"Mind what?"

"Going back early."

It's quiet for a spell. I tap the tobacco in my pipe with my finger to keep it tamped down.

Then Penny says, "She ain't in school. Myra said she'd show her how to bake cookies." She sits down at the table. She's wearing them tight jeans and a yellow bandanna on her head. A crispy white blouse, too big for her, bunched up at the waist. She has the tail of the shirt tied in a big knot in front of her. When she notices me looking at her, she puts her chin in her hand and glares at me. "Why didn't you come up?"

I light the pipe. She sits there watching me. When I got it going pretty good, I say, "I told you. I been looking for signs. The stone ain't going nowhere."

She shrugs then stands up and goes over to stand in front of the sink. She's as nervous as a horse in a storm. It don't seem like she can sit still. She stares out the window, her back to me. She sighs and puts her hands in the back pockets of her jeans.

"You still ain't seen your aunt Clare?" I ask.

"No."

I don't say nothing.

"I don't know what's going on," she says.

I sit back and puff on my pipe. She stands there, watching out the window. Then she turns and leans herself against the sink, staring at me.

A man gets to a certain age and almost everything is an inconvenience. You know there's work—chickens to feed, maybe a board or two on the back porch that needs replacing, and the house could stand another coat of paint—but you been doing things like that all your life. After a while it gets to be like shaving or cutting your fingernails. You let it go a day. Nothing bad happens. Then another day. A week. And pretty soon you get to feeling like it really don't matter one way or the other whether you ever do any of it.

When tomorrow's big—when you feel like you've got thousands of them—it's easy to dream about what you can make of it and get busy trying to do that. You work and sweat. You don't think about much. Maybe the weekend or payday. But when tomorrow shrinks, when every night might be your last, you get a little bit like a dog. You eat and then you sleep. You walk around, drink a little water, scratch. Then maybe later in the day you eat some more. When you feel like it you sleep again for a while. You ain't thinking of days like other people. It don't even seem like days. It all seems like something you dreamed or remembered after a dream. Ain't none of it very real.

I just don't feel like another visit from the Gypsy Man. I know if I *did* look for signs, I might find another one. I tore up the one I found, and I made up my mind I wasn't going to tell Penny nothing about it. It'd just make her worry more.

"Well," Penny said. "What should we do?"

"I guess we'll see what we can see."

She keeps her hands tucked in the jeans. She is sure a well-shaped young woman, with good hips. Dressed in those jeans as she is, I am trying not to stare at her. I hope I never get so old I don't appreciate the shape of a woman's body. Something in the way a woman's hips and thighs, the stomach and calves, seem to be all a part of a single, curving line that suggests—I don't know. Time without end, maybe. A young woman means all the earth. And truth, too. A young woman is as much truth as there is in the whole big world.

"I dug out part of the stone," she says. "This morning."

I take the pipe out of my mouth and tamp the tobacco down a little bit with my thumb.

"It's not just a stone," she says.

"What is it?"

She comes around in front of me and sits down. "It's a tombstone."

"I'll be," I say.

"You know what that means?"

"Yes."

"It's a goddamned grave."

I hate to hear her talk like that, but it don't really bother me right then because the word *grave* settles in my head like something wet and cold. I hear her say *tombstone* and all, but I don't think *grave* until I hear the word.

"Well," I say.

"In my backyard, not more than a hundred feet from the back porch. I think I could reach it with the garden hose."

"Well," I say again. "I figured if it had lettering on it that's what it was. Didn't you?"

"I guess."

"It's probably pretty old. Years ago, a lot more folks buried their own around here."

"Aunt Clare goes missing," she says, "and then I find out that stone in my backyard is a grave. It's spooky."

"A really old grave. Ain't that what you said?"

"I don't know. I never seen the lettering on it before. That stone's been there as long as I can remember."

"So, now you know what it is. That's all," I say. "What's changed?"

"How'd it get to poking out of the ground so far that you can see the lettering?"

I puff on my pipe again. "Maybe just time and the earth shifting and such."

"It's so rocky up there, how'd anybody dig a hole deep enough to make a grave?"

"Maybe that's the one place on the Crawford farm where dirt's piled just right."

She looks at me. I keep puffing the pipe, calmly. It's quiet for a spell, then I say, "Your aunt Clare's gone missing before."

"Not this long. And not without saying nothing."

"Not ever? She never run off without letting you know?" I know the answer to the question.

Penny stares at her hands. The hair not covered by the bandanna hangs down by her face, so I can't see her eyes no more. "Sometimes," she says.

"Sometimes, what?"

"Sometimes she left without telling me."

"There you go," I say.

"Still. It scares the hell out of me."

"I can't believe it. You ain't scared of nothing, Penny Bone."

She looks kind of puzzled. "You know," she says. "People are always saying things like that to me. Like I ain't never been scared. But you know I don't know why they could think such a thing."

"Really?"

"I'm scared a lot."

"You don't show it."

"You lose your husband a month after your first child is born, and about anything will scare the wits out of you."

I nod, looking at her.

"Just about anything can happen, can't it?" Her voice is soft and almost sweet.

"I guess so."

"And so ain't you scared, too?"

"If'n I think about some things, some dark and dangerous things, I expect so."

"Is that story about Gypsy Crawford and the Gypsies true?"

"You mean that he got taken by Gypsies when he was a baby?"

"And they brought him back?"

I nod. "My daddy said it was."

"And there really is a Gypsy Man?"

"You know there is."

"And he leaves signs before he starts taking children?"

"Fires. Piles of leaves and broken branches that look like scarecrows or Lord knows what. I've seen the signs. Sometimes the leaves and branches look just like a man sitting down, Indian style, you know?" I draw more smoke from the pipe. She stares at the table, places her hands in front of her. The way her hair covers her eyes, she looks like a little girl.

"John never believed it," she says. She stares off out the window, now. Thinking of him probably. "He never believed any of it. And as long as I was with him, I didn't neither. But now..."

"Now what?"

"I got to think of Tory."

"Yes, you do."

"John said it was just folklore and ought to be called 'foolishlore,' because the folks that believed in it was all fools."

I give a short laugh. "That's John," I say. I tap the edge of the bowl of my pipe on an ashtray and knock out some of the ash. I say, "You think I'm a fool?"

Her eyes get real bright. Like she seen something that scared her. "No."

"I'm glad to hear it," I say.

It's quiet for a spell, then she says, "They really brought Wilbur Crawford back after three years? Put a sign on him and all?"

"That's how the story goes."

"The idea just gives me the creeps," she says.

"We'll have a look at the old Crawford place," I say.

"I thought you said you'd already looked for signs."

"Not up there."

She waves smoke away from her eyes. "I don't think we should—I don't—we shouldn't just go up there."

"I'll come have a look at that tombstone you found, and then we'll see." I put the pipe on the table. It's still smoking a bit. It don't relax me like it always used to. I don't like the idea of a grave. That piece of land Clare's cabin is on used to be Crawford property, and Lord knows who's buried up there.

"I think we should call the sheriff," Penny says after a while.

"We'll go on up," I say. "If there's need for it, we'll call the sheriff."

"I don't like the thing so close to the house."

"No sense bothering the sheriff, now." I get up, pull my suspenders up over my shoulders.

"The lettering says something, don't it?" she says.

"Bound to. If it's a tombstone."

We walk out on the front porch. I pull the door shut behind me and lock it. She notices me do that.

"I lock it now," I say. "I always do."

She has nothing to say. We stand there for a minute, then I say, "I don't take no chances if the Gypsy Man might be about."

I can see from the look on her face that she ain't locked her place. "You say you uncovered more of the stone," I say. "Does the lettering spell something?"

"I can't make nothing out. It's just some letters."

"Well, I'll just have to see it, I guess." We walk up the road. We don't say nothing for a long time. We pass her aunt Clare's little store, and then go up the long hill toward her place. When we pass the store, Penny says, "Clare's going to kill me when she finds out how many days I've kept the store closed."

"I expect Gault's wife ain't too happy about it neither. She don't like going all the way down to Lebanon Church for—"

"I brought her a bag of groceries when I took Tory down there this morning."

"Oh."

"She was complaining then."

"Well," I say. "She's a good customer." We walk on. It's almost cold in the shade. The hill seems longer and higher and my knees start hurting again. After a while, I'm glad of the cooler air, because I can't get enough breath to say words. Penny keeps talking about her aunt Clare.

"I just think she's gone too far this time."

"One of her binges." I'm puffing when I talk now. "You should be used to it."

"It's never taken this long. She always got her fun and come home."

I don't have nothing to say to that.

"She wouldn't stay away this long, would she?" Penny says. She ain't really talking to me. She's trying to convince herself and not doing very well.

The sun ain't high enough. It's dark under the trees along the road and all the way to the cabin.

"She wouldn't do that," Penny says.

"She got a mind?" I say.

"What?"

"Your aunt Clare got a brain?"

"Everybody's got a brain," she says. She seems restless, but now she, too, is puffing a bit.

"That's why everybody's so . . ." I take a deep breath. "So damned unpredictable."

"Sure."

"That's right," I say. I stop. Take another deep breath. We're in front of the thin, broken sidewalk that leads up to her cabin. A three-step cement stair breaks up in the grass here. I sit down on the top step—the only one still intact—and wipe my brow with a handkerchief. "Let me get my breath."

She places herself in front of me, her arms folded across her chest. I love the way her hips and legs look as she leans on one leg then the other in the dark shade of the trees. She bites her lower lip, staring back down the hill.

When I can breathe again I say, "If people was predictable, we wouldn't need laws or courts or nothing like that. We'd only have to read each person like a sign and decide from *that* whether to leave them walking around free or not."

She shrugs her shoulders.

"You see what I mean?" I say.

"Clare's in trouble," she says. "I know it."

"You ain't listening," I say as I stand up again. I take another deep breath and then lead the way up the broken walk to the cabin and on into the backyard.

"There it is," she says.

The stone is in the far corner of the yard, almost off the line where Clare regularly mows the grass. It sticks up out of the dirt sideways—like the fellow buried there tried to roll over and took the stone with him.

The top line of letters reads *I N M*.

Penny brushes her hand over the face of the stone—or at least the part of it that juts out of the ground. "It's as clean as I could get it."

Beneath the top letters is another group of letters. *W I L E L*.

"What do you suppose *wilel* means?" I ask.

"I don't know."

"Is it a word?"

"I was hoping you'd know."

"Maybe it's a name," I say.

"Really?"

"Yeah. The top one is probably *In Memory of*, don't you think?"

She nods, but I can see she ain't thought of it.

Below the second line is the letters *B O*. "Look here," I say. "This here's probably the first two letters of *Born*. You uncover more of it, and you'll see. I bet the next letter is an *R*."

"That would make the next line—" Penny stops herself.

"Well, yes," I say. "Look at it. It's a *D* right? That must be for *Died*."

She starts digging around the base of the stone with her hands.

"Take a long time that way," I say.

"I've got a shovel."

"Go get it."

"I don't want to dig the whole thing up," she says. "I just want to be sure what it says."

"Okay."

She stands up, brushes the knees of her jeans, then wipes her hands on her backside. She walks toward the back porch and I follow her. I am just about to sit myself down on the top step, when I hear a low, weak moan from inside the cabin.

Penny is rooting in a shed on the back porch. I ain't sure she heard it. I get up and step toward the back door. Penny straightens up and says, "Here it is."

I hear the sound again. It's louder this time, but it don't sound like a moan no more. I can't figure out what it might be.

"You hear that?" I say.

She don't say nothing, but she grabs my arm. "What do you think it is?" she whispers.

I hear it again, softer now, and very faint. "You get yourself a cat?" I ask.

"No."

"There's somebody in the house," I say.

"Let's go," Penny says.

"Where?"

She's pulling my arm. "Get the sheriff."

"You afraid of it, and you don't know what it is?"

"That's when I'm *most* afraid."

"Whatever that is, it's too weak to be dangerous," I say. I reach for the door handle, but Penny says, "Wait."

She moves back into the shed and comes out with the shovel. "Take this."

"Whatever's in there," I say. "It already got hit with something like that. I don't need it."

She seems disappointed.

I try the door but it's locked. I look at Penny. She shakes her head. "I never lock the door," she whispers.

"You left this unlocked?"

She frowns as if to say it's a silly question. "Yes."

"Well, it's locked now."

We go around to the front door, but it's locked, too.

Penny's face turns white. She stands next to me close enough that I think I can feel her trembling.

"I guess you do get scared sometimes," I say.

She only frowns at me. Then she shakes her head as if to clear it of thought.

"Well," I say. "Maybe somebody's come home finally."

I start to knock, but Penny stops me. She walks slowly to the far end of the porch. A flowerpot sits on the railing down there and she lifts it and gets a key, then walks back and hands it to me. She don't seem as frightened as before, but she gets around behind me again. I feel her hand on my arm. I open the door.

The room is dimly lit, with the shades drawn and a lone bare bulb burning over the kitchen table, but I can see a shape on the couch, curled up like a pile of dirty laundry.

"Lookee here," I say. "It's your aunt Clare."

PENNY

She is unconscious when we find her. Curled up with her face buried against the back of the couch.

I put my hand on her shoulder, try to wake her gently, and she says, "Don't. Don't touch me."

"You all right?" Morgan says.

"It ain't my fault," she says. "I didn't start it."

"She doesn't know where she is," I say.

"Her eyes open?" Morgan says.

"She can't see us really. Her eyes are all glassy."

73

"I ain't all right," Clare says. "You leave me be."

"She's way off somewhere," Morgan says.

"I ain't gone nowhere."

"Been hitting the bottle," Morgan says.

"Don't," she moans.

Morgan leans over her. "Clare. You been hitting the bottle?"

She turns toward us slightly and then I see her face. Her right eye is swollen shut and blue as a grape. What I thought was smeared lipstick on her mouth turns out to be dried blood.

"My God," I say.

Morgan just stands there shaking his head. "She's mighty beat up."

I go into the kitchen and get a towel. I soak it in warm water and come back and sort of pile it on Clare's forehead.

"What's that?" she says.

I look at Morgan. "What should I do?"

"Maybe if you folded it."

"No. What should I do with her?"

"Maybe we should take her to a hospital. She might be bleeding inside."

"Should we move her?"

"That probably ain't such a good idea."

"You think we should get an ambulance up here?"

Clare moans, then puts her hand up over mine.

"She's coming around," Morgan says. "Maybe we don't have to."

"She won't let me take her to a hospital. And she'll be fit to be tied if she wakes up in one."

"Yeah, well."

"She'll blame me. I know it."

"You can't let her stay here like that."

I go back to the kitchen and put cold water on the towel. I squeeze it out and fold it so it will rest on her forehead better. When I come back, Morgan is dialing the phone.

"Turn the radio down, honey," Clare says. Her eyes are still closed, but when I put the wet towel on her, she takes my hand and holds onto it. "I'm all right, baby," she says.

"Clare?" I say.

Morgan talks quietly into the phone.

I go over to him.

"What are you doing?"

He holds up his hand. "No," he says into the phone. "She's breathing okay."

He is quiet for a minute, then he says, "No, there ain't no blood neither. Maybe a little dried on her mouth."

Clare groans, then seems to struggle to get closer to the back of the couch. Morgan says, "Just a minute." He puts the phone down and walks over to her. I follow him. "Help me get the uninjured eye open," he says.

"What for?"

"Just do it." He leans down and turns her head back toward him.

"Don't," Clare says.

He gently pushes her hair back a bit, and I hold her head still. He puts his thumb on the healthy eyelid. When he opens it, Clare looks right at him. "What the hell you doing?" she says.

"I'm looking in your eye," he says.

She tries to close it, but he holds it open. "Get away from me," she says.

"Looks okay to me," he says. Then he goes back and picks up the receiver on the phone. "The one eye I can get open looks normal."

He listens for a second, then he says, "That's right. The

pupil's right normal looking, not too big nor too small. She looks pretty mean, if you ask me."

Clare turns back against the couch. "Son of a bitch," she says.

"Nope, she ain't coughed once. She's breathing and cussing up a storm," Morgan says. "Okay, thank you kindly." Then he hangs up the phone and comes over next to me. I look up at him. His face is calm, like he's been trying to stay awake and he's made up his mind to go to bed. "That was a doctor in Lebanon Church. A friend of mine. He still makes house calls."

I nod.

"He says he can't come by until later this afternoon."

I stand up. Clare moans again. Then cries out, "Penny! Get me a drink of water this instant."

Morgan turns as if he is going to leave.

"Where you going?" I say.

"What's happened?" Clare says.

Morgan shakes his head. "Well," he says. His face is blank. "I was headed home, I guess."

"Don't go now."

"I figured this was private."

"Don't go," I say. "Please. Wait until the doctor or the sheriff get here."

He shrugs. It is quiet for a while, then he seems to shuffle his feet a bit. "You know," he says. "This ain't..." I wait for him to finish but he falls quiet again.

"What?" I say.

"This probably ain't what you think it is."

"What do you mean?"

"I know you're pretty scared right now, but I wouldn't call the sheriff just yet."

"I'm not afraid," I say.

"I wouldn't blame this on the Gypsy Man."

"I won't."

I move the towel on Clare's forehead. She tries to turn away from me. I say, almost to myself, "Somebody's got to stay with her while I go open the store."

"All day?" Morgan says.

"Just for a few hours. And then I got to go get Tory."

"Oh." He seems to weaken a bit. "I'm sorry. Of course."

"Don't," Clare says.

"I'm here, hon," I say.

"Who's that? Who's there?"

"It's me, Clare. It's Penny."

She opens her one eye, slightly. "Who's that?" She tries to point at Morgan.

"It's Morgan Tiller," I say.

"What's that awful smell?" She puts her head further back into the pillow and closes the eye tightly. Seconds later she is snoring.

MORGAN STAYS with her and I go down the hill and open the store. Hardly no reason for it, because only a few customers come in the whole time. Around three in the afternoon, I close it up again and go to Myra's and pick up Tory.

As soon as we get back Tory tries to bolt over to the couch and pounce on Clare. I grab her arm, and she almost swings up into the air. She thinks I want to play, and it breaks my heart to see the look on her face when I scold her. "Sit still, now," I say. "You have to be quiet."

She goes into her room to pout. "Tory," I say. "You can go into my room if you want."

She has always liked jumping on my double bed, and I know if she goes in there she'll stay for a long time, if I check after her every few minutes.

The doctor comes about a half hour later. His name is Sam. That's what he wants to be called: Dr. Sam. He is taller than Morgan and a lot younger. His hair is dark brown and he has a wide, smooth face. He wears a white shirt with the sleeves rolled up to the elbows, and a pair of gray corduroy trousers. A white Panama hat with a black band tilts back on his head. He looks more like one of them wags that hang around a race-track than a medical doctor, except he's carrying a black leather bag and has a stethoscope around his neck. When he comes in he throws the hat onto the dining room table and then shoos me and Morgan out of there so he can examine Clare.

We wait in the kitchen while I make a pot of coffee. When the doctor is done he calls us back into the room. He says Clare has suffered a severe concussion and we shouldn't let her sleep.

"Will she die if I just leave her on the couch like this?"

He shakes his head, then seems to nod a bit. "It's not a good thing to let her sleep. You're not supposed to do that after a concussion. But her eyes look okay."

He isn't saying something and I can tell it. "What else?" I say.

"She's been drinking."

"So?"

"That may be why she's sleeping," he says. He pulls the stethoscope from his ears and lets it drape again around his neck. Then he starts rooting around in his black bag. "Her heart rate is good. I've cleaned the wound and put some stitches in the cut on her eye. You've done the right thing putting cold compresses on her head."

"The first one was warm," I say.

"Cold is better. If you want her to stay awake."

"I don't want her to go to the hospital."

"Okay."

"I want to leave her here with me."

"She's probably not in any danger," he says. "But she's going to be in a lot of pain when she's fully awake." He takes a small bottle of pills out of the bag. "Give these to her—two every four hours—for pain."

I take the bottle from him and put it in my pocket.

"If you need more, just call me and I'll give you a prescription." He bends down and looks in her one good eye again. "Pupils still look fine. She can stay right here until she's feeling better."

"Thank you," I say.

"Make sure you keep that medicine away from your little girl."

"Of course, I will," I say. Tory is having a high time jumping on my bed. The noise shakes the room sometimes, but it don't disturb Clare none.

"It's a powerful painkiller, but a small amount of it can really make a child sick. Too much and . . ." He don't finish the sentence.

I slip my hand into my pocket and close it over the bottle. "I'll keep it right close," I say. "You don't have to worry."

"Have you talked to Sheriff Paxton about this?" Dr. Sam says, closing up his bag.

"Not yet."

"I have to report this sort of injury."

"What sort of injury?"

"She's clearly been beaten up by somebody."

"I reckon I'll call the sheriff," I say. Morgan sits in a chair across the room, sipping coffee. When the doctor moves toward the door, he stands up and shakes the doctor's hand. "Send the bill to me, Sam," he says.

"You don't have to do that," I say.

Doctor Sam smiles at me. "I'll send it to Miss Bone, here, and you two can work it out."

"How'd you know my name?" I say.

"Oh, I know everybody's name in this town—and Lebanon Church, too."

"You don't say."

"I knew your dad," he says.

I have nothing to say to that.

"Don't forget to let the sheriff know about this."

"Should I worry about the stitches?" I ask him.

"No. When she's up and around, have her stop down to see me and I'll remove them."

Clare says, "Get me a drink of water, honey." Her voice is strong, but she don't know where she is.

"You should try and wake her," Doctor Sam says. "It's okay to give her plenty of water if she'll drink it. She's going to be in a lot of pain..."

"You already said that," I tell him.

He nods. "Well," he says. "I'll be going." He pats Morgan on the arm, then takes his bag and walks out.

Morgan and I sit near Clare for a while and watch her gradually waking up. She won't say nothing but she keeps opening her eyes and looking at us, and I keep giving her sips of water. She don't seem to be in much pain.

After a while, Morgan says, "I've got to go up there." He glances over his shoulder and I know he is talking about the old Crawford Place. "I wish my leg felt better."

"What do you think happened to her?" I ask him.

"I got to start looking for signs again."

"You think it was the Gypsy Man?"

"There's something I ain't told you."

I look at him.

His eyes are dark and sad. "I seen a sign the other day."

"You did?"

"No mistake. I didn't want to tell you about it."

"Why?"

"I didn't want you to fret over it until I seen another one. He always leaves more than one." He shakes his head and gets to his feet. It ain't easy because of his bad leg. "Ain't no Gypsy

Man beat her up, but somebody did," he says. He turns and limps over to the door and takes a deep breath. He stands there for a while, looking up the road. Then he says, "That's not what bothers me."

"What do you mean?"

"It don't worry me none that she got beat up. Anybody might have done it." He brushes his hand over the top of his head. He stands in the open door frame, gazing out, his back to me. "I just think you can't let a thing like this go. You have to pay attention to it."

"You don't really know what to think of it, do you?"

He turns and looks at me. "I'd sure like to talk to her when she wakes up and makes some sense."

"You think it might have been the Gypsy Man, don't you?"

"You get that shovel and lock your door when I go."

I go outside and get the shovel, and then he comes out behind me.

"Where you going?" I say.

"I'm going on up there," he says. "Before it gets too late in the day."

I watch him work his way further up the hill, then I pick up the shovel and go back inside the cabin and lock the door. It takes me awhile, but I push the big green chair over in front of the door so if a body does try to break it in, they'll have even more work to get inside.

I move over to Clare and shake her gently. "Clare," I say. "You have to be awake. You can't sleep now."

"What's the matter with you?" Clare says. "For Lord's sake. What's got into you?"

"You just have to be awake," I say.

"I'm awake, honey."

"No, you ain't."

"I'm right here, glory be."

"You have to open your eyes and stay awake."

"Where's Penny?"

"I'm right here," I say. I am just setting here, holding the shovel real tight, listening to Tory in the next room, jumping up and down on my bed.

In all the confusion, I almost forget about that tombstone sticking up out of the ground in my backyard.

GAULT

From a distance, Crawford looks like a town right out of the nineteenth century. Even in June smoke rises from the chimneys of some of the cabins along the highway. There's a mill you come to first, on Route 13 on the right, smoke rising from it, too—then back in the trees beyond it a white house, tall and stately, with a rock path and brick driveway. That's where I live.

Beyond my house, which is also a school, are other houses—smaller and well spread out, even further from the highway. In the center of town there's a small post office, a gas station, a bank, and a long flat building under a Goodyear sign. Turn right on Lookout Road, and you scale another hill, up along a winding, single-lane pavement until you reach a small house on the right, back a long way from the road. There's a broken and tilted sidewalk leading to the front porch. The sagging roof of the house gives it the appearance of quaintness—as though it were a romanticized version of a country house you might find on the cover of *Saturday Evening Post*. That's where Penny Bone lives with her daughter and her aunt Clare. Further up the road, on the left, you come to a driveway with two great stone pillars on either side of it. That's the old Crawford place—or what's left of it. It occupies the entire area of the great circle that Lookout Road makes between where it branches off Route 13, then meets it again. It must be more than a hundred acres of land. The tip of the mountain is there, rising above the town and even the lookout, like some sort of balding tower. You can see it for miles before you start to ascend this mountain, and it always looks as though it's covered in snow. In truth, it's so rocky at the summit, the trees can't get a foothold there. Or perhaps the mill had something to do with the lack of trees.

Just below where the house was, there's a gazebo, leaning over and dragging its rotten posts to the ground, but if you get close to it, you can see as far as the rim of the world. The valley below seems to stretch into a blue infinity, and the clouds that hover over it sweep along with such slow grandeur, you feel like God gazing at his creation. Also, to be honest, you have the sensation that you are in a place that has completely rejected God—since, over the years, we have abandoned this overlook to the devouring forest.

Directly below the overlook, deep down in the ravine under it, runs a swiftly moving, blue, snaking river that winds through the trees and, with the help of a few steep waterfalls along the way, to the valley below. All the young men of Crawford, and most of the girls, too, have fished in that river. They scramble down the side of the ravine hanging onto trees and twisted branches, leaping in the air sometimes from one small tree to another, risking everything, as the young do, carrying towels and picnic baskets and bottles of soda and beer.

East and back down the mountain the other way, the road winding like a tightly folded ribbon, is Lebanon Church, a true township, with a county courthouse (where I maintain a legal office), two schools, several churches, a synagogue, four hotels, and a sheriff's office. The county sheriff is a fellow named Theodore Paxton. He's elected, but he's a very competent police officer. Everyone in Lebanon Church says he's one of the best, and that's probably how he keeps getting reelected.

In the mountains you can smell rain long before it comes. Also, you can see it sometimes, far in the distance, drenching the fields or the scattered houses in the valley. You can actually see above the clouds that have loosed the rain and thunder, and the dark places underneath where everything is pelted and shoved by the storm. You can watch it come up the mountain, making its way to you in a slow, almost respectful approach.

My house doubles as both a courthouse and a school. The school is in the basement, and the courthouse on the first floor. I am both a teacher and a lawyer. I've practiced both professions with, I like to think, equal skill and passion. I was born in Lebanon Church, but have now lived in Crawford most of my life. I went to George Washington University before the war, continued in the law school there, then brought my new bride up here to set up a law practice. I bought the house right after the war from the Crowly family, who own the mill—and as far as anyone knows, always will own it.

This evening, I'm sitting in my living room with Myra, and cool air blows through two wide-open windows across the room, stirring the leaves of her potted palms, umbrella plants, and tall green Schefflera. The light breaks into shadows of the windowpanes on the floor, and the curtains rise and fall softly while we talk. I can hear the little girl laughing at something in the kitchen, and then she comes in and climbs up on the couch across from me.

"Well, Miss Tory Bone," Myra says. "What's so funny in there?"

"I ate a cookie."

"Shame on you."

Tory bows slightly from the waist. She sits all the way back in the couch so her legs splay straight out in front of her. She wears shiny black pumps, with white socks and a denim dress. Her neatly combed brown hair is gathered above each ear with a small yellow ribbon.

"You look very pretty today," I say to her.

"Her momma always dresses her up when she visits, doesn't she?" Myra says. "Of course I gave her the ribbons."

"Well, they look very nice." I watch Myra staring at the little girl and wish again that we had been luckier.

A little later, while Tory sits at the dining room table drawing pictures on a white legal pad, Myra says, "Penny is afraid the Gypsy Man has returned to Crawford." She speaks in a low voice so Tory won't hear.

"You don't say."

"I told her it was nonsense. But she believes it."

My chair occupies a shaft of sunlight that cuts through the sheer curtains over the two large windows on my right. Outside, I can see the strip of road rising toward the town. This room is my favorite, with its plants and broad furniture, ornate and somber, with dark oak paneling. It looks as if, with very little redecorating, it would make a fine lawyer's office, rather than a living room. Books fill the shelves of dark oak bookcases along three walls.

"I just know this will get people talking about the little Landon child again," Myra whispers.

"It was the worst thing that ever happened in this town," I say, softly.

"And Terry Landon was such a beautiful child, a truly beautiful child."

"Yes, he was."

She looks at me and I say, "No more, dear."

One of the curtains fans out fully in the room, looks almost like a ghost swirling up toward the ceiling.

"Yes, I'm sorry," she says.

"School's starting up in only a few days. We both have a lot to do."

"Yes."

We are silent for a while, watching Tory as she concentrates on the paper in front of her.

Then Myra says, "It is such an odd story—about the Gypsies and all."

"What do you mean?"

"I wonder if there's any truth to the original story—you know, about Wilbur."

"Let me read you something." I get up and walk to the bookcase directly behind her. She remains seated, waiting, not watching me.

"Here," I say. She turns and I withdraw a book from the top shelf. I go around and sit down next to her, flipping the pages in it. When I find what I want, I say, "This is a book by a fellow named Gilbertson. William Walker Gilbertson. It's called *The Gipsies*. See?" I hold the book up so she can see the cover. "Mr. Gilbertson spells the word with an *i* because he's from England, I think."

She nods.

I reach into my breast pocket, get my wire spectacles, and put them on. I hold the book so she can read along with me. "You ready?"

"Go ahead." She is watching me warily. She doesn't understand my apparent fervor over this, but I really won't brook such talk coming from her, and I want what I'm about to read to her to make an end of it.

I read out loud, "*Gipsies don't call themselves that. They refer to themselves as 'rom,' which means 'man,' in the generic sense. All other people are called 'Gadje.' This word has Indian origins and means 'yokel,' or 'bumpkin.'*"

"Indian as in India," she says.

"Wait. There's more." I find my place and go on.

Gipsies have no nationality, and until the twentieth century, were found only in Europe and Africa. Most scholars think they originated in India. They are nomadic, live in groups or families they call 'Vitsas.' There are three main groups which comprise all Gipsies: the Kalderesh, the Gitanos, and the Manush, or Sinti. Of the three groups, the Kalderesh, which originated in central Europe and the Balkans, are the most populous—followed by the Gitanos, from the Iberian peninsula, Northern Africa, and southern France—and the Manush, from northern France and Germany.

The Gipsies sometimes leave signs, or what they call 'Patterans,' in the forest to announce their presence. Sometimes it is a kind of warning to stay away. They pile leaves and branches in an odd way—often to suggest a man sitting straight up, or perhaps an animal down on its knees. No one is really sure what these signs mean, although they are supposed to have meaning for each of the vitsas. Although Gipsies did migrate to Mexico early in this century, as far as anyone knows, there have been no Gipsy populations of any significance anywhere else in the Americas.

I stop and look at her, slowly closing the book. "You see, don't you, what the problem is with the original story—the one about Wilbur being taken by Gypsies?"

"I guess so."

"The original legend is just that—a legend."

Now she smiles. "Of course I knew that, darling."

"We live in the easternmost mountain range in the United States and well north of Mexico."

"You have to admit, the legends are intriguing," she says.

"No, I don't. I don't have to admit that at all."

"I mean just as legends."

"I'm more interested in the truth," I say. "As you should be."

"Yes, of course."

"Search for that, and you won't find a Gypsy Man."

"I wasn't looking for one, dear," she smiles.

"Good," I say. I kiss her on the cheek.

At times like this, when she is questioning me about things, trying my patience with her apparent naiveté, I love her all the more.

MYRA

Morgan Tiller used to drive the school bus for Henry. Imagine a man like that, driving the county's young children around every day. That's the one thing I've never agreed with or shared with Henry: his trust in human beings. At the time, he just felt that Morgan would be good for the children, since he had apparently been classified a war hero by some authority beyond my comprehension.

But I turned out to be right about Mr. Tiller. I told my husband that it was clear from his appearance alone that the man just could not be trusted. Sure enough, Henry had to fire him one day, right on the spot, because he said something very physical about me. I happened to walk down to the garage where both of them were working on the bus to keep the thing running, I suppose, and I saw Morgan lean over and whisper something in Henry's ear. He was grinning when he said it—a leering, lecherous grin, if you ask me.

Doubtless, Mr. Tiller said something I'd rather not contemplate or hear spoken out loud, and I think I can pretty well guess what it was. I walked into the garage then, and I saw that my husband was instantly angry, even though Morgan didn't notice it at first. He just laughed and went back to his work.

"You just don't have any idea, do you?" Henry said.

Mr. Tiller tried to apologize, of course. "It was just a joke. You know, between men." You should have seen the red smile on his dirty face.

"I do not think your joke was funny," said Henry.

"Just a way of complimenting you," Mr. Tiller said. "That's all. I didn't mean nothing by it."

I've been around men like him, and I know what they notice about a woman, so Henry didn't have to tell me what he said. Even when a woman is dressed properly, some men can look at her as if she were wearing nothing at all. And the thought that a man like Morgan Tiller finds me attractive is enough to make my bones turn to powder.

So he was fired that very day. Henry didn't raise his voice, he merely stepped back from him slightly, regarded him with a curious frown, then he said, "Morgan, I don't think we'll be needing a bus driver anymore." He was very mannerly.

"I'm sorry to hear it," Tiller said. "If it's because of what I said, I . . ."

"It's got nothing to do with that," Henry said, waving his hand dismissively and moving away from him. "I was meaning to tell you this morning anyway."

Morgan shrugged his shoulders, put his hands in his pockets, and walked out. He acted like it didn't bother him, but he hasn't spoken more than a few words to Mr. Gault or me since then, and that was thirteen years ago. Henry hired Morgan in 1946, right after we founded the school, and fired him the same year.

And then when the little Landon boy got lost a few years ago, Morgan Tiller made as if to help out, but he was busy trying to make it look as though we were at fault. The boy disappeared in the early morning, on his way to school, not while he was here. In fact, I don't know if he ever got on the bus. My husband said he picked the boy up that morning, but he couldn't really be certain. It's quite possible he never saw the boy. I can tell you no one saw him here at the school, once the bus arrived.

I think whatever happened to Terry Landon happened between his house and the spot next to the road where he waited for the bus.

But I hate to even think of those times. Henry undervalued the hatred in these people; he is so prone to seeing only the good in a person. Even a man like Morgan Tiller. And I suppose, if I were to be truthful, and if I could resist the shudder of embarrassment I feel every time I see the man walking like a peddler down the middle of the street, I'd have to admit there might be good even in Morgan Tiller. Lord knows, Penny Bone sure depends on him, and if she sees something good in him, who am I to dispute it?

Oh, but Henry and I were so proud of the Landon child. He was the first Negro student to attend our school. Of course that was Henry's doing. I wondered at the time if it was a wise thing to do. I have to tell you, no one around here was very happy about it. Even I was against it—not because of any silly racial notions—but because I just knew something awful was going to happen.

You know, if people think one way long enough, it's like nature; an opinion can somehow take on the vigor and energy of genetics. When you go against a thing people have been compelled to believe for generations, you pit yourself against heredity in a way. At least it might seem that way to less-fortunate people who have no willing intellect and who do not want to question a single thought they might have inherited from their parents.

The net result is, of course, that you appear to be "unnatural" in the eyes of such people and as we all know, unnatural things are almost always kindred to the work of Satan. It was precisely this peculiar trick of the human imagination that caused ignorant people to see my husband, who was trying to do a good thing, as an instrument of Satan, and a nine-year-old boy like Terry Landon as the very embodiment of evil. And no matter what Pastor Sloan read from Scriptures on Sunday about brotherhood and the bond of love between Christ and all men, folks looked at Henry and me as if we might hurt them in some way.

You feel that sort of thing in your heart, when it is quiet and you've just settled down to watch the front lawn and see who decides to stroll up the walk to say hello. Silences start to accumulate in a town where people think the devil may be at work, small silences. You say hello to a chatterbox you've always known, and the reply is shorter, less interested. It's a kind of detachment that you get used to, although you begin to feel that you are straining the very kindness and civility that you've always embraced because you live in a small town and everybody knows you; it's the same kindness and civility that you've taken for granted year after year without ever calculating what might be left of it.

Something of the warmth goes out of a town when civility is consciously applied, and people stop looking each other in the eye. My Lord, when that happens, a simple hair appointment can take on the weight and significance of a political meeting.

The whole country was about to be ordered to do exactly what we did—only one year after we admitted the Landon boy, the Supreme Court ordered that colored children be admitted to white schools all over the south. Henry and I have no doubt that we did the right thing. No doubt at all. In spite of the outcome. But I was so afraid of the trouble it would bring.

THE MORNING Penny dropped Tory off to stay for a while, I told Penny I'd keep a good eye on her, as I always do.

"Don't let her out of your sight," Penny said.

"I certainly won't," I said. Then I looked in her eyes, and she stood there watching me, as if she expected me to say something else. "Are you okay, honey?" I said.

"I'm worried about Clare."

I took Tory's hand. "Well, we'll have a fine time today."

"I got to open the store."

Tory put her thumb in her mouth and leaned against my leg.

"Can you keep her until this evening?" Penny said.

"Of course. I'll enjoy the company."

"If I don't open the store at least for a while, when Clare does come back she'll really give me hell."

I patted Tory's head. "Don't let's have talk like that in front of the little one," I said.

Penny just stood there looking at me.

"You learned better manners than that in this school, young lady."

Tory said, "I want a drink of water."

"I'm sorry," Penny said. "I forgot my manners." It cost her something to say that to me, and I instantly felt bad about reproaching her.

"Your aunt Clare will come back very soon," I said. "And I'm sure she'll be none the worse for the wear."

"Yes, ma'am."

"My, she is a traveler though, isn't she?"

"Yes, ma'am."

"I declare, sometimes I wish I had the adventurer's heart like your aunt Clare," I said. I retreated into the kitchen to get Tory a glass of water.

I like Penny. I think Henry likes her. She can be a bit of a wild one, but she's smart and has a good heart. I helped her with arithmetic when she was in the school and we had good fun with it. She learned fast and seemed to understand instinctively that criticism is an act of love. I was very sorry that she married John Bone and never went to college, although now that she's alone and struggling to keep herself sane while raising a very feisty little girl all by herself, perhaps she's learning more than any of the best universities could teach her.

I brought the water for Tory. Penny remained in the living room, quiet, with her hands in her pockets. Tory drank the water as though she was afraid I'd snatch it away from her before she finished it.

"We'll make some chocolate chip cookies today, how would you like that?" I said to her.

Tory gulped, then said, "Thank you."

She handed me the empty glass. Penny came to the arch between the kitchen and the living room. "Do you believe in the Gypsy Man?" she said.

"I don't even think about him, honey," I said.

Tory said, "What's the Gypsy Man?"

I could see Penny wished she hadn't said the name out loud. She went to Tory and bent down in front of her. She brushed the little girl's hair back off her forehead and smiled. "It ain't nothing," she said. "I was just asking Mrs. Gault about a story I heard."

"Would you like to make some cookies today?" I said.

Tory smiled. "Yes, ma'am."

Penny stood up and looked at me. She had her thumbs hooked in the front pockets of her jeans. "Don't let her out of your sight," she said.

"I won't, honey," I said. "You come on back here when you close the store and I'll fix you some supper. You don't look like you've had a decent meal in days."

"I will," she said. Then she leaned down and kissed Tory on the forehead. "Behave yourself, you hear me?"

"Yes, ma'am," Tory said.

"I may stop up at the store later," I told her. "I'm going to need some sugar and flour."

"Could you make it in the afternoon?" she said.

"Well, sure. We got enough here for the cookies."

"I'm fixing to go over to Morgan's place first," she said.

"Really?"

"I won't be there long."

"I'll wait until noon, then. Will that be okay, honey? I just need a little flour and sugar. And molasses. I can't keep enough molasses. I think the ghosts in this house drink it."

"Ghosts?"

"It's just an expression, honey."

She cast her eyes down. Then she absently started patting and caressing Tory's hair and the back of her neck. "Bye, honey," she said.

"You got plenty of flour up at that store?" I asked.

"I think we still got some."

"Bye, Mom," Tory said.

Penny touched the top of her head again, then turned to leave.

"You come back for supper," I said. I really did expect to set her down in my dining room and feed her the best meal I could put together.

But now, it's a little before noon, and Tory and I have just cleaned up the mess we made baking the cookies, and Penny comes back early. She opens the screen door, loses her grip on it and lets it slam, then opens it again and swings open the front door. "Tory?" she hollers.

Tory runs out of the kitchen and greets her mother, who is standing on the foyer entry rug, and looks to be haggard, dirty, and fairly sullen. But when she sees me, she says, "I can't stay. We found Clare." She's in a big hurry. She doesn't want anything but Tory.

"Are you all right?" I say.

"I got to get back home," she says. "Clare's been hurt."

"My Lord, honey. Is she going to be all right?"

"Morgan called the doctor. We don't know yet."

"What happened?"

"She got beat up pretty bad."

I notice Tory's face change. "You're upsetting the little one."

Penny lays her hand on Tory's head. "Your aunt Clare'll be okay, honey," she says.

She lets the screen door slam behind her when she goes out. It's only her careless need to rush out, but it seems like an angry response, nonetheless. I register it as just her usual country way of doing things. She probably lets her own screen door slam just as hard, even when she's just headed out to the yard to hang out the wash. And to be truthful, I've never really minded the sound of a slamming screen door.

Henry doesn't like it, though. He comes into the kitchen. "What was that?"

"Just Penny taking Tory back home."

"She came back already?"

"Her aunt Clare came home."

"Oh, good." He went to the cabinet and got the coffeepot, then filled it with water and put it on the stove. I watched him getting his own coffee. He does things like that. Takes care of himself when he wants things and never bothers me.

"Penny said Clare was hurt. Somebody beat her up."

"Oh?" He doesn't say any more.

HENRY'S FATHER was a doctor and his mother, an artist—she was a consultant to none other than Mr. Teddy Roosevelt. So Henry presents a curious amalgam of logic and imagination, of cognition and intuition. I met him in college—at George Washington University. I was a drama major and performed in

95

several plays. The *Washington Times Herald* said I had a future. But there was Henry when he was young: he looked a lot different then. He was lean and very strong, with dark brown hair cut evenly and not too short. A southern girl I knew back then said once, "His arms hang by his sides like the stocks of rifles in a gun rack." He carried himself with such tension—as if he might explode any minute—yet his voice was as smooth as the bass string on a violin. And he was so eloquent. It just thrilled me to hear him say anything. Anything at all.

And I know I can depend on him. I have that as knowledge and always have. And we live the kind of life I've always wanted in this house, back in the country, away from the rude city.

I don't have a lot of strange encounters with people back here. Our company is almost always the right kind of company, if you know what I mean. I believe a person has to be polite. That's how we have become civilized, finally, as Henry will tell you. But you have to admit, some strands of the human race are not as fully developed as others. I'm not talking about the differences between races or anything foolish like that. Good Lord, these days a person would have to be pretty ignorant to insist on the kind of separation we've become accustomed to in these hills. I'm not a segregationist. No, I'm simply talking about people—individual people. You can't account for the differences between a person like my husband—refined, educated, humane, mannerly, and kind—and a man like Morgan Tiller.

Now Mr. Tiller is—well, there's no polite way to say this—he's itinerant. Your average handyman or laborer. I don't think it matters that he owns that ramshackle place down the road or that he's lived there as long as anyone in Crawford. He's itinerant. That's how I think of him: a wanderer, with no idea what to do or where he's going. He walks around in those filthy coveralls, with tools hanging from every loop and scraps of white paper and measuring tape dangling out of every pocket, and he looks like some sort of peddler. He never combs his hair, so it sticks up like gray wire, and he stands in the middle of the road sometimes, just trying to get his balance—leaning back and forth like a sapling about to fall. One time he stood right in front of my walk and just stared at my rose bed. I was clipping some of the buds, and you know, pruning and such, and he pointed to the stone border that surrounded the front of the rose garden. "Got some stones missing," he said.

"I know it," I said. "Probably some kids around here took them. They were always loose."

"I'll put you two more in there for ten dollars," he said. Just like that. And I told him heavens, no. Just leave it alone. To tell the truth, I was surprised he noticed it. But then he said, "Looks like a mouth with teeth missing. I'll find stones that will fit right close into the cement there."

He just wanted my money, and I knew he'd only get two rocks and force them in where the two white stones used to be, breaking up the cement in the process. The white stones fit exactly, and it would take either those stones or new cement to make it look right, and I told him so.

"I guarantee I can make it look right," he said. "I'll crush the cement there."

He may have been drinking. A lot of the folks up here drink too much whiskey and they smell as if they just crawled out of a bottle.

Morgan's pants are always a little too long, or they're too short, or they hang on him like they're two or three sizes too big. At all events, he is simply sloppy. That's the difference, finally, between good people and folks who just haven't had the privileges of a decent upbringing.

I'm not judging though. I merely point out the difference between my husband and a man like Morgan Tiller because the difference is there and truly unmistakable. You have to take a difference like that into account if you're going to be listening to Morgan Tiller.

I've never seen the man in church, so he doesn't believe in God. And yet, he's willing to go around talking about this mythical creature who steals children and sets fires on the old Crawford place. It's hard not to feel sorry for him. Maybe whatever was noble or civilized in his heart just withered with the rest of him, or he forgot it. I know a man has certain brute instincts that battle with his education and upbringing. Without knowledge, with nothing in a man's head to distract him and occupy his more primitive inclinations, and when there is a lack of development—I hesitate to say breeding, but of course that's what I'm talking about—nothing can save a man.

Or a woman for that matter. I am not a prude, but certainly the stories I've heard about Clare Richmond are enough to make a person ponder how Penny can save Tory or herself from the same sort of future. Of course I refuse to add to the legends, or the gossip, but I think it's important for me to spend as much time with Tory as I can.

It would take common sense, and perhaps a dash of native intelligence, for even the dullest person to doubt such illogical superstitions as the boogey man or whatever name you want to give it. Morgan Tiller would be more likely to develop a goiter on each fingernail than a little common sense. I've known him for a long time and what I know for certain is, one simply cannot believe a single thing he says.

PARCHMAN

One man escaping from prison can cause enough trouble that it can seem like fifty. And fifty can be so confused and scared they don't even get the feeling they're free. It just turns out to be one kind of prison, moving away from another, until the other prison finds them and swallows them up again.

I'm a goddamned fool.

MORGAN

I'm out of breath by the time I get up the road to the old Crawford place. Have to sit down in the dirt by the front gate. I have some time before the sun gets too low, but it's already sinking toward the crest of the mountain. Still it bakes the dry grass, and by the time I sit down, it's not much cooler in the shade. The air is dry and stone still.

Penny looked a little frightened when I left her. I don't know what she thought she could do with that dang shovel. I wish I could just wave my hand and make her happy, bring John back to be with her and the child. That's what I wish.

After a while, I get up and root around in all the weeds and undergrowth along the path to the old house. I pick up a dry, thin, dead branch and poke the vines and bushes with it as I walk. I'm looking for a "pattern"—a small fire, maybe, or sometimes just a pile of leaves and broken branches that looks like a man sitting down Indian style, or a fella on all fours looking for a contact lens or something. The Gypsy Man wants me to find the signs, I think. Not just anybody. Only me. He knows I'll come looking, and I'm pretty sure he keeps an eye on me whenever I follow one of his trails. It's a game we play. The winner gets to take a life—or save one. I don't know how many times I might have won, but he ain't always stealing a child.

I know I lost with the little Landon boy. He disappeared right into thin air—off one of Gault's school buses. I didn't see no signs until after the Landon boy was already gone, but I wasn't looking neither. It'd been years since I'd seen any. I got to thinking that maybe that part of our history was over, if you know what I mean. I been pretty vigilant since the Landon boy, by God. I ain't going to let it happen again if I can help it. We got no damned shortage of missing children in this world. I don't know if the Gypsy Man don't wander around somewhere in West Virginia and take children over there. Who knows what goes on in West Virginia—especially back in some of them hollers where no stranger ever sets foot?

Now I look for a pattern, stumbling around the broken bricks and beaten boards of that dead mansion until it's so hot I can't keep the sweat out of my eyes. I figure I'll probably find something if I stop looking so durn hard. I walk around in front of the old hulk and shake my head. "Well," I say. "I hope you can hear me."

The low, flat sun cuts through the split boards in the front wall and the fallen roof. The front of the house is pretty much intact, but everything behind it is rubble; moss, twisted vines, shattered bricks, and piles of old boards. Folks come up here looking for buried treasure and dug holes even in the basement floor of this place. Ain't a speck of concrete, nor board, nor stone that ain't been turned over, dug up, or slammed with a pickax.

"I hope you can hear me," I say a little louder. "You got me stumped this time."

I kick the dirt in front of me, start back down the dirt path to the road. Then I see it. Just off the road, back in the underbrush, piled up next to the base of a huge oak: a pile of cut brush and tree branches shaped like a man just a setting there, watching me.

"I'll be goddamned," I say to myself. My heart's beating like a bull's. I walk up to it careful, lean down, and pick up one of the leaves. It's still attached to a small branch, and it's covered in a kind of oil, sticky and black. That's what holds the pattern together. The leaves and branches are piled up over a stump, so that it really looks like a man who's been tarred and covered with leaves, sitting there cross-legged, arms folded in his lap. The Gypsy Man went to a lot of trouble with this one. There's so much of the black sticky stuff, has to be a million flies buzzing around it, and the whole thing's taking on a sweet, sickening odor by the time I find it.

I'm just placing the leaf back on the pile, when I hear, or think I hear, something moving in the underbrush behind me. I stand straight up and listen. It's still broad daylight, so there ain't no earthly reason for nobody to think they can hide from me, even in the thick growth of the bushes and trees around the dead mansion. *Okay,* I say to myself. *I got to pay homage to this little trick of my imagination.* I know ain't nothing there, but I hear the leaves crackling slightly. "Sure," I say. "Probably a squirrel." I ain't afraid it's the Gypsy Man, because he don't work that way.

Then I hear a louder noise—the bushes move. It sounds like somebody pushing a house through the woods. I turn to my left, and just off the path on that side, a black bear rises up out of the thicket.

"Goddamn," I say. I look for a cub. I take a quick peek at the pattern hoping there ain't no little cub licking up the leaves on the other side or something. You get between a bear and her cub and you're a goner. I know that. Even if there ain't a cub nearby, if I make the wrong move, I'll be in real trouble.

The bear makes this noise—a sort of exhalation of air, then shakes its head at me. I still don't see no cub. I know I can't run fast enough to get away if the bear decides to come over here and take a piece of me.

I stare at it. Standing on its hind legs, it's almost as tall as I am. Its eyes are black and glittering like polished buttons. It glares at me, moves its head slightly left then right, never taking its eyes from mine. I can see that, like me, the bear's pretty confused about what to do.

"Well," I say out loud. "What's it gonna be?"

It raises up a bit higher, moves its head back, as if to get a better angle to look at me.

"I can't run and I sure as hell can't hide. I ain't gonna charge at you, neither."

The bear makes another sound, a sort of whimper, then it tilts its head and rubs both sides of its nose with its paws. I can't think of nothing to compare them long, black, sharp nails with—but I'm pretty sure it can just poke me in the belly with one of them and cut me all the way to my spine. I'm thinking, *this is a goddamned silly way to die.*

I don't know how long we stand there looking at each other. After a while, it really is sort of comical—but I ain't laughing.

I figure the way my heart's beating I'll probably die of a heart attack, anyway.

"Well," I say. "What's it gonna be?"

The bear snorts, but I don't move.

"It's been nice seeing you. I got to go."

It drops down on all fours and makes a loud grunt, like a foghorn.

"Tell them I was in to see you," I say. I take a slow step back. Then I turn and take another and another.

The bear moves out into the path behind me. Not fast or nothing, but even so, I freeze. He's about ten feet behind me, ambling along. It ain't in no hurry, but I can see it's gaining on me. I have my back to it, but I watch over my shoulder. "For Christ's sake," I say. "I still got all my teeth."

The bear suddenly roars and I see it still has all its teeth, too.

I swear I think I'm a goner.

But a bright blue pickup truck roars down the road up at the end of the path, and the sound and dust and flying gravel sends the bear back into the vines. I hear him running a long time, and while I walk back down the road, I search the sky for some sort of providence that might be smiling on me. Nobody I know ever been as lucky as I feel right now.

I think I'd like to be home now, so I pick up my pace a bit, and let the downhill walk have its way with me. I feel as light as a dry leaf.

I never wonder why a truck would be going so fast on that worn-out stretch of road, all the way up by the old Crawford place.

BOOK II

SHERIFF PAXTON

When I find out about Clare, I ain't surprised none. People she hangs around and all. I told Penny I'd be by on Saturday or maybe Sunday. Whenever Clare was feeling more clearheaded. I didn't see no point in wandering up there if the old woman was still fuzzy about everything. Penny says she was having a hell of a time keeping her awake.

I was probably going to wait until Sunday, but then I get to thinking about it—how my wife sort of slants her week toward that day—so I decide to go on up there Saturday morning. You know, take a chance that Clare'll be awake. I should wait until the following weekend—till after Labor Day. Then the little brat will be in Gault's school and the whole interview might go off a bit more smoothly.

You might as well know this right off, I don't think much of them mountain folks. Maybe especially them people up there in Crawford. The world has just deprived them of vital brain circuits or something—the air's much thinner up there—so you never know if what you've said ever makes it far enough between their ears to make any sense to them. You speak, and most times they act like you ain't said nothing at all, and you just stand there waiting for something to happen. Then you say it again. After a while, talking to them is about like trying to untie a very small knot with fat fingers, you know what I'm saying? It's enough to make a religious man curse.

One feller right here in Lebanon Church is so old he can't talk no more. When he wants something, he just writes it down on a piece of paper and half the time you can't figure out what he wants. His name is Stooch. That's what everybody calls him. I run when I see him coming. One time he had to write the same thing five times before I figured it out. He come down to this town from Crawford, and don't you know anybody can guess it just from looking at the notes he writes. Once, he wrote *yesterday you find brown gloves give me*. It took me a half hour to figure out he'd lost a pair of gloves and wanted to know if I'd found them.

I don't like the way mountain folks look at you, neither. They never look you right in the eye. They focus on your chest, or your shoulder, or even your throat—which can make you shudder if you ain't used to it—and they stay that way. You'd think you had a stain on your shirt, or a bone sticking out somewhere, the way those eyes fix on you and don't move.

When I get to Clare's store the place is all closed up, so I drive on up the hill to the cabin. I figure it don't matter if I wake everybody. Hell, it's near seven. I knock on the door and Penny hollers, "Who is that?"

"It's me," I say. "Sheriff Paxton."

She opens the door, stands there in front of me with a shovel in her hand, and a vicious look on her face. If you happened along right at that moment, you'd think I hit her with that shovel and she just wrestled it away from me, and now she's going to give me a little of it.

"What's the matter with you?" I say.

"Just come on in." She puts the shovel behind the door.

I have to push this huge green chair out of my way and back against the far wall. "What's this here for?"

"I'm letting Clare sleep, now."

"What's the chair for?" I say. "And that 'ere shovel. You waiting for somebody?"

"I don't know what I'm waiting for." She walks over to the couch, points at Clare all trussed up in the blankets there. "Well, here she is, half dead when we found her."

The old girl is snoring like a lumberjack. She smells of cheap whiskey and she looks a lot healthier than me *or* her niece, if you ask me. Her fingers are all curled up around her nose and she's snuggled up there against the back of the couch enjoying her sleep just like a child.

I take out a pad of paper and my new Paper Mate. "A gift from my wife," I say, holding it up. "Thursday was my birthday."

She don't say nothing.

"I just turned forty. What do you think of that?"

Penny shakes her head, then walks back into one of the bedrooms. I stand there looking at Clare. Maybe her eye is a little swollen, and I can see she has a fat lip. Stitches stick out above her eye. I wonder what the hell I'm supposed to do with my pad and pen if Penny don't come back out. It wouldn't be kind to try and wake Clare. Anyway, I think it might scare her to see me sitting here in my uniform.

I watch her eyes awhile, then lean down and pull the cover back away from the couch where her knees are curled up. Just as I thought. It's a bottle stuffed down in between the cushions. Old Granddad. You just know Penny has no idea about it, too. A drunk is a lying son of a bitch once he starts hiding bottles. And a woman drunk? Hell. A woman already ain't that chummy with the truth. When a woman is also a drunk— well, there ain't nothing worse in this world if you ask me. Especially a sloppy one like Clare. It's a goddamned shame if you ask me. She used to be so pretty. Now, I can see where she tried to put makeup on her face and smeared it every which way. She stirs a bit, so I put the covers back over her.

You might find this hard to believe but a few years ago she was a right beautiful woman. When she was younger and all and didn't drink so much. But age and booze have wore her out, and that's the truth. I feel sorry for her. I swear to God, old age is a son of a bitch.

I hear the little one jabbering in the bedroom, and I figure out where Penny went. I sit down in the green chair, and when Penny comes back out I say, "I'm sorry I got here so early. I thought you'd want me here soon as possible."

"Yesterday was sooner," she says.

"It wasn't possible." I try to catch her eyes and freeze them on mine.

"Doctor Sam was here yesterday."

"She looks pretty good to me."

"Had to keep her up most the night. Now she can sleep, and you show up."

Clare moves onto her back, lets out a groan.

"Well," I say. "I'm sorry I come so early. I really am."

"Now you're here, so it don't matter," Penny says.

"I ain't even had my coffee this morning."

"The doctor said I should keep her awake so that's what I done," she says, no hint that maybe she might offer me a cup.

"Sure do hate to do without my coffee," I say. "I should of stopped and got a cup before I come up here."

"Well, do you want me to go ahead and try to wake her?"

"Who?"

She looks at me. "Aunt Clare."

"Sure," I say. "Sure, go ahead. Maybe she'll want some coffee when she wakes up."

Penny leans over the couch, starts whispering Clare's name—like she is trying to wake up Snow White or Sleeping Beauty. Let me tell you, that old girl is so unconscious you'd have to drop her off the back of a moving wagon just to stir her more than a little bit.

"Hell," I say. "You got to be louder than that. She probably drank a lot."

Penny says, "She was beaten senseless, Mr. Sheriff Paxton! I had to walk the floor with her all last night because she has a concussive."

"You mean a concussion."

"She needs her rest."

"Sure," I say. "But maybe it was a few drinks she had before everything got started."

"I don't have time for this," Penny says. "I got to go to the tire store and work all day."

Clare turns her head around, makes a noise out of her throat that sounds like somebody stabbed a shoat.

"Clare," Penny says. "Are you waking up, honey?"

"It sure don't look like it," I say.

"She ain't going to be no help with Tory today," Penny says. "That's all I know."

Well, it takes her near a half hour to rouse the old girl, and I still don't have no coffee. By the time Clare can talk, the little girl is all around asking me fool questions about my gun, my badge, my shiny boots, my gold nameplate, and just about anything else you can think of. I swear children can get on your nerves more than just a little bit. Tory already looks at me the way mountain folks do. When I show her my nameplate, I put it right up in front of her face, then get my eyes behind it so we have to be eyeball to eyeball if she wants to see it close up. She concentrates on that little strip of gold so hard her eyes cross. I don't care if she is only six or seven years old, she knows what I'm trying to do and sets herself against it. She's just like her daddy. He was stubborn and proud, too.

Clare is just glad to be alive. That's how she puts it. I don't have the nerve to tell her that if I had to live a life like hers, I'd rather be dead. Even when she looks good she looks on the verge of awful, you know what I mean? One day soon she ain't just going to look like a man, she's gonna look like an ugly man.

"Tell me everything that happened," I tell her. "And go slow, I want to write it all down."

"Wait a minute," Penny says. Then she starts shooing Tory into her room. "This is going to be grown-up talk," she says. "You play on my bed. You can jump if you want, but don't jump too high."

"Ain't you going to get that child some breakfast?" I say.

"When we're done here."

"This might take a long time," I say. Then I look at Clare, who's drifting off into space, remembering something. "Don't you want a cup of coffee?"

"I can't remember the name he give me," she says.

"Who?"

"The fella who beat me."

"Wait a minute," I say.

"Was it the Gypsy Man?" Penny asks.

"It wasn't no half-red face. I don't think it was the Gypsy Man," Clare says. "But I don't know."

"Wait a minute," I say again. I write *man face not half red* in my book. Then I say, "What do you mean when you say 'half-red face'? What's that mean?"

"It wasn't no half-red face. Like the Gypsy Man's."

"Well. But I don't understand it. Do you mean he didn't have no face that was red on one side and some other color on the other side? Or that his face wasn't almost red, it was all the way red?"

"The man didn't have no half-red face," she says. "Red on one side and ordinary on the other."

"You don't have to speak so loudly," I say. "I can hear you."

"Can you?"

"Yes, I can," I say calmly.

"So it wasn't the Gypsy Man," Penny says.

"Sure," I say. "It was the Gypsy Man. A hundred-year-old ghost that makes bruises."

Clare coughs a little. It looks like a soul forces its way out of her the way she clenches up in pain from it. Then she says, "It might of been him. I ain't so sure. I never seen the Gypsy Man. Not since I was a little girl. But maybe this fellow was, he was just as crazy." There's a look on her face that ain't exactly serious.

"I need just the truth," I say.

"I reckon you ain't heard the story they tell around here," Clare says. Her voice cracks, then she winces in pain. I catch her eye for a split second, and I can tell she don't like having that bottle pinched between her and the couch. She wants it a little closer at hand, you know what I mean? "You old enough to remember the Crawford family?" she says.

"I know where you're going with this, and I ain't gonna do it. Just tell me what the fellow looked like."

"They helped settle this mountain," Clare says. "You go up the road there about half a mile and you'll see a driveway all covered with brambles and honeysuckle. That's the entrance to the old Crawford place."

"I know where it is."

"Up that road you'll find what's left of it. The house used to be as white as a dogwood blossom and almost as big as the state capitol building."

"I've heard all about the house white as a dogwood blossom and whatnot. You ain't old enough to remember it neither. You ain't but a few years older than me."

"I ain't older than you!" She like to come up at me.

"Settle down," I say. "Maybe you ought to have something warm to drink." I turn to Penny. "She ought to have something to soothe her, what do you think?"

"Old man Crawford's little boy was kidnapped by Gypsies," Clare says. "I don't remember it, but my daddy told me the story."

"I've heard the story."

"And I remember Wilbur Crawford. Everybody called him the Gypsy Man, until he disappeared."

"More than forty years ago. I was a baby."

"Well."

"Was you a baby?"

"I was a little girl."

"So you are older than me, ain't you?"

"Maybe it was the Gypsy Man that come and took me. I was took. He brought me back. That's supposed to be what happened to Wilbur when he was a little boy."

"Now, it ain't no Gypsies around here," I say.

Clare turns a bit toward the back of the couch. She reaches down in there, you know, kind of secretly. She wants to make sure the bottle is still there.

"Your daddy could sure tell some stories," I say.

Clare coughs, then she says, "My daddy can be left out of this, thank you kindly."

Penny says, "The Gypsy Man used to haunt this mountain. He stole children from their homes. They were never found again. He killed livestock and—"

"Livestock. I never heard nothing about no livestock."

"He burned down houses," Penny goes on. "Only nobody ever really seen him except..."

"Except who?" I say.

"The Gypsy Man is evil. He's a hundred years old. And maybe he's back, he's..."

"If he's a hundred years old, you don't have to be afraid of him," I say.

"They say this all used to be his land," Clare says.

"He kills children." Penny speaks to herself when she says this, staring out the window.

"Ain't no children ever killed around here," I say.

"What about the Landon boy?" Clare says.

"He ain't never been found. It can't be murder if it ain't no body. And the only other child that ever got killed around here…"

Penny looks at me.

"Well, if it *was* an accident, it don't change nothing," I say.

"It was an accident," Penny says.

"Still. It was a dead child. And John admitted it. It wasn't no Gypsy Man."

"But the Landon boy is still missing."

"You don't have to tell me that. I know that."

"Well, there you go," Penny says.

"I'll find that Landon boy, or know what happened to him," I said. "I been working the case all these years. I ain't never gonna give up."

They both set there looking at me. Then Penny says, "You don't have to get angry."

"Anyway," I said. "Maybe the Gypsy Man will bring him back. Ain't that the story?"

Penny puts her hand on Clare's forehead. "Was it the Gypsy Man?"

"I don't know, honey… only…"

"Only what?"

"He didn't look natural. He didn't have no birthmark, but his eyes was flat and dark and almost lifeless. They looked like flat, brown fish eyes. You know? But he was, he wasn't no…" She stops and looks right at me, and I think she can tell I ain't buying any of it. Then she says, "That's all I'm saying."

"Just tell me what happened," I say.

"I ain't saying no more."

"Clare," Penny says. "You have to."

"No, I don't."

"Look here," I say. "All I want you to do is tell me exactly what happened. I don't want no speculation, nor stories, nor nothing like that. Just what happened."

"Please, Clare," Penny says.

"Okay," she says.

"You were with this here man."

"I was." She holds her head up, like she might be proud of it. Then she looks at Penny. "Maybe it wasn't no Gypsy Man, honey. I bet he wasn't much older than forty. Maybe it was just a crazy man."

"And he beat you up?" I say.

"Yes."

"And what else?"

She blinks the one bruised eye. I swear she looks like a hen, blinking one eye at a time. "He come into the store, late in the day—that was—it seems so long ago. What's today?"

Me and Penny both say, "Saturday."

"It was a week or two ago?"

"Three weeks," Penny says.

"He come in the store on a Monday. A few weeks ago, I don't know. A body loses track of time when death walks into the place." She stops, thinking. Then she says, "Of course, I didn't know he was death or any such thing at first."

"I see."

"His eyes just clutched me the moment he looked at me, like they could stop everything, like in a movie or something. I just froze. There was something grand about him, in a way. I couldn't speak, but my face was just burning when he looked at me."

"I ain't going to write none of that down, if you don't mind," I say.

"He beat me up on Thursday, this week. I know, because he made me buy him a newspaper."

"Just this past Thursday?" I say.

She nods.

I say, "My birthday."

"What?"

"Nothing. Go on."

116

She looks at me. It's real quiet for a spell. Then I say, "Why'd he want a newspaper?"

"I don't know. I think he wanted to see if there was something about me being gone. Or maybe he wanted to read about the election next year. He talked a lot about that. He thinks a Catholic's going to run for president."

"Really?"

"That's right."

"Why does that matter?" I ask.

"Why does what matter?"

"Who cares what the fellow thinks."

"It's why he bought the newspaper is all."

I try to be patient. "Go on," I say.

"Go on, what?"

"Tell the rest of what happened."

"Well, on Thursday..." She starts coughing again. Penny gets up and goes to the kitchen. I hear the back door slam, then the pump outside. She comes back in with a glass of water and hands it to Clare.

"She should have something warm to drink," I say.

Clare sips the water, then she says, "I thought I'd talked him into taking me home, but he just come after me."

"What do you mean he come after you?"

"He just started hitting me." She gets all teary eyed. It's enough to break your heart, if you believe her. But I know about the Old Granddad nestled there in the couch under her ass, behind her knees.

Penny moves around and sits in a wooden rocker next to the couch. I'm writing in my notebook and it's quiet for a bit, and then I think I hear somebody's stomach growl.

"Now, did you hear that?" I ask.

They both look at me. "Hear what?" Penny says.

"Somebody in this room besides me is hungry."

Penny just glares at the floor, then she reaches out and

brushes the hair away from Clare's eyes. Clare rolls her head and moans, "Ohhh, I've had a terrible time." It's beginning to dawn on her what has happened and all. I think she wants a drink real bad, too. It makes me very happy to watch her face, knowing how bad she wants to get her mouth on the end of that bottle.

I lean over and whisper to Penny. "I think you should get her a cup of coffee or something, what do you think?"

She rubs the old girl's forehead. "There," she says. "You're safe now."

"We should get her some nourishment." I click my pen a bit.

"Just finish telling the sheriff what happened," Penny says. "Go on, now."

"I was so scared when he come into the store. I can't remember if he said something to me when he first come in. He looked at me and I could swear he knew who I was."

"What made you think that?" I say.

"I don't know. Just the way he looked."

"That don't tell me a lot."

Penny sighs real loud.

"Well, it don't," I say.

"Maybe it was just that he could see I recognized him," Clare says.

"You recognized him?"

"Well, no," she says real fast. "Not that. Just that maybe he thought the way I looked at him that I recognized him."

"That is possible," I say. "Had you seen him before?"

"No."

"But you said you recognized him."

"I ain't seen him before."

"You know there's a fellow escaped from Richard Bland not long ago—from up around here. I got a piece of paper on him. Was this fellow a big, stocky man with tattoos up both arms?"

She looks at me. "Tattoos?"

"That's what I said."

"I don't recollect no tattoos."

"Was he a stocky fellow?"

"He was very rugged looking." Now she actually smiles.

"Is this a pleasant memory?" I say.

She glares at me. Her eyes are still dark and beautiful, at least.

"Did you say something to him?" I say.

"No. I just went on doing what I was doing."

"And what was that?"

"I was dusting off the canned goods."

"Why do you think he thought you recognized him?"

She looks at me. "I didn't say I recognized him."

"Yes, you did."

"I never did."

I turn to Penny. "Did *you* hear her say she recognized him?"

"Clare," Penny says. "Was it somebody you seen before?"

"It was a stranger."

"Well," I say, "I think we got that clear. But you said maybe he thought you recognized him. Why do you suppose he thought that?"

She raises her head up and looks at me directly again, like she ain't sure I'm really there in front of her. Then she lets her head fall back on the pillow. "I just meant that I—I should of seen he was bad. That's all."

"Yeah, well. It don't make no sense," I say.

So she goes on and tells me the story, and I take notes. She says when he first come in he walked around looking at packages of peanuts and Twinkies, and every time she looked at him, she caught him looking at her. She started putting bread out on the counters. (She drives all the way down to Lebanon Church early Monday mornings and buys boxes of cheap, day-old bread at the bakery, then she comes back up to Crawford and sets three or four loaves each day out on the counter under a sign that says FRESH, HOMEMADE BREAD.) Anyway, she was setting out some of that bread, watching the man who ain't got a half-red face, but who does have flat brown eyes. Then he come over to her, put his hands on the counter in front of her, leaning toward her real slow, like he was trying to break the counter with his weight.

"What you doing?" he says.

"Nothing." She tried to look away from him, but he moved slightly toward her, and this made her wary of taking her eyes off him. Then he says, "If'n I ask you to put that loaf down and come with me, what would you say?"

"I'd say, no."

"Well, I guess I won't ask you then."

She thought she was safe, but then, after a few minutes of staring at her, and her heart beating like a "frightened sparrow's heart," as she put it, he says, "I'm telling you."

"Just like that?" I say.

"Just like that," she says. "He said, 'I'm telling you,' and I figured I had to go."

"But why?"

"I thought it might be . . ." She don't finish.

"Go on," I say.

"I just didn't want him to hurt me."

"Well, but he did hurt you. Just a little bit."

Neither one of them says a thing.

"Did he have a weapon of some kind?" I ask.

"No. None I seen."

So she didn't think nothing of closing the store in the middle of the day to go off with him. Never mind that everybody in Crawford would have to drive all the way to Lebanon Church if they needed any groceries.

"He had no weapon and you went with him, anyway?"

"It was a command," Clare says.

"That store run a lot better when your brother was alive," I say.

"Oh, who cares about that old store?" she says. "It's only just enough to keep us alive."

I am tempted to say, "You mean to keep you in booze," but I think better of it. I say, "Well, you'd never get rich closing it up at all hours of the day."

"I was forced to," she says. "Ain't you heard a word I said?"

"It's just that I ain't seen the man yet that could get you to do nothing you didn't have a mind to do," I say.

"What's the matter with you?" Penny says.

"We don't keep the store open for you," Clare says.

"I don't mean to be critical," I say. "Hell, it ain't nothing but your store."

Clare blinks the one eye again. It's quiet for a time, and then the little girl suddenly bursts through the door behind me. Like to scare me to death.

The little brat stands there staring at me and I got my gun half out of the holster.

"Put that thing away," Penny says. Then she starts patting the little one. "What you want, sugar?"

Tory watches me snap the holster over the top of the gun, then she says, "I'm hungry."

"We'll have breakfast in a little while."

"You ought to feed that child," I say.

"She don't drink coffee, Mr. Sheriff Paxton," Penny says. She makes it a point to look me straight in the eye, which takes me back some. I know she's just being mean—the way poor folks get when life thumps them a bit too much and they ain't got nothing to show them the difference between being polite and being weak. She probably thinks I'll take it wrong if she offers me a cup of coffee.

"How about you, Miss Clare. Don't you want a cup of coffee?" I say.

Penny takes the little one out of the room, then comes back in and sits down.

"You let her play all alone like that? Before she's had breakfast?"

Clare says, "Do you want to hear what happened or not?"

"She'll fall off that bed in there and hurt herself," I say. "Then how will you feel?"

"Can we go on with this?" Penny says.

I swear, if some people had manners it would look like a feather bonnet on a cow. Clare goes on about how the fellow got mean, then he'd be real nice, then he'd get mean again.

"All for no reason," Clare says. "I didn't know how to keep him being nice, or how to make him be nice once he started getting mean. He'd just change, snap, like that."

I write down what she says.

Clare turns her head back and tries to look at Penny. "I wanted so bad to call you, honey. So you wouldn't worry."

Penny is creeping up on a smile, but it gets away.

"What would you have said to her?" I ask. "I'm okay, Penny, I'm just with the Gypsy Man?"

"That ain't funny," Penny says.

"I was just making an observation," I say.

"Funny way to do it."

"Mr. Paxton don't take any of this very seriously," Clare says.

"I do," I say. "I surely do."

"Sometimes, I felt like I was with a dog that figured out he's chained to something. He'd just start pulling and barking."

"You say he barked?"

"He'd yell at me." She smooths the covers a bit. She's thinking about that bottle, all right.

"Just stick to what happened," I tell her. I cross out *barked* in my notes and write *yelled*.

"He'd grab my arm and pull me wherever he was going. He

wouldn't let go of me unless we was in his truck and it was moving."

"Did he drag you off?" I say.

"Not at first, no."

"You went along anyway?"

"We went through this already," Penny says.

I didn't pay no attention to her. "Did he hold a gun on you at any time?" I ask.

"No." She tries to sit up, then puts her head back. "You just know, sometimes," she moans. "You just know. If I tried to get away from him, he'd hurt me. So I went."

"Did you—did he—excuse me for saying this. Did he rape you?" I have to know what sort of laws got broke, you know? But she seems insulted—like I've just complained about her cooking or something.

"Nothing like that happened," she says.

"I got to know."

She looks up at the ceiling. "At first I thought he might—well, you know."

"Yes," I say. "I do."

"But he never seemed to want that."

"Well, what'd he want then?"

"He said he knew me. He kept saying, 'I know you,' like he expected me to hurt him in some way." She stops.

Penny stoops over her. "He knew you?"

"I don't think he meant it that way, honey. Just that he could—he could—you know, predict what I might do."

"What'd he want?" I say.

"You don't think it was the Gypsy Man?" Penny whispers. She sits straight up, her hands working together in her lap.

"What'd he want?" I ask again.

"I don't really know what he wanted. The whole time we was together, he didn't talk much."

"Did he take any money?"

She shakes her head.

"Did he take something from the store?"

"No."

"So far," I say. "We ain't got no crime."

"He drove me way back into West Virginia. He kept me against my will. He beat me." She tries to yell when she says this, but she ain't got the steam for it. She falls back into the cushions. "Up into those mountains north and east of here. After a while, I didn't know where we was. I was a nervous wreck, and that's the truth."

"Oh, I believe you," I say. "Tell me how tall he was. What color was his hair? Did he have any marks or scars and such? How about that?"

"He was average height. Maybe a little taller. Shorter than you."

"I'm over six feet."

"He might of been shorter'n you."

"So. Six feet or so?"

"I guess."

"And his hair?"

"Brown."

"Did he have all of it?"

"I don't know." She is getting kind of winded—or maybe impatient. She don't seem like she can sit still. She tells me he fed her by stopping at cider stands and gas station grocers. She can't name any of the places he stopped, there was so many. She thinks he must of been driving around in circles because she kept expecting to see the other side of the mountain—a valley or a river—and she never did. Also, she says he may of stopped at one of the cider stands more than once. She'd been driven around so much, she couldn't tell if she'd seen a certain place or not. "He probably come to the cider stands from different directions," she says. "You know, from the south the first time and then a few hours later from the north."

"How'd he do that in these mountains?"

"I don't know."

"He give you something to drink?"

She don't answer that. She turns her face away in disgust.

"All them cider stands got signs," I say. "Where'd you sleep?"

"A trailer."

"A trailer?"

"We stayed in a rented trailer somewhere over there in one of them hollers. I don't know where. Sometimes we slept in the back of his truck. He's got a truck."

"What kind of truck?"

"It had a camper on the back, you know."

"A pickup?"

"Sort of," she says. "But when you opened up the camper, it was nothing in it. Just the bed of the truck."

"He didn't have no tools nor nothing else in the bed of that truck?"

Penny mumbles something about the difference it makes.

"What'd you say?"

"Nothing," she says.

"I heard it."

"Then why'd you ask?"

"I didn't hear all of it."

"I just wonder what the big deal is about tools in the truck and all."

I turn back to Clare. "What kind of truck was it?"

She don't know. But it was blue and she thinks it may of been a Ford.

"Why'd he beat you up?" Penny says.

"I don't know," Clare says.

"You don't know?" I say.

"It's a funny thing," Clare says.

"Funny?" I say.

"He kept saying he was sorry. He'd feel so bad and try so hard to get me to forgive him. Then, he'd break into a rage again."

"And he'd just start beating on you?" Penny asks her.

"Excuse me," I say. "I have to ask the questions here."

"He didn't talk very much," Clare goes on. "And when he did, something about his voice sounded—it sounded far away, like it was something soft and padded between me and him. He wasn't ashamed of nothing, but a lot of things made him sad. That's what I think."

"Did you ever call him the Gypsy Man?"

"I don't remember. I don't think I did. But he said I should know who he was. Said he worked at the mill and come from up near Quincy."

"Well," I say. "Now we're getting somewhere. Did he tell you his name?"

"No."

"There's a fellow named Middleton, Paul James Middleton. Escaped from Bland a few weeks ago. He's from Quincy," I say. "You sure this man didn't have no tattoos."

"I didn't say there weren't no tattoos."

"Yes, you did."

"I did not."

I look at Penny.

Penny says, "Clare, you said he didn't have no tattoos."

"Well, he didn't."

"That's all I need to know."

"And he wasn't stocky or fat, neither."

"I never said the fellow was fat."

"Whatever."

"Tell me about his face."

"What about it?" She's annoyed.

"I have to ask you to describe it."

"It was a face. What do you want me to say? Glory be."

126

Penny starts to say something, but I look at her. "Please," I say.

"It was round. It had two dead-looking eyes, like a dead dog's eyes. It didn't smile. It was unshaved. The nose was average looking—maybe a little flat."

"Right," I say.

"He didn't talk much about nothing, except Catholics running for president, and Sputnik, and what we was going to eat or drink. He'd get mad at me for nothing, then he'd be tender—like he known me all my life. He never touched me, except the first day when he twisted my arm, and the last day when he did this." She points to her face, which, as I said, don't look all that beat up to me. I mean, you can see she's been beaten, but it ain't no more than a little bit.

"Did what?" I say.

"Beat me. Blacked my eye."

"Your eye ain't black."

"It ain't?"

"It might be slightly bruised, but that's all."

"You should of saw it yesterday," Penny says.

"I'll take your word for it."

"He beat me to within an inch of my life."

I write everything she says as best I can. I'm thinking maybe he beat her within a mile of her life, but he didn't get no closer than that. "Go on," I say.

"When I asked for—when I needed something for my nerves..."

"You mean when you wanted a drink," I say.

"Or cigarettes or whatever. He'd get it for me. He seemed to like doing that."

"So you sent him for booze pretty frequently?"

"No, I didn't."

"But you did drink just a little bit."

She adjusts herself a bit on the couch. I almost pull the

covers back and point to the bottle and say, "This here's what I'm talking about."

Then she gets this puzzled look on her face. "He never took nothing to drink after that first day. It was like he was just taking care of me, when he was being tender and all. But I was tired, worn to the bone from lack of sleep. Once, when we was sleeping on the hard bed of that truck it got freezing cold, and he wouldn't let me go up to the cab of the truck, turn it on, and get warm." She raises herself up a bit on one elbow. "I tell you what—I was laying there, shaking all over, like I might die right there, and he never showed the slightest sign that he was even alive, much less cold. If he didn't snort once in a while in his sleep, I couldn't tell if he was even breathing."

"It's him," Penny says. "He ain't human."

I say, "If it drives a pickup and snorts in its sleep, it's human."

"I was so cold," Clare says.

"In the dead of summer."

"It gets cold up here at night," she says. "We're a lot higher up."

"Well, you ain't that much closer to heaven. It don't ever seem much colder up here than it does in Lebanon Church."

"I was cold. You want the truth or not. I was cold. At night it got all dewy and wet and I got cold. I'm sorry."

"So what happened on my birthday?"

"What?" They both speak at the same time.

"On Thursday," I say. "When he beat you up."

"I told him I wanted to go home."

"You never said that before?"

"Sure, I did. And he'd just grunt and go on with what he was doing." She lets herself back down, blows out this breath of air that would peel the paint off a brick.

"Whew," I say. I turn to Penny. "Why don't you get her some chewing gum or something at least?"

"On Thursday," Clare says, "I told him I wasn't going to take no more. I said, 'I don't know who you are and I don't care.' Then I told him if he wanted to stop me he was just going to have to kill me."

"That was smart," I say.

She looks at me.

"I mean that," I say. "It got you out of it, right?"

"Well he—he—he just started laughing."

I don't see no point in writing that down. "Go on," I say.

"I thought he might take me home. I thought I was—I thought I'd done it. We got in the truck, and he was still laughing, shaking his head. 'You're quite a girl,' he said. After a while, I was kind of laughing, too. So I reached across and slapped him on the shoulder, you know, the way you do when you're laughing with a person, just to share in it—that's all. I wasn't even thinking of my own safety, no more."

"Well, you should of been," Penny says.

I look at Penny. "If you don't mind."

She takes a deep breath and folds her arms in front of her.

I say, "You're going to have to let me do my job here. The sooner I finish, the sooner I can be out of your hair."

She turns herself away, staring out the window.

"I just wanted to laugh with him," Clare goes on. "I said, 'you're all right, honey,' and he..." She closes her eyes. She looks like she's tasting something in her mouth, working it behind her teeth. Then she says, "He stopped the truck, got out, and come around my side. He wasn't laughing no more. He stood there for a minute, looking at me, then he opened the door and took me down out of the truck like I was only a pile of dirty laundry." She stares at me directly now, and I can tell she wants me to think it hurts her to remember it. You know how dramatic some people can get when they're feeling sorry for their selves. "He just kept hitting me," she says. "Even when—even when I fell down. He sat on top of me and just kept..." She breaks off in tears. Then she starts coughing again.

"Be careful, or you'll choke yourself to death," I say.

Penny keeps stroking the old girl's forehead, trying to soothe her.

"Before he commenced to beating you, didn't you say you slapped his shoulder?"

"Haven't you been listening?"

"Yes, I have. I been writing it all down, too. It just ain't real clear is all."

"We was laughing. I clapped him on the shoulder."

"Did it feel like you maybe hit him pretty hard?"

She don't say nothing. She just looks at me.

"Did his shoulder feel like it was skin and bone underneath it?"

"It just felt like a body's shoulder. A normal person's shoulder. Glory be. What kind of question is that?"

"And that's the only time he hit you? After you smacked him?"

"I didn't smack him," she says.

Penny shifts a bit, lets out a loud sigh, but she don't say nothing.

"Did he hit you any other time?"

"No. He'd be real nice, then he'd yell at me or act like he might hit me. Then he'd be real nice again. But he never really beat me up until the last day."

I write on my pad, *there was only one real beating the last day.*

"I woke up here," Clare says. "Just all by myself. I didn't know where I was."

"You're safe now," Penny says.

"Did you cover her?" I ask Penny.

"What?"

"Did you put that cover on her?"

"What difference does that make?"

Clare moans. She's run out of tears. She keeps her hands over her face, but I watch her. Probably just the thought of that bottle behind her knees makes her squirm.

"I just want to know if this is the way you found her," I say.

"Yes."

"You didn't move her or touch her."

"Well, I had her up walking all around most the night."

"She had this cover on her when you found her?"

Penny looks at Clare and then back to me. "I guess so. Why?"

"And she was unconscious."

"Yes! What're you getting at?"

"What's that right there?" I point to a piece of paper sticking out from under the cover. It's in the side pocket of the sweater that Clare's wearing.

Penny reaches for it and Clare says, "What's that?"

"What is it?" I say.

"It's a note," Penny says. She hands it to me. I can barely make it out, but it says, *I'll be back. I can be useful.*

"What's this?" I say.

Clare won't look at me, now. "I don't know." It seems to me like she's trying not to smile.

"Your fellow leave this for you?"

She looks at it. "I guess. It don't make sense that nobody else would put that in the pocket of my sweater."

"So, you think this here's a threat or a promise?" I say.

Penny is very quiet.

Clare says, "I don't know. I wouldn't pay it no mind, though."

I put the Paper Mate back in my shirt pocket. I ain't going to worry about any of this none. Hell, I figure the old girl probably just got drunk and fell down a flight of stairs. Whoever put her back on that couch was kind enough to leave something to sip on, and she's been sipping it, too. I can see that.

Hell, you know what I think? Clare put herself on that couch, and she was mighty careful to make sure she was comfortable. She wasn't beat up by no Gypsy Man; she just wants her niece to think so. She never got roughed up by nobody. If a man beat on her the way she says she was beat on, she'd be a mite worse off than a cut lip and a bruised eye. She fell down, or bumped into a tree maybe. It's easier to explain a disappearance if you've got somebody to blame it on.

These hill people, I swear to God.

"Well," I say. "Ain't nothing left for me to do here." I get up to leave. Suddenly Penny gets this wide-eyed look on her face and says, "My Lord."

"My Lord, what?" I say.

"He's got a key."

"Who's got a key?"

"The Gypsy Man. He must have used Clare's key to lock the door after he put her back here, and now he's got it. He's got the key."

I say, "Looks like you ought to get yourself new locks for this place, and stay awake until you do."

If I had my coffee, I might try to settle her some. I might tell her what I know. But I feel mean, and that's the unfortunate truth.

Outside, as I'm getting ready to leave, Penny says, "It was the Gypsy Man, and he's got a key." She can't get over it.

"Now I know why you greeted me with that shovel," I say. "You got that little girl to think of, and the Gypsy Man takes little children."

"I know it."

"You might worry just a little bit," I say. "What with your being alone up here and all. Course, you got your aunt Clare."

"Ain't you supposed to look out?"

"Well, I can't just park here. There's other places in the county, you know, and other problems I got to look into."

"You think he'll come back?"

"Who?"

"The Gypsy Man. You think he'll come back here?"

"Who knows," I say. "What's he need that key for? I'd wonder about that. Except he's a spirit and all, so why would he need a key? You see what I'm saying. Maybe he's watching us right now."

"What should I do?"

"I wouldn't sleep none, until you change them locks."

"Ain't you a big help."

"I can't be everywhere at once, Miss Penny. But you call me if anything happens, you hear? You call me right away."

"You think the Gypsy Man's come back?"

"I don't think there ever was a Gypsy Man, if you want to know the truth."

She slowly shakes her head. She wants to believe it ain't true. She wants that very much, I think.

"But," I say. "Whoever put your aunt Clare on that couch, he's got a key. Why wouldn't he come back?"

"Would you help me if you thought there *was* a Gypsy Man? Would you do that?"

I don't know if I ever seen a mountain woman so afraid. Maybe I did sometime. I try to forget about it whenever I have to deal with them people. But I swear to Christ, her eyes look just like a horse's eyes in a barn fire when she asks me that.

PAYNE

We were working up near Charlottesville, in the high mountains along Route 33. McCarthy was the head of the detail, and he had two other guards with him each holding a shotgun and wearing dark glasses. Peach and Bone, me and Parchman, and a few others worked in the ditch by the road. We had to cut down thick patches of saw grass, ivy, and underbrush to clear the shoulder of the road. Poison ivy was all over the place, and nobody liked working in it. We were using hand scythes, so we had to bend down in the black heat from the highway, and we were wearing elbow-length leather gloves, canvas trousers, and thick wool socks because of the poison ivy. Cars snarled by fast, kids eyeballing us while we worked.

Sometimes, whenever I'm on the road gang I wonder if anybody I know will drive by, if I'll see somebody from the past and they'll know what happened to me.

I never meant to harm anyone, but I'm a creature of temper and action. I never think before I react to things, and when I got out of the army after the war, I didn't last long in civilian life. I got into a fight in a bar down in Falmouth, Virginia, and somehow in the heat of it all, I choked a man to death. I don't really remember it. I was drunk, angry, and trying to hang on so he wouldn't be able to hit me again. He may have punched me to begin it; I really don't remember. I can't even remember his face. I just found out later that when the police got there, I was still holding onto his throat, and he was cold dead. That's what I was told.

So here I am. I went from the University of Ohio, premed, to the army, to that bar in Falmouth, then to jail, and now here. My life has been one long episode of trouble, and it's mostly trouble I blame myself for. I don't make excuses.

Working on the road gangs is the worst thing that can happen to you in Bland. Whenever you misbehave, or they're not satisfied with how quickly you follow orders, you end up on the road gang. That's how Warden Buchanan keeps order in this place. It's not that he's cruel. I think he's a humane man, that he thinks about things and considers something other than his own power when he makes decisions. Still, the threat of roadwork keeps everybody in line.

It isn't the way the guards treat you out on the road, either. Some of them don't care very much what's happening to you, but the lead man out there, Mac McCarthy, is not a bad fellow if you don't cause any trouble. He understands when you're really suffering, and he'll let up a little when it gets too hot to breathe. He keeps the other guards in line, too. Doesn't let any punishments go on too long or get too brutal. McCarthy's a man with a soul and it shows, you know what I mean? Most of the men respect him and listen to him. And it seems like he really doesn't mind the road gang. That's all he wants to do: get outside of the prison and be somewhere else all day.

But you know most of the men will do almost anything to keep off the road gang. Working in that heat, you don't need to be beaten or tortured by one of the guards. The work and the sun will do it for them. People just don't have any idea. Walking up mountain roads in Italy during the war, thinking I was going to be blown to bits any second, was more tolerable than standing on the hot, black asphalt of a Virginia highway at eleven-thirty in the morning, dripping sweat, with another six hours of backbreaking work in front of me; shoveling pebbles, or tar, or even sand onto a steaming roadbed, or bending over to swing a hand scythe through dense unyielding grass; even painting the roadway made you fall in love with the idea of a painless death. I never want to look at or smell a can of fresh paint or tar again as long as I live.

And in the winter, with the cold wind or the rain—with the air so cold it stabs you when you take it in—you almost wish for summer.

I don't remember what I did to get on the road gang that day. It may have been just my turn. Peach had a regular rotation that divvied up the work pretty fairly, even among the inmates who behaved.

Anyway, I was on the gang that made the prison break, although I didn't run. I only got five more years before I'm eligible for parole, and I'm not going to mess that up. The other fellow who didn't run was John Bone, but I think he had a different reason for sticking around. To tell the truth, I don't think running even crossed his mind.

We were almost finished in the ditch by the road, and me and Bone were picking up trash and cutting the low tree branches that jutted into the highway. Everything we were wearing, except the leather gloves and the wool socks, was bright yellow—standard prison issue. Even our boots were stained a dull lemon color, although some of the men, perhaps to preserve at least some dignity, insisted the boots were tan.

It was a pretty big detail. Maybe twenty of us in all, plus the two guards and McCarthy who stood across the road with his shotgun slung over his shoulder. Another guard named Daigle was positioned up the hill a little from where we were working. I think the third guard was walking farther ahead of us. We'd been out there for most of the day, and it was getting near quitting time. We'd worked our way up the long slope of a mountain, followed the road around several bends and switchbacks, and were almost to where the yellow prison bus waited to pick us up. In other words, we thought we could see the end of our day.

I was struggling for air in the heat and the sight of the bus exhilarated me, made me briefly feel genuinely happy. It had been a long day, but it went faster than most. I'd be able to eat something soon and sleep.

I was just getting ready to cut a long thin branch hanging over the ditch where we were standing when I heard Daigle say, "Mac. You mind if me and Frank go on up to the bus and get a cold drink?"

McCarthy smiled. "Go ahead. Save me some."

Daigle and the other guard went on up the road. All of us

were still working. Peach stood in behind the gang, carrying one of the coolers of water. There were three trustees out there with us, helping the guards keep track of us. None of them had to work, but I could see Peach was sweating and breathing heavy. He'd had enough, too. He loved carrying the water, though. He called it his "muscle-building work." He believed it made him stronger.

McCarthy took out a cigarette and lit it. He moved his rifle under the right arm, with the barrel pointed down to the road. His cap was tilted back on his head, and he just stood there, puffing the cigarette. It was late enough in the day that the shadows from the mountain made it dark on one side of the hill in front of us. Bone stopped for a second, wiped his brow. McCarthy said, "We're almost done, boys."

Bone went back to work, but he was all in. His face was soaked with sweat. Twenty of us, working there by the road, and only McCarthy and three unarmed trustees to watch us. The other two guards were way ahead of us, walking fast now, approaching the bus far in the distance.

I remember thinking it was going to be a long time anyway. We were near done, the bus was in sight, and still it would take most of another hour to work our way to where it waited for us. Then I heard a funny sound—like somebody trying to puke or something. I turned and saw McCarthy on the ground, lying on his face across his shotgun. Bone was standing there in the road, looking down at him.

"What'd you do?" I said.

"He just fell down," Bone said. "He grabbed his chest and fell down."

Everybody stopped and stared at Bone, who knelt down, slowly, and turned McCarthy over. Bone took a handkerchief out of McCarthy's shirt pocket and wiped the old man's face with it. He was very careful. We were all just standing there, watching him. Bone said, "He's still breathing." He put his head on McCarthy's chest, then sat back and looked at him. "He's still breathing," he said again. "I think he had a heart attack."

"Christ," somebody said.

"Get some help," said Bone.

The other guards were way up the road. Bone hollered once. They didn't hear him, or maybe they thought Mac was calling them back. But they kept walking. They were almost at the bus.

A black Chevy came along, slowing as it approached. Peach waved and flagged it down. It stopped next to where McCarthy was lying there on his back. "You need me to call somebody?" the driver said. He was a gray-haired man with a white mustache. Rimless glasses teetered on the edge of his nose.

"We need an ambulance up here," Bone said.

"I'll stop ahead and call for help," the man said.

"There's a radio on that bus up there," I said. "If you could..." Just then the driver realized who and what we were. His face changed when he noticed the gun next to McCarthy. "We didn't do this," I said. "The man had a heart attack or something." Then Peach stepped up, opened the car door, and said, "move over."

The old man just looked at him.

"I said move over," Peach said, and he pushed him to the passenger side.

"Please," the old man said. "Please don't hurt me."

Peach got in behind the wheel. "Goddamn," he said. "We got wheels," but he slammed the door, turned the car around, and drove on back the other way. He didn't even wait for the others. Parchman started running. He ran down the hill and into the trees and the rest of us just stood there watching him.

Peach disappeared down the road in the opposite direction from the bus, and then I saw another car—a long, green Ford station wagon—coming from that way. Before I could think what to do, John kicked the shotgun out of the way and then stood in the middle of the road. The car squealed to a stop. A young woman sat behind the wheel, a horrified look on her face. Bone went around to the driver's side and knocked on the glass.

The girl didn't know what to do.

Bone said, "Roll the window down. I ain't going to hurt you."

She shook her head.

"Look, miss," Bone said. "If you would just drive your car on down yonder to where that bus is sitting, and tell one of them guards down there that we need an ambulance, he'll radio for one. Tell him to get one up here right away. That's all I want you to do."

She said nothing.

"Will you do that for me? For us?" He let his hands fall to his sides.

She nodded real fast, tears in her eyes.

"Just tell them," he said. "We need help here."

Then he looked at me. "He ain't gonna die."

McCarthy started stirring a bit, but he was still unconscious.

"He'll die," I said, "if we don't get him to a hospital damned quick."

The car started to move a little, but suddenly Bone told her to stop.

"Wait a minute," he said.

She stopped the car.

"Get out," Bone said. I was looking at the shocked look on the girl's face, then I realized that Bone had opened the door himself. "Please. Get out of the car," he said.

The girl never took her eyes off John. She got out and stood there. Bone moved her gently back away from the door. She came around the back of the car, looking at me as if I should do something. The car was still running. Bone opened the back door and I realized what he was up to. I helped him put Mac in the backseat. Then he slammed the door and looked at me. "You coming?"

"Where we going?" I said.

"We're gonna get some help."

I picked up the shotgun and got in and he got behind the wheel. "You want this?" I said, holding up the gun.

"Hell, no," he said. I put it outside the window and rested the stock on the pavement, then I let it fall to the ground. Bone said, "Ask her if she wants to go with us."

I leaned out the window. "We're just taking him up the road a piece. To get help. That's all. We're borrowing your car. You want to go with us?"

She shook her head.

"Why don't you?" I said. "It'll go easier on everybody if you ride along." She shook her head again, and I said, "Get in the car."

"Please," she said.

"We're trying to help a man here. That's all."

She didn't know what to do. Her hands came together and she started moving them as though she were washing them under real hot water.

"I don't know what to do."

John leaned over from the driver's seat and said, "You stay with your car and you get it back a lot sooner than if you stay here." She went around to John's side of the car and got in the back beside Mac, who was slumped back against the cushions still unconscious. I slammed the door shut and we started off. As we did, another inmate took off, following the path Parchman had taken. Then the others just sort of scattered, most of them down the hill next to the road.

I watched the young girl in the backseat trying to prop McCarthy up better, and I felt like part of this rescue—not dangerous, not criminal or anything—just people helping, and I had not felt like that in a long time. I was scared. It was something like being at war again, because I was excited, but also very afraid. Bone was driving right down the mountain toward the bus and the other guards.

He went right by them. They were crouched in the shade of the bus, sipping cold drinks, smoking cigarettes, and they didn't even look up. We could have been home free if we'd wanted. You know what I mean? We could have just kept going, but John drove right down into Charlottesville to the hospital there.

We never would have found it if it weren't for the girl. She turned out to be all right. I think we didn't make a mistake leaving McCarthy's shotgun on the road. Once she saw that, she stopped being so afraid and eventually started trying to help. She was fairly plain looking, but when she started tending to McCarthy—wiping his brow with a handkerchief, holding his head against her breast—I thought she was lovely. She just understood what we were trying to do, and so she wasn't afraid anymore. By the time we got to Charlottesville it was like we were all three part of a rescue team, working together. She was calling out directions, eyeing the road and McCarthy at the same time. She looked at me and said, "Is my cooler still on the seat up there?"

I picked up a small red cooler that was on the floor by my feet. "This?"

She reached for it without looking at me. McCarthy started moaning, and she tried to give him a sip of cold water from a bottle she had in the cooler.

"I could sure use some of that," I said.

She smiled and handed me the bottle.

McCarthy seemed to draw in a lot of air all of a sudden. Then he moaned again.

"We're almost there," she said.

I swear I fell in love with her then. It's sad to think of, though. I don't even know her name.

When we got to the hospital and took McCarthy inside, somebody called the police and Bone and I found ourselves sitting in the back of a squad car before the nurses finished admitting the patient. But we were heroes and we knew it. Even the girl told them she volunteered to help us. We had saved Mac's life, and we didn't run. The rest of the gang was in trouble, but we were headed for what I hoped would be a kind of reprieve. It's the first thing I've done since I got out of the army that feels really good. You know what I mean?

That should be reward enough.

PENNY

I can't believe I forgot to tell Sheriff Paxton about the stone. I watched his car pull out and move on down the hill toward town, then I remembered it. He wasn't very obliging before he left, so maybe I was too angry to think about nothing. He stood there on the front walk, kind of smirking at me, and told me I should get a locksmith up here and change the locks on the doors.

"Sure," I said. "I can get a locksmith up here on a Saturday. Sure."

"It'll probably cost extra, but you can do it. You can't sit up all night long holding that there shovel."

"What about you?"

"I don't need no shovel," he says.

"I don't mean that. Ain't you supposed to be the law?"

"Oh, I'll drive by every now and then, sure. And I can have the state police keep a lookout when they're up this way, especially at night." He winked at me, like he was telling me something secret. "But you live almost all the way to the top of this here mountain. It's a long haul up here, even for folks like me down in Lebanon Church. The state police won't be coming up if there ain't no occasion, know what I mean?"

"I know," I said. "I figured that."

"Ain't nobody can be here every minute," he says.

"Well, I guess I know what my situation is."

"And with the store closed, there ain't no place to get some coffee around here."

I didn't say nothing, and he stood there looking at me for a while. Then he says, "I ain't no baby-sitter, young lady." He shrugged, then turned and went and got in his Ford, and I never said a word about the stone. I guess I was too mad to remember it. I hate it when a man calls me "young lady." Like I'm a child that needs to be scolded. I already have a child of my own. I'm a mother and I was a wife and I take care of my aunt as good as anybody probably ever done, and he calls me "young lady." Tells me he ain't no baby-sitter.

Times like that, I still miss John. I try not to, because it ain't no point to it, finally. He's gone just like he was dead. That's what he said to me: "I may as well be dead to you. You're gonna be dead to me." But he was all the storms in my life, all flashes of lightning and thunder.

I remember when I first seen him. The first time I knew there was a John Bone. That was way back in 1951.

He walked into Miss Demera's class late, and she stopped everything to look at him. Something in her eyes, in the way she gazed at him, was very strange. It was a sudden kind of being ready for something—you know, a wide-eyed expectation—as soon as she seen who opened the door. Then he stepped in. His long, thin legs in dark jeans made him look taller somehow—although he really wasn't more than a inch or two taller than me. It was the first day of school, and I was promoted that year to the sophomore class, even though I just turned fifteen. John had been going to Gault's school all the time, but I never paid him no mind until that year. He was seventeen, almost eighteen. And he grown over the summer. His hair was dark brown, not long or greasy looking. It covered his head though, evenly all around, and come to a perfect point in the center above his forehead. He was lean and angular and the long muscles down his arms seemed to be gripped by arteries and veins from his elbow to his wrists. He wore a T-shirt, blue jeans, black work boots. He just stood there for a minute, looking at all of us, then he turned toward Miss Demera.

"Sit down, John," she says.

"Where?"

We was all looking at him. Miss Demera says, "Just take any empty seat."

He walked over to a seat just the other side of me and sat down. Miss Demera went on about China and tea and tungsten and I glanced over to where he was sitting.

He ignored me most of that class, but then just when I was about to give up, he looked at me. I smiled, and he smiled back.

His eyes was so light blue they glowed, like they'd glow in the dark. He had thin, dark eyebrows, but his face was not as angular as the rest of him. It was almost almond shaped, with very pale, smooth skin that looked like alabaster in the sunlight. Most of the time his expression was determined, almost angry. But when he smiled, his face would change so drastically you couldn't take your eyes off it. His brows would rise and twitch, and then the straight white teeth would show, and you didn't want to ever look away from him. It was a mischief in his smile, and devilry. You knew it was there, but no meanness, no savagery, nor nothing like that. Just a kind of mischief.

Later I found out why he was late to school that first day. He was in jail until that very morning. I heard this story from my aunt Clare, who run around with people who seen it, but I also heard some of it from John, himself. When I found out what he done, I thought it was amazing they didn't lock him up and throw away the key. Some folks thought what he done was stupid, but I don't think so. I think it was real smart and perverse; a lawless act that made a point too sharp for anybody to get very well. It was all I ever heard about him before I actually got to know him: just the story about what he done when he was down at the Moose Club in Lebanon Church.

He'd gone there to work for the summer. Wasn't nothing to do up in Crawford, so he hitched down the mountain and got a job working in the yard and on the "grounds" of the Moose Club. He worked most the whole summer there, and when August come, when he knew he'd be coming back to school, he counted up what they had paid him. What he said was, "It ain't near enough."

They asked him, "Didn't you agree to work for seventy-five cents an hour?"

"But I ain't got paid that much," he says.

"Sure you did," they argued.

"What's this here?" He pointed to some deductions on his last check.

And one of the other folks who was talking to him—it was supposed to be the manager—says, "Why that's a clothing allotment—for the green uniform you been wearing all summer."

"You said the clothing was included," John says, just to remind him. And the manager says, "Who said that? I never said that."

"Yes, you did. You told me seventy-five cents an hour including the uniform."

"I said 'plus' the uniform."

"I didn't hear 'plus.'"

The manager folded his arms and just looked at him. "Whose fault is that?" he says.

Then John smiled. Everybody said he just smiled at them—the Moose Club folks—and says, "Thank you kindly. I'll see to it myself."

"What do you mean by that?" somebody asked him.

And what I was told was, he says, "I'm going into business for myself, fellers."

So picture this: What happened was, the next day was a Sunday, and they had this big meeting at the club. It was a Labor Day weekend, so lots of members and guests was there and the parking lot was packed. The sun was high and just starting to fall to the other side of the mountain. It was a hot day—even for September. The meeting broke up, and people started coming outside to climb into their baking cars. They're squirming on hot seats, trying to get their engines to start, and nothing's happening. Most of them are soaked in sweat, cursing to beat all, even if it was a Sunday. First one, then the other raises the hood on his car. A few more follow. Pretty soon, most of them got their hoods raised up and now, they are getting angry—mob angry. John said they was, "hot, sweaty, and absolutely lynch mob pissed off." He laughed when he told me about it. Finally, somebody noticed him. He was setting in the shade of a giant oak tree just up the hill and off the grounds, but in plain sight of the parking lot. He was relaxed, leaning back in a lawn chair, next to a big orange cooler full of lemonade and Coca Cola. In front of him was a small, white table, with stacks of Dixie cups piled high on it. He fanned himself with a beautiful Japanese paper fan. On his left was a stack of those fans—with a sign that says FOR SALE: COOLING FANS. ONE DOLLAR. To his right, it was another sign that says ICE COLD LEMONADE OR COCA COLA. BY THE CUP. FIFTY CENTS.

But none of that's what got him in trouble. In fact, he might of sold a few drinks and fans, but for what was piled up behind him—stacked against the tree and around the roots like something to hold the old oak upright. You know what it was?

Car batteries. More than thirty of them. All kinds of car batteries.

And it ain't hard to guess what was missing from every car in the Moose Club parking lot.

John had made a big sign, bigger than the signs for fans or drinks, and it says BATTERIES FOR SALE: ALMOST NEW. TEN DOLLARS OR BEST OFFER.

I heard it really was like a lynch mob. They come up that hill at him as if they was one beast. He set there with his arms folded across his chest and refused to budge. People saying things like, "I think that's my goddamned battery right there," and John saying, "It can be if you got ten dollars."

I can just see him grinning at them.

"Where'd you get all these dad-burned batteries, son?" somebody says.

"Fair and square," John says. "That's where I got them."

"That don't answer the question."

"I reckon I don't have to share my business secrets with you nor nobody else," John says. "Let's just say my distributor is a local fellow and let it go at that."

Somebody called the police, and a few stout hearts kept the mob from killing him. But John stayed seated in the chair, staring them all down. When a few of them started looking over the batteries he just let them have at it. He knew they wouldn't get nowhere. People don't want to take just any battery. They want their own personal battery, the one that come standard equipment, or the one they bought at Sears, or JCPenney, or Pep Boys, or wherever. Have you ever tried to root through a pile of batteries? It was a god awful mess.

And John says, "Anything you take from that pile, you owe me ten dollars or your best offer."

"You stole my goddamned battery," somebody says.

"It wasn't me. I come upon these batteries."

"How?"

"I hunted them."

"Goddamn it boy, you're in a heap of trouble."

"No, I ain't," John says. "I'm in business. That's what I'm in."

He didn't get into as much trouble as everybody wanted him to get in. Eventually they sorted it all out and most people got the battery they personally owned, or close to it anyway. And they got to drive on home in their own cars. But it took a long time. Days for some people. And Sheriff Paxton only kept John in the county lockup until the next day, when school started. Really wasn't much he could do about him, what with his father being drunk all the time and not ever knowing what John was up to and all. The Moose Club considered formal charges, but Paxton talked them out of it. He figured John would be in Korea before long, getting shot at, and it wouldn't be the fairest thing, taking his last year or two on earth away from him. Or something like that. That's the way Paxton tells it, anyway. When he was younger I reckon Paxton was a better man.

Anyway, John got out in time to hitch his way back up the mountain, and when he got home his father told him to go onto school, and that's why he was late that day when I first noticed him. If his father hadn't of told him to go, he wouldn't of gone. That was his way. He liked his father and seemed to understand what was lost in him after John's mother died.

It took me awhile to get to know John that first year I taken to him. I don't think he said five words to me. But he'd look at me, or I'd be outside watching the little kids playing tetherball during recess, and I'd catch him staring at me. Those dazzling blue eyes stopped on me like the bright reflections of the sun off distant water. I just admired him so. Not just the way he looked—even though he was the best-looking boy I'd ever seen in person—but the way he was. The way he talked to Mr. Gault, or Miss Demera, or anybody. Calm and friendly like—but also like he was equal to them. Like he knew what they knew and more. Once I heard Miss Demera tell Mr. Gault that she thought he was a bomb with a short fuse and one day he was going to explode. But that wasn't the feeling. She just misunderstood the tension in him.

John was kind. That's what I remember most about him. He could get himself into so much trouble because he hated being told what to do, and he blamed the whole world for taking his momma away from him. All of these was definite faults. I understand that. He ain't never been faultless. Probably there's better young men in the world, but I never met nary a one of them. He was really kind when he had to be, and he never wanted to hurt nobody.

I remember when I found out what kind of man John was going to be. It was the year he graduated.

That was when Terry Landon first come to the school.

A lot of people didn't like it that Mr. Gault had gone and let a Negro child into the school. I don't know if they wrote letters or what they might of said or done to Mr. Gault, but one day during recess he come outside and called all of us over to where he was standing. John stepped away from a tree he'd been leaning on and walked across the yard, and everybody followed him. Mr. Gault says, "No doubt you've all noticed that we have a new student in the school." Miss Demera stood behind him, her hands behind her back, and a look on her face that was both sad and angry, like she'd been scolded for something and resented it.

"Terry, please come here," Mr. Gault says.

Terry worked his way through the other children and stood in front of Mr. Gault. Mr. Gault put both hands on Terry's shoulders and Terry's wide, dark eyes shifted down to his feet. "This here's Terry," Mr. Gault says. "Terry Landon." Then he let his hands fall down in front of Terry, so that his arms was draped next to Terry's head. He leaned over the boy and says, "Say hello, now."

Terry says, "Hi," like that, real soft and embarrassed.
None of the other children said nothing.

"Terry's not only new, he's different."

It was still quiet. Miss Demera moved forward a little and patted Terry on the top of his head. Terry turned to look back at her but she'd stepped away, and so he stared at the ground again.

"There are things in this world," Mr. Gault says, "that you don't know about yet. Things changing. Maybe for the better. And bad things. Bad things, too. You see, we can't know whether a change is a bad thing unless we go ahead and try it."

Some of the children looked around, sort of making faces at each other. They didn't know what he was getting at.

"We'd like it not to be that way," Mr. Gault went on. "But it just is." He paused, looking at all of us. Terry didn't know what to do with his hands. "Terry's family lives down the mountain a little, and his daddy works in the mill."

We all knew that. Some of the kids begun to fidget.

"It may be better for our school, better for Terry, and better for those bad things I mentioned if Terry joins us in our endeavors, and if we welcome him . . ."

One of the girls says, "What's end evers?"

"Pardon?" Mr. Gault says.

She repeated it.

"Endeavors," Mr. Gault says. "Work. Study. What we're doing here, every day."

It got quiet again.

Brad Crowly was the same age as me. He was in my class the year before and he used to tease me about my short hair. He told me he already smoked cigarettes and that he could drive a car. He said his daddy even let him go down to Lebanon Church and shoot pool. He stepped in front of Mr. Gault and looked down at Terry. "Well, he's right puny, ain't he?"

It was quiet. Mr. Gault started to say something and then Crowly says, "Do we eat with him at the same table?"

"Well," Mr. Gault says. "Of course we'll..."

Miss Demera says, "He'll eat at the same table. That's right." Mr. Gault nodded.

"And wash in the same toilet with him and whatnot?" The whole time Crowly didn't take his eyes off Terry and Terry was looking at him right back.

"We are going to welcome him," Mr. Gault says. "Soon the whole country is going to have to do what we're doing right here in Crawford." He rested his hands on Terry's shoulders again.

"I ain't going to do it," Crowly says. "We don't none of us have to do it."

Terry seemed to get shorter, backing a bit into Mr. Gault's legs. I thought he might start to cry. His chin quivered.

Crowly says, "I ain't going to be welcoming no niggers into my school." He just stood there looking at Terry, like he might suddenly hit him or something. The Crowlys always took pride in their appearance. Brad wore new blue jeans and a heavy starched white shirt, and his hair was combed straight back. It almost glittered in the sun. The hate in him almost glittered, too. Sometimes you could just about hear it, like loud awful music just when he walked by. He had his hands in the back pockets of the jeans, and his head tilted to the side a little, still looking in Terry's eyes. "My daddy says we don't belong with no niggers," he says. He pronounced the *n* with such venom it seemed like I could see hate dripping from his sneering mouth. Then he says, "We supposed to keep away from them because they cursed by God. And that's why they're all black." His voice was quiet, like he was praying out loud. It was silent for a second or two, and I seen Terry blink. Then Crowly looked up at Mr. Gault and says, "And now you just trying to start something."

Terry's eyes was so wide and frightened, I thought he might start crying.

Miss Demera shook her head, a look of disgust on her face.

Mr. Gault looked like he was trying to remember something. His mouth was closed tight in a thin line and he just stood there, watching Brad Crowly. It wasn't like he was afraid or nothing. He just seemed to be waiting there until Brad said everything he was going to say; like he wanted to hear all of it before he did whatever he was going to do. Miss Demera whispered something to Terry, to calm him down. It seemed like I could smell the dirt, and I just hated that day. I knew I hated it right then.

"Ain't you trying to start something," Brad says. He was talking to Terry, now, completely ignoring everybody else. Mr. Gault started to speak. "Now listen, young man," or something like that, and then suddenly there was John.

He stepped in between Terry and Brad, with that smile on his face, and says, "What's the matter, Crowly? Is your whole family afraid of this here little fellow?" He reached down, picked Terry up, and put him on his shoulders. "Look it here," he says. "He don't weigh more than fifty pounds."

Crowly just glared at him. Terry put his small black hands on John's forehead, trying to steady himself. John says, "My my my. You better go warn the rest of your family about the serious business I got here on my shoulders. I've lifted the devil up high. Good Lord. There ain't no way of knowing if he might break loose or not." John still had that smile on his face, but now he leaned a little bit toward Brad and says in a deep, fearful whisper, "And then there's no telling what might happen."

"That's enough," Mr. Gault says.

Miss Demera says to John, "Put him down this instant," but Mr. Gault turned to her and the expression on his face did something to her. She let her arms fall to her sides, but her face softened.

"I'm just going over here with my friend to play a little tetherball," John says. Then he walked off, and Terry bounced on his shoulders, smiling for the first time.

Mr. Gault says, "You all take a notion from John there. It's the best way to improve the world just a little bit. And that's what education is all about."

Miss Demera even smiled then.

I thought John was a hero. But Brad Crowly just kicked at the dust and walked over to the seesaws.

I knew then what kind of man John Bone was. I had no idea he'd one day be my husband and that I'd lose him before we had a year together.

AFTER SHERIFF PAXTON'S car disappears down the road, I go on back in the house and close the door. I figure I'll wait and see if Morgan will come back this morning before I fool with the stone. If he don't come I can always call him later on. To tell the truth, I'm afraid to dig it completely out of the ground unless Morgan is there.

I wait a long time. About noon, Mr. Gault comes by. I watch him drive past the cabin three or four times, and then finally he turns up the hill and parks in front.

"Good morning," he says. He strolls across the grass toward where I'm hanging clothes on the line. I have the shovel leaning against the clothesline pole just in case.

Mr. Gault wears a white shirt, tan pants, and a white straw hat with a navy blue band and the brim bent very low. He tips the hat back on his head when he gets to where I'm standing.

"What you want?" I say.

"I heard about your aunt Clare." He stands there looking at Tory with his hands on his hips. Then he turns back to me. "I'm very sorry she got hurt."

"She'll be okay."

"Myra said you were upset when you came for Tory the other day. Then she ran into Doc Hardesty's Missus."

"I don't know any Doc Hardesty."

"Doctor Sam Hardesty. People call him Dr. Sam."

I shrug. He don't say nothing for a while, then he points at Tory. "She's gotten a bit taller I think."

I'm just hanging clothes, being quiet.

"Over the summer."

Tory stops and looks at him. "You're a good girl," he says, "helping your momma with the wash and all."

"I can do it all by myself," Tory says.

"I bet you can." He's quiet for a while, then he says, "You looking forward to coming back to school?"

"No, sir," Tory says. "I ain't."

"You *aren't*," he says.

"I aren't."

"No. *You* say 'I'm not.'"

"You're not," Tory says.

I laugh.

Tory picks one of my bras out of the basket. He looks at it. I take it from her and hang it up on the line. He looks away, tries to pretend I didn't see him looking at it.

"Is there something I can do for you?" I say.

"I just wanted to make sure everything was okay."

"Everything's *not* okay."

"I mean about Clare and all."

"You know who may of done it?" I say. "It was—" I start to say it, but then I realize Tory is right there, listening, and I don't want to frighten her. "It was bad," I tell him. "But she'll be all right."

"And how about you?" he says, in a real soft voice.

"Momma didn't get hurt," Tory says, handing me a long white slip that belongs to Clare. I hang it up, and he stands there looking at me as if he expects me to start crying and fall in his arms or something.

"I just want you to know," he says. He reaches out, sort of unconsciously, and touches the slip, runs his hand lightly up and down the edge of it. "If there's anything I can do—you can depend on me and Myra."

"I sure do thank you," I say. I take a pillowcase from Tory and step toward him with it, and he backs away and gives me room so I can hang it next to the slip.

"Myra was saying just this morning that—well, we care about you."

I don't say nothing.

"You're important to me," he almost whispers.

I face him. "You looking to sweet-talk me?"

That sets him back a bit. "Well," he stammers. "There's nothing I *want.*" He seems insulted.

"I don't know," I say. "I never met a man under seventy that didn't want something."

"I care about all my former students."

I don't know what I'm supposed to say, so I take the last article of clothing out of the basket and hang it on the line.

"I don't want you to get the wrong idea, young lady," he says.

"I ain't no 'young lady' to you nor nobody else," I say.

"Well, you're not an *old* lady now are you?"

"I'm grown," I say. "I ain't no child."

"I didn't mean to insinuate that you were."

"What's that mean?"

"What?"

"What you just said there."

"Insinuate?"

"That's it."

"It means—well, it means I didn't mean to call you young—I wasn't trying to suggest that you are a child."

"Well, that's what it felt like."

"I know you can take care of yourself, Penny."

"Right now, I have to take care of Clare," I say. I pick up the empty basket and the bag of clothespins and move back toward the cabin. "Do me a favor and bring that there shovel," I say to Mr. Gault. I tell Tory she can have cookies and milk, so she runs in front of me, and Mr. Gault walks a little behind me, muttering to himself.

Tory runs in the house and slams the screen door. I'm afraid she'll wake Clare, but when I get up to the porch I can see through the screen door that she's still sleeping peacefully on the couch. I put the basket on the bottom step and wait for Mr. Gault.

He comes up to me. "You didn't hear what I said?"

"I heard you talking to yourself. I didn't hear what you was saying."

"I was just wondering what the shovel's for." He leans it against the porch railing.

Behind him I can see the sky beginning to darken, and a light breeze pushes the hair up around his ears, but his hat stays on. The leaves of the trees start turning over and swishing in the wind. "You want to help me?" I say.

"That's why I came up here."

"It's going to rain soon." I point behind him. He seems surprised at the bruised sky on the other side of the mountain.

"And you just hung out the wash," he says.

"It looked like a good day for it an hour ago."

"That it did." He waits there with his hands in his pockets, not saying nothing. I think he's embarrassed. Then he says, "Well, you want me to help you take it all down?"

"That ain't what I want help with."

"What can I do?" he says.

"Come with me," I say.

I take him around back to the stone. "I want to get this here stone out of the ground before it rains."

156

He leans over it. "I'll be," he says. "Look at that."

"Can you help me?"

"It looks pretty big."

"If you could dig it out for me, I'd appreciate it."

"Isn't it a tombstone?" he says.

I say, "Yes."

He hesitates, looking at me. Then he walks back out front and gets the shovel, and when he comes around the corner of the house he's walking slowly, as if he has to think about each step before he takes it. He comes up next to me again, sets the shovel down, and leans on it, the palm of his hand over the top of the handle.

"What's the matter?" I say.

"Well, it's probably a grave."

"So?"

"I had rather not disturb—it's probably what we would call consecrated ground."

"Ain't you the pious one."

"Well," he says. "If it *is* a grave, it wouldn't do to disturb it. There's probably laws against it, I would think."

"What else would it be with a tombstone a-setting over it?"

"That's my point."

"Ain't you a lawyer and a judge and all?"

"That doesn't matter. I can't take the law into my own hands and..."

"I don't want to disturb the grave," I say. "I just want to dig up the stone. If I don't, Tory will play around it and keep digging at it. Then you mostly *will* have a disturbed grave."

He seems to think that's reasonable. It's quiet for a while, then I say, "I'll fix you something for lunch."

He takes off his hat and picks up the shovel. "It's a deal," he says.

He hands me his hat, spits into his hands, and then starts digging. I walk back across the yard to the porch, put his hat on the railing there, and sit down on the steps to watch him. I know I'll never know for sure what goes on in his mind—but he'll never figure out what goes on in mine neither. Maybe he really does want to help me because I was once a student in his school. It don't really matter to me. I need him just now, and not just to dig up the stone. No, I need him for something far more important than that.

When he's nearly finished, I go into the house and make him a sliced chicken sandwich. I bring it out with a cold beer. He stops digging to eat—comes over and sits on the back porch next to me watching the sky seem to close over the mountain like a blanket. But we can both tell there's plenty of time. The breezes haven't really got going yet, and the birds are still chattering away in the trees.

"Looks like it's going to be a bad one," Mr. Gault says.

"I reckon it will get cold, too."

Tory comes out and before long she has wandered over by the stone. She's pawing dirt from around it, getting herself all dirty.

"Tory, get away from there," I holler.

"Oh, let her play," Mr. Gault says. He throws his head back and finishes the beer. I see crumbs on the corner of his mouth. When he looks directly at me I say, "I want to talk to you."

He puts his hands on his knees and leans back. I look over at Tory and even though she's too far away to hear me, I whisper, "I need another favor. It's about Tory." I feel Gault's eyes on me, but I ain't looking at him. He stares at the side of my face like a dog waiting for a milkbone.

Tory comes back slowly, daydreaming and singing to herself.

"Shouldn't you finish?" I say to Mr. Gault.

"I thought you wanted to talk."

"I can talk while you dig."

He seems disappointed.

"You've almost got it out," I say.

"All right." He gets up and strolls back to the hole. I shoo Tory inside, then go over to where he can see me while he works.

"I don't want to keep Tory here tonight," I say.

"Why not?" He stops and leans on the shovel.

"You'll never finish that if you don't keep going."

"All right. All right." He smiles. "You're about as demanding as a first sergeant I knew in the army."

After a while, I say, "Whoever beat Clare up got a key."

"Really."

I tell him the story. Then I say, "I don't know, but what if she got beat up by the Gypsy Man?"

He shakes his head, but he don't say nothing.

"Maybe he's come back," I say. "Morgan's looking for signs."

Now he digs around the stone as if he's angry at it or the shovel. "Did Clare tell you it was the Gypsy Man?"

"She ain't made much sense. She don't know."

"Well, where'd you get this idea about a—about a Gypsy Man?"

"She don't know. She don't know nothing. She don't believe in it half the time."

"I don't understand why you do, Penny."

"I remember the Landon boy."

He frowns and stops digging again. He holds the top of the handle on the shovel far out away from his body—as if he hangs from it.

"I got Tory to think of."

"Was this fellow who beat up Clare a hundred years old?" he says.

"I know you don't believe it neither," I say.

159

"Was he a hundred years old? Did she say that?" He starts digging again. He's a little out of breath, but he's getting all the dirt from around the stone, digging now at the base of it. "Well, did she?" he says.

"It don't matter what she said. If it wasn't him I got to act like it was. I can't take no chances."

He strikes the shovel into the dirt. "Well, if he's a hundred years old, you don't have to worry about him."

"Maybe he don't age," I say. "You ever think of that? Maybe he ain't human anymore and he don't age."

"I'm surprised you believe in all that hocus-pocus," he says. "You're smarter than that." He gets the shovel under the bottom edge of the stone and leans hard on the handle. "It's moving," he groans.

"Don't hurt yourself," I say.

The stone won't give much. He wipes his forehead with the back of his arm and starts digging around it again. "Son of a gun is really in there."

"Whoever beat up Clare has a key to the cabin now."

He stops. "I understand that."

"He brought her back here, set her there on the couch, covered her with a blanket, then locked the door when he went out."

"Huh," he says. "That's not so good, is it?" He works the shovel under the edge of the stone again, leans on the handle so hard I see it bend. I wait for him to offer what I need, but when he don't I just blurt it out.

"You and Myra got to take Tory for a while."

Suddenly the stone comes out. It just lifts up out of the ground on the tip of the shovel, and Mr. Gault falls down on the handle. "I got it," he says. His face is only inches out of the dirt, and it takes him awhile to get back up. He has grass stains on his tan pants, but I don't think he minds much. He's amazed at the name on the stone. I have to get the hose and wash it off clean before we can make it out completely. The top says,

IN MEMORIUM

and under that, in very small, hard-to-read script is

Gone but Not Forgotten

and the next line don't say W I L E L, like Morgan and I thought. When Mr. Gault washes all the accumulated dirt out of the letters it says,

WILBUR

and there's a name next to that. It says,

CRAWFORD

Under the name, as me and Morgan thought, is the word B O R N, and then the day and year,

APRIL 28, 1867

Under that is the word,

DIED

And then,

19—.

The rest is blank.

"This is—this is strange," Mr. Gault says. "It's a tombstone, but there's no date of death on it."

I feel my heart beginning to stammer.

He looks at me with serious eyes. "You leave this alone," he says. "I think maybe we ought to get somebody up here to look at it."

"Who? Sheriff Paxton?"

"I could call Paxton. Maybe he should see this, too."

"Paxton's been here. He was here this morning."

"You showed him the stone?"

"He ain't gonna take kindly to the idea of coming back up here. I don't want him back up here anyhow."

"Well. It's best you leave this alone. Maybe we should just do that. Leave it here."

"It's on my property."

He rubs his jaw, then puts the shovel down on the ground. "I just wouldn't touch it, that's all. I think it's probably more on the old Crawford property."

"What would be the harm in taking it out of here?"

"You looking for things to be afraid of?"

"No, I ain't. I got a child to look after, and right now I wish we didn't dig that thing out of the ground."

He looks at the stone, touches it with the toe of his shoe. "It may really be a grave. It seems like—for something like this—ought to be an official of some kind present."

"Ain't you an official?"

"I don't understand," he says, but he ain't talking to me. He stares off behind me, at the cabin, or the hill beyond and the old Crawford place. "I don't understand why there's no date of death on this stone."

"It's because he ain't dead yet," I say. "Don't you see? It's the Gypsy Man's stone." Thunder murmurs low, quiets down for a short spell, then rumbles in the black clouds over the top of the far-off trees. The air smells like rust, and spring water, and new mowed grass. "I wish we didn't disturb it. That's what I wish."

He don't say nothing. I know it will be useless to bury it again, and I know he ain't about to suggest it, neither. For a second I hate everything I can see. Now I have the damn stone to contend with.

Finally I say, "Why don't you lay it out flat at the base of that tree and leave it there?"

"Why don't I just carry it down and put it in the trunk of my car?"

"I don't care what you do with it. I don't want to look at it."

The air starts to move. Mr. Gault picks up the stone and carries it down the hill. He puts it in the trunk of his car. Then he comes back up the hill like he done something heroic. He almost claps his hands rubbing the dirt off them. "There."

He reaches up and grabs his hat. The air kicks up and swirls into a steady wind that comes swiftly down the mountain, herding the fallen leaves and scattering the branches of the trees. The wind rushes around and shoves things like something alive and angry.

"We best get inside," Gault says.

Then it starts to rain.

GAULT

I'll never forget the look on Penny's face when I lifted the stone out of the ground and she saw the name on it. She looked as terrified as any child I've ever seen. Her fear was real, you understand. A clap of thunder shook her as though lightning had cut its hot way right to her bones.

"It's all right," I said. I put the shovel down and took her in my arms. She shuddered against me, her head in the hollow of my shoulder. She trembled like a small bird. I took her hand and moved her across the yard and gently up onto the porch. My hat blew off the railing and hit the wall. The trees started hissing. "I'm going to do a little paperwork and then get some people up here to look at this thing," I said.

Her eyes got even wider.

"Now don't be afraid," I said.

"You've got to take Tory with you," she said. "He's got a key."

"Who's got a key?"

"The Gypsy Man." Her chin quivered, her teeth chattering. She looked cold, as if she'd already gotten wet in the storm.

I almost reached for her again. The impulse to take her in my arms and just comfort her, get her warm and calm, was almost too much to resist.

"That's a goddamned grave," she said.

"Well, we don't know that now, do we? There's no date of death on the stone."

"Whatever's buried there ain't dead yet."

"Now, you know better than that." I picked up my hat. "You just know better than that, Penny."

"He's got a key, goddamn it. He's got a key." She flashed her black eyes at me. The wind lifted her hair and blew strands of it across her face. She looked back to where the stone leaned against the tree. "Take that thing out of here. I don't want to look at it."

She was serious.

"It's just a stone," I told her.

I ASK YOU: what is your experience with devils, spooks, ghosts, and gods? You think it is truly experience? Knowing what we know about our primitive ancestors and their childlike superstitions and fears?

Is there any difference at all between what a man *wishes* he could do, or what he *imagines* his experience might have been, and what he has *actually* done? It strikes me that both exist in exactly the same way: a simple feature of imagination. Both the memory of an event and the imagined wish for it exist only in a man's head; both are, in the truest sense of the word, imaginary.

Oh, but experience is preferable, you say. Experience leaves scars, physical evidence of the event. It changes us, perhaps. Certainly the person who cannot distinguish between experience and imagination suffers from some form of mania. But what is the difference, truly? You see the problem, don't you? Both the man who remembers living quietly and happily in the same house for twenty years, and the man who wishes he had done so and only imagines it, are contemplating it in their thoughts. Both are merely engaged in thinking. Experience is preferable to imagination only in the full flower of the present moment—that elusive flicker of sensation that, like flame, cannot be arrested or stilled. Once experience gets into the past, once each microsecond passes into memory, it becomes imaginary. That's all. It has the same flavor and force in the mind as anything one might dream or conceive. So finally, it's *all* in the imagination and *not real.*

Perhaps we are all victims of an elemental human need to believe in things greater or more lasting than a single life— some notion of immortality and eternal, ongoing history. Perhaps from such a need and from the sheer force of imagination, we got the idea of God.

If we didn't know that death waits at the end to arrest life, we'd have no real interest in history or God. Isn't it just possible that we created the dear Lord because of all we *cannot* know, not because of all we know? Would the primitives have believed in gods and spirits if they knew what we now know? I would not make the point very loudly or publicly, of course. Privately, however, I've often wondered about the superstitious nature of religion. My wife would merely register such meditations as doubt and attribute it to a lack of faith, but sometimes I think there's a real similarity between the myths and fables of primitive people and the religious pieties of the more civilized.

What would make a man who grunts and sweats every day under the sun raise his eyes to the moon at dusk and put his faith in a spirit he cannot see and a future no one has ever come back from?

No doubt I'm reacting to the fact that my own little village has its own myths. I can't help how I feel about that. I am sometimes angered by what people choose to believe. And belief *is* a choice. The Landon boy's been missing for six years, and still Sheriff Paxton persists in the belief that he will find him. So, of course, every few weeks or so, he feels like he has to talk to me about it. As if he's involved in some sort of ongoing investigation and I'm one of his possible witnesses or suspects. He promises me he'll find out what happened, and when he says it, he always has this glint in his eye as if he were threatening me with something.

"Why go all over it again?" I said once. "What's the point?" We were sitting in front of my house, by my wife's rose garden. This was a long time ago. It was late in the afternoon, at least a week or so before Clare wandered off and got Penny talking about the Gypsy Man again. Paxton had pulled his car up in front and stopped by the curb.

"I ain't satisfied about it," Paxton said. "I'm a little surprised you are."

"I'm not satisfied," I said. "I just don't know what else we can do but what we've done."

"Don't it bother you a little bit?" he said.

"It's a crying shame," I said. "But I don't know what it will serve, opening these old wounds all over again."

"Six years is a long time," he said. "But there ain't no statute of limitations on murder."

"If murder it was," I said.

"You think he run off by himself?"

"No," I said. "He wouldn't do that."

"You think it was the Gypsy Man?"

I frowned at him.

"I didn't think so," he said. "But something happened."

"Yes, it did," I said. I just wanted him to put his car in gear and drive on up the hill. I felt sick thinking about it again. "You let me know if you find out anything more," I said.

"I will." He smiled.

I said, "I have to tell you, it looks like all you can do is go around asking the same questions over and over again."

He nodded. Then he said, "Some folks don't get it just the same way every time."

I said nothing.

"Well, so long, your honor." He waved as he pulled off. I've never liked his attitude toward me and what I do, not my teaching, but my work as a lawyer. He cheapens it by everything he says and does that *appears* to be respectful, but is, in reality an ironic kind of derision. I watched him drive on up the road and turn back toward Lebanon Church.

Saturday, I noticed he was up at Penny's place, so that's why I drove up there this morning after church. I wanted to be sure everything was all right. I knew her aunt Clare had come back, but I wasn't sure how bad off she was. Penny was pretty upset when she came to get Tory yesterday. She didn't say anything to me, but she wore an expression on her face that made me think of auto accidents and hospitals.

"What's wrong with you?" I asked. I just wanted her to know that I could see through her tough exterior. Myra had planned a delicious supper for her, but she came early to get Tory. She announced that Clare had returned and that she was mighty beat up. Then she rounded up her little one, thanked us both "very kindly," got in her little VW Beetle, and started back up the hill toward her place. I figured she'd been talking to old man Tiller again.

Of course, Myra had been insisting that I go over there, anyway. "See if that poor young girl needs anything," she said.

"If she wants you to open the store for her, let me know. I can spend a few hours over there."

"Honey, you know how those people react when you offer to help," I said.

"It won't hurt to offer it," she said.

"I guess a lot of people are beginning to wonder when the old store will be open again. It's a fairly long drive to Lebanon Church."

"Yes, it is."

I kissed her on the cheek.

She smiled briefly. Then she said, "If Penny needs help I'll give it."

"I'll ask her," I said.

So I go up there and bring back the stone. And that isn't all I bring back with me. I also have Tory, which makes Myra very happy. She is waiting at the end of the sidewalk when we pull up, even though it's still raining pretty steadily. "What a nice surprise," she says, when Tory gets out of the car. She embraces her and then starts back toward the house, covering the little girl's head with part of her cloak.

"Hey," I say. "Wait. I want to show you something."

"It's raining," she says. "Show me later."

It isn't raining all that hard. I lay the stone down in the tall grass next to Myra's rose garden in the front yard. The rain pelts it steadily, and I see more dirt is beginning to melt away. I know exactly what Morgan Tiller will say about this. In spite of myself, it almost pleases me to think of it. I turn away from it and walk on up to the house.

When I come in the door, Myra says, "Good Lord, look at you."

"What?" I say.

"You're covered with dirt."

"I've been digging."

Tory says, "Can I have some water?"

"And you're soaking wet," Myra says. "Where on earth have you been digging?" She goes to the linen cabinet and throws me a towel. Then she runs water in the sink until it's cold, fills a glass for Tory, and hands it to her. "Your Sunday best, too."

"It's just dirt," I say.

"What were you doing up there?"

"That's what I want to show you."

"Dry yourself off," she says. "And get out of those dirty clothes."

Later, when the rain starts to slow a bit more, I walk back out and stand there looking at the stone. The rain has washed it further, and it is as clean and bright as the new moon.

CLARE

If she could just take the little one out of here for a spell. I can't stand the racket. It don't matter if she's reading a picture book or jumping on the bed, the noise is the same. And Penny won't sit on her to make her stop.

Penny comes in out of the rain like she's getting away from a fire—slams the door shut. I feel the wind of it. Tory is braiding the hair on one of her dolls. The sound of the slamming door makes her cry out.

"I'm sorry, honey, did I scare you?" Penny says. Then she looks at me. "You're awake."

"Even if I was unconscious, I couldn't stay that way for long in this house."

"You done all right so far."

"I'm hurt," I say. "What's the matter with you?"

"Nothing." She scoots Tory into her room. I reach under the cushion and get myself a little medicine. I hate to drink it from the bottle, but it's so warm going down. It soothes me.

"What're you drinking?" Penny says, behind me. I didn't hear her come back in the room so her voice frightens me a little bit.

"It's just some medicine," I say. I put the cap back on and push it back under the covers, but she sees it.

"Old Granddad," she says. "That's some medicine."

"It's good for my nerves," I say.

She goes back in her room for a spell. I take a few more sips. It is quiet for a long time.

"Penny, honey, what're you doing in there?"

Neither one of them makes a sound.

Then Penny comes out carrying a small suitcase.

"Where you going?"

"I ain't going nowhere." She puts the bag down by the door and disappears again. I hear Tory start up, chattering and laughing. Then she comes skipping into the room, pulling her mother by the hand.

"What's going on?" I say.

"I'm sending Tory to stay with Mr. and Mrs. Gault tonight."

"Why you doing that?"

"I have to."

"I don't want to go to school," Tory says.

"It ain't school," Penny says. "You're going for a visit." She goes to the window, watches the rain scatter on the glass in a light spray. She don't even blink. "I left the wash on the line, and now the wind's going to blow it all away."

"It'll be there tomorrow."

It's quiet for a minute. Then I say, "You ought to open the store today."

"There's people down there right now," she says.

"Who is it?"

"I can't see in the rain. They run up to the door and tried it. They're pulling off now. I think it's one of the Crowlys."

"Well, they'll come back."

"I don't know what we'll live on if we don't open that store and keep it open for a while." She talks to the window in front of her. It seems like she's trying to make up her mind about something. She stands still, but she keeps shifting her feet— like she's on the deck of a rocking ship or something. I see a shadow move across the glass.

"What're you looking at out there?"

"Mr. Gault. He's waiting for us."

"Well, don't leave him out there in the rain."

"He's standing on the porch." She leans against the window frame, her head down now, but she's still looking through the glass. She looks sad.

"We'll make out, honey," I say. "We got your dad's annuity. And what you get down at Goodyear."

"It ain't enough."

"Did you go to work yesterday?"

"I worked in the store for a while. I had to call in sick at Goodyear."

"What'd you do that for?"

She still gazes out the window as if she thinks my voice is coming from there. She don't answer me.

"Penny."

"I called in sick because I had to stay here and take care of you." She don't say it mean, but that's how I take it.

"I'm sorry," I say. "I can't help what happened to me."

Now she turns around and faces me. "Did I say a word about that?"

"Well, you can open the store. I'll be okay here."

Tory picks up the suitcase, then sets it back down again with a loud bang. "That's heavy, Mommy," she says.

"I'll carry it."

"I want to carry it."

"Well, then I'll help you."

"What'd you leave the wash out there for?" I say.

"I don't know what I'm..." Penny stops, puts her hand up to her cheek as if something burns there. "Damn it. We're trapped in here."

"It's just rain," I say. Sometimes, even when you love a person and you know you love them, you can't make yourself care the way you should. It seems like ever since I told Penny about what happened to me, she's got this anger in her. Like when she made Tory wait for breakfast until Sheriff Paxton had gone. That ain't like her. I guess even your blood kin can wear on your nerves bad enough that you end up treating them like strangers.

Tory picks up the suitcase again, makes a big show of how heavy it is, grunting and panting with the stress of holding it off the floor. Then she drops it again.

"Tory, if you do that one more time," I say.

"I can't sit up *every* night," Penny says.

"What do you mean?"

She kneels down in front of Tory and straightens the collar on her dress.

"I don't want to go to Mrs. Gault's," Tory says, letting her lower lip stick out.

"I know, honey," Penny says. "But it won't be for long. She likes so much to have your company."

"Why you sending her away from you?" I say. "Good God, girl. That's the last thing I ever thought you'd do."

She turns to me, frowning. "Mrs. Gault is lonesome. Mr. Gault asked if Tory could keep her company, just for tonight."

"What's the matter with you?"

"I can't stay awake every night," she says.

"Who said you have to do that?"

"Never mind." She gets up and opens the front door. Gault stands on the porch with his back to us, watching the rain. He turns around and smiles down on Tory. "Well, aren't you the picture of loveliness."

Then he looks over Penny's shoulder and sees me. "You feeling better, Miss Clare?"

"A mite," I say. Mud all over his tan pants. He has his hand up on the brim of his hat, holding it on against the wind. I say, "What you been doing?"

"Digging."

"Penny, why'd you leave him standing out there all this time?"

Penny kneels down again and kisses Tory on the cheek. Gault takes the little one's hand, then nods at me. Tory walks on in front of him, pulling him down the steps and out into the rain.

"Hurry up," Penny says to Gault. "Get her to the car before she gets soaked."

He waves his hand and steps after her. It looks like she's dragging him where he don't want to go.

Penny shuts the door, then goes to the window and watches them get into Gault's car and pull away.

"Now why'd you do that?" I say.

"I had to." She ain't looking at me.

"Why? I'm going to be all right."

"It ain't for you."

"Well, what for then?"

"The Gypsy Man." She starts to wave out the window, but then just holds her hand up by her face. Her breathing fogs the glass, and she wipes it with her hand. She keeps looking off in the distance, like she wants to find Tory's face in the thicket of rain and dripping water. Then she slowly puts her hands in her pockets and leans against the frame in a sudden sort of collapse, like she's given up something and just quit. "He's got a key. I can't leave you here by yourself, and I don't want Tory here if he comes back." She turns and faces me. "If John was here, I wouldn't have done it."

"I ain't afraid," I say. "And honey, that fella wasn't no Gypsy Man. I told you."

She looks like she might want to believe me. Then she says, "I can't take the chance. You can't hardly get up off the couch. If the Gypsy Man is running around this mountain he's got a key to this cabin." She stops, seems to taste something in her mouth. Then she stares out the window again. I swear I think she might cry, and I ain't seen her do that since she was eleven years old. "I trust Mr. Gault," she says. "He's tall and strong. He's been in the army. His house is big. Myra keeps it clean, and she loves to cook. Maybe she'll teach Tory some things . . ."

I try to sit up, but my back and shoulders feel like they are nailed together. "What can that Miss Priss teach Tory? Glory be, Penny."

She just stands there, her face lit by the gray sky and flashes of lightning.

"Don't send that child away on my account. You want to leave me here, leave me here. I can take care of myself."

"Where would I go?"

"Go down to Richard Bland Prison."

Penny bows her head, like she found something to stare at on the floor.

"Go on down there and see your husband," I say.

She don't move.

"You go see John," I say. "That's what you should do."

She comes back and stands over me. "You said you wouldn't bring that up again."

"I'm not bringing it up. I know what you and John agreed on, and I ain't said you should change any of it."

She starts to put her hands back in her pockets, but the tight jeans ain't too willing so she sets her hands on her hips.

That don't feel right, so she crosses her arms in front of her. She can't be still, and I know why.

"I'm sorry if it makes you nervous," I say.

"I ain't nervous."

"He's your husband," I say. "You don't have to change nothing just to make one visit."

Penny says, "He's got fourteen more years."

"You're young. You think that's a long time. I understand."

"No, you don't understand."

"I never seen two people more in love than you two," I say. "That's all. And you know it. Even your mommy and daddy didn't get on like you and John."

Her face don't show a thing. But the corners of her mouth move a little bit. I can't tell if she's about to smile or cry.

"It ain't a long time," I say. "Hell, twenty years is nothing. Nothing at all."

"You don't understand what it's like not to have him. To love a man so much and never to have him." Her voice starts to tremble.

"No. How could I understand?"

She looks at me. "I'm sorry. I don't mean..."

"You don't mean what?"

"Nothing."

"Well, it's crazy," I say.

"We done what we had to, Clare. Don't you see?" She's looking at me as if she caught me at something shameful. "Don't let's talk about this no more," she says.

"It ain't what love is supposed to be."

"It's what John wanted."

"Why? Did he tell you that?"

"Yes, and you know what he told me."

"It don't make sense."

"He didn't want me to be alone. He wanted me to be—he wanted me to have a life."

"So. Is that what you been doing?"

She has no answer for that.

"For the past six years, you been having a life?"

She still don't answer.

"Looks like grieving and waiting if you ask me," I say.

"Don't," she says.

"You go down to that tire store on Saturdays. You running with anybody down there?"

"I ain't going to talk about this no more."

She starts toward the kitchen, but I say, "You ain't going with nobody up this way," and she stops. I say, "You been just like you'd be if you promised John you'd wait. Ain't that the truth?"

She don't say nothing. She just stands there, thinking, not really looking at me no more.

"Ain't it?"

"I got nobody," she says, and I see tears in her eyes. "You know it."

"And it's sure John's got nobody where he is."

"Oh, hell," she says. She sets down on the green chair, leans back, and drapes her arms over the side of it. She looks sick, but she fights back the tears.

"So," I say. "Looks like you and John didn't decide nothing but that you'd never visit him while he's in jail. That don't make sense."

She gets up and goes into the kitchen. I hear her in there for a spell, making coffee or something. I force myself to sit up, even though it feels like I have to break bones to do it. I take another sip of the medicine and put the bottle back just as she comes back in, carrying a cup of coffee on a saucer. She's combed her hair and she looks calmer.

"Seems like you're waiting for him anyways," I say. "Don't it?"

She sets down again on the chair. Thunder rolls over the top of the house, and the rain gets worse.

"One visit wouldn't hurt nothing," I say. "Maybe he'd be glad to see you."

"We done what we said we was going to do," she says. "It's been six years. I ain't written him a word. I ain't talked to him."

"But you don't got no life, neither. Ain't that just the opposite of what he wanted?"

"Maybe I don't. But I can't expect to just go on like this. For fourteen years."

"You been doing it for more than half a decade," I say.

She is quiet for a while. I'm feeling good to be upright finally. I'm a bit light-headed and groggy, but I've been sleeping off and on for a long time, so it don't worry me none.

Finally I say, "Suit yourself."

"I got the Gypsy Man to worry about."

"He ain't no Gypsy Man," I say. "He was flesh and blood. A man. Strong and strange, but still a man."

"You don't know. You said yourself he wasn't human."

I look away from her dark, accusing eyes. "Well, I was upset."

"And whoever he is, he's got a key."

"Who told you he's got a key?"

"He put you here, didn't he?"

"I don't know how I got here. It's where I woke up."

"You didn't lock the door, did you?"

"No."

"I didn't neither. But the door was locked when we found you. I had to use the key in the flowerpot to get in. And he wrote that note. He *said* he was coming back."

I think about everything for a minute. I want some more medicine, but I don't want her worrying about it. She balances her coffee on the arm of the chair, gets up, and comes over next to me. She sets herself down on the coffee table. "Do we have a gun?" she says.

"No."

She don't look away. Her face is only inches from mine, and she studies me, like she can see through me if she gets close enough.

"I don't know. Seems like your father had one," I say. "I don't know where he kept it."

"Think," she says.

"I'm trying. I don't know. I seem to remember a pistol."

"Did he keep it somewhere in the attic?"

"No."

"In his closet? The pantry?"

"No."

"The cellar?"

I close my eyes, try to picture the gun and my brother. He 'most never took it out, but he showed it to me one time. In case I ever needed it. Then I watched him put it away. "Where were we? Was it in this house or some other place? The store, maybe? I think I need another sip of medicine, that'll help me remember."

She don't say nothing. I take out the Old Granddad and treat myself to just a few sips. When I put the cap back on, she reaches over and takes the bottle out of my hands.

"You might as well leave it out here on the table," she says.

I look at her.

She sets it down next to her. "I'll leave it here, where you can reach it. Now think."

I say, "There was a time, a long time ago, when your daddy said he was going to shoot Jack Crowly in the ass."

She almost laughs. The smile on her face makes her eyes shine again. "When?"

"It was back before you was running around with John, when you was just a little thing."

She don't say nothing, but her eyes seem to narrow and soften.

"Your daddy never got along with Jack and a few of that—

that trash down that way." I reach for the bottle, but she moves it back away from me.

"Daddy was really going to shoot him?"

"No. He was just showing off, you know, giving me to think of him as a kind of hero because Jack had said some things about me."

"I never knew that."

"Well, it's true."

"And he had a gun?"

"In my recollection, your daddy had a pistol. And I think he went down to the store to get it. So he must have kept it somewhere in the back. Maybe the storage cabinet or the toolbox."

I can't believe the look on Penny's face. You would think I just told her that her daddy was alive. She reaches out and moves the bottle back to where I can get a hold of it.

"I'm going outside to get the shovel," she says, getting up.

"Don't go out there, now. You'll get soaking wet."

She's already at the door, holding it wide open. "I'm going to take the shovel with me down to the store and find that pistol."

"You ought to wait for the rain to let up."

"I'll be back in a minute."

"It ain't going nowhere."

"I want it now."

"Wait until the rain stops."

"I don't care about the rain." She goes out and leaves the door open. The screen door slams, and bounces open again. "Shut the damn door," I holler. She's running so fast, I don't think she hears me.

I take a big sip of my medicine. It feels so smooth going down. It makes me warm as a cat in a wood box. The rain is loud, now, spattering against the windows and roaring on the roof. I try to think about some good day in my life—some time when I felt good and young and permanent and beautiful. The sound of the rain reminds me of death. I know in my heart I will die, and no matter how far away in time it might be, I know it will be soon. I wonder what the weather will be like when it happens, what kind of day I will die on. You start getting old and it does something to the person inside of you. Like your soul gains weight and weakens. Gets sharp, too, like it might slip out of your body altogether, cut its way to the surface just from its own weight. You don't care about things like you used to. You look at the world all the time as if it was a book you might just put down, might just give up on. It ain't worth fighting with nobody, even people you love. And why not throw caution to the wind when you have a chance? Why not go off and see what you can see, if a gentleman expresses an interest in you, makes you feel like a woman, like you ain't used up. With the wind in your hair, a cigarette in your hand, and a few sips of whiskey, you can get to feeling young and sassy again. The winding road can feel wonderful.

I'll be fifty this November. And I ain't had a easy life.

MORGAN

I think it was the first rain cloud blocking the sun and the lost light that woke me. I was dreaming, and knew I was. A bear had a hold of my bow tie. Ain't worn one of those things since before the war. He swung me around like I was only made of straw, but I couldn't feel nothing. I knew when the pain started, I'd wake up. You ever notice that? You never feel no real pain in a dream—fear maybe, *real* fear, or grief. But as soon as the pain should begin, you wake up.

I was afraid I might die in the dream. They say if you die in your dreams, you never wake up, you really do die. Nobody ever remembers dying in a dream, so maybe it's true.

Sometimes I dream that I'm beginning to die. It ain't one of those pleasant dreams where you go to this pillow-filled room and get into a white gown and take a comfortable seat next to a harp or nothing. Most of the time I end up in a bare room with cold, white tile and mirrors on the wall and silver sinks. I have to stand up until my feet turn blue, and everything's cold. I can actually see my breath, and I hear this woman saying, "Pass this way; you must pass this way," but I can't find her nowhere and I can't move. There ain't no clock I can see, and I don't know what time it is, or even if it's light or dark outside. That usually wakes me up.

I don't have that exact dream all the time, but like that. And in this last dream the bear had me—so I was afraid I'd end up in the cold room, listening to that woman. I actually had that fear in the dream. You know what I mean? So when I roll over and look at the clock, I can't believe the time. It ain't even six in the morning yet. I planned on sleeping until noon. "Well, there's another sign of your age," I tell myself. You know you can't hold onto nothing—hell, you got to let go of some things just to grab on to others. (Of course, some folks hold on to one thing all their lives—until it rots.) I figure if this is going to be a new way of life, I'll just have to go to bed earlier. I roll back over and sit up on the edge of the bed. I have to admit, I'm tired. Since that useless trek up to the old Crawford place I've been running up and down the mountain every day for a week. I drive the old Chevy pickup everywhere, but you got to walk back in the woods to see signs of the Gypsy Man. You can't see it from the road. So between Quincy and Lebanon Church, I done a lot of walking. I mean a lot of walking. Plus, with the bear throwing me around in my dream, I didn't sleep all that good neither. So I am bone tired.

I'm just sitting down to a cup of coffee and a piece of toast when it starts to rain again. Second Sunday in a row, the clouds empty out. I watch the ground turn yellow, puddles forming in all the ruts and gullies. Every time it rains like that I tell myself I got to plant grass out by the fence in front of the house. The posts are starting to lean. The water carries away so much dirt. But hell, I know I'll never get to it. I just wish sometimes it was done. I think I'm afraid that fence will outlast me. Maybe it pleases me to see it starting to lose its footing.

I figure I'll have to go on up to Penny's place, see what's going on there. I thought she might call me last night, and the fact that she didn't sort of bothers me. Not that I am worried or nothing. I just thought she might call me and was disappointed she didn't.

After I spent a long week of looking for signs, the new rain makes me feel like I haven't had those days at all; like the week never happened. I am watching the fence, in front of the house, thinking about everything when a blue pickup truck comes down the road and slows to a stop in front. It's a big Ford, with a wood cab on the back. It stops just beyond the front gate, then seems to shiver there in the rain.

I wait to see who my visitor is, but nobody moves. Sheets of rain swirl around the truck like smoke in the wind. Water moves like a dance—a fine white, sheer curtain. "It ain't gonna let up for quite a spell," I say out loud. "Whoever you are, you got a long wait."

I finish my coffee, eat the last scrap of bread, then sit back in my chair. The window is right in front of me, but I'm far enough back away from it I'm sure my visitor can't see me. But that makes us even, because the rain is so dense I can't see into the cab of the truck neither. I can't tell if it's one or two people in it. I might go for more coffee, but I don't want to leave the window.

The rain seems to increase—like it has something heavy in

it. The wheels of the truck start to turn, slowly, and it inches forward a little bit, then goes on up the road. I don't know what he thought he wanted, stopping right there in front of the house.

Gault don't have no pickup. Paxton's is a big red Dodge. The Crowlys have an old Ford stake bed. I can't remember nobody who owns a truck like that.

It takes me awhile before I realize I seen that same pickup on the old road in front of the Crawford place just the week before. It had scared the bear away. Of course I can't tell for sure if it's the same truck or not—it moved too fast on that road, and I was still pretty shaky from my run-in with the bear. But here I am watching one in front of my house in the middle of a rainstorm. I lean a little closer to the window, trying to see if it stopped again up the road. As the wind-swept rain keeps throwing curtains in front of me, I can't see very much but the brown water running in the ditches by the road.

Then I hear it coming down the road, and it goes by in the other direction, moving slow.

"Well, I'll be goddamned," I say out loud. "The Gypsy Man's gone and gotten his self a truck."

I stand up and creep over to the window. I have to laugh at myself, trying not to make noise in my own house while that truck rolls by, its occupant a mere shadow in the white mist, sixty-five feet away in the center of a storm that sounds like a damn battle both of us might run from.

Next to the window I peak around the curtain. Now, the road is empty. I shake my head and go back to my chair. I'm getting nervous in my old age. It was just a pickup truck that drove by—probably headed for Clare's store. It come back down the hill when the driver seen the store was closed. Still, I watch out the window and listen for noises. You ever tried to do that? In the racket of a thunderstorm, while rain rattles every board and tin roof and windowpane in the world, you listen for some noise that's different; some sound that's foreign and not supposed to be there.

I got doors everywhere in this old house. A back door, a cellar door, a side door, and the front door next to the window I am keeping lookout from. And that's what I feel like I'm doing. I can't remember if I've locked any of the doors. I go to the back door just to be sure it's locked. Then I lock the side door. I don't have any doubt about the cellar. Anybody coming in that way, I'd hear him. When I come back to the window and look out, the road is still empty. But the windows are all fogged up and it's even harder to see. And now my mind is playing tricks on me. I'm wondering if I seen a driver in that truck.

Then I hear the front screen door squeal open and shut. It might be the wind. There's a stepladder on the porch—the paint buckets. Two of the wooden lawn chairs I'd just painted. I wait for some other sound.

I hear the door again.

Is somebody standing there banging on it? I try to see out the window, but it's just the door, blowing open in the wind. Nothing else. It ain't moving much, just enough to make the noise. The wind is loud and picking up pace. It sounds like a train.

I fetch a good long butcher knife and go on over to the door. This time it slams like somebody threw it hard against the jam. I'm going to open it. If it is the Gypsy Man, I'll meet him face-to-face and we can just have at it. But I wait a minute, listening. He might be going around back. I'm here in front of the door, watching the windows, but it's just too gray and foggy and the glass, with water running down, only makes me feel trapped and blind.

I lean against the wall and wait. Whoever it is, if he comes in the back way he'll have to open the outer door and then work his way down the hallway to the front of the house and across this room to get to me. I'll be ready for him. I wish I hadn't sold my shotgun, but I hold pretty tightly to the knife. I step back a bit to move the curtain aside and look out on the front porch again. The screen door sits open a bit, but nobody's there. When I turn back around, I think I see a shadow on the wall across from me. Then a clap of thunder shakes the whole house and me with it, too. It's like an explosion. The whole room lights up with it, and I feel the vibration and shock in my chest. I crouch down, waiting for whatever might happen. Then it seems to get quiet, except the storm still howls outside. I wait and listen a long time. Then I see the hallway is lit up in a strange yellow light.

I look out the window again and see the door slam against the jamb. Ain't nothing on the road.

Something behind me makes a crackling sound, and I turn to see the yellow light is much brighter now, and it gives off heat. The back porch is on fire. Flames lick along the door frame and the heat is starting to curl the wallpaper in the hallway.

The odor of gasoline comes to me long before I smell the smoke.

It don't matter that rain is pouring down like water over a dam, or that I'm here and know exactly what to do.

The Gypsy Man done set his first fire.

BRADWELL

It's been raining all day, second weekend in a row. One of the old houses near the center of town catches fire. It might be Morgan Tiller's place. Maybe it got hit by lightning. The fire can't be too bad because it's raining to beat all. Like somebody pouring piss out of a boot onto a flat rock. It ain't long before a small detachment of volunteer firemen comes roaring up

Route 13 and right into the white clouds of steam and smoke from the fire and rain. I been down to Quincy to get coffee, and when I drive up the road to the house, I stop the car and watch the excitement for a spell.

We was about the first to live on this here mountain. My daddy's the grandson of the first owner of the mill—back when it was a planing mill—and he probably knows as much about the town and its history as any man alive. Also, I went to Gault's school and was there when that nigger boy disappeared.

Our house is about a quarter mile beyond Gault's place, and sits back a long way from the road. We got both a front and back porch, and both of them screened in as tightly as you please. We keep the place clean, but the yard does have its fair supply of old car parts—wheels and transmission housing and such. But the house itself seems to rise above it all. When I pull up in the car and see it standing high in the rain, white and spotless, it makes me think of a gentleman in a white suit, standing in a shorn field looking at the wreckage of a battle.

I run from my car to the front porch. The screen door ain't locked, but when I open it to approach the front door, it makes a loud squeak. The front door opens and my old man steps into the frame. His hair is white, piled high on his forehead. He has white brows and a thin, white beard. His light blue eyes are stained yellow around the edges from years of smoking tobacco, and when he opens his mouth to speak, his teeth are the same shade of yellow. "Where you been?" he says. The old coot knows he sent me out to find fresh coffee, and here he is acting like I'm a cherry pie he found on the porch.

"I got your coffee," I say, rainwater dripping from my hair. I brush it off my shoulders and arms. "Don't you remember? You said you wanted fresh coffee."

"Where is it?" He waits, looking hard at me.

"Right here." I hold up the small white bag.

"You get coffee up at Clare's place?"

"She wasn't open. I drove on out to Quincy."

"No wonder it took you so damn long."

"I got you coffee, didn't I?"

His face changes. It is almost a smile, but not quite.

"It'll only take a little time to percolate it," I say.

"Well," he says, moving over to a white wooden chair on the porch. He struggles to sit down. I wait for some signal of what he expects, but he sits back and places his thin, knotted arms on the armrests and stares out at the rain. "I ain't got nothing but time."

The door is still open. I smell the strong scent of cooking bacon and fresh baked bread. "Mom's already started breakfast," I say.

"Hell, we ate already," he says. "Go ahead and get yourself some."

"You want coffee?"

"Sure," he waves his hand, like he's telling me to go away.

"I'm sorry," I say. "I don't know what else you think I could of done."

He says nothing.

I go in the house and put the coffee on the counter. "Fresh coffee," I say to my mama. She looks up, smiling. Her hair is white, too, now, but she still keeps it curled and pretty.

"Thank you kindly," she says. "Now sit down and I'll fix you some eggs."

"No, I'll just have the coffee," I say. "Whenever it's ready."

She nods, takes the coffee, and moves over to the stove. "I'll get it going," she says.

I go back out on the porch to watch the rain.

"What's all the excitement down there?" the old man says.

"Pardon?"

He points towards the town, the white smoke and steam rising over the far-off rooftops.

"Oh," I say. "It's a fire."

"I'll be damned."

We sit there for a spell, then I say, "You know people are talking about the Gypsy Man again."

"You don't say."

"And that nigger that disappeared, too."

The old man turns and faces me. "Sit down."

It is definitely a command, so I take the chair right next to him.

"You got yourself a bit wet. Want a towel or something?" he says.

"I'm all right. Just a little damp." In front of us is a great trunk, also painted white, that serves as a kind of table. The porch's got a waist-high wall, and then only screen attached tightly to the support beams that hold up the roof. I helped my daddy put that screen on only a few years ago, and we done it right. It's still tight and it ain't got no holes in it.

"You know, son," the old man says. "All around here, it was a forest. When the planing mill switched to paper and pulp, it wasn't a tree left standing more than ten years old. Those trees up yonder by the lookout are the oldest trees we got, and they ain't but more than twenty years old or so."

The wind shifts and sends a volley of raindrops against the screen, spraying us with cold water. I push my chair back a bit, but Daddy seems to enjoy it. He rubs his leathery arms and pushes his short sleeves all the way to the shoulder. There's a tattoo of a Confederate flag just above the biceps on his left arm.

"We still make paper," I say. "But it ain't the same, is it?"

"Go see if she's got that coffee ready," he says. It's definitely an order. He looks at me, "You had your coffee?"

"I'll go see if it's ready," I say.

I get up to go inside, and as I do a sudden loud clap of thunder seems to heat up the air. Trees shed bits of leaf and lean over in the wind like they might just rattle themselves empty.

"I believe it's worse this week than it was last," the old man says.

"The wind is definitely worse," I say.

There's a long silence, then he says, "You want to know about the Gypsy Man?"

"Yes, sir." He's told me things before, but each time there's something else. Something I ain't heard. He was alive back then. He knew Wilbur Crawford.

"My family come up to this here place long before there was a Gypsy Man."

"And that was..."

"The Civil War—my granddaddy fought with John Singleton Mosby. You ever hear of him?"

"The Gray Ghost. Yes."

"Well, he wasn't no ghost. A Crowly was with him at Fairfax Station. Up and down the valley. And when the war was over, they come up here to get away from all the free nigras."

"Wait a minute," I say. "Let me get the coffee."

I go get two cups. I kiss my mother on the cheek and take it back outside. I set the coffee on the trunk, then sit down next to him, leaning forward a bit so I can see his face.

"You ain't a sissy about your coffee, are you?" the old man says.

"Pardon?"

"You take cream and sugar?"

"This is fine," I say. It sometimes scares me what he forgets.

The old man makes this growling noise when he sips his coffee, then he says, "Goddamned nigras and Yankees. They ruined this country."

I say nothing.

It's quiet for a spell, then he looks at me. "Did I tell you this before?"

"No, sir," I lie. I take a long sip of my coffee, which is strong and bitter.

"It ain't nothing but perdition, plain and simple," he says.

"What's perdition again, daddy?"

"Damnation, boy. Ain't you learned nothing I taught you?"

"About the Gypsy Man," I say, trying to change the subject.

"You think I don't know what's going on in this country? Nigras in baseball, basketball. The White Sox might win the pennant this year, and they got a nigra outfield."

"Well," I say. "I don't follow baseball."

He looks at me real hard. "What kind of man don't follow baseball?"

"It's just the way things turned out for me," I say. "It ain't no disrespect."

"Yeah, well."

"It ain't. If'n I liked it, I'd follow it."

He's quiet again, sipping his coffee. Then he says, "I don't have nothing against nigras because of the color of their skin, you know. That's where the integrationists got it all wrong. They think I don't like nigras because of blackness—but color ain't got nothing to do with it. Hell, in the summertime, you get as black as a two-year-old banana. I was the same way. No, it ain't blackness nor color neither. It's behavior. It ain't nothing but rudeness and sloth and single-minded stupidity, or at its worst, downright barbarian behavior in all the nigras I've ever known. Honest to God. I've never known a single nigra you could trust or that had an ounce of manners. I've never known one who couldn't fly into a rage and kill another nigra just for the hell of it, neither. I'm telling you."

I take another sip of my coffee. I can't interrupt him when he gets going on the nigras, and I can't get him off it neither. I just have to wait. But he settles a little and it gets quiet. He watches the rain, the patterns of it in the air and how it seems to just dance around the trees.

"And that Landon boy's father ain't no good neither," he says.

"Not since his boy disappeared."

Daddy looks at me.

"I keep him on down there just because I feel sorry for him."

He laughs, briefly. "What the fuck we got here?" His smile is ruined by missing teeth on the left side. He looks at me again. I feel suddenly very embarrassed for noticing his teeth, and for being afraid of him. He's my father, and he ain't never done me no harm at all. He was always like a friend of mine in the house.

"I agree with you," I say.

"We still got him over at the mill?" he says. "I thought I told you to fire him."

"You did, sir."

"So what's he doing there?"

I look away. I wish the rain would shift and scatter against the screen, drive us inside.

"Well?" he says.

"I been meaning to tell you," I say. "I didn't fire him yet."

He shakes his head.

"I been meaning to. I just feel sorry for him."

He leans toward me, pointing his finger at me as he speaks. "And he never done nothing but think about that little boy every goddamned day of his life. He don't do a full day's work no more, and that's the truth."

"But he did once," I say, unable to resist pushing it a bit.

"We ought to fire him," the old man says. "He don't show up for work half the time. Sometimes he disappears for days and even weeks at a time. Says he's looking for that boy of his. Josh ain't worth a penny of the money we pay him. You can't keep a man on just because you feel sorry for him."

I reach down and brush the top of my shoes. "I run the mill, now," I say. "I'll keep him on a while longer."

He looks out through the screen at the smoke in the distance. It's quiet for a while, except for the clatter of the rain. I have the feeling that he is considering what he should say to me and the silence gets longer, kind of big, while the rain washes against the screen.

"I understand how you feel about nigras," I say, finally. "It's just that I thought you was going to tell me about the Gypsy Man." My voice sounds loud even in the racket of the rain and wind, and I realize I am ashamed of it; of the way I know it will sound in my memory when I recollect that I didn't just tell him that I ain't going to fire Josh Landon. I can't fire him. He's the only one down there that knows what he's doing, and when he *does* work, it's worth every penny we pay him.

The old man stares at me, thinking. Then he says, "Might of been the Gypsy Man that run off with that little Landon nigra."

I put my coffee cup down on the white trunk. "You know what I think?" I say.

He don't say nothing.

"I think it was John Bone that killed the Landon boy. Hell, he killed that little girl on the highway."

"Yes, he did."

"And he was always hanging around the nigger in school."

"Well, if'n he *did* do it, then he's where he belongs, ain't he?"

"I think he did. He never fooled me. Acting like he taken the nigra's side and all."

He nods, looking out at the rain, the smoke, and steam across the way.

"You remember much about the Landon boy, Bradwell?" the old man says.

"No. Not much."

"Wasn't he close to your age?"

"He was a lot younger, Daddy. You know that."

"But ya'll went to the same school, though."

"For a while," I say. "He wasn't there long."

"I thought you was in the same class."

"He was four years behind me, Daddy. You know all this."

He sips his coffee, slurping it over his lips from the edge of the cup. The rain is steady, now, but the wind has calmed a bit, and all we can hear is the splashing water running down the hillside and dripping out of gutters and spouts all around the house. The air smells like smoke, iron, and green pine. Finally, I say, "I was down at the Goodyear store and the folks there said Penny's aunt Clare got beaten up by the Gypsy Man."

"You looking for the Gypsy Man?" the old man asks.

"No, not exactly. But I'm interested."

"Why?"

I shrug. I point to the rain. "There ain't nothing else to do."

He hands me a odd-looking smile.

"And you known him. Most folks can't say that."

He shakes his head. Then he seems to remember something. He takes hold of the arms of the chair and scoots it around a bit, so that it faces me, but he doesn't say nothing right away. He drinks from the coffee cup, eyeing me over the brim. When he's done, he sets the cup on the trunk and says, "Did I ever tell you about Wilbur's father?"

"What about him?" I say.

"You know, the story about Wilbur and his father and the whipping."

"No," I say.

"Are you sure?"

"Oh," I say. "Yeah, the whipping. Wilbur told you that story himself."

"That's right." He seems disappointed.

"I'd be interested to hear it again," I say.

CROWLY

Josiah Crawford, Wilbur's father, was a hard sort of man. Like he was made of ice and had a contraption in his head that allowed him to move from place to place. He kept accounts of everything. I mean everything. If you got something over on him, he'd remember it and write it down in a ledger. Then he'd find a way to get himself even. He really did have a ledger, a book he wrote things down in to be sure he was even with folks.

Once I sold him a load of firewood. This was back in 1912. I was not even twenty yet, but I was already in business for myself. He come down here complaining that it was too fresh.

"You sold me a cord of unseasoned, green wood," he says.

I told him I didn't claim it was seasoned. I say, "Why don't you let it set a spell. I reckon it'll get seasoned soon enough."

He takes out this little book and writes it down. He's scowling at me the whole time he's writing.

"I wonder what you think you owe me now," I say. But he had nothing to say, spoke no more. He walked back up the hill to his big house and I forgot about it.

About a year or so later—had to be at least a year, because it was getting to be winter again, and I remember thinking he'd had his satisfaction not buying no wood from me that year—anyway, a year later our generator broke. Back then, we was one of the few families that had electricity, but it weren't no electric company that provided it. We used generators, and the power come from a gas motor. My daddy had a Chrysler six-cylinder engine running ours.

Anyway, the Chrysler quit running. Come to find out, it wasn't nothing wrong with the generator. Somebody'd put sugar in the gas tank on the engine. I reckon I know who it was.

For a year he don't talk to me. Pass me by even in church. Then after the engine gone bad, he is all civil again, nodding his head when he seen me in church, or tipping his hat whenever he happened to pass me on the street. I mean he didn't seek me out nor nothing, but there it was. He was friendly again. He got his account even, you see.

But that's not my story. This is something I heard from Wilbur himself.

Oh, sure, I've talked to Wilbur many times. Before he took off and become the Gypsy Man. He wasn't no crazier than nobody else in that family. Except for the birthmark on his face, I'd say he was less than peculiar. I reckon some folks would even call him ordinary. Like most young mountain men, he got into his share of trouble. More than most and most the time, and not just with his old man. People talked about him a lot and didn't like him much. But he wasn't no ghost back then, nor nothing like it. He was spooky to look at, and some folks thought he was mean. But I didn't think so. I believe he was used to being an outcast, and that made him behave like one. Besides, he had his old man for a role model, and the old man was a damn sight peculiar himself. Wilbur was different in one way though. He didn't mind talking to folks. It didn't matter if he knew you or not, he'd just start a conversation about the weather or dogs or horses or electricity. He'd look right in your eyes and try to catch you staring at the birthmark on his face, like he was challenging you to look at it. This was a long time ago. Before the war. The first one, what we used to call the Great War, before we come to see there'd be another one much worse.

No. Wilbur wasn't crazy. Wasn't nothing wrong with him at all. His old man, though. Goddamn.

This is what Wilbur told me.

The old man took him out to the shed to punish him one time—I don't know what Wilbur done wrong. Seems to me he sold something belonged to his daddy or some fool thing like that. Or maybe he'd set one of them fires he was always settin'. Wilbur liked to burn things. Anyway, the old man took him into the shed, made him take off his shirt, and then bent him over a sawhorse and whipped him with a belt. The buckle end of it, mind you. His bare back, just like a slave or something.

And then, you know what? Old man Crawford commenced to weeping. He dropped the belt and fell down at his son's feet. Wilbur don't know what to do. After a while, he just put his shirt back on and walked back up to the house so his mama could dress the wounds on his back. He said he didn't hate his father no more. He just felt pity for him.

But that ain't the story neither. You know what happened then? About a month or so later the old man called to Wilbur as he was coming in from the field, and Wilbur went over to the barn again—to the place where he'd suffered at his father's hands, and the wounds still ain't completely healed—and he stepped inside, not knowing what to expect. He said he wasn't afraid, exactly—but he was ready; the way a cat is ready, all his senses astir—and the old man was standing there by the sawhorse, the belt in his hands again. But this time, Wilbur ain't going to stand for it; this time he won't let his father come near him. He started to back out, but his father spoke. "Wait, son."

"What?" Wilbur said, almost whispering. He said he felt as though the barn, with all of its tools and hay and even dumb animals, listened to him, waited for him to move, and if he spoke too loudly, it would swallow him.

"Come here," old man Crawford said.

Wilbur said, "I ain't."

And the old man held out the belt, reached it out to his son, from a distance. The old man had to lean toward him, stretch to make him take it. Wilbur held his ground, but then finally, rather than run out of there, he carefully touched the belt, felt the cool leather on his fingers, and the old man dropped it, so Wilbur had to grab on, so it wouldn't hit the hay-covered floor.

Old man Crawford took off his own shirt, draped himself over the same sawhorse, and give his son leave to have at him. Said it pained him so much to whip his only son, he wanted to be purged of it by the same pain.

"You owe this to me," he said. "And I owe whatever pain I suffer to you. Hit me."

Wilbur said he didn't know what he should do. He didn't have no idea how he felt. He was not angry or sad. He said it was possible he felt nothing at all. He stood there, holding the belt, and his father said again, "Hit me. Hit me." So he stepped up to him, raised the belt, and brought it down. It slapped against his father's upper back.

"Harder," the old man said.

Wilbur had to keep whipping him until the skin begun to bleed. When he saw the blood starting to come, he dropped the belt in the hay and walked out of the barn.

He said his father come up to the house, set himself down at the kitchen table, and wrote it all down in his little book. That's right. He took the book down off the shelf and wrote in the ledger. He was even.

Wilbur himself told me that story. I don't know as I believe it, but that's what he told me.

Sometimes I think it's probably true—knowing what I know about old man Crawford. And then again, sometimes I think it ain't true, knowing what I know about Wilbur.

Except for maybe John Bone, there ain't never been nobody on this mountain that seemed more determined to get in trouble than Wilbur Crawford. When he took off it wasn't a soul that mourned him. He wasn't crazy, nor a ghost yet, nor anything like that. He was just a big, strong, lonely son of a bitch. But he wasn't all quiet and inside himself like John Bone was. If he had something to say, he said it. Like I said, he'd corner complete strangers and talk to them, the whole time acting like it didn't matter to no one what his face looked like with that mark all down the side of it. He was the same color as a football on one side. And if'n he had nothing to say to nobody, he'd whistle. If he was quiet more than two or three minutes in a day, it was a miracle. And he told me that story one afternoon right after I'd got a haircut. I come out of the barbershop in Lebanon Church, brushing the hair back under my hat, and there he was setting there on the steps, staring out at the road, whistling a tune. He looked up at me, and I said, "Hey," and he said, "I beat my daddy with a belt," like that. And I said, "You did?" and he said, "He made me do it."

I just stood there looking at him. Then he told me the story. When he finished, he shut up a minute, like he was waiting for me to say something. When I didn't, he looked out at the high clouds over the top of the mountain and started whistling again. Then he says, "You think my daddy's crazy?"

"Well, he ain't ordinary," I said. "That's all."

It wasn't long after that, only a few years, if that, his daddy and momma passed, and he disappeared and become the Gypsy Man.

And he *is* the Gypsy Man. You better believe it. Wilbur Crawford.

Some folks say, "Maybe he ain't come back and maybe he has." But if he has or not, he's older than I am. He'd be close to ninety, in fact. He was near fifty when he took off—and that was back in 1917. I was twenty-three. I'm sixty-five now. So, you tell me. Do you think he's anything but what folks say he is? It ain't natural for a man to live that long and still he can scramble around the hills and gullies of this mountain. If he ain't a ghost, he's something ungodly, something evil. Plain and simple. I reckon it don't take much sense to put two and two together about it and get four.

I know some folks say he don't exist, but I seen him. Back when John Bone went to jail for killing that colored girl, I seen him. Remember I knew Gypsy Crawford. And the Monday when they took John Bone off for good, I was crossing the street in town, down near the lookout, and a white Pontiac pulled up to the intersection there, stopped to wait for me. I started to cross in front of it, and then I seen the multicolored face through the windshield, the one side as red as a football, and the other pale and ghostly white. He was just looking at me with dark, lifeless eyes, his hands on the wheel in front of him, one knuckle curling up and then down again with a slow rhythm, like he was writing a song in his head. I stopped. The sun disappeared behind a dark blue cloud, and then I heard the engine start to increase and I thought he might run me over. I moved as fast as I could to the other side of the street, and when the car pulled away, I seen the Gypsy Man had transformed himself into just an elderly gentleman with gray hair and a slight beard. But he didn't fool me none. He was whistling when he drove by. I heard it. He knew. He knew I seen him, so he made himself into some other shape and thought to fool me, but he had the window open and I heard him whistling. I seen his eyes as he passed, too—the same dull, colorless eyes, like a scarecrow's black buttons, and I know who it was. So he's came back here before. Maybe he's back again.

I wouldn't be surprised none.

BOOK III

JOHN BONE

I never went to Korea. I was drafted, but while I was at basic training at Ft. Gordon, North Carolina, my mother's death and the loneliness finally started to get to my old man. He'd call me—emergency calls through the dayroom, involving priests and chaplains and the first sergeant—and then when I came to the phone he'd just be breathing heavy, as though he fell asleep, or he'd be crying so hard his breathing sounded like a dog's panting. Then I'd call Penny and ask her to go up there and look out for him, check to see how he was doing.

He was always passed out when she got there. Bottles all around him, and him laying on the floor, either in the kitchen or the dining room, or next to the bed against the wall in his room. Penny'd get him up and into bed, then she'd clean the place and go home. I know she must have hated having to do that. I was afraid of what it would do to her—to us—having to take care of him like that.

He always drank a lot before my mother died, but never like that.

The first time I came home on leave, I found him again, in the dining room, laying under the table, passed out. An empty bottle of Old Crow on the floor and another empty bottle laying sideways on the table.

I picked him up and carried him to the bedroom. My mother's picture, her smiling face with the aqua blue eyes, witnessed the little scene of me lying him on the bed, cleaning him up, putting the covers on him. "My boy," he whispered. "I'm sorry."

He was never a mean drunk.

The next day he got out of bed, threw the bottles away, and cleaned up the whole house. I waked to the smell of fresh coffee. When I came downstairs, he said, "I'm so glad you're home." He put his arms around me, and I stood there not knowing really what to do with my hands. Then he slapped me on the shoulder, a little too hard, stood back, and looked at me. I could see it hurt him that I did not hug him back, that I was prepared not to believe him. "Well, young man. We've got some work to do today."

"We do?"

"First, we're throwing out all the bottles, all the whiskey in this house."

"Good."

"I'm done with that, now. For good, son."

I didn't know what to say. He'd made this promise before.

"I really mean it," he said.

"I know you do."

"And I'll prove it." He smiled. Still looking at me, he backed away—moved to the corner cupboard he'd built for my mother with his own hands, opened it, and retrieved a full bottle of Old Crow. "See this?" He was still smiling, but he looked at the bottle now. His face was almost entranced by the label, by the smiling glint of the copper liquid so full to the brim in the bottle. His eyes went up and down, as if he were scrutinizing a woman, and he paused a moment, contemplating it.

"Dad," I started to say something to him—something about all those times when I was little and fetched his whiskey for him, those times we were allies against my mother's wishes or knowledge. I remembered all those times he took a jug from me, smiling just as he was smiling now, and how he'd say, "Just our little secret, lad. Eh? Our little secret."

He held the bottle now in front of him, and his eyes met mine again. "Watch this." And he walked past me, into the kitchen. I heard him open it, and when I came in behind him, he was in front of the sink, looking at the bottle again. Only this time he held it the way a man does right before he takes a sip out of it. I know the odor of it must have seemed like a call from my mother, like her voice saying, "Come here, hon."

But he hesitated only a moment. Then he began pouring it out. He looked back at me, still pouring, that smile on his face. "See? I mean it. I'm through with it."

I wished I could just be a kid again for a while, so he could pick me up in his arms, let me ride on his shoulders like he used to. I wished we could have just one of those innocent, long, slow, and hot summer days sitting on the bank of the river, fishing. Just the smell of the mud banks of that river can bring it back to me—the sweet and tender alliance of father and son as I believed it must be for every boy, for every worthy child. I felt so powerful back then. So ready for the big world, because the entire small new world had my father in it, had my dad being with me. And my mother loving him. It was all too perfect, too good to last. It finally provided nothing but a kind of exquisite suffering, just remembering it. I wanted to talk to him just once more in that time before the whiskey swallowed him, before he went so far into grief that he no longer recognized loveliness. I didn't want to have this problem with him now. It didn't seem possible that I could help, that I could find a way to watch over him. There was still so much I needed and expected from him.

"I'll never take another drink," he said when he was done pouring it out.

"You don't have any other bottles hidden?"

He seemed disappointed.

"A jug somewhere you haven't told me about?"

He put the empty bottle down in the sink. "No, son. I really don't."

I didn't say anything. My throat ached a little, and I realized I was fighting back tears. Not just for him, and not for the situation we found ourselves in that weekend, but for my mother, and for our loss, and for all the numberless days ahead when I knew he would fail me again.

"I give you my word this day and this hour."

"I know it," I said.

"You have my word."

"Great."

He sat down at the kitchen table. "Come on, pour yourself some coffee. Let's talk."

"I want to go see Penny," I told him.

"She's—she's still in school, right?" he said. " 'Til three?"

"She knows I'm here. She'll want to see me."

He had his head down now, and I saw that he was avoiding my gaze. He didn't want me to know how it made him feel to leave him there by himself.

"Why don't you get dressed and come along?" I said. I hoped he couldn't see how certain I was that he wouldn't go with me.

He brightened a bit, looking up at me. "Really?"

"Sure."

"Ahh," he said, remembering himself. "You're courting, ain't you?"

"She's my friend," I said. "It ain't exactly a courtship."

"You don't want me to be hanging about."

"She won't mind."

He shook his head. "I wish she didn't have to remember coming over here to clean me up."

I said nothing.

"Last weekend, it was?"

"And the weekend before that," I said. "And the Wednesday before that. And remember the day I left for the army?"

He looked away. It was a cruel thing to say, but I couldn't help it. He'd promised me so many times, and each time he'd convince me. I'd believe him.

"Well," he said, after a while, his voice almost a whisper. "She'll never have to do it again."

I was quiet, watching him. I wished I could wave my hand and make him happy.

"And you won't neither."

I knelt down in front of him. "Dad," I said. "Why don't you come with me? So you're not here by yourself, thinking about things."

He put his hand up and lightly touched his forehead, like he was thinking, but then he said, "You go on." He was smiling. "Go see your girl. Hell, I remember when me and your mother..." He stopped, his eyes beginning to swim. He got control of himself. "It's a wonderful time. You don't need an old former drunk complicating things."

I rose and stood there for a moment. I put my hand on his shoulder. With a hand that trembled, he raised the coffee cup to his lips and took a sip. Then he set the cup down very carefully in front of him. I looked at the crown of his head, the puffed skin of the back of his neck, and felt desolate and sad.

Outside the sun made shadows on bright green pastures and tree-lined roads. Gentle but much warmer breezes seemed to hiss in the trees, and the last vestige of spring began to give way to summer. I would go back to Ft. Gordon in two days, and he would find his way back to the bottle before my train crossed over the state line into North Carolina. I knew this. And still I said, "I'm proud of you, Dad."

He smiled, put his hand on mine. "Do me a favor, son," he said. I saw tears in his eyes.

"Anything," I said.

"Don't ever let it get to this."

I didn't know what he meant.

"You hear?"

"Okay," I said. Then, "What do you mean?"

"Don't get like me," he whispered. "Don't let this happen to you."

"I won't."

"I mean it." He faced me, but he reached for the cup again. "Watch this," he said. "Look at my hand." He held the cup up and his hand was shaking so much, it began to spill. "See?"

"Don't," I said. I started to take the cup from him, but he put it down again. It had not spilled much, but I got him a dish towel and he wiped the coffee up very carefully, studying the surface of the table as if it was the most important thing to get all of it up. I knew he was avoiding looking at me. He had his head down, studying his hand, and I saw his lower teeth, his tongue lolling against them, as if he was out of breath from a long run, but he was breathing normally.

"Dad," I said.

He made a sound, a bare acknowledgment. He was lost in thought.

"Why don't we go fishing today?"

He looked at me, his eyes brighter, more awake. "Really?"

"We can go down to the bottom of the lookout and fish for trout."

"I don't even know if I can find my gear," he said.

"You can use mine."

It was quiet for a while. He sipped his coffee, and I stood there not knowing what to say. I was afraid he'd really want to go fishing, and I'd miss seeing Penny. I hated myself for not saying anything else. The last thing I said hung in the air like an echo between us.

When he was finished his coffee, I turned to leave and he said, "Promise me, son."

"What?"

"You won't ever drink."

He had fed me drinks since I was fifteen. He knew I'd had Old Crow with him, beer with friends. He knew I drank.

"I won't ever let myself get like y—" I stopped. This seemed a harsh judgment on him. "I'll stay away from the booze, Dad," I said. "Okay?"

"That's all I ask," he said.

"I won't get drunk," I said. This seemed a promise I could keep, since I hated being drunk, anyway.

"You have a good time," he said, smiling again. "And kiss Penny for me."

"If I ever kiss her, I'll give her one for you." I was saddened to realize that I was anxious to get out of there. I wanted to run from him, get him as far away from me as possible.

And I wanted to keep him safe forever.

TWO WEEKS after that visit, I was called home again. An emergency. He had passed out on the front porch of the house and the next day the postman found him. Penny had to go up there again to clean him up and put him in bed. She called me—again it was an emergency call—and asked if she should take him to a hospital or something.

"No," I said. "He'll never stand for that."

"He told me this morning he'd never let this happen to him again."

"I know," I said.

"I think he really means it this time."

209

"He *does* mean it."

She was silent. I heard her breathing. Then I said, "I miss you."

"Should I maybe call a doctor or something?"

"There ain't nothing can be done," I said. "Leave it."

"I just feel..."

"I know," I said.

Then she said, "I miss you, too."

A little while after that—after a few more emergency calls, and weekend passes—the army gave me a hardship discharge.

I was allowed to go home and take care of an "invalid father." That's what they told me, anyway. But the Korean War was almost over—the peace talks had already started—so maybe the army figured they really didn't have no use for me. I didn't care. I got to go home.

That's how Penny and I got together.

The drinking never did stop, but it seemed to level off after I came home. I'd return from visiting Penny in the evening, and he'd be sitting on the front porch, drinking from a jug. He'd be happy to see me, and we'd talk about going fishing again like we did so often when I was a boy. He'd talk about my mother. At night, he'd fall into bed with the light on and go to sleep. He never turned the light out, and he never let me turn it out. "Leave it on," he'd say.

"Why?"

"Just leave it on."

One night I said, "You afraid of the dark?"

He smiled. "No."

"Well what, then?"

He seemed sheepish, and he'd been drinking, so maybe it was the booze talking, but he smiled broadly—as if he was having a little joke on himself—and said, "I lay here at night, like I'm waiting for your mother to finish brushing her teeth, like she'll join me in a minute."

I said nothing.

"It helps me fall asleep," he said, wistfully.

Then one night late, I crept in there to turn off the light, and he moaned in his sleep, turned over, and whispered, "Honey, is that you?"

Very softly I said, "Go back to sleep, Dad."

"Helen?" he said.

I went out and left the light burning.

IT WASN'T long after that, and Penny and I were married. Dad was my best man, and Mr. Gault gave Penny away. He walked down the aisle with her, wearing a white tuxedo, smiling as if Penny was his own daughter. She looked like a spirit in her white gown—her dark hair glistening in the sun under the veil. Mrs. Gault had helped her pick out a dress, had bought and arranged all the wedding flowers, and she baked the cake.

It was the happiest day of my life.

MORGAN

"Might of been lightning, I don't know yet," the fireman says.

"Sure it was," I tell him. "You don't smell that gasoline?"

"Well, you had gasoline on the porch, right?"

"That's right. And it was somebody poured it all over and lit it, too."

"Maybe," he says. "But it really don't look like it. I think you got hit by lightning, and then the gas got to burning. But we'll take a close look at it."

"You do that."

The porch smells like somebody lit a flock of sheep with that gasoline. I can't stand to be near it. They got the fire under control before the porch roof fell in, but it don't look like it will stand too much longer. The firemen put yellow tape around the back of the house.

"You got anyplace you can stay for a while?" one of the firemen asks me.

"No, I don't."

"Well, the house is probably safe, but I don't think you'll be able to lock that back door anytime soon, much less close the damn thing."

It is pretty bad. Black scarred wood all the way to the shingles. One post burned almost all the way through, and the screen hanging down like torn flesh. The rain let up a bit when they finished putting out the fire. The hallway beside the kitchen is blackened, and the kitchen door looks like a chip of wood attached to coal black hinges. I'm afraid to try and shut it.

"You're lucky it was raining. The whole house might of burned down," the fireman says.

"With me in it."

They clean up their equipment, roll the hoses back up, and use crowbars to drag down all the hanging wood and Sheetrock. The rain has stopped, and now the sun is bright and absolutely clean—like the air was washed of every speck of dust or pollen or ash. The trees are green and look like they're dripping diamonds.

I go back inside and walk to the front room and sit down by the window. In all the excitement I forget how old I am, and now it's difficult to get my breath. I think I'll enjoy a sip of whiskey, but when I go to the sideboard and pour myself a glass, it tastes smoky and like it was cooked in the fire. It's durn warm, too.

Once the firemen take off, I decide to ride up to Penny's

place. Maybe she'll put me up until I can get somebody over to have a look at my back door.

I don't know what I'm going to do about the porch. It's dangerous to walk on it, although the floorboards are the only wood not burned black and rippled by the fire. The foundation looks pretty solid. It's going to be a major job, cleaning it all up, and I don't want to think about it.

I have to talk to my insurance company—nothing I ever want to do—and then it'll be probably weeks of people milling around and working noisily with hammers and saws and whatnot. All the wooden chairs I just finished painting burned to ash or down to bony skeletons that look pitiful and sad, dripping black water from the rain and the fire hoses. The whole problem makes me hate the simple notion of the next few hours, much less tomorrow, and then the next tomorrow, and all the others to follow.

I walk down to the road. Brown water runs down in all the drains and ditches. As I climb into my truck, I realize my stomach is commencing to hurt pretty bad. I ain't hurt nor nothing. I'm just hungry. Like a bear in springtime. The whiskey I drank burns my pipes, and only makes the ache in my stomach worse.

I drive slowly up the side of the mountain to Penny's place. When I pull up out in front, I see her standing in the window. I wave to her, but she don't seem to see me. The walk in front of her place is slippery, so I take my time going up.

She opens the front door before I can knock on it. "Get in here," she says. She takes my arm and pulls me inside the house.

"Lordy," I say. "What's the matter?"

"Look." She points out the window. I notice she has a pistol in her other hand.

"Be careful with that thing."

"Look. He's there."

I turn and look out the window. Down the road a piece, I see it. A blue pickup truck with a cap on the back of it. "I'll be goddamned," I say. It's coming up the road slowly, just barely moving, pretty as you please.

"It's him, ain't it?" Penny says. "He's looking for this place."

"Whoever it is," I say, "I think he set my house afire this morning."

"He did?"

"I seen the truck," I say. "It stopped in front of my house, then went on real slow."

Clare says, "What are you two whispering about?"

"Gimme that gun," I say.

Penny hesitates for a minute. The truck comes up the hill, still in that steady, slow movement. Like the driver is looking for an address or something.

"We got him," I say.

"We do?" Penny says.

"Gimme the gun."

She hands it to me. I pop the cylinder on it, see that it's loaded. It feels pretty good in my hand. "This here's just what we need," I say and start for the door. "Call Sheriff Paxton."

"What are you going to do?"

"I'm going out there and have a talk with that fellow."

"The Gypsy Man?"

"That's right. If it drives a truck, maybe I can shoot it."

"You ain't going to shoot him," Clare says. In fact, she fairly screams it.

"What are you so all fired upset about?" I say.

"What if it's just somebody wandered up here by accident?"

"He don't look like he got here by accident," I say.

Clare is frantic. She comes over and grabs me by the arm. "You ain't going to shoot nobody," she says.

"I'm going to see who it is. I ain't been this close to the Gypsy Man in a long time. Maybe never."

"It ain't no Gypsy Man," she says.

"How do you know?"

She stammers, looking at me. She can't think of what to say.

"How do you know?" I ask her again.

"I just know it ain't no Gypsy Man."

I open the door. Outside the sun is still bright, although it has commenced to weaken and sink toward the mountains just over the valley. I don't know what I will do. I ain't thinking of nothing. I just want to get up to the thing and get a close look at it. See if it's a ghost or a man or what. I recognize the truck, and maybe the smell of my burning house is fresh enough in my nostrils to make me a little crazy. I'll grant that. I walk down the hill in front of Penny's place toward the road. I cross behind my own truck to the other side of the street and start toward the truck with the pistol in my hand. The shadow in the cab seems to grow, then I hear the gears grind, and the truck stops and starts moving backwards.

I raise the gun, aiming for the front windshield.

I yell, "Stop!" But I can see he's in a hurry to get away. I don't think I try to shoot the window, but it's possible. I ain't thinking about much of anything, I just want him to stop. When the gun fires, it's a shock. Even when you've fired a pistol before, you never expect the noise to be so loud and final. You don't expect the recoil to be so violent neither. Like a small cannon in your hand. I don't know if I hit nothing. The truck spins around pretty fast, then tears down the hill toward town. I can't very well run after it, but I fire another shot, aiming now for the back of the cab, for the shadow itself.

PEACH

I like it sometimes the way it makes me feel to holler. Just scream real loud and let the air out like that. I wonder why you can always feel it when you smile, but you don't know when you got a frown on your face. My momma used to say, "Why you scowlin' at the world?" And I swear I wasn't feelin' nothing at all. Not a dad-burned thing.

But I feel a smile in my jaw. Like a part of my face goes up. You think dogs laugh?

Like if'n a dog seen another one trying to take a piss, and when he raised his hind leg he fell over, I wonder would the other dog just a-set there and pay no attention to it? You know he's got to be laughing somehow.

Don't you?

I swear.

SHERIFF PAXTON

You mean to tell me you fired that gun right there in the middle of the street?"

"I might of got him," Morgan says.

"Give me that thing." He hands it over to me. "I swear to God. If you had a durn brain it'd be awful lonely."

"That's my gun," Penny says. She stands there with her arms crossed in front of herself. Clare rests against the white porch railing to hold herself up.

"Your friend here just committed a felony," I say.

Morgan grunts with disgust and looks hard at me.

"It's the truth," I say. "You can't go discharging firearms in the middle of the street."

"I was shooting at somebody," he says.

"I know," I say. "That's worse."

"I was shooting at the Gypsy Man." It's like a pronounce-ment from on high—just like if he's some kind of judge in a contest, like if he's explaining the taste of a mighty fine wine or something.

"You ain't heard that haints can't be killed with guns, I suppose?"

"That haint set fire to my back porch today," Morgan says. "If he can do that, I can shoot him."

"I knew I hadn't ought to of called the law," Penny says.

"Nobody got hurt," Clare says. "Thank the Lord for that."

"Glad to see you can stand up again, Miss Clare," I say.

"It wasn't no haint nor Gypsy Man that beat me up," she says. "This is all just plain nonsense."

Morgan looks at her.

"I'm sorry," she says. "I mean it. Just plain nonsense."

Penny says, "I'm glad Morgan shot at that fellow. Maybe he was the one that beat you to an inch of your life."

"Well, a yard maybe," I say. "Or even a foot or two. It wasn't no inch."

Penny throws her hand in the air. "Ain't it a felony to beat a innocent woman half to death?"

"It wasn't no half to death," I say. "Maybe it was a thirty-second, or at worse, a sixteenth. It wasn't no half."

Clare just leans there, glaring at me.

"You're not funny nor clever," Penny says.

"I'm confiscating this here gun," I say.

"Ain't it a felony what happened to Clare?" Penny says again.

"I have to deal with each felony one at a time," I say. "I'm taking this here gun."

"No, you ain't," Penny says. She comes up close to where I'm standing, but I don't give no ground.

"Go on," I say. "What you going to do?"

The light on my car still flashes behind me. I never took time to turn it off. I come up the mountain in a hurry. Somebody tells me there's a fellow gonna make a citizen's arrest with his own gun, I move pretty fast. I never did see the truck, though. When I got there, Penny and Morgan was setting on the porch steps, and Clare stood behind them holding the railing.

Now Penny says, "That there's my father's gun."

"Well, I'm right sorry," I say. "But this here's a bad thing. You can't just shoot at any soul you've a mind to."

"It was the Gypsy Man," Morgan says. "I'm sure of it."

"There ain't no such thing as a Gypsy Man," I say. "And even if there was, you got no right to shoot at him."

"That's my father's gun," Penny says again. "I need it for protection."

"I don't doubt that," I say. "It's a damn sight better than a shovel, too, ain't it?"

"That's why I want it."

I open the cylinder and empty the shells into my hand. It's a .38-caliber, long-barreled revolver with a fancy handle and shiny gray finish. Two of the shells are spent, and the other four are still bright as pennies. You wouldn't think a tiny piece of metal like that could make scrambled eggs out of a man's brains, but it sure can.

"This ain't nothing but trouble," I say. "And it's my job to prevent trouble."

She gets this fierce look on her face.

"It's my job," I say. "No two ways about it."

"So you take my gun and leave me up here waiting for him to come back."

"I can't have you up here shooting at anything that moves. Not right here in town."

"I'm smarter than that," she says.

Clare says, "Don't bother arguing with him, honey."

"You listen to your aunt Clare," I say.

"I'm smarter than that," she says again, real loud now.

"I ain't going to argue about how smart nobody is, but maybe you can figure this out." I hold the gun up by the trigger guard, let it dangle upside down from my own trigger finger. "This here's evidence. If I want to, I can slap cuffs on Mr. Tiller here and drive him down to Lebanon Church and let him spend the night at county expense. It's a crime to discharge a firearm in a public place or on public property. I'm talking about a felony, here. You understand? I can arrest him right now."

All three of them nod. I can see I'm beginning to break through. "But I ain't going to do that."

Penny looks at me. She has such hope in her eyes, I actually feel sorry for her.

I say, "I'm only gonna confiscate this here pistol." Her face changes so fast, it's eerie, almost like she changes herself into some other kind of thing. Her fierce eyes grow small as mustard seeds. I look right into them seeds and say, "I'm confiscating it in the name of public safety, and to keep you three from committing any more felonies."

"It's my goddamned gun," Penny says. "It's my property."

"What I'm doing here is for your own good, little lady," I say. "Besides, what do you need it for now? The fellow you shot at's probably still wetting his pants and well toward the bottom of the mountain by now."

"Don't call me 'little lady,'" she says. "I ain't your little lady."

I move on down the walk, still holding the pistol. She follows me, with Morgan behind her. Clare comes on after them.

"Wait a minute," Morgan says. "This fellow set fire to my house. I seen him."

I stopped. "You absolutely sure you seen him?"

He pushes himself up beside Penny, so both of them are on the sidewalk in front of me. I can barely see their faces in the sinking sunlight, but I realize that she's almost as tall as he is. "You seen him set the fire?"

"I seen him in front of my house. Then he drives by real slow, so he can see that what he done got started. The damn porch almost blew up."

"So you didn't see him set the fire."

"I smelled the gasoline. I smelled it with the fire. I know he done it."

"And Aunt Clare just said he might be the one kidnapped her," Penny says.

I look at Clare. "That right?"

"I never said that directly." She stares at her feet. "They think he might be the one."

"You seen him?"

She looks at me now. "Of course not."

"And the truck? Was that the truck you was talking about?"

"I don't rightly know." She seems annoyed that I asked the question.

"Nobody kidnapped nobody," I say. "You went with the fellow, didn't you?"

"It mighta been him," she says. "The truck looked familiar."

"Did you go with the fellow or didn't you?"

"I went with him."

"And you're sure that was the same fellow in the truck?"

"I said it mighta been him," Clare says.

"Where was you standing when you seen the truck?"

"What do you mean?"

"You was on the porch? Or out here in front, or maybe you was down yonder in the road? Where was you standing?"

She knows where I'm going with my questions. She makes this face, looks back up at the house, then at me again. "I was inside, by the window."

"And the sun just went down right over yonder," I say, pointing across the road. "You was looking out the window, right into the sun, and you seen a truck probably seventy-five yards from the house, and you recognized the truck. That's what you're telling me."

"No."

"No, what?"

"No, that ain't what I'm saying. Morgan said it was him."

"How the hell does he know? Was he with you when you got roughed up?"

"I just thought it might be him, is all." She lowers her head again. "I don't know for sure if that was him."

"You said he drove a pickup truck with a cap on it," Penny says.

"Oh, I don't know, honey. What do you want me to say? I just don't know."

I swear at one time she had good sense, but it ain't no evidence of it no more. "Sure," I say. "So Morgan here takes a shot at him."

Nobody says nothing. I look at Penny. "You see why I'm taking this here pistol?"

She has nothing to say.

"Well," I say. "It don't look like you seen what you thought you seen, any of you. Whoever that shadow was that you shot at, it wasn't looking for no trouble. It just had the misfortune of wandering up here to where you three lunatics could point a pistol at it and give it a taste of the hospitality of mountain folks."

"How come he took off when he seen me coming?" Morgan says.

"Did you have the gun in your hand?"

He ain't got no answer for that.

"This here's a pretty shiny piece, ain't it? Make sunlight fly every which way."

"It was him," Penny says. "I know it."

"I seen that truck in front of my house," Morgan says.

"You're sure of it?"

"Yes."

"You seen the tags on it?"

"No."

"You recognized the fellow inside driving it?"

"It was raining," Morgan says. "Christ a' mighty. You want the whole trial and jury and all before you do anything?"

"Oh, I'm doing something," I say. "I'm confiscating this here gun." I smile. Nobody likes it very much, but they just stand there, frustrated. Clare starts moving back toward the house.

Morgan says, "I'm the one who misused that thing. It ain't no reason to punish her for it."

"Who's being punished?"

"I need the gun," Penny says. "For my own safety." It's quiet for a while, and when she realizes I ain't going to answer her, she says, "I paid to have the locks changed and everything." Then she gets real loud. "I've got a small child to look after."

I swear it looks like she's gonna start crying. Morgan puts his arm around her shoulders and she leans into him. She won't look at me. Just like every mountain girl I've ever known. Then Morgan says to her, "I'll stay with you tonight. You needn't be afraid, honey."

"There you go," I say. "You got a war hero to watch over you." I throw the pistol on the seat in my car and slam the door shut. I go around to the other side of the car and start to get in.

"Next time there's trouble," Penny says, "we won't call you."

"Well," I say. "Then I'll thank the Lord for big favors." I get in the car and turn the emergency lights off. I roll the window down and both of them turn and look at me. "You know old man Stooch?" I say.

"What?" Morgan says.

"Old man Stooch, down in Lebanon Church. He used to be from up around here."

"Yeah," Morgan says. "I remember him."

"Maybe he's the Gypsy Man. He's sure old enough."

Neither of them has a thing to say.

"Likely you could get him to confess it. He can't walk much faster than he writes on that pad a his. It might take him a hour or two to write 'it's me,' and then you could shoot him down pretty easy."

"You ain't even amusing," Penny says.

"I don't know," I say. "The idea makes me laugh." I put the car in gear and start back down the hill. I see them moving slowly up the walk toward where Clare waits for them on the porch. Morgan still has his arm around Penny's shoulders. They look like a grieving couple, walking away from a grave.

PARCHMAN

I flew down that hill. I was running faster than I ever did. I'd been walking everywhere for almost ten years, and now for what seemed like the first time I was running. I felt already free, you know what I mean? I run so hard my legs begun to quiver. I fell forward and rolled several times, but then I hopped up and just kept going. At first it was just running, but after a while, I was trying to get myself away from the others. I wanted to be by myself, in the woods, so I could sit still in the free air and listen to the birds and breezes in the leaves and branches all around. I wanted that stillness more than food. Then I'd decide what to do. I didn't want nobody near me. I dodged in the trees, and when the ground leveled out I stopped a bit, to catch my breath and see where everybody else was.

A fellow named Griggs panted and chuffed next to me. Beyond him, leaning on a tree was a black named Jewell. I didn't see nobody else.

"What we gonna do?" Griggs said.

"I ain't studying nothing with you nor nobody else," I said.

Jewell said, "We got to get out these clothes."

I commenced walking further down the hill. I wanted to be under the trees in the shadows. I hoped if I just kept walking down the mountain, I'd come to a road, or a house. Griggs and Jewell followed me. I stopped.

"Where you think you're going?" I said.

"We got to find a house or something," Griggs said.

"I ain't going nowhere with you," Jewell said.

"Well, why you following me then?"

"I ain't following nobody."

"You know where you are?" I said.

"We is high up, in the mountains," Jewell said.

"I think we should stick together," Griggs said.

Up the hill, I seen two others coming—staggering from tree to tree, trying not to fall.

"Goddamn it," I said. "We got to split up."

"You're the fastest runner here," Griggs said. "Everybody's following you."

"Why? Go your own way."

"Maybe they figure you know where you're going. You run down this hill so fast and all," Griggs said. "And it's a whole lot easier to run down this mountain than up it."

I started moving again. I didn't want the others to catch up. "You all are on your own," I said. "We can't be wandering the countryside in groups."

I was walking now, but Jewell and Griggs moved over a bit, as if they was going to gradually get off in a different direction, but the underbrush sort of forced them back into the path I was on. Griggs looked at me. "I guess we're stuck until we find another path."

I started running again, and they followed. I felt like I was already running from the dogs. And like the whole prison was chasing me.

In a space of light under the trees in front of me, down off to the right a ways, I seen the sagging roof of a cabin. The boards that leaned into it didn't seem to give it no support. One window on the side was cracked, but I could see sunlight reflected from the glass even through the dark canopy of leaves overhead. I slid down the embankment behind the cabin. I didn't see a car nor nothing around it.

I went to the front and found it open. I ain't lying. No door nor nothing, but again it was glass in the windows on the front side. I was trying to catch my breath. I staggered up three broken-down wooden steps to the porch and went inside the cabin. It wasn't nothing in there, not even an old sack or a pile of hay. It might of stored bottles and jars at one time, because broken glass was scattered on the floor and empty shelves lined both side walls. It wasn't a place nobody ever lived because it wasn't no place for a stove nor a fireplace nor nothing like that.

I was standing there, panting and gasping when Griggs come around the corner with Jewell.

"What's this place?" Griggs said.

I didn't answer him. I thought if this was a storage shed, must be a house or another cabin nearby. I just wanted to catch my breath before I kept going. I never felt like I was just running from the law. Right at that moment, I was running from Griggs and Jewell and the rest of them fellas a-coming down the mountain behind them.

"We can rest here," Jewell said. "We be fine here for a while."

"I wish I had some water," Griggs said.

I could hear the woods beginning to crash with the rest of

them. I sat down with my back against the wall. Griggs and Jewell done the same. It was quiet for a small spell, then we could hear the others stirring the leaves as they come toward the cabin.

"How far you think we're going to get with this crowd?" I said.

"Be quiet," Griggs said. "Maybe they'll go right on by."

We waited, setting against the wall. The open door invited everybody up the porch steps, until they was just standing there peering in at us.

"Get the fuck out of here," I said.

The first man turned to leave, but a big fellow behind him—a guy they called Shovel—said, "Who you think you are?"

"There ain't enough room in here," I said.

He looked around. "You find anything in here?"

Griggs said, "Like what, food? Water?"

Shovel shook his head, then turned and walked back down the steps. The others followed him. They was all breathing hard and sweating. Shovel said something I couldn't hear, then they was all talking out there. It was pretty noisy. I figure we was probably a mile or two down the side of the mountain. I heard Shovel say something about finding a road or a house. I was afraid he'd find the house that went with this cabin and strip it of what I'd need: clothing, food, water. All I wanted was to wear a plain shirt and a pair of dungarees so I could get out on the highway and see if I could catch a ride out west—somewhere flat. I was thinking about Peach, how he'd taken off in that car and was probably halfway to Tennessee by now.

"I ain't staying here," Griggs said, getting up.

"Go on," I said. "I'm just taking a rest." I pushed myself down along the wall until I was almost flat. "I'm going to stay here until dark."

The rest of them started moving off through the trees.

"I wish I hadn't run, now," Griggs said.

"Anybody see Bone?" I said. "Did he run, too?"

Jewell sat up more straight against the wall. "It be cool here," he said. "I don't care if they catch me tomorra. I be cool now."

"They'll give you more time," Griggs said. "They'll give all of us more time."

"Well," Jewell said. "They can't no way possible give me no more time. They say 'life' to a nigger, they means it."

Griggs laughed. "I guess it may as well be life for me, too. In twenty years I'll be over fifty."

"You better had stayed in and learned a trade," I said.

Now Jewell laughed. "No," he said. "They can't add no time to me. I done got all they got to give."

I moved to the door and looked out. The clearing in front of the cabin was empty. I couldn't see none of the others, but I could still hear them moving through the underbrush further down the mountain. I didn't think they'd found the house that went with the cabin. They just kept getting further and further away, moving leaves and bushes so loudly it sounded like they was pushing a truck through the woods.

"Must be a path around here somewheres," I said.

"A path," Jewell said.

I didn't answer him. I stepped out onto the porch and looked around. The sun broke through the leaves overhead in fiery beams of light. The straight lines of yellow light fanned down toward the clearing like a great rake and reminded me once again of the cage I lived in. I walked to the rear of the cabin, kicked the underbrush there. I was looking for a place where it was a path or the remnants of one. Someplace where the underbrush was thinner, less tangled. The others was still in the cabin when I found my path.

I stepped over what was probably a hedge at one time and went down the hill slightly to the left of the cabin, and the rocks on the forest floor become visible in front of me. I had to duck down, under prickly bushes and vines, but it was a path. As I moved along, the vines thinned out and eventually I could stand upright. I walked a long time, along the mountain, never really going downwards, but not climbing much neither. I might of walked a half hour. I don't know. I was constantly pushing branches away, and pulling against the stickers that caught my pants, but eventually I seen it. A small house in the distance, by a road that wound like a pale snake away from it and down the mountain. I knew it was somebody living in the house because laundry hung on a line in the backyard. The clearing in front of the house wasn't much bigger than a swimming pool, but it was a black car sitting on blocks there in the grass by a big tree that towered over the porch. In front of the house, you could see all the way across the valley to the Blue Ridge Mountains, and beyond that was even more mountains. I was not interested in sightseeing though. What caught my interest was the clothing hanging on the line. I thought I might get all I needed without bothering nobody.

I watched the house for a little while, thinking about what to do, and then I heard a car coming up the winding road. It was the black Chevrolet and, I swear to God, Peach was behind the wheel. He pulled right into the driveway and got out. I come out of the trees and when he seen me he crouched by the car for a minute, like he might jump back in and start it up again. The old man just sat there in the front seat staring at me.

"How'd you get all the way down here?" I said.

He stood up when he recognized me. "Anybody following you?"

"Maybe some of the other men, but I don't think so."

He stood there a minute, looking at me. Then he come around the front of the car and opened the door on the passenger side. He didn't say nothing, but the old man got out of the car like he'd been told to do it in a hurry. "Come on," Peach said, moving him toward the house.

"How'd you get down here?" I said again.

"I took the first left off the highway and it led me here."

We walked up the steps and onto the porch.

"You sure none of them guards are following you?" Peach said.

"Yeah, I'm sure. I don't know how far I run, but it's a long climb back up."

The old man had a key to the door.

"You live here?" I said.

"That's why we took the first left," Peach said. "I told this gentleman to take me home." He was smiling.

Inside was warm and damp. An old woman come out of a small back room and the old man said, "Don't fret yourself none, Dolly. They ain't going to hurt nobody."

She made a small sound in the back of her throat, and Peach said, "Sit down please, ma'am."

Her husband went to her and put his arm over her shoulder, and both of them moved to a small table next to a woodstove. She was wearing a white robe, kind of fluffed at the edges, and white slippers. The house smelled like wheat, like a bakery in the morning. The old woman kept looking up at her husband, her mouth half open. She wore lipstick, but it looked almost dirty on her. She was whispering something to the old man. Her hands shook, and she was mighty afraid, I ain't lying.

Her husband said, "It'll be all right, honey."

"Shut up," Peach said.

"I'm just explaining to her," the old man said.

"Nothing bad's going to happen to nobody. Okay?" I said. "We just need a few things is all."

"Open a window," Peach said. "It's kind of close in here."

The old man opened a window by the stove. Peach said,

"You know when I was a kid, my daddy built a shed near the house with a chimney pipe, and we put the stove in that."

The old man looked at him.

"On hot summer days, we just cooked all we wanted and the house was cool as could be."

"What about in winter?" I said. "Wasn't it cold walking out to the stove in the winter. And how'd you keep the house warm?"

The old man seemed to nod with this, like he thought of the question, too.

"It worked just fine," Peach said. "The fireplace kept the house warm."

"Got anything to eat?" I said to the woman.

Peach went to one of the front windows and opened it, too. He had to take a stick that was sitting on the sill and set it in the window to keep it up.

"Got anything to eat?" I said again.

The old man nodded, and pointed to a bread box on the counter. I found a small, stale loaf of bread there. "Where's a knife to cut this?" I said.

Peach took it out of my hand and bit an end off it. "Fuck a knife," he said. Then he broke it in half and gave some to me. I opened a drawer in one of the cabinets, and the old man said, "Not that one. The one next to it."

"Thank you kindly," I said. I found a long butcher knife in the second drawer and used it to slice the bread. "You want some?" I said to the old man.

"No, thank you. I'm just fine."

The old woman was crying. Tears run down her face and her mouth—I ain't going to ever forget her mouth. Even with the lipstick, it looked like a kid's mouth, crying at birth, you know what I mean? But silent. No sound at all. I ain't lying.

PENNY

I felt better when I had the gun. It was sure better than a shovel. When I found it, I couldn't wait to tell Morgan about it, and now I wish I didn't put it so easily in his hands. I wish I didn't let him take it out there and shoot at the man in the truck. And I wish Aunt Clare never called the law.

It would only take a damn fool not to see what was happening. Old Gypsy Crawford's tombstone shows up in my yard, just about right under my back porch, and then Clare disappears with a man who kindly places her back on the couch, locks the house, and takes a key with him. He brung her back. Just like what happened to Wilbur Crawford. Then Morgan's house catches fire. Why couldn't nobody but me and Morgan see it? I wonder what John would say about this. What it looks like—it just ain't something I can ignore.

I know if I had to shoot somebody with that gun, I'd a done it.

Tonight, the rain comes back and don't seem like it will ever stop. It beats against the windows. I listen to the radio for a while, then the wind, the rain, Clare's snoring. Or maybe it's Morgan's. He sleeps in my room. I told him I'd take the couch, and that's where I spend most of the night. But I can't sleep. I get up and sit in the chair by the window. Sometime near toward morning, I fall asleep. I don't know how long. I dream that Clare screams, but when I finally get my eyes open, she is still sound asleep in her room. I don't know if I actually get back to sleep after that. Maybe I drift a bit, listening to the clock ticking in the kitchen.

When I finally decide the day has started, I get Tory out of bed. I tell her to be extra quiet, help her dress, then take her back down to Gault's school. Mrs. Gault is up already, sitting in her kitchen with coffee steaming on the stove.

"Can you believe it? Rain again," she says. "You want to help me bake again today?" she asks Tory.

"I'll get done late this afternoon," I say. "I'm going to open the store for a while."

"That's fine, honey," she says. Tory looks like she might pout if she was awake enough to think about her last day before school starts. But she just leans against Mrs. Gault, who pats her shoulder and smiles down on her like a Madonna. She really is happy to have Tory with her, and I never feel bad about leaving her there. "We'll be in the kitchen," Mrs. Gault says. "Won't we, honey? And we'll make something fine and sweet to eat."

I kiss Tory on the cheek and go out. When I get back to the cabin, Clare is still sleeping and so is Morgan. I go and sit down at the kitchen table. From where I sit I can see out the front window and down the hill to the store.

I'm thinking about the gun when Clare finally wakes up and comes out of her room. She tries to be quiet, too.

"You up already?" she asks. She comes into where I'm sitting, her slippers sliding on the floor. It sounds like air leaking out of something with each step she takes. Then she stretches a bit and lets out a loud, long sigh. More of a yawn, I guess, but it sounds like she is happy with the morning and ready for the day, like she just woke from a long, restful night's sleep and nothing bad ever happens to her.

"I'm going to open the store again today," I say. I set my chin in my hand and keep on looking out the window. Light breaks through the gray wall of clouds that covers the mountain and fills the valley below. Sunlight, fanning out in thin sprays, cuts through the black branches on the trees and makes jewels of the leaves.

"When I feel better, I'll open it." She seems almost insulted, as if my saying I'm going to open the store is a kind of criticism.

232

"I just want you to get better," I tell her.

"What time is it?"

"I don't know. It's pretty late. Way past seven, I expect."

"What've you been doing in here all by yourself?"

"Nothing," I say.

"Tory up yet?"

"I took her down to Myra's again."

"What time did Morgan go home?"

"He didn't. He's sleeping in my room."

She sighs again. "I need some coffee."

How can I make anyone understand why it bothers me that I have to take care of her, too. She's my daddy's older sister, and she always tried to be a mother to me, even before he went off to war and got killed by the Germans. I ought to love her, and I reckon, on some days, when she laughs about one of her "boyfriends," or when we're working hard on something in the store—doing the inventory or stocking the shelves—and she sings old songs I never heard before, I feel sort of close to her. Maybe it's more than just kinship. I don't know. I understand what she expected when she was my age, and I reckon I know how I'd feel if my life turned out like hers did: a hundred different "boyfriends"—even if he's fifty years old, a man is a "boyfriend" if he runs around with my aunt Clare. I swear men follow her around like hound dogs; like they get a scent from her and can't help themselves. She's had so many of them, and not one of them ever really cared about her. I know how I'd feel. I remember the sickness in my heart when I found out that John Bone was going to have to leave me, when I knew I was going to have to give him up. So every once in a great while, I feel sorry for Clare. Maybe that is just loving her in the only way I can love her. Still, I hate taking care of her now. It wasn't so bad the first day, when I was afraid she wouldn't wake up at all. But the next day, and the day after that, when I had all those other things to worry about, and she didn't seem to notice it. All she could do was lay there and ask me to get her water, and warm rags, and coffee, and just about everything else. Twice I had to help her go to the outhouse and I almost got sick. The first time, I sat her down and she says, "Hold me up, hold me up." She placed her hand over her heart. "I'm afraid I might fall in there," she says.

"For Lord's sake, Clare, you ain't going nowhere. The hole in that seat ain't big enough."

She looked at me as if I'd screamed at her.

"Really," I said. "How can you fall in?" I was standing there with the door open, and a right smart breeze blew it against the side of the house and then back against my legs.

"Honey," she laughed. "I'm brittle as a candy cane. I might break in two."

I think it hurt her that I didn't laugh, but it just wasn't funny. It was downright shameful, if you want to know the truth.

"I'm all right, honey," she says. "It's just the way my head spins. I get dizzy. It'll pass, once I get used to walking upright again."

I wanted to say, "When's that going to be?" but I didn't. I held my tongue. I helped her back into the house, wondering how long I was going to have to be her personal nurse.

NOW, CLARE GOES into the living room and sits down on the couch. She puts her feet up, sort of bunches her legs under herself, then she turns and looks at me. "So." She blinks her eyes, slowly. "You lost the gun. Now what are we going to do?"

"I don't rightly know."

It's quiet for a while. I watch the sun cutting through the high clouds and what's left of the misty rain. "Looks like it's getting ready to quit raining for a spell," I say.

Clare don't say nothing. I can't tell if she's falling asleep again or not. She lays her head back on the cushion and closes her eyes, but she's breathing quietly.

"Clare?"

"Hmmmm."

"You awake?"

"Yeah."

"Why'd you go with him?"

She says nothing.

"Didn't you know who it was?"

"What?" She opens her eyes and looks hard at me.

"Why'd you go off like that without telling me?"

"It was just one of them things, honey. You know, spur of the moment."

"Right."

"I never know what I'm going to do from one minute to the next." She laughs, then sighs. "Ain't it the truth?"

"I wish I didn't give the gun to Morgan."

"You don't need that old gun, honey. Don't be so blue."

"I've got Tory to think about. If it's the Gypsy Man . . ."

"Aww, honey." She waves her hand. "I never did believe any of that talk about a ghost. I knew Gypsy Crawford. I seen him most every day when I was a little girl. I was eight or nine when he left this town for good, and I ain't never seen him since. The man I went with wasn't no Gypsy Man. He didn't even have no birthmark."

"He didn't? You're sure he didn't?"

"Lord, no. He needed a shave. That's all."

"It wasn't a red mark on half his face?"

"I told you it wasn't no mark."

"Yeah, well," I say.

"Hell no, honey," she says, settling herself more comfortably in the cushions. Then I realize she's reaching for her bottle. "If I remember right, you couldn't miss a mark like Gypsy Crawford's. It run all down along the side of his neck and around his cheekbone. And it wasn't red, neither, no matter what folks tell you about it. It was really purple." She twists and turns, reaching in back of herself.

"It's not there," I say.

"What's not there?"

"What you been squirming there trying to find."

"Well, where is it? I need some medicine."

"Ain't you hungry? Don't you want to eat nothing?"

"I will," she says. "As soon as I have some medicine."

"Stop calling it medicine," I say, getting up. "It's really aggravating that you call it medicine."

She sighs again, this time a little louder. It's a way of letting me know she is truly unhappy.

I get the bottle for her.

After she sips a bit of it she asks me if I'm going to make coffee.

"Oh, for heaven's sake."

"Well, if you don't want to, I will." Her voice is wistful and sad.

"I'm sorry," I say. "I'll make you some if you want."

While I'm making the coffee I tell Clare I'm going to get a dead bolt lock put on the door. "Either a locksmith or maybe Mr. Tiller will help me do it," I say, "but I'm going to get it done first thing today. I thought I was going to get it done yesterday, but Morgan never showed up until late in the afternoon, and then he went and shot the pistol and all. So today I'll do it."

She says nothing.

"I'll feel safer with Tory here and all," I say.

"Well," Clare says. "Now that school's starting, you won't have her with you at all then. Not during the day."

"I know it," I say.

I wait next to the stove for the coffee to start perking. It's quiet for a long time. I miss Tory. Suddenly I want to have her in my arms, her legs wrapped around my hips, and her arms around my neck. She's so small and light. Holding her makes me feel like the earth, like all of history and everything bright in the whole universe. Like I am a happy God. I want to feel the skin of her cheek on my lips and smell the fall in her hair.

"Maybe *I'll* open the store," Clare says.

"You want breakfast, hon?" I say, thinking to smooth things over a bit.

"Nooo," Clare says. "Just the coffee."

"Your hair's a mess," I say. "You want me to do a hundred strokes on it with a brush this morning?"

"Nooo," she says lazily. "I'm fixing to take a bath."

I pour the coffee when it's ready and bring it into Clare. She thanks me, sets it on the table in front of her. I sit down in the green chair across the room. Then she says, "The safest place you can be is on top of this mountain, girl. Don't you know that?"

"Sure," I say. "Look what happened to you."

"Well," she says. "I just don't know nothing about that except that it wouldn't a happened to me if I hadn't a gone with that fellow."

"I felt safe, holding that gun," I say. "I felt safe." I'm telling the truth, partially. As long as I had the gun, I believed at least that I was not going to be afraid.

"Except for that little Landon boy, ain't nothing much ever happened up here," Clare says.

"What about John?"

"John went his own way, and made his own trouble. You wouldn't be afraid of him, would you?"

"You know what I meant. And you know I wouldn't."

"No, I didn't think you would. And the fellow I went with wasn't no Gypsy Man, neither. I seen him, and I know what I'm talking about. He was just a drifter, you know. Probably just back from Korea, or something."

"And he's got a key to this cabin."

"Well, it don't matter no more. You gone and changed all the locks."

I don't say nothing.

"And if'n you go and put a dead bolt on the door, well then..." She fluffs her robe so that it covers her legs, holding the whiskey bottle up high as she speaks.

"Still," I say. "If'n he's got a key, he'll think to come back here. The note said he'd be back."

"And maybe that was him yesterday. He already come back and we damn near blew his head off. You think he'll come back after that?"

"What if it wasn't him? And what does he mean he can be useful?"

"Useful?"

"That's what the note said."

She shrugs. I watch her look at the whiskey in the bottle, check the level of it.

"How *did* you get back here?" I ask.

"The truth is, honey, I don't remember. Maybe I let myself in and locked the door."

"Where's the key then?"

"I don't know. How could I know if I don't remember how I got here?"

"You don't need to get mad," I say.

"Well, I ain't. I ain't mad."

"So maybe it's the Gypsy Man and maybe not. I still wish I had the gun."

"It ain't the Gypsy Man." She seems offended, like I'm accusing her. What she says about Gypsy Crawford should calm me but it don't. I keep going over it in my head, as the clouds continue to break up and the wind settles. Now the sun shines through the clouds in long, scattered columns. The air outside will be much warmer now, and the soaked trees will dry out before dark tonight.

I think of Tory again. Sometimes, thinking of her makes an ache in my heart—a real pain, like a disease almost—and whenever I feel like that I want to cry, even though I know I am happy. If I let myself, I'd hug Tory so tight she'd just melt into me and then she wouldn't be Tory no more, she'd just be a part of me again, like she was when she begun, before life. You have to be so careful when you love a person.

Then I'm remembering John. I picture his smile, try to recall his voice.

Clare sits up and puts her feet back on the floor. Her hair is all mixed up and piled wrong on her head. With no makeup she looks much older. "It's Labor Day," she says. "You sure you want to open the store today?"

"Right now I'm just gonna sit here and think."

"Did you sleep at all?" She picks up her coffee and starts to sip it.

"I slept fine," I tell her.

"You ain't been setting here on guard all night?"

"No," I lie. "I been thinking about John."

It's quiet for a spell. Then Clare says, "You really afraid, honey?"

"I don't know."

"You sure was full of spit and fire when you had that pistol."

I try to smile, but what she says only reminds me how angry I am at Sheriff Paxton.

"And you setting here all morning thinking about John," Clare says. "Maybe that's a good sign. Maybe he's thinking of you."

"I can't remember the sound of his voice, but I wish he was here, right now. I wouldn't be so afraid if he was here."

"I don't recollect you being afraid of nothing, ever. You

least of all. Why, when your daddy went to—" She stops. It's quiet. I don't look at her. "When we lost your daddy you were the one. You carried both of us through it."

I look at her. She sits back, then gets up and goes to the cabinets over the sink. "I'm going to have sugar this morning."

She comes back in with the sugar and puts two teaspoons in her coffee. She sets the sugar bowl down and stirs the coffee, almost lovingly, just leaning over and staring at the cup. I can see she's remembering something. She sits down again still staring at the cup. Then she says, "Honey, I got to tell you something."

"What?"

"You got to promise you won't tell nobody."

"I promise. Who would I tell?"

"I don't want you to be mad at me neither."

"Okay."

"You promise you won't get mad at me?" She looks at me now, raising the cup to her lips. I can see steam coming from the top of the cup in her hand, and the new sunlight scatters through her thin hair so it looks like a halo around her head. She has tears in her eyes.

"I ain't going to get mad."

"It wasn't no Gypsy Man that I run off with."

"You told me that."

"No, I mean he didn't beat me up nor nothing like that. It wasn't him."

"What do you mean?"

"What I said."

"He didn't hit you or nothing?"

"He didn't."

"Well, how'd you get like that?"

She starts crying. The cup begins to tremble in her hands, so I lean over and take it away from her. I put it down carefully on the table and wait. She covers her face with her hands and cries silently for a spell. Then she wipes her eyes with the sleeve of her gown and looks at me. "I'm sorry," she says.

"Don't do that," I say. "Just tell me."

"Well, we was dancing. I was dancing with him, and then he was dancing with this other woman. Some hillbilly and I couldn't stand it. I'd had a bit too much to drink."

She starts crying again. I get up and get her a dish towel, and she wipes her face with it.

"Just tell me," I say. "I won't get mad."

"I was happy for a spell," she says. "You see?"

"I see." I sure do see. I see as well as a person can when they're looking at somebody inside a bottle.

"I got mad," Clare says. "So I socked her. Then . . . then we was fighting."

"Lord sakes, Clare," I say.

"All the men was cheering and she was pulling my hair and hitting me." She wipes her eyes very carefully with her hand.

"Just use the towel," I say. "That's what it's for."

"It was in a bar over in West Virginia somewhere," she says. She takes a breath or two, then wipes her nose. In a stronger voice she says, "Up near Ohio, I think."

I just look at her. It ain't nothing you can do when you promise not to get mad and you get mad. I want to scream at her. She just sets there, gaping at me, like a bird trapped on a barbed wire fence. Finally I say, "Why'd you do it?"

"I was ashamed," she says.

"Ashamed," I say. "Ashamed."

"I figured you'd get mad," she says.

"I ain't mad."

"It don't look like it."

"I said I ain't mad."

"Well."

It's quiet a while. Then I say, "I don't guess I'll ever understand . . ."

But she breaks in. "What was I to do? I am waked up in the condition I was in—the woman did beat me you know. I was beaten. That part was true. And I am waked up with you and Morgan Tiller..." She stops, looks back at the door on my room.

"He's still sleeping," I say.

She goes on, almost whispering now. "You was all staring at me. You and him, and the doctor and then Sheriff Paxton. I just couldn't tell it like it happened. I couldn't tell..." She stops again, for a brief second, like she can't get the words out, then she says, "*Them.*" She waves her hand like she can point to them on the other side of the room. With that gesture, she looks exactly like my father, and I feel something drop in my heart. Recognizing him in her makes me want to cry. "I couldn't tell them people what I done," she says. "Not with you there, and Lord knows where Tory was."

It's real quiet for a spell, and I can't think of what to say to her. I hear Morgan snoring. The sun seems to break through the window and lights her whole face—like the light comes from behind the bones and skin and not the sun at all. The coffee is still steaming in her cup.

"Well," I say. "I reckon maybe someday I *will* understand."

She don't say nothing.

"I'm alone, too," I say. "I'm alone, too."

She takes a sip of the coffee and then sets it down on the table again. She looks at me for a second, pulling her legs up next to herself again. She has stopped crying. The sunlight still crosses the room and bathes her. It's like she's in a spotlight on a stage or something. Outside the window, the sky looks like it was shattered into purple clouds by long shafts of sunlight.

"It's a beautiful morning," she says, putting her hand up to shade her red eyes. She looks back at my room again.

I get up and go to the window and pull the blind down. Then I say, "It's all right, Aunt Clare."

"You know," she says. "The fellow brought me back here out of kindness."

I don't want to talk about it no more. I say nothing.

"Pure and simple." She sips her coffee.

"And we almost shot him yesterday," I say, returning to the green chair.

"I was so terrified," she says. "You don't know."

"*Was* that him yesterday?"

I watch her face, the way she just barely touches the cup to her lips and then puts it right back down each time she takes a sip of the coffee. She gets this expression, like we're both involved in some kind of secret plan. Then she nods. "I think it was him. I recognized the truck. That's why I was so afraid when he . . ." She tilted her head back toward my room. "I could have killed him yesterday."

I shake my head. "It might a been nice to ask your fellow what he meant by that note he put in your pocket," I say.

"Well, he sure ain't coming back now," she says. "Not after Morgan taken a potshot at him."

"What was his name?" I say.

"Peach."

"Peach?"

She nods.

"What was his first name?"

"Just Peach. I don't think he had a first name."

"Peach," I say.

"I tell you what, honey," she says. "He really was a peach. I mean he knew how to treat a lady."

"He did?"

"I ain't never been with nobody that exciting."

I don't say nothing.

"He was—he just knew what he wanted. He took command of me."

"You want that?"

243

"Well, it's not like he ordered me around or nothing. He was just all fire and passion and on the go. Like a engine, charged with fire. It was like he took a hold of life and made it please him. You know?"

"I don't know."

"Like John with you."

"John never commanded me."

"You know what I mean. He had a passion. A kind of subdued violence—on the edge, kind of. You know? Like he was dynamite."

"He sounds dangerous."

"That's what was fun," she says. "On the edge of danger. Never knowing from one minute to the next what we'd do. He lived by no rules but his own. It was exciting."

"Really?"

"I ain't never felt so young. You'd of liked him."

"He didn't beat you at all, then."

"He was a gentleman," she says. "I mean, he'd been around and all. You could see that. But he was smart and as kind as you please."

"Long as it wasn't the Gypsy Man," I say.

She's smiling. "I bet he was coming back up here to return that key."

"What's he gonna do now that Morgan taken a shot at him?"

"I don't expect we'll ever see him again," she says, sadness creeping into her voice. But it ain't real sadness. It's kind of like a wistful sort of giving in or surrender in her voice. Like she just accepts what she knows is true.

"If'n he lives by his own rules, he'll be back," I say.

"You think so?"

"I sure do."

She smiles.

"Anyway it don't matter that he ain't the Gypsy Man," I

say. "Morgan says he's seen signs and he's been on this mountain longer than anybody. He don't lie and he's smart."

"He's a mite superstitious, too," she says.

"I still got to think about Tory. I'm putting a dead bolt on that door."

She thinks about it, not looking at me. Her eyes are still red from crying, and I think she looks so sad she is almost young and beautiful again. "I'm sorry, hon," she says.

"It's okay," I say.

She tries to smile once more and says, "You go ahead and get a dead bolt if you want. But I'm telling you, honey. There ain't nothing to be afraid of."

PARCHMAN

The old man said, "You boys in some kind of trouble?"

"What do you think," Peach said. "You think we'd wear these yellow trousers just for the style of it?" He went off into one of the back rooms. He was gone for a while. I noticed the old woman looking at me. I offered her a slice of the bread, and she just started crying silently again, shaking her head.

"Really," I said. "We ain't going to hurt nobody. We just want some clothes and food and any money you got."

"I was going down to Charlottesville, to the market," the old man said, and he reached into his pocket and come out with a handful of one-dollar bills.

I took it. "This all you got?"

"Yes, sir."

"Sir," I repeated. It made me laugh a little.

"Please," the woman said. "I have a heart condition."

Peach come out of the room. He was wearing denim jeans and a red flannel shirt with the sleeves rolled halfway up his arm. The shirt was way too tight for him, but he buttoned all the buttons just the same. It looked like he might burst out of the thing and start shooting buttons every which way if he just took a deep breath. "You got a gun, old man?" he said.

The woman shook her head, but the old man nodded, pointed to a tall cabinet next to the front door.

"This is a nice little house," I said. "You keep it nice."

"I have a heart condition," the old woman said. She was sitting there trembling, and the old man kept patting her shoulder and brushing her gray hair back off her forehead. "It'll be all right, honey," he was saying. "They just want some things and then they'll leave us."

"That other car belong to you?" Peach said. He opened the cabinet, took out a small rifle. "What's this?"

"It's a .22," the old man said. "I don't use it much."

"You got ammunition for it?"

"It's in there."

"What about the other car?"

"It's my old Buick. It don't run."

"The damn thing's on blocks," I said. "You didn't see that?"

Peach said nothing. He was looking at the gun, holding it up, aiming out the window.

"It was a good car once. That's why I keep it yonder." The old man was being as nice as he could be. "You know, for parts and all."

"You got tags for that old thing?"

"No, sir."

"You hear that?" Peach said, smiling at me. "He calls me sir."

"Yes, sir," the old man said, more assurance in his voice. He was almost pleased. "I respect your position," he said. "I know—I understand..."

"You don't know nothing," Peach said. "So just shut the fuck up."

"That ain't the way to talk in front of the lady," I said.

"Oh, Lord," she said. "Oh, Lord. Oh, Lord."

"It'll be okay, honey," the old man said. "Just be still, now."

"The Lord ain't no help," Peach said. "I can kick the Lord's ass."

The old man fell silent. I was watching the way his hand kept moving across and over his wife's shoulders, while he soothed her. She was trembling, staring at the far wall like she was afraid it might collapse on her or something. On the table next to the couch I seen a picture of them holding each other in front of a big cake. They was young, and you could see they liked the world. To people like that, they don't know what a miracle is. You know? They get happy and smile at a camera and make a record of the happiness; like it needs to be recorded for some courtroom later in life. They live so many years thinking somebody owes them that same goddamned smile, and all the time the world don't care no more than a squirrel or a skunk cares about it. These folks go year after year *believing* a prayer to the Lord helps them find a pair of shoes, or a postage stamp, or even a gas station on the road. They think goodness is what they have when they pray and their prayers have been answered. And they think it's a miracle. That's what they think. Ain't nothing for it neither. Folks like that never know about real miracles, until they run into somebody like Peach.

"I'm sorry, but she just gets herself all worked up," the old man said looking at his wife. "Okay, honey? Don't be worrying yourself for no reason. These fellas don't want no more trouble than they already got."

Peach looked at me. "Go on in that other room and get some different clothes on."

I didn't want to leave Peach alone with them folks. I really didn't. I said, "What are you going to do?"

He rested the gun on his shoulder and stood straight at

attention, like he was in the army or something. "I'm going to stand guard, sir." He smiled. His voice was so high, I could tell he was excited. When his blood was up he always sounded like he could belt out a Peggy Lee song. "Go on," he said. "Go in there and change out of them state issues."

"I'm gonna eat some more bread first," I said.

"Cut me a piece of that," he said.

I cut him a piece then I cut another one for me. I looked at the old woman. "This here's mighty good bread."

I don't know. Maybe she started to smile a little. The old man said, "Thank you kindly. She makes a loaf 'most every day, but she's been so sick lately. I expect that there's pretty stale."

"It's better'n what they serve in the prison," I said. "A damn sight better." I set the bread and knife on the table and went on into the back room. The closet was tore all up and clothes was all over the floor and on the bed. I found a short-sleeved shirt—a blue cotton thing that fit me pretty good—and a pair of blue overalls. I was changing clothes as fast as I could. I heard the old man say, "Yes, sir!" real loud. Then I think he said, "Anything you say." The wife said something I couldn't hear, and the old man said, "She's just frightened is all." I was changing clothes as fast as I could, I ain't lying. I threw the yellow prison issue on the floor, then thought better of it. I didn't want to leave nothing there. I balled them up and picked up Peach's, too.

When I come out I slipped and nearly lost my balance.

"Be careful," Peach said.

The old man and woman was laying on the floor next to the stove. Peach lounged in the chair by the table, with the gun on his lap, watching them. It was blood I slipped in. Peach had slit both of them across the throat and the floor wasn't exactly level. The blood had run all the way across the room to where

I was standing. I walked around it and handed him his prison clothes.

"Oh, yeah, good thinking," Peach said. "We probably shouldn't leave nothing here."

Blood was all over the place.

"For Christ's sake," I said. I went to a small rug on the floor by the front door and wiped it off the bottom of my shoes. "Goddamn it to hell anyway."

"What's the matter with you?" he said.

"Nothing."

"It ain't nothing but the safest way to go here," he said.

"You didn't have to do that."

"Sure, I did."

"Now we're murderers."

"You ain't," he said.

"You didn't have to do that."

"Look at them," he said. "Ain't they peaceful?"

I didn't want to look at him or them nor nothing. I hated everything in sight.

Peach started going through the cupboards, getting cans and jars of food. "Take what you think you'll need," he said.

"I wish I had not done this," I said.

"You didn't do nothing."

"I wish I had not run. That's what I wish." I felt sick to the stomach, and that's no lie. I wasn't no killer and I seen enough. "I ain't no killer," I said.

He got up and stepped over the bodies. "We're gonna take the old man's car and drive all the way to California. Then you can go wherever you want to go and thank you kindly."

"I ain't going no place," I said. "No way."

"You ain't coming with me, then?" he said.

"No, I ain't."

"Where you think you're going?"

I still had my prison issues bundled in my arm. "Back out into the woods, I guess."

He seemed to think about that. I thought he might try to finish me the same way he done the old man and his wife. "I ain't going to tell nobody about this," I said. "If that's what's worrying you."

He stood there with the gun cradled under one arm. I didn't know if he'd loaded it or not, so I was afraid to move. "I'm just going on back into the woods," I said again, moving toward the door. I didn't take my eyes off him. When I opened the door, he said, "I reckon you might ought to go with me."

It never occurred to him that he was going to be running in the old man's car and the old man's clothes, and whenever they caught up to him they'd know he done it. I had a second there when I almost give up and went with him. I was finished and I knew it. What would I do now? I was wearing the old man's clothes, too.

"Now why don't you get on down there and hop in that car and we'll be off," Peach said.

"We really going to California?"

"Why not?"

I kept myself very calm. I nodded toward the knife on the counter. "Better get that," I said.

He looked at it. "Oh, right." When he turned to pick it up, I took off down the steps and into the woods as fast as I could. When I got into the trees, I only scurried a ways up the hill, then I turned into the thicket and run like a crazy man. I got all cut up. But I never heard nothing behind me. When I was sure he wasn't going to shoot me, I stopped there back in the trees to catch my breath. I couldn't see the house no more, but I thought I heard the car start up and pull down the road away from where I was standing. I don't know how long I sit there listening. Then I got up and changed back into my prison clothes. I got down on all fours and with my bare hands I dug a small hole in the damp forest floor. I covered up the clothes with black dirt and pine needles and leaves. I realized I was crying while I was doing this. I wasn't thinking about nothing, but I was crying anyway. I wished I could go back in time and start the day over again. That's all I wanted. I never wanted nothing more than to just begin that one day over again. I started the long climb back up the mountain to where I come from.

I forgot all about the goddamned blood on my shoes.

PEACH

Sonbitch run. I laughed a long time. Parchman run up the hill and gone in the trees just like a deer. Like a doe. He leaped up high, too. Goddamn I laughed. Don't understand folks. Never will. A dog is better. Sometimes I don't get it. I swear, I just don't get it.

Sonbitch flew up the hill. Every time I think about it, I start laughing.

What'd he think. I'd shoot him in the ass?

Ain't never *shot* nobody.

GAULT

This year we're going to be covering the Declaration of Independence. I'm going to devote half the year to it. By Christmas these kids will know the meaning of this country. We're going to talk about satellites in space and the Cuban thing, too.

In spite of everything that's happened, I am proud of the fact that I had a black child attending my school even before the state of Virginia was ordered to admit Negro students into white schools, "with all deliberate speed," whatever that means. What is deliberate speed, anyway? You can almost interpret the phrase any way you want. A man walking down a steep incline, at an inch every half hour, could be moving as fast as he can under the circumstances—the circumstances being that he does not want to fall. You could say that he is taking each careful step with "all deliberate speed," then, couldn't you?

Don't get me wrong. Integration is the right thing to do, I'm certain of that, but to be truthful, I have to confess that I was glad for other reasons besides philosophic ones.

At the time my school was still private—waiting for state approval—and I needed all the students I could get. I was competing with the public school down in Lebanon Church, and even all the way over beyond Quincy, on the other side of the mountain. No state or county money whatsoever. The people around here couldn't afford the normal tuition of a private school, so we just barely scraped by. I bought most of the textbooks and other materials out of my own pocket. I never did recoup those expenses. And that was a lot of money, believe me. But let's just say it was an investment, and let it go at that. I got a loan, of course, and Myra helped out. She had a small inheritance.

At any rate, I made my share of mistakes. I was wrong about having a war veteran—even if he was a hero—driving the school bus. It didn't help business, and when I realized what kind of man Morgan Tiller was, I had no compunction about firing him. He wasn't bad with the children, or undependable—I mean he showed up for work on time every morning, and he was good at taking care of the bus. But he made a lewd comment about Myra one afternoon. She came into the shed where we were working on the bus—changing the spark plugs I think—and he looked at me kind of leeringly and said, "Lovely. Just lovely," and I knew what he was thinking.

But it didn't do any real harm having Morgan Tiller as a bus driver. He didn't work for me long enough. What hurt my school, almost drove me out of education all together, was the disappearance of Terry Landon.

Nineteen fifty-four. You should have seen the uproar around here then. A lot of folks weren't happy about the fact that he was attending my school with the white children. I let Terry into the school in 1953—before the Supreme Court said anything about integration. I didn't call it integration, either. I'm not even sure if I'd heard the word yet. I just figured since the Negroes and whites worked together at the mill, and their children played baseball against each other during the yearly spring picnic and Labor Day outing, it wouldn't matter overmuch if they went to school together. I wasn't naïve—and doubtless you've probably already figured out that the increased enrollment was foremost in my mind, as I've already stipulated—but I was also conscious of the good it would do. I really was. Perhaps you have some idea how people can get when they think an age-old practice is about to be discarded.

Terry Landon was one of the most beautiful children I've ever seen. Tall for his age, with dark, smooth, almost perfect skin. His eyes were large and luminously black. You know how the lenses of a dark pair of sunglasses glisten in the sun? That's what his eyes looked like. He was a bright boy, too. The kind of child you want to work with just to see the way his face changes when he learns something new. It just makes me furious that Morgan Tiller blames his disappearance on the Gypsy Man. That boy's name didn't need to be added to the local lore, especially the way his parents took the loss.

I don't think anybody ever really gets over a thing like that. Terry wasn't there anymore—a nine-year-old boy who was so alive you couldn't picture him sitting still, or sleeping, or— well, it was hard enough for those of us who only knew him. You can imagine what it must have been like for his parents.

He was the kind of boy that defines a family, gives it character and interest and purpose.

Nobody ever figured out what happened to him, and although Sheriff Paxton keeps picking at the wound, it didn't take long for Terry to get counted among the Gypsy Man's victims. This only makes the boy a subject of conversation and superstition and keeps his name on everybody's lips. Would you want to live in a town that was constantly worrying over your lost boy? A town that admitted him into its mythology and continued to remind you every day of your loss? Can you imagine the lasting vitality of your grief and fear? But as long as Paxton keeps worrying it, as long as he keeps the wound open and festering, the boy will be on people's lips, and stories about the Gypsy Man will increase and endure. If you try to bring people to their senses about the Gypsy Man, it only appears to Paxton as if you want to steer him from his quest.

I guess that's another reason I don't really have any use for Morgan Tiller. I don't bear him ill will, but I just wish people like him would find a way to look more clearly on the world.

Of course, what I'm talking about is education.

The Landon family lived in a small, tidy little house about three miles down the southwestern side of the mountain— down toward Quincy. The nearest school for coloreds was all the way down on the eastern side in Lebanon Church. It was almost to the valley. Even so, it took a lot of persuasion to get his mother and father to let him come to my school. They said they didn't want to cause trouble.

"This is such a small town," I said. "All of the children play together at the company outings, anyway."

"That don't matter," Mrs. Landon said. Her name was Julia, and she stood fully a foot taller than her husband. She had dark skin and black glistening eyes, like her son. She always wore a white scarf around her head, and the contrast with her skin was entrancing, almost as if she understood the great difference between black and white and wanted to demonstrate it to the world.

"You know almost everybody in Crawford, anyway," I said. "What trouble could there be?"

Josh Landon, Terry's dad, looked at me as though I was crazy.

"Seriously," I said. "No one cares up in Crawford."

"You just don't know," Josh said.

"It would be a good thing," I said. "Don't you see?"

They said nothing. "Look," I went on. "It would be good not just for Terry and more convenient for you. It would be good for..." I hesitated to say it. "Good for your people."

"Lord, that's all I need," Julia said. "Do something good for my people."

"What people?" Josh said. "What people we got to worry about except ourself?"

Julia stared at me. "It would be good for our people," she said, disgustedly, shaking her head slightly. To be honest, I was astonished at my embarrassment.

"I'm sorry," I said. "I do think it would be a good thing. I truly believe that. But it would be good for me, too."

"Now we're getting somewhere," she said.

"It's the right thing to do, even if it is good for me," I said.

"How much?" Julia said. Her head was tilted slightly, and a smile played around the corners of her mouth. She regarded me as if she wasn't sure what I might do next, and she better watch for it. But her expression was also tolerant and almost affectionate.

"How much?" I said.

"What's it going to cost us?" She looked briefly at her husband and then back to me.

"Well, in the beginning," I said, "Not too much at all. If you could pay maybe, ten dollars a week?"

They looked at each other.

"You wouldn't have to make that trip over the mountain every day," I said. "And Josh makes enough money at the mill, right?"

"Ten dollars a week is a lot of money," Julia said.

She just wouldn't give in at first. I even asked the Reverend Sloan to go down there and have a talk with her, try to make her see that it would be the right thing to do. When he came back, he stopped by the house. "She's a fine woman," he said. "I expect she'll do what's best."

"You talked her into it?" I said.

"No, sir. I didn't. But she listened well enough."

Finally, Julia started to see my point of view. It might be she saw it would save them money in the long run. And maybe she, too, saw that it was time. Time for this country to wake up and be what it claimed to be. Although Dr. Martin Luther King, Jr., hadn't made himself too well-known yet, anyone with any sense could see where this country was heading, where it was bound to go. It couldn't fail: too many white people were in favor of it. And Negroes weren't going to take no for an answer anymore. Anyone could see it. They had been to war and fought and bled for this country, so they figured they had it coming.

The Landons really were such clean people. The best kind of people, colored or otherwise. He was a foreman at the mill, no less. Julia made and sold the most beautiful cloth flower arrangements you ever saw. Everyone in Crawford knew and respected them.

Now, I know there was talk when Terry came to our school. Some people objected, I suppose. We got a few unsigned letters, and one of the Crowly boys said a few things that led me to believe his parents were talking about it. I don't know exactly what he said in class, but when his teacher brought Brad Crowly to me he said, "Why do we have to go to school with that nigra?" I could have compounded the trouble, had I punished him, so I said nothing for a while. I let him sit across from me and wait for me to say something. Then I sent for Terry Landon, and when he came in I asked him to take a seat next to Brad. I told Brad to turn his chair so that it faced Terry's, and then I asked Terry to do the same. "Now, you two just look at each other for a while," I said.

I left the office and took care of some business, then came back in and sat down. They were still staring at each other, arms folded and feet planted. They weren't more than a foot apart. I think the toes of their shoes must have been touching. Then Terry started to smile. He fought it, but it was there, and when Brad noticed it, he laughed. Pretty soon, they were both laughing.

"There, you see?" I said. They both looked at me, still fighting the laughter. "You see? There's really no difference between you two but the color of Terry's skin."

"Or the color of *my* skin," Brad said.

"Well, yes. That's what I mean," I said. "Now if young Terry here is willing to go to school with you, why aren't you reasonable enough to go to school with him?"

"It's okay," he said. I think he was embarrassed that he'd said anything at all. To tell you the truth, I kept the children so busy they didn't have time to cause any trouble.

No. Most of the trouble came from parents. And it was manageable trouble mostly. I'm telling the truth. No threats of violence. No church fires or crosses burning on any lawns or anything. No dramatic withdrawals of children from school. (That was my main worry, but apparently, even having to go to school with the minions of the devil was better than having to drive to the nearest school for white children, which was all the way down past Lebanon Church, almost in the next county.) It's not really fair to call it trouble. What happened was, fewer and fewer parents participated in school activities. We had no PTA that year. The Halloween party never got off the ground. There was no Christmas pageant or play that year, and the Spring Festival was so sparsely attended we decided to cancel it after one day. I think, if you consider how it went in other parts of the South, integration would have come rather smoothly to Crawford County, if Terry Landon hadn't turned up missing.

To tell you the truth, I was very proud of the people in this community. They all turned out to help look for Terry. I remember the week he disappeared. It was cold and rainy for three or four straight days. I was driving the bus that day. This was late in the fall—a damp, misty November, Terry's second year in the school—and he came out to the bus the way he always did: running. You never saw his legs together except when he was sitting down and that wasn't often. During school hours I used to put a book in his lap and make him hold onto it just to keep him in one place and stop him from moving his feet.

He was in the third grade when it happened. He came to the bus that morning, carrying a small umbrella his mother had given him. Every morning I looked forward to seeing him come down the path from his house. I felt as if I was moving our little town into the future, beginning a correction long overdue. I never believed in segregation.

He wore a yellow raincoat. He got on the bus and went on back and sat by himself as he always did. The children left him alone and he didn't bother any of them. It was an arrangement children make between themselves—a kind of separate peace that leaves adults out of it.

Terry never showed up inside the school. Or at least I think that's what happened. I can't be sure of anything because I had some business in Quincy that morning and after I dropped the children off and parked the bus, I drove on up there. I had made an appointment to see a fellow about buying a new, smaller school bus, and I had Myra teaching my classes that day. When I got back early that afternoon, I walked into my classroom, and Terry simply wasn't there. No yellow plastic raincoat among the coats. No one in the school saw him coming in or going out. Myra said, "Was he here today?"

"Of course he was," I said. I immediately went down the hall to Miss Demera's room. She was a young woman from Ohio who taught the fourth graders that year. Marty Demera. I went to her room to see if Terry had wandered down there. Sometimes he'd go to her classroom because she had a lot of live animals in there: a squirrel, a rabbit, and even a black snake.

"He hasn't been here," Marty said.

"You haven't seen him?"

"No." She looked at me, wondering I suppose if I was testing her in some way. I expected all my teachers to be vigilant, and I'd corrected her earlier that year for letting one of the children remain in the lunchroom when lunch was over. "You really don't know where he is?" she said.

"Well, he was on the bus this morning," I said. "Did you see him come into the school?"

"No. I didn't notice him."

It was her job to stand at the door and watch the children come in. I said, "You were on door duty, right?"

"Yes, I was."

"And you didn't see him?"

She looked like she might start to cry. "I was there until all the children came in the door," she said.

"You saw them all come right from the bus."

"Yes."

"And you didn't see Terry Landon. Our one Negro student."

She just looked at me.

"Well, where could he be?" I said.

"I didn't see him."

I searched everywhere. All I can remember thinking was, "Oh, my God."

Just about everybody in Crawford joined the search in the days following that. I was among them. The sheriff, the state police, and eventually even the FBI got involved. None of us believed we'd fail.

Morgan Tiller helped in the search, too, but it was the kind of help a child gives you. He just got in the way—said he knew all the "haunts" of the Gypsy Man, and he'd be looking there. He combed the old Crawford place, crawled up and down the side of the mountain up there. Of course he never found a single thing. But he went on about how it was the Gypsy Man taking "another" child. I remember a state trooper looked at him and said, "What other child ever got taken around here?"

"The story goes that he takes children," Morgan said. "I've heard about them."

"When?" The trooper seemed as if he might lose his temper and I didn't blame him.

"I've lived around here a long time," Morgan said. "I've been hearing stories."

The trooper shook his head. "Me, too, and I don't recollect nothing like this."

"Well."

"I don't. I got no idea what in the hell you're talking about."

It was quiet for a while, then Morgan said, "It's a horrible thing, ain't it?"

The trooper put his hat on and walked away from him. Morgan kept his mouth shut after that. If you demonstrate that you know what you're talking about, and if you show Morgan that you're probably smarter than a parrot, he backs off. The trooper knew there hadn't been that sort of trouble around here in a long time, and he wasn't about to let Morgan suggest otherwise.

They never did find that little boy. The police were very hard on me and Marty for a while. Questions and questions, hour after hour—did we miss anything, was there anything we'd forgotten? Finally, Miss Demera broke down. She admitted that, while the children were filing into the building, she'd left the door for a few minutes to help one of the little boys with the metal buttons on his raincoat; that she had not been as vigilant as I had always insisted. She had not seen all the children come into the building.

Some lapses in judgment just cannot be forgiven, and although she was an excellent teacher, and the children missed her dearly, I'm sad to say I had to let Miss Demera go. She went back to Cleveland, I think, or someplace out west, away from the memory of what she had inadvertently let happen.

Terry's parents grieved implacably—it was almost as if something in their bones had turned soft and it had become difficult to stand or walk. Josh seemed to lose the capacity to smile, and grief robbed him of speech. He walked around like a man who goes on living after his own death. Eventually, Julia couldn't take it anymore. Last year, she packed her things and went home—wherever that was. Josh still works at the mill, still a foreman as far as I know. They keep him on over there because they feel sorry for him. Sometimes he'll get into his pickup truck and drive off down the road and nobody will see him for days, even weeks. Then he'll come back, unshaven, his eyes yellow and ruined, asking for a dollar so he can get some breakfast. "I been lookin' fer my son," he'd say. "Yassir, been tryin' to fine my boy."

Without Julia around to take care of it, he's let the house go all to pieces.

Like Myra says, Josh is a dead man. He died the day his son disappeared. He sure did love that little boy.

JOHN BONE

B oone," Daigle says. "You got a visitor."
"It's Bone," Parchman says. "His name is Bone."

Daigle lets a smile cross his face as he unlocks the cell door. "Whatever," he says. "Your old man's here."

I walk down the hall with him behind me. I hear his keys jangling. Yesterday we were out on the road again, and now I feel all the hours in the small of my back. I walk by cell after cell of almost white bars, with dark shadows behind them. It's quiet for this late in the morning.

In the visiting room, I take a seat at a long rectangular table. In the middle of it, running across like a Ping-Pong net is a wire mesh barrier about eight inches high. Anyone sitting on the other side can easily hand me anything they want over the barrier, but they can't slide anything across the table. Everyone, including the guards, thinks the wire net is ridiculous, but that's what separates visitors from prisoners. Guards stand at either end of the table and watch, and almost everything is taboo. So you really can't pull any funny stuff anyway.

Another guard brings my father in and then leans on the wall behind me. Daigle is by the window, watching both of us. There are no other visitors in the room. My father sits across from me, as he has almost every third Thursday of every month since I got here. He holds his gray fedora in his lap, his trembling hands resting lightly on the top of it. His hair is thin and seems soft and limp on his head, but all of it is there. His face is a little too worn-out, a little too jaundiced to look healthy, but he always seems in good spirits. I know he works very hard to sober up and get himself clean and presentable so he can make these visits. It saddens me to think of him doing that; to consider what it costs him, but I am also reluctant to tell him not to come. I know how much it would hurt him. It is also possible that I need his visits. I am sometimes happy at the beginning of a visiting week, when I realize I am going to see him.

"It's good to see you, son," he says.

I nod. I hate the guards listening to everything we say. On so many of these visits, we sit and stare at each other. I never know what to say to him, and he always tries to make small talk. Most of what he says dies in the air almost the instant it leaves his lips. He has no news of home I want to hear, and he knows nothing of my experience here. We sometimes only say hello, and then he'll talk a bit about the Washington Senators or the New York Yankees. He'll tell me what he's been doing around the house, that he's been behaving himself very well. I worry every day that he's drinking again and passing out in the house some evenings, and there's no one to wake him up and put him in bed, no one to listen to his convincing promises. Sometimes, he arrives smelling of bile or stale urine, and I feel so sorry for him. Sorry that the guards make faces when they turn to leave him sitting in front of me, sorry that he thinks he has to come here to see me once a month. Sorry that he is alone and I have let him down.

Now, after a long silence, while we just sort of stare at each other, he says, "How you been?"

I tell him I have news. I can't suppress what feels like a bit of a smile, even though I am afraid to feel anything.

"You do?" he says.

"Yes."

He waits.

"The warden thinks he can do something for me."

"Really." He only half believes me, and I can see he isn't aware of all that has happened. I tell him the story—the long haul down the mountain in a commandeered car with Mac barely breathing in the back. I tell him how me and Payne saved Mac's life, and how the warden thinks we are heroes.

I sit back when I'm done. It's the most I've said to him

since I was sentenced, so he takes awhile, sitting back in his chair looking in my eyes. I see the sun beginning to burn outside the window behind him. It's already hazy, and the distant hills are barely visible through the thickening air. My father turns the hat in his hand. His long face, smooth even where light down is beginning to show around his jaw and chin, seems always ready for a smile, as if he is anticipating the end of a long joke. His blue eyes are bright and wide, almost playful.

"So, you're a hero," he says.

"I'm surprised you didn't read it in the papers."

"It wasn't in no papers I saw."

"They got it plastered all over the walls when you first come in here. You didn't see it?"

"Oh," he says. "I seen those." He lowers his head, then looks at me. "I only glanced at it. I didn't notice it said anything about you."

"You don't believe me?"

"No. I believe you. I noticed it said something about two inmates saving a guard's life. I saw that. That was you?"

"That's what we did. Me and Payne."

He's looking in my eyes, waiting for me to continue.

"I want you to do something for me," I say.

"What?"

"You seen Penny?"

"She don't come around."

"You ain't seen her at all?"

"Not since you come here."

"You talk to her at all?"

"You said I should leave her alone," he says. "I ain't seen her." He sits back and puts the hat on the table in front of him. "I send a Christmas present every year to the little one. I don't deliver it myself."

"Keep the hat off the table, sir," Daigle says.

Dad looks up sharply, shocked that someone else has spoken. He puts the hat back on his lap, then runs his hand over the top of his head, pushing the fine gray hair back. "You told her not to wait, so I guess she ain't."

"You know anything that's going on with her?"

"I know you got a six-year-old daughter that's going to Gault's school."

I don't say anything, but he watches my face, tries to see if I'll react. I'm thinking about what it would be like to hold Penny in my arms, to smell her hair. "You ain't heard anything about her?"

"Far as I know they're both doing fine. Tory started back to school a few days ago, and she's doing just fine."

"How come you know so much about her?"

"I keep an eye on things. Folks know what's going on."

"You know if she's—if Penny's still..." I don't know how to finish the sentence. It's been six years, and I have no expectations at all. If anything I have fears, maybe. Things I don't want to know but I have to ask anyway—because if I do get a pardon or paroled, where will I go? Somewhere in the back of my thoughts, I suppose I want to know if she's been with anyone, but I won't let such thinking get into words.

"I know she's still living by herself with that aunt of hers," Dad says.

"You think you might go see her?"

He leans forward, his eyes getting brighter. "Sure. I'll go see her."

"I think I want you to tell her about this."

"All right."

"If the warden—you see what I'm thinking?"

"You might not have to be here as long as you thought?"

"I'm going to get a chance, now," I say, and instantly feel as though I've done something to ruin it. I have put the purity of my dream into words and sullied it with hope. Right away I feel lifeless and sad—as if I've thrown everything away by wishing for it. "You never know," I say. "Probably nothing will come of it."

"Well, they've got to do something, right?"

"No. They don't." I don't want him talking like that. His urgent hope makes me sick. And why should I strike Penny with this news—with this trick of expectation? As soon as I ask myself this question, I have my answer: What if she hasn't yet given herself to the future without me? What if circumstances have kept me in her scarred and clouded heart in spite of the distance and time between us? Shouldn't she know there might be at least a chance? What if she has worked very hard to rid herself of any memory of me; what if she has set herself against all possibilities right when a real possibility arises? I realize maybe I have to let her know.

"You think I should tell Penny about all this?" I say.

"Why wouldn't you?"

"I mean about the possibility I might get out early now."

"Is that what the warden said might happen?"

"He talked about a parole. About talking to the governor about what me and Payne did."

"You thinking what I'm thinking?"

"What?"

"The governor can pardon you straight away. You could be home by Christmas." He's not smiling, but I can see the thought pleases him, excites him with hope. "Goddamn son. That ain't far off."

"I don't want to get her hopes up."

"Penny's a big girl," he says. "She can stand up to more than you think."

"But if nothing's going to happen..."

"What a Christmas present that would make." Now he is smiling, and I can see he is excited. "Goddamn son," he says, and tears begin to fill his eyes.

"I'm afraid if nothing comes of this. What will that do to her?"

"You want me to go over there? See her?"

"And do what?"

"Have a talk with her. Tell her the truth."

"The truth," I say ruefully. "And what's that?"

"Just that you done something very fine, and the state may reward you for it. That you're a kind of hero." He wipes his eyes with both hands. Still, he is smiling, happier than I can remember seeing him in a long time. I realize I'm getting his hopes up, too.

"It may not happen, Dad."

"Hell, wouldn't it be a great Christmas? We could go fishing again in the spring."

"Don't talk like that. It's only a bare possibility."

He seems puzzled. Then he says, "What should I say to Penny?"

"Don't tell her nothing about pardons or paroles. Just..."

He looks into my eyes, waiting.

"Just go see her. Tell her what I—tell her what happened."

Suddenly my father stands up. "I'll do it," he says. "I'll go see her as soon as I get home." He is so excited he doesn't notice the guard who comes up behind him.

"Sir," the guard says, giving him a start.

"Good Lord. Don't creep up on a man like that." He is flustered, his blue eyes wide and indignant.

"You must sit down sir, or..."

"There's something else," I say. "Sit down."

He sets himself back in the chair, makes an effort to regain his dignity. I realize I am embarrassed for him.

"It's all right, Dad," I say.

He says nothing. I watch his fingers move a little on the brim of the hat that he holds now, absently, against his chest.

"A fellow got out of here when we... one of the inmates

got out when Mac had the heart attack," I say. "A fellow named P. J. Middleton. They call him Peach."

"You mean they let him out?"

"No, listen," I say. "This fellow escaped from the same gang. When Mac had his heart attack. Back in July."

He says nothing, looking at me.

"He's from up around Crawford. He knows I lived there."

Dad stares at me, unconsciously thrumming his fingers on the brim of the hat. He can't wait to tell Penny the news, and I'm not sure he is listening to me.

"Did you hear me?" I ask.

"Sure."

I don't know what to say to him. I feel so helpless and caged. I am hoping Peach will go to Crawford, because that is where I told Warden Buchanan he might go. But I don't want Peach anywhere near Penny and the baby.

"This is a bad fellow," I say.

"What do you want me to do?"

"Just, maybe you can watch out for her a little."

"I will."

"Don't let her know it," I say.

"I won't."

"You understand what I'm asking you?"

"Yes." He looks hard at me. "You don't have to say it."

"You need to stay sober for a while," I say.

He shakes his head and I feel as though I've stricken him. I am instantly sorry for saying what we were both thinking. But I *had* to; he is as helpless against the booze as he would be up against Peach.

I reach over the barrier and touch his arm. I see the guard move to speak, but I take my hand away.

"I'm sorry, Dad. I know you'll stay sober," I lie. "Anyway, Peach don't know about Penny and the baby."

He leans forward, waiting for me to continue. His eyes

look almost gray in the shadows of his brow, and they are so sad it makes my heart ache to look at him. My father, with all the power gone out of him. It's a thing no son should ever see.

I say, "If Peach does show up there, don't mess with him. He's dangerous."

"When I come back—in October—you want me to bring Penny?"

"No. No, don't do that. Not if..."

Neither one of us speaks for a time. Then I say, "I'd like to know what she says." I sit back and look out the high windows. I can't meet his gaze. He stares intently at me. "You know," I say. "If she's... I'd like to know what she says when you tell her."

"What am I telling her?"

"I might be getting out before... the warden said he was going to do everything in his power."

"Okay."

"Should I get her hopes up? You think that's the right thing to do?"

"You two ought to forget that goddamn promise you made on the Bible," he says, rising again.

"Sir," the guard says. "You must remain seated."

"We're done here," I say to him. Then to my father, "See what she says."

"I'll go right soon," Dad says. "Soon's I get back home." The guard puts his hand on my father's arm, turns him toward the door. "My son's a hero," Dad says to him. "Did you know?"

"We all know about the hero," the guard says. He escorts my father to the door, still gently holding his elbow.

Daigle comes over and stands next to me. "Come on, hero," he says.

I watch my father as he passes through the door, and I remember how much I have always loved him. When he puts his hat on, he looks like a younger version of himself, and he walks at a kind of jaunty pace, as though he is reporting for his first real job. He holds his head high, moving down the corridor with the steady gait of a man who knows exactly where he is going and why.

"Short visit today," Daigle says, as he follows me back to my cell.

"I guess so," I say.

"Your father's a good man to visit you so regularly."

I say nothing.

Daigle sighs as he opens the cell door for me. "You know, Boone," he says. "I really do hope the warden can do something to get you out of here."

"So do I."

He pats me on the shoulder. "I'll pray for it," he says. "I truly will."

I don't answer him. I move to the bed in my cell and sit down. Parchman sleeps on his back with his hands up behind his head. He does not hear Daigle's keys or the metallic clang of the lock on the door. I lay down and close my eyes. The bare bulb at the top of the cell, still burning as it always does at this time of day, rain or shine, seems to give off heat like a small sun. In the back of my mind, I gradually come to hear the murmuring of hope and sorrow, and not quite refusing it, I am dismayed to discover that a small inexhaustible voice in my skull, is saying *please god,* over and over again. *Please god, please god, please god.*

GAULT

Myra was always so happy to have little Tory stay for a while. She'd be grateful for the company of course, but perhaps some element of vicarious fulfillment lifted her spirits as well, as if Tory was her child, and this was how her life had gone. It couldn't be anything of which she'd be aware, but it was probably there, nonetheless. If it had been possible, if things had worked out differently, she would have made a very fine and capable mother.

This Monday morning, she makes up her mind to teach Tory how to bake an apple pie when you don't have fresh apples. She soaks dried apples in brandy and cinnamon, and then makes a light crust with just a touch of cheddar cheese. She drains the apples and then simmers them in honey and more cinnamon with a bit of nutmeg and mace. The house smells like a bakery. Tory makes the top of the piecrust, getting flour all over herself and the kitchen, but Myra doesn't mind. She's brimming with happiness the whole time. It makes me regret, again, our misfortune. Neither of us knows whose fault it is—I mean we never went to a doctor and tried to find the problem. We made the effort for a number of years, and finally, without words, or recriminations, we gave up. Or at least we gave up thinking about it.

I expect Penny will want Tory back before the day is out, but there's no way I can file the paperwork necessary to dig up where the stone was before Tuesday morning. In the bright green grass it is whiter than the stones around Myra's rose garden. When I wash it with the hose it is almost sparkling white. The grains of white rock and sand in it seem to capture a tiny fraction of the bright morning sun and then reflect it back.

Myra comes out in the middle of the baking project and asks me what I'm up to.

"Look at that," I say. I point to the stone.

"What is it?" She bends over a bit and seems to regard it suspiciously. Then she says, "Oh, you finally going to fix my border?"

"What?"

She points to the place where two of the white rocks around her rose garden are missing.

"No. This. Look at this," I say.

"You don't have to be impatient."

"I'm not." I shake my head. She looks at me, and I smile. "Look at the thing," I say.

She studies it again.

"You know what it is?" I ask.

"Yes, I see that it's a tombstone."

"Of course."

She crosses her arms and leans to the side, one leg straight and the other bent just right. In that position, her hips tilted just right, she looks beautiful to me again. "You notice something," I say.

"What?"

"Look at it."

"I am looking at it."

"There's no date of death on it."

"So?"

"Penny found it in her backyard."

She just stands there staring down at it, reading the inscription. She has flour on her hands and all over her apron. "Gone but not forgotten," she says, almost to herself.

"Penny's a bit spooked," I say.

Myra leaves the walk and comes over next to me.

"Spooked?" she says, quoting not only the word I used but the tone and accent she heard in my voice. "Listen to you."

I shrug. "I don't notice it half the time."

"You only sound like a country hick half the time."

It's quiet for a while, then she says, "What's that thing doing here?" She crosses her arms in front of her again. The air is pleasantly warm and dry, but she seems cold the way she folds her arms and holds herself.

"I don't know. I just wanted to get it away from her place. Penny was pretty upset about it."

"It's just a stone nobody needed to use."

"Well, I thought of that. Maybe the Crawfords way back had this made up for Wilbur and then they just never..."

"What do you want with it?"

"Well," I say. "I guess I'll just keep it as a kind of curiosity. I think I'd like to do some digging under where we found this."

"Digging?"

"Nothing official. I don't want to involve the county or the state. But I'm curious. Seems like there ought to be somebody who could tell us about this." I touch a corner of the stone with my shoe. "I mean, there ought to be a record of some kind about burials, or deaths, or—you know."

"That stone's so old."

"But look," I say. "It says Wilbur Crawford. Don't you think it's sort of suspicious that the town's oldest family's last surviving son wanders off into the hills and trees and is never heard from again, and then we find a tombstone with his name on it, right there in the ground that used to be one of the Crawford's orchards?"

"I don't know if it's suspicious or not. There's no date of death on it, and anyway, wasn't Wilbur born around that time? It probably is a stone they had made for him."

"It must be. He left Crawford in 1917—he'd be exactly fifty by then."

"I know," she says. "They thought he was dead, didn't they? Wasn't he gone for three or four years? Isn't that what the legend says? Maybe there's some truth to it. Maybe old man Crawford had it made and they just didn't want to admit a date of death on it..."

"It's a curiosity though, isn't it?"

She looks at me. "Are you serious?"

"What do you mean?"

"Now you sound like these people around here with their myths and superstitions."

I laugh. "I guess I do."

"So what are you up to, my dear?"

"It sure frightened Penny."

"Yes, I guess so."

I reach over and put my arm across her shoulder. "It's a mystery," I say. "That's all. I'm not falling for any myths or wondering about the Gypsy Man. It's just a mystery and I love a good mystery. I understand there's a perfectly reasonable explanation for it. I also understand that I won't ever know it, probably."

She pats my hand and I withdraw my arm and let it drop to my side. I reach in my shirt pocket, get a cigarette, and light it. There are four more in the pack so I offer one to her, but she shakes her head. "Not so early in the day."

I smoke for a while. Myra gazes toward the hill up to the Crawford place. A slight breeze moves her hair. Sweat is beginning to dampen the fine hair around her ears. She wears a light blue scarf around her neck.

"What are you going to do with it?" she says.

"I guess I'll just keep it here. Some stonemason made it. Maybe if I make a few phone calls, I can find out who it was that ordered it."

"It's a god-awful-looking thing."

"You think so?"

"All tombstones are awful looking to me."

It's quiet for a while. When I finish the cigarette I flip it out into the grass. "You know," I say. "Maybe I can get somebody to confirm whether or not there was a grave there where we found it."

Just then we hear a clatter from the house. "I'd better get

back inside," Myra says. "There's no telling what Tory has gotten into."

She starts to turn from me, but then she catches my eye. We look at each other for a time, neither of us saying anything. She is still as attractive as any woman I've ever seen. She is tall and strong and very fine, and once again I realize how lucky I am that she loves me.

"You're so good with children," I say. "With all the children."

She smiles but says nothing. I know she understands that I am once again apologizing for what we have unwillingly missed in our lives. Although, as I said, we don't know whose fault it is and don't want to know. I always believed it was me. I think she knows that.

"When our pie is done, won't you come in and have a piece?"

"Sure."

She starts to leave again, and I say, "You think I should call Sheriff Paxton about this?"

"What would he know?"

"Well, I think maybe we should do some excavating up there. See if there's a coffin or not."

"If you can get Penny to do that, what would you need Mr. Paxton for?"

"I told Penny I was going to do something about it, that's all. I'm really just thinking out loud I guess. Maybe I should call the health department."

"You could do that, too," she says. Then she turns and goes back into the house.

I sit down by the stone. I don't like the idea of waiting to find out. A part of me wants to drive back up to Penny's place and start digging with a pick and shovel.

On the other side of the mountain, high white clouds shift in the blue. It doesn't look like a hot day, but it might get to be.

Presently a pale yellow Volkswagen comes down the highway, slows at the entrance to the school, and then turns in. As it comes up the driveway, I realize it is the old Negro who runs the Sunoco station outside Lebanon Church. His name is Ambrose, and I forgot I had asked him to come up on this day and help me change the spark plugs on the school bus. He struggles to get out of his small car and then waves to me. His frameless glasses gleam in the sun, and his dull gray hair looks as though it is painted on his head. He pushes the glasses back on his nose as he approaches me. He is wearing penny loafers, light blue slacks, and a sleeveless sweatshirt. He has this lean, beatnik sort of look about him, although he's clean shaven, and when his yellow eyes glare at you through the thick lenses he looks like a wasted man, a drunk. "Good morning," he says.

"It's pretty well past morning," I tell him.

"Well, it still a good ways 'fore noon."

"I thought you'd be here around noon." I sit back down on the steps and he stands in front of me.

"I was going by and see you standing out here."

I nod, reach for another cigarette, and light it.

He seems to shrug, turns away. In all the years he's been in Lebanon Church, and he's been there since the war, he's still just Ambrose to everybody. No one knows if that's his first name or his last. But he's the best mechanic in the valley or on the mountain, and most people depend on him.

"What can I do for you?" I say.

This almost gives him a start. He says, "Oh. Well. You say you got work for me."

I puff on my cigarette, looking at him.

"So." He clasps his hands together in front of himself. "I guess I'll..."

"Look here," I say, pointing to the stone.

"What?"

"Look at the dates on it."

He leans over the stone, studying it hard.

"What do it mean?" he asks, finally.

"You tell me."

He looks at it again. "I don't know."

"I dug this up from under an old tree in Penny Bone's backyard. Just out of her yard really, on the old Crawford place," I say.

He tilts his head a bit, regarding me. The sun's gradual ascent to the top of the sky already seems to produce a kind of bright wind. The breezes are cool, but in the still air the sun begins to burn pretty steadily. Ambrose studies the stone again, waiting for me to continue. He takes a handkerchief out of his pocket and wipes his brow. At the moment there is not even a whisper of a breeze. The leaves hang from the trees like dried paper.

Behind me the door slams, and when we turn, there, coming down the walk with a tray and two glasses of cold iced tea, is Tory Bone. She walks carefully, smiling at both of us as she approaches.

"Well," I say, taking the tray from her. "What a nice surprise."

"One for you and one for me." She sits down in the grass next to the sidewalk.

"Is it okay if I give mine to our guest here?"

She looks at the Negro and then determinedly reaches for her tea. I hand mine to Ambrose. "Go ahead."

He looks at it, then at Tory, then back to me. "That's okay," he says. "I got a Thermos of cold RC in the car." He hands the glass back to me and walks down to his car to retrieve the thermos.

I turn to Tory and say, "You know what the polite thing to do was here, don't you?"

She drinks her tea, staring off at nothing.

"It's polite to offer your drink to a guest, and go back in the house and get another one for yourself, honey."

277

She stands up, almost spilling the tea.

"You don't have to do it now," I say. I throw my cigarette away. It lands near the other one and smokes in the grass. She watches it for a moment, then she says, "Yes, Mr. Gault." It sounds sarcastic, but I can't be sure. Hell, Tory is so much like her mother—and I don't mean her mother when she was Tory's age, either. I mean Penny Bone after she'd lived for a time with her husband, John. It didn't take much exposure to that young man to convert a person—especially a young and impressionable girl—into a proud and willful foe of anything that might be construed as conventional. Now Tory strolls up the walk, sipping her drink, obviously finished with me.

Ambrose comes back and sits down. "That be Tory, right?"

I look at him. "Yes."

"Penny Bone's baby girl."

"Right again."

He's smiling now, satisfied with his memory.

"You haven't worked for Penny, much," I say.

"She ain't a regular." There's a long pause, then he says, "I used to see her in with that older woman she live with. Down to the Sunoco station or over to the A&P buyin' bread for they own store."

"She dropped Tory off this morning, so it'll probably be open," I say.

He is quiet again, not looking at me. He rubs his arms, seems to find it difficult to sit still. Each time he takes a sip of his drink, he carefully puts the top back on the thermos and then sets it next to him, concentrates on getting it to sit upright by itself. I wonder if there is whiskey in it.

"Yes," he says. "I come up here 'cause you say you got some work for me."

"Maybe we'll work on the bus some other time," I say.

"Okay." He opens his thermos and takes a big gulp. When

he sees me looking at him he says, "It hot sitting out in the sun like this. It really do feel like we closer to it up here."

"Most of the time, it's colder up here than it is down below," I say.

"Yes." He seems embarrassed.

"Not that I'm contradicting you," I say. "It *does* seem hotter this morning."

He puts the cap back on the thermos, studies it as he sits it up in the grass.

"You feel like doing a little digging?" I say.

He looks at me.

"It's in the shade of a big tree. It will be cooler." I stare out at the haze forming at the foot of the valley and over the brown trees in the foothills. "It's going to get worse in the afternoon."

He is still waiting for me to go on.

"I want to prove something. About the Gypsy Man."

This registers. His face seems to lengthen a bit. He shakes his head.

"I want to dig up under where we found this stone."

"You want to dig up a grave?"

"It isn't a grave," I say. "That's what I want to prove."

"Really? Who does you want to prove it to?"

"We'll just go up there and dig for a while. We'll be on a mission, you and I."

He seems puzzled.

"A mission to put an end to at least one superstition."

"Not the kind of mission I be interested in."

"Come on," I say. "You said you needed the work. I'll pay you, same as if you worked on the bus."

"But digging in the dirt? I do mechanical work. Not hard labor."

"Come on. We've had so much rain lately the ground will be good and soft," I say. "Besides, I'll do most of the digging."

I can see he doesn't believe me, but he needs the money. He comes along anyway. He talks to me while I get the pick and shovel out of the shed in back of the house. I hand him the pick and he walks next to me, muttering to himself. "Is I going to be digging up a grave? Hell, no. Is I going to be digging up around a grave? Hell, no. Is I going to be digging up where a grave used to be? Hell, no. Is I going to get paid for goin' up there with you, whether or not I does any digging? Hell, yes."

"I'll pay you," I say. "Don't worry."

MORGAN

I see them coming up the walk, carrying shovels and a pickax. Penny is just getting ready to go on down the hill and open the store. She stands in front of a small wall mirror in the hallway between her bedroom and Clare's, brushing her hair. I woke up with an ache in the small of my back like a bone broke, and my mouth so dry it's hard to move my tongue in it. I stagger over to the open front door. "Lookee here," I say.

Clare sets at the kitchen table, smoking a cigarette and sipping coffee. I don't think she noticed me get up. Likely I startled her, but she puts the cup down and calmly moves from her seat. "What are you going on about?" she says.

Gault steps up onto the porch, starts for the door, then notices me standing there behind the screen.

"Well," he says. "Good morning."

"Morning."

"What are you doing here this early?"

"I stayed here last night."

"You did?"

"My place smells of smoke. It's all tore up while they're a-fixing it."

He don't say nothing. The nigra nods my way.

"Penny," I say, turning to her, "you got company."

She comes to the door. "I was just about to go down and open up," she says.

Gault stands there smiling. The nigra puts his foot on the bottom step, sets the pickax down, and leans on it.

"What do you want?" Penny says.

Gault removes his hat. Sweat has collected all around the top of his skull, and his hair is all twisted and matted down. "Remember I said I was going to get somebody up here to have a look at the grave out yonder?"

"So you get ... ?" She don't finish the sentence.

"This is Ambrose," Gault says. "You know him, don't you? Runs the gas station ..."

"I know him."

The nigra don't say a thing. He don't even look at Penny. He may as well be a grave digger the way he looks a leaning on that pickax. He's a damn beanpole, bent over at the top like a sunflower.

"I'm quite certain it's not a grave," Gault says.

"What would that prove?" Penny says.

"Well, that the Gypsy Man is ..." He stops.

Penny says, "If it ain't a body there, then the Gypsy Man is what?"

Ambrose looks up for just a second, then back down. "I ain't working 'round no ghost," he says.

"It ain't no ghost I'm worried about," Penny says.

"It's a mystery," Gault says. "Don't you want to know it?"

I pull my suspenders up over my shoulders. The ache in my back feels like a saw, a cutting through me. I don't want to stand up no more. Penny looks at me, then at Ambrose. "You studying the Gypsy Man?"

He frowns. "No ma'am."

"He's going to help me dig up whatever's buried under that

tree back there," Gault says. "You remember? I said I was going to bring..."

"You said you'd bring some 'official' up here. You didn't say it was no mechanic, and you didn't say you was going to dig up my yard."

"I ain't digging around no grave," Ambrose says.

"Well, now, strictly speaking, it isn't really in your yard, is it?" Gault says.

"It's close enough you'll make a mess if you start digging holes," Penny says.

"You want to know what's there, don't you?" Gault says. "We'll put everything back neat as you please when we finish."

Penny leans against the doorjamb, her hands in the back pockets of her jeans. Ambrose puts his foot down and hefts the pickax up over his shoulder. "To tell you the truth," he says. "It's awful hot out here, and if you doesn't want us to be digging just now, I understands."

Gault turns around and looks at him.

Penny says, "Where's Tory?"

Gault faces her again, with that smile on his face. "Why, she's making an apple pie with Myra and having the time of her life."

I open the screen door and Gault steps back. He takes hold of the door as I walk out on the porch and set myself in the wooden rocker there. "What you think you going to find?" I say.

Gault don't look at me. He lets the door close slow and gentle so it don't slam. He almost whispers to Penny, "Did you tell him what we found out there?"

"I know all about it," I say.

"Well, maybe you'd want to help us," he says.

"Go ahead," Penny says. "But it better look exactly the way you found it when you get done."

"We'll fill any hole we dig, and pat it down nice and smooth," Gault says.

So they walk back to the corner of the yard and start. Ambrose lets Gault swing a pickax for a while, but he don't make no progress. Finally Gault says, "Why don't you give it a try?"

Ambrose shakes his head. "No, sir. I ain't."

"Well, what'd you come up here for?"

"Well, I don't know," he says.

"Here," Gault says. "Just dig for a while. If we get deep enough you got to worry, I'll take over."

Ambrose don't want to, but he takes the pickax and starts using it. He's not much use, though. He's an old man, and he don't have the strength no more. He don't exactly pound the dirt with the pickax. He keeps dropping the thing down like he don't have the strength to hold it up. But it breaks up the soft earth there, and Gault shovels it out for him. At first it's heavy work because the ground's so wet and a single shovelful of it likely weighs thirty pounds or so. But then they get down to dry dirt and it starts to go more smoothly. I watch from the back porch, setting in a chair from Penny's kitchen. Gault finally just takes over, and he digs for more than an hour. He keeps looking over at me, wiping his brow, drinking water Penny fetches him. Ambrose don't do nothing now, except when Gault gets down in the hole to shovel the dirt out. He helps move the dirt out of the way when Gault throws it up out of the hole. But you can see Ambrose is scared. The whites of his eyes show like stones, and he's ready to take off if he has to. Gault keeps staring over at me. Finally he hollers, "You want to join in here?"

"What for?" I yell.

"This is pretty heavy work."

"I'm possessed of good sense," I say. "And I'm too old."

I sip a little whiskey and branch that Clare makes for me. I think she is drinking the whiskey without water, but she don't stay outside very long.

"I'm going in," she says. "The sun's just too bright out here."

It's cool in the shade of the porch, but I can see the heat is beginning to get to Gault. Sweat darkens his hair and runs down the sides of his face and soaks through his shirt. Nobody says nothing for a long time.

I am about to get up and go on back in the house when Gault hits something with the ax. It makes a dull thud, and everybody stops moving for a second.

"We hit something," Gault says.

Ambrose drops the pickax and starts walking back toward the house. He don't make a sound.

"Where you going?" I ask.

He stops, turns back toward the hole.

Gault scrambles out of the ditch and gets the shovel. He lets himself back down and starts digging. He's in a hurry. The hole is deep enough I can only see the tops of his shoulders, and when he bends down and starts digging with his hands, he disappears altogether. I am surprised he could make a hole so deep in the side of the mountain. He ain't even hit a rock yet.

I set my cup down, get up, and walk over there.

"See?" Gault says, out of breath, talking to nobody in particular. "The tree's roots have made a little cavelike opening in the mountain here, in the dirt and all."

"We be committin' a sin if you in a grave," Ambrose says.

Gault says, "See how the roots are here? You can just keep digging down, into earth. We're in the lee of a big stone." Now he gets down on all fours, scraping at the dirt with his hands.

"Well," he says. "It's a casket all right. A wooden one."

"That ain't deep enough for no grave," I say.

"Well," he says, all out of breath, still digging. "It's a box. And it's a wooden one. I don't know how big it is."

He stops and wipes his brow. He looks at Ambrose, who stands back from the hole, still ready to run. "If this is a grave, it might be illegal to go any further," Gault says. Ambrose don't say nothing. He just stands there, looking down at the rotted wood in the bottom of the hole. Gault sets back on his haunches, his dirt-caked hands resting on his thighs and soiling his blue pants.

Penny comes out to look at it. Clare is with her. The old girl has another cup of the whiskey and she smiles at me and says, "Good morning," like she is seeing me for the first time.

"We got a grave here," I say. "What do you think of that?"

Penny steps up to the edge of the hole and looks down in it. "Good Lord," she says.

"What do you want us to do?" Gault says.

"I got to be going on back down to the station," Ambrose says.

Gault commences to scraping the top of it again, clearing dirt away around the edges. "I don't think we should open that thing if there's a body in there," he says.

"Mr. Gault," Ambrose says. "I got to be going now. You can pay me later."

Gault stops what he's doing and stands up. He throws the shovel on the ground next to the hole and then climbs out himself. He lifts the tail of his shirt up and wipes his face with it. Nobody says nothing for the longest time.

"Well," Clare says. "It ain't no business of ours." She is wearing a white robe and white slippers. Her black hair has got streaks of gray starting to show at the roots, and it is piled up on top of her head now, but still, without the makeup she looks like she might of been the one that crawled up out of that coffin.

"What ain't?" I say.

"Who's laid out there." She points at it. "I'd call Sheriff Paxton. Let him figure out what to do with it."

"That might be a good idea," Gault says.

"It's a wonder it don't smell," I say.

Gault smiles at me in his superior way and says, "It wouldn't smell after all this time. All I smelled down there was dirt."

"Well, you open it," I say. "Then tell me what you smell."

"I think I'll just call the sheriff," Penny says. I look at her. She's been quiet for a pretty long spell, but I can't figure out what's working in her. She looks calm—as though we been talking about what to do with clothing hanging on a line. "That's what I'm gonna do. I'm gonna call the sheriff."

"Do that," Gault says. Then to me he says, "You know this is probably the grave of Wilbur Crawford, don't you?"

"You don't say."

"Maybe he didn't wander off like everybody says."

"What'd he do?" I say. "Bury his self?"

Penny turns to go back in the house.

"Maybe it's his grave," I say. "Maybe not. I bet he ain't in it."

Gault shakes his head.

Clare says, "How can it be Wilbur's grave?"

"It ain't for sure that it's a grave at all," I say.

SHERIFF PAXTON

The last thing I want to do, on any kind of day, is open a wooden casket that's been underground for nobody knows how long. As a matter of fact, the last thing I want to do is open a casket of *any* kind—even a new one that don't have a permanent resident yet. The sight of a coffin is repugnant to me, pure and simple. It makes me recoil, if you want to know the truth. So here I am, on a clear, very warm Monday, a holiday, thank you kindly, all the way at the top of the mountain again, standing over what looks like an open grave.

"You still got Penny's gun?" Tiller says.

"I do. And I'm going to keep it for a while."

He makes this sound in the back of his throat. Then he says, quietlike, like it's a secret between me and him, "This here ain't deep enough to be a grave."

I say, "It looks like I should've confiscated that dad-burned pick and shovel, too."

"I didn't do this," he says.

I shake my head. Gault says, "Don't you think it's important to find out what's here?"

"Why?" I say.

He don't answer me. He just looks at me.

"Why?" I say again.

"Well...," he says. He can't think of nothing. He's a college-educated man. A lawyer, a judge, a teacher and he can't think of nothing.

"You ain't got no reason, do you?"

"There was a stone here. Penny found it."

"A stone."

"Yes. It had Wilbur Crawford's name on it. It was a gravestone."

"And you felt like you wanted to dig it up."

He shakes his head, as if he's just as disgusted with himself as I am.

"I know," I say. "Why don't you go on down to Arlington Cemetery and do some investigating there, too? Bound to be some caskets buried down there."

"This was just about in Penny's backyard," Gault says.

"Well, that explains why everybody, including this here damn nigra—excuse me Ambrose—is out here digging."

Gault says, "If you saw the tombstone that was buried here, you'd want to dig it up, too."

"No, I wouldn't," I say. "You got to have papers to do this sort of *investigating*."

"Papers," Gault says.

"You might be a teacher in that all-fired school of yours, and you might think you know the law as well as you pretend when you set in that flower shop down yonder and give tickets to speeders and such, but you really don't."

"What papers?"

"From a real judge?" Clare says.

"From *some* authority. Hell, I don't know," I say. "Nobody never done nothing like this since I been sheriff. I don't have no idea what laws you broke. I mean I can't name them nor nothing like that. But you gotta have a court order to exhume a body. I know that. And you ought to know it, too. You broke the law here, and it's my job to apprehend lawbreakers."

They all get real quiet when I say that. Then Morgan Tiller says, "So, now we're all about to be arrested."

"I don't rightly know what I'm supposed to do here," I say. "I ain't never been up against the problem."

"Why don't you have them just cover it up again," Tiller says.

"No," Penny says. "I don't want it there."

"I swear to God you people beat all," I say.

Penny looks at me.

"Any of you all been to church lately?" I say. It's quiet. I can hear the birds singing way down the mountain. Nobody says nothing. Penny is still eyeing me. "Yesterday was Sunday, you see. And today's a holiday, ain't it? A holiday. And you all ought to find someplace to kneel down and pray. You ought to be in the front row, by God. Instead of robbing a damned grave."

Gault lights a cigarette and puffs on it, slowly shaking his head. Since I told them they broke the law, they're all kind of waiting to see what I'll do. Finally Penny says, "Can't you please do something about this?"

"What you want me to do?"

She shuts up. She don't know, neither.

"You know, if you hadn't dug it up, we wouldn't have the problem," I say.

"Well, but we *have* dug it up," she says.

"Why don't you *un*dig it," I say.

She has no answer for that.

"Why don't you folks just cover the damn thing back up and forget about it?"

Gault comes around the hole and puts his arm over her shoulders. "Come on," he says. "We'll figure out what to do here. Don't get yourself upset."

"She ain't upset," Tiller says, but to tell the truth, she looks like she's about to throw a conniption fit.

I walk over to the side of the hole and study the box. There ain't no writing on it. It's only partially uncovered—the top half probably. The dirt is pretty well cleared off it, but I can see a lot of it has begun to seep into the grain and seams of the wood. It's an old grave all right, if that's what it is. I pick up the shovel and reach it down to catch the edge of the lid, then I lever it a bit to see if it will move. The lid comes up a crack, and I realize I'm either opening the top half of the casket, or the box ain't long enough to be a casket. I think I hear a rush of air escape from the box, but none of the dirt moves.

"It's already open," I say. "Any of you do that?"

All of them come to look over the edge. "We didn't do anything but scrape the dirt off it," Gault says. "Maybe I hit it with the pickax."

I look at Gault. He's covered with sweat, and his pants have dark patches on the knees. He looks like he's ashamed of what he done now, like he knows he's a better class of person—you wouldn't expect to see his type standing here with a pickax and the soil of a grave on his hands and knees. Like he don't know how he got here.

"You was digging in here, too?" I say to Ambrose.

He nods.

"I reckon you stirred up enough trouble around here, what do you think?"

"It ain't true," he says. "This wasn't none of my idea..."

"Well, but it's trouble though. Ain't it?"

He looks at Gault, then at the others and keeps his mouth shut.

"What the hell you doing all the way up here, anyhow?"

"Mister Gault say he got work for me," he says. "And he say he pay me, too. No matter what. He promise he pay me."

"I'll pay you," Gault says.

"Well, you did some work, by God, didn't you?" I say.

"It don't matter," Clare says.

Gault says, "We might as well see what we have here."

I look at Clare, but she don't even glance my way. She just gazes at the hole in the ground.

Nobody says nothing.

Sweat runs down my neck. All I can hear is everybody breathing and the birds and insects chattering in the woods. The lid looks like it will swing open if I just push on it a little bit with the tip of the shovel.

"You want me to open it?" I say.

"Go ahead," Gault says.

At the same time, Penny and Tiller say, "No. Don't."

I look at them. "What you want me to do? Lift the box out of there and put it in the trunk of my car?"

"The box would probably fall apart if we tried to lift it," Gault says.

"It ain't going to fit in the trunk of no car neither," I say.

"Of course," Gault says.

Then I go ahead and lift the tip of the shovel. The lid comes up some and I push the shovel further under it. "Here goes," I say. I take it slow so the wood don't break up. It's really rotted and soft. I raise the lid straight up and the hinges creak like an old door. It really is spooky.

"I'll be goddamned," I say.

The damn thing is empty. At the bottom of it is just a rumpled old rag covered in black dirt and nothing else. I take the shovel and move the rotted cloth around.

"What *is* that?" Gault says.

"It ain't nothing," I say. "It's just a pile of old cloth." I try to lift it with the tip end of the shovel, but it falls off. I turn it over. "It's just an old sack." There's a drawstring on the tattered end of it. "Just a damn sack of some kind." I hear a sound come from Penny, like she's holding in some sort of pain. She's looking hard at Morgan Tiller.

"Well," Gault says. "I guess it isn't a grave after all."

"Not unless a midget was buried here," I say. "This here box is too small for a casket."

Penny turns and goes back toward the house. Tiller follows on behind her, moving more slowly—as if he is afraid he might fall crossing the lumpy grass. He shakes his head as he moves.

"I guess you ain't broken no law here," I say. "It's a good thing." I try to lift the sack with the tip of the shovel, and it seems to come apart. It ain't empty after all.

"Look," Gault says. "Is that what I think it is?"

"Yessir," I say. "It's a right smart pile of money." The bills are clean and wrapped with some kind of white paper, but it's a stack of them. I hand the shovel to Gault. "Hold this here," I say. I let myself down onto the edge of the box, balance myself, and lean down to pick up the money. I get most of it in the first try and put it on the ground next to the hole. I drop down into box itself and scrape up the rest of it. Then I reach down and feel all around the box. It's only about four foot long.

Gault is going through the money when I climb out. "There's papers here, too," he says. "Notes with writing on it."

"Just put them down there," I say. "I'll take care of it."

"It could be..." He stops.

"Look," I say when I'm standing up again. "Why don't you take this here shovel and fix this mess you made in her yard."

Gault says, "Why would anybody just bury a bagful of money and then put a stone over it?"

"It ain't no grave," I say. "It's just money buried in a box. You've heard of that, ain't you? Folks been up here digging up this old place for as long as I can remember."

He stands there looking at it.

"I guess that explains why there was no date of death on the stone," Gault says. He reaches down with the edge of the shovel and closes the lid of the box.

"What stone?" I ask.

"The gravestone that was in the ground over this hole. Have you been listening?"

"I been listening," I say. "I'm about to do some talking."

Penny comes back out with Tiller still following her. He's saying something to her as they walk. When she gets to us, she says to Gault, "You put the dirt back in that hole."

"Look here," I say. I kick at the pile of money and paper with the toe of my shoe.

"What's that?" she says, but then I see she figures it out. "Where'd that come from?"

"It was in the box."

"It's yours, Penny," Gault says.

"No it ain't," I say. "We don't know exactly who it belongs to."

"It's on my property."

"This here's your property?"

"Well, it's right on the edge of it," she says.

"That don't count." I turn to Clare. "Go get me something to put all this in, will you?"

Nobody says nothing for a long time. Clare comes back out and hands me a large paper bag. "Thank you kindly," I say.

Morgan Tiller says, "It's the Gypsy Man's box. His stone was above it. And I guess it's the Gypsy Man's money."

"It ain't nothing to find out who it belongs to," I say. I kneel down and start gathering the money and papers. "These here papers will tell the tale, I expect."

"He's out there," Tiller says. "And now maybe he knows what we done."

I put the money and papers into the bag gently, then I fold the top of it. I can't wait to sit down by myself and read what is on them papers. As I'm about to stand up, I look down in the hole again, and I notice something yellow sticking out of the dirt in the side of the hole. "What's that?"

"What?" Gault says.

"That yellow thing right there. It ain't buried half as deep."

"You want us to dig that up?" Gault says.

I turn to leave. "It ain't no grave," I say. "You want to dig up her yard some more, go ahead." I go to the squad car and put the bag on the front seat, but I don't leave. I turn and see Gault down in the hole, digging again. It's a wonder the lid of the empty box supports him. I walk back up there. I watch Gault with the shovel, chipping at the dirt in the side of the hole. The shovel is too long, so he can't get it to work right.

"It's too much of an angle," he says. "I need a shorter-handled shovel."

"Don't," Penny says, "Leave it alone."

"Wait a minute," Gault says. He is breathing hard, leaning against the side of the hole, chipping the dirt in front of him away with the shovel. It is more cloth. He uncovers it, slowly, and dirt falls onto the lid of the empty box in the bottom of the hole. The dirt makes a hollow sound that echoes like a fist on a closed casket. You dig a hole deep enough, and shape it right, and put a box in it, empty or no, and it sure is spooky, even if there ain't no body in the box.

I turn to leave, but Gault hits something while he's digging, and then he bends down and pulls on the yellow cloth. Dirt falls away from it. A strange minute passes, while Gault pulls on the cloth, and then I realize it ain't cloth at all but a kind of plastic or rubber.

"My God," Gault says.

Beneath the dirt, I see long white splinters of wood. The yellow rubber is a raincoat.

It's real quiet. Everybody stares at me.

Gault leans back and sets the shovel against the side of the hole.

I hunker down to get a closer look. Gault has a kind of shocked horror on his face.

"What?" I say.

Then I realize it ain't wood all scattered there in the brown dirt. It's a small collection of shattered, white bones.

I think I can hear the insects breathing. Gault shakes his head. He don't look like he can get the kind of air he needs; his skin is as pale as an October moon, and his hands start to shake. "Is that what I think it is?"

"Yep," I say. "Likely, this here's what's left of the Landon boy."

BOOK IV

CLARE

The last time I seen Penny's daddy he was standing in front of the house, where the sidewalk breaks up in the grass, and he had a green pack slung over his back, his service cap tilted back on his head, and a look on his face so sad it like to broke my heart.

"I'll be back," he says. "I know I will."

I believed him. I'm not a Baptist or a Church a Christer or a Methodist, or nothing like that. I don't visit the good reverend's church very religiously, if you know what I mean. Growing up I was a good Catholic girl, and I give that up once I was grown. But something in the sunlight made me feel like the Lord was with us, witness and protector, so it pleased me at the time to realize that I believed and expected that God would surely abide by what we was hoping. You know what I mean? Like the Lord was listening and would see to our needing and hoping. It was an absolutely beautiful morning in the spring: cloudless with a bright, clean sun, and the air moving tenderly, warm and soft, fragrant with honeysuckle, wildflowers, and mountain laurel. One of those days that just means peace and walking along under trees on shade-splashed lawns, and ain't nothing unholy in the world. My brother stood tall, his spotless uniform starched and pressed, his short hair combed, his boots glistening black. But he was going off to war.

I come down the steps and walked out to where he stood in

the yard. Penny was upstairs asleep still. "Why don't you wake her before you go and say good-bye," I said.

"I said good-bye last night," he whispered. His voice broke. "I can't. I just can't right now. I don't want my daughter to see me like this." It was quiet for a spell. We stared at each other for what seemed like the longest time, then he smiled half-heartedly, tears in his eyes, and said, "Besides, if I saw her face right now, I don't think I could leave."

"It's some country that'll take a father away from his children so he can go off to be shot at."

"I'm going to shoot back," he said, not looking at me.

"I never could have had a better brother," I said.

He said nothing.

I touched the smooth sleeve of his uniform. "You know I'll miss you, too."

"Just being away in training was bad enough. I didn't think this would happen so fast." He tried to force a smile. "I'll dig the deepest foxholes, and I'll do what I'm told. I'm coming back." He hugged me tight. Then he turned and walked down to the bottom of the hill where two other boys from Crawford was waiting for him in a black Ford sedan. I seen him lean over to get in the car, and he extended his arm and waved. I waved back, just as his arm drawn back into the car, and then he was gone.

I never seen him again. He was killed somewhere in France.

Since that day—no, since that morning—the world is mostly just cold, empty, and dark, like a dried-up well.

I done the best I could with Penny and the store and all. I thought maybe we would get to someplace where we'd feel like a peaceful spring morning again—like there was something tender in the world after all, even if it was only a skittish breeze.

Now, I don't know what I should be doing with myself. This thing, this evil thing. The whole time Gault and that nigra was digging up the ground I couldn't get the sight of my brother's boots out of my mind. The way they glistened in the dirt and sparse grass under that gentle sun. I would sometimes walk out in the backyard and stand under that tree and think about the last time I touched him. I had this yard in my mind as the spot on earth where he left this world, and some nights, when the sky was bruised and sinking into night, I'd stand there under the tree down yonder and think of him. He was the only man I ever known that I trusted.

How can I ever stand under that tree again? That's what I keep asking myself. Now there's a mystery underneath, a kind of temple in my heart, a place that over the years I come to think of as sacred. Now there's bones there, the bones of a child.

When Paxton got to his knees and pulled the rest of that yellow raincoat out of the dirt, something in my stomach seemed to bubble and perk. I had to breathe deep just to keep my head up. If I'd had any whiskey left I'd of finished it that very minute.

I sit on the top step of the back porch and wait for the state police. I watch Gault and Ambrose staring off into space. Gault is soaked in sweat, and he sits on the high pile of brown dirt he created when he dug the hole. Ambrose stands next to him. He looks like he might start to cry or fall asleep. His yellow eyes sag under thick brows. He smokes a cigarette, not looking at anybody if he can help it. The dirt is damp and clotted next to the long scar they've made in the ground. Nobody speaks much. Finally Gault says, "What would cause a family to bury a goddamned gunnysack full of money in a pine box and then put a gravestone over it?"

Ambrose shakes his gray head, but he don't say nothing.

Morgan says, "Likely that's a sure way to keep folks from digging around there."

Gault looks at him.

"If'n I was going to bury treasure, I'd put it under a tombstone, myself."

There's a long silence again. Gault takes a deep breath, then shifts himself nervously. "This is a terrible thing," he says. He almost gasps it. He isn't talking to nobody, but he can't sit still. He wants to calm himself down, but his mind won't leave him alone. I think he is trying not to cry. "Terry was a good boy," he says, quietly, shaking his head. He flips his cigarette out into the grass. "Jesus. I brought him into my school."

Sheriff Paxton comes back up from his car where he's been on the radio. "How do you suppose that boy's body ended up down yonder, Miss Clare?" he says.

"What?"

"You know what." He points at the smaller, shallow grave. I just stare at him.

"Six years is a long time," Paxton says. "Maybe you'll remember something before long."

"What do you mean by that?"

"I'm just telling you, they'll be questions. That's all."

Penny comes out and sits down next to me. When I look into her eyes, I can tell she's been crying her own self.

Gault lights another cigarette. Then he whispers something to Ambrose and they both come across the yard and approach the porch. "I should call Myra," Gault says. He steps on past me and goes into the house, and Ambrose stands there for a moment, then I say, "Why don't you sit down?" He nods his head, glances at Penny, then sits down on the bottom step below me.

Penny looks hard at me, but I don't want to face her. Finally I turn slightly and say, "What?"

"What are you going to do?"

"There's nothing to do, honey," I say. I brush my hair back, then rest the palm of my hand on my forehead. This always calms me. When I was younger, it made me think of God's hands. "We'll wait for the state police."

"What are we going to do about Tory?"

"What do you mean?"

"I can't bring her back here. To this." She points at the grave.

I reach back and put my arm over her shoulder. "Once the police are done here, they'll—then they'll..." I realize I am fighting back tears and I can't finish what I want to say.

"They'll what?" Penny says.

"They'll take it all away, and then we can put the dirt back and just go on."

"How did it get there?"

I look at her. "Honey, how would I know that?"

"Well, *somebody* knows."

"Yes, they do." I let go of her and turn away. She's upset, so I decide to leave her be. I really need a drink.

Paxton comes closer, leaning down in front of Penny.

"When was the last time you seen John?" he asks.

"I don't see him no more. I divorced him."

"No, you didn't."

"We swore on the Bible," she says. "It don't matter about the law. We're divorced."

"Before he got sent away though. You remember when that was?"

Penny straightens up and sets her chin toward him. "Why you want to know that?"

"Wasn't it four or five years ago?"

"He was sent away exactly six years ago," I say. "You know it, too."

"Well, Miss Clare," he says to me. "You were here then, too. What do you remember?"

"Nothing," I say.

"I wonder where John was when the little Landon boy disappeared?"

"It wasn't him," Penny says. "No way was it him."

"Still," Paxton says. "I wonder if he was in custody and all when this happened. I can't recollect. Can you?"

Penny ignores him. He leans over even closer, speaking in a very gentle voice. "I really can't recollect. I ain't looking to agitate nobody here, but it would help if I knew just what John was up to, and where he was when all this here happened."

Penny won't look at him.

He gestures toward the grave. "Maybe John knows something about all this."

Penny shakes her head. I look at Paxton. "Why don't you leave it alone?"

"It's right here," Paxton says. "Almost at your back door. Folks are going to wonder just how in heaven's name such a thing could happen, and you don't know nothing about it."

"John was here," I say. "He helped look for the boy, every night. You know it, too."

"That's right," Paxton says. "I remember it now. It all comes back to me."

"He hadn't gone to trial yet," Penny says. Her voice is so soft, it sounds like she's coming back from death. "But he was with me."

"Here?" Paxton says.

"Yes."

"So, how do you suppose anybody dug a hole over yonder and you and him don't know about it?"

Gault comes back outside. Ambrose gets up and brushes his pants off. He looks scared. The sun goes behind a cloud, and we're all in shadow for a spell, but then a hot breeze seems to come from where the sun has gone, and the cloud starts to slowly scatter. Nobody can look at nobody else, nor can none of us look at the grave or the yellow raincoat with the white bones in it. After a while, we're all standing in the yard, as though tethered to the little white hand bones that glisten in the bright sun.

When the state police arrive, they very carefully lift each bone, each fragment of clothing, and place it in its own small, clear plastic bag.

Penny is still crying.

I feel like God's been killed and whatever got him is coming our way.

JOHN BONE

The warden isn't smiling. "Sit down," he says. I can't read anything in his expression.

I take a chair across from his desk. He stands by the window, looking out. He turns and nods at Daigle who quietly gets up and steps out. The warden and I are alone.

My heart sputters like a choking motor. I wait. I have hoped and prayed for this moment so long I am afraid of it. I've dreamed of nothing else since we drove that young girl's car down the mountain and deposited McCarthy in the Charlottesville hospital. They have already reduced Payne's sentence to ten years. That means he'll get out on parole in only a year. He killed somebody to get in here, the same way I did. Manslaughter. It was an accident. On the next visiting day, when my father comes to visit, I will hear news of Penny. That is the only other thing in the future that I can think about. I don't want to make words for what I am hoping for, but right this second, the future is like a great, predatory animal, lolling before me in the sun, beginning to stretch and wake, with hungry, pitiless eyes staring blankly at me. It might swallow me, but then again, it might not. Warden Buchanan has his back to me. He gazes out the window in silence. I wait for him to say it. I wish he would just say something. I start to speak, but he turns and looks at me.

"John," he says. "I don't have good news."

Everything seems to freeze. My eyes burn, and I smell a pencil eraser, ballpoint ink, and fresh paper. His whole office seems to constrict on me.

The warden's head is bowed slightly as he moves to sit at his desk, but he looks at me through his brows. It's like he's ashamed. His glance is almost furtive, but it is expectant, too. Like he expects me to react in some way he has earlier predicted, and he is waiting for it. He picks up a piece of paper.

"It's like this," he says. "The governor said no. Plain and simple."

"But I don't understand. I was . . ."

He raises his hand. "It don't look good for parole, neither. This hijacking—I prefer to call it 'commandeering'—of the car, that girl's car—well, it's getting to be pretty embarrassing."

"I saved Mac's life. We saved his life."

"I know. I know."

It's quiet for a while, then he says, "And I will admire you to the end of my days for it, too."

I don't say anything, but I'm thinking about how much good that will do me.

"I truly will, John."

I nod.

"But another problem's cropped up."

"What's that?"

"Seems there was a boy missing up there where you lived before you came here."

"The Landon boy. I know about it."

"What do you know?"

"That he was missing."

"That's all you know?"

"I helped look for him."

"You don't know nothing else about it?"

"No, I don't."

"Well," he sits back. "They found him. Or what was left of him."

I don't know what to say. After a short spell, while the warden watches my face, I say, "What do you mean, 'what was left of him'?"

"John, it's a bad deal all around. They found his body on your property—buried right behind your house."

"I didn't have nothing to do with it," I say. "I didn't kill him."

"No, I don't expect you did. But they're going to be looking into it—and well, you see the governor'd have a hell of a time if he was to—you can see the problem, can't you?"

"I can't believe it," I say.

"They're going to want to talk to you and all."

I shake my head. "How'd they find it?"

"Did you say you knew the boy?"

"I was there when—he went to the same school I did."

"I'm sure you can straighten it all out eventually, but until then..."

I look at him.

"You can see my hands are tied."

"I guess so."

"What you did, though—saving Mac's life. That's a right definite accomplishment, and we all sure do thank you for it."

I don't say anything.

"I'm sure you'll be hearing from Mac, once he recovers. He's going to retire, you know."

Still, I remain silent. I just stare at him. I'm thinking of the Landon boy and where they found him. The whole world is getting ready to swallow me, and I know I have to stay calm and think. I have to be ready for it.

"Now I know what you're thinking," he says. "Maybe it woulda been better if you just run on down the road like those other fellas."

"I ain't thinking about that," I say.

"Well, I still think you should be rewarded somehow. And that's what I said to the governor. He wanted to know when your first parole hearing was."

"It's a long way off," I say.

"I told him that. It'll be too long. The governor won't be in office no more by the time it rolls around."

"So," I say. "That's it?"

"John, I was on the phone with him all day. Yesterday and today. He just won't budge."

I try to smile at him. My mind is already moving toward the deadened emptiness I always need to get from morning to night in this place, a kind of dumb animal resolve to blink and squint my way through all experience, like something driven by genetics alone.

"The whole thing's getting to be kind of embarrassing to him. That girl's parents are suing the state, you know."

"No. I didn't know."

"Ain't that the damnedest thing you ever heard of?"

"I don't think she's behind it," I say.

"No. Probably not. But you see what the governor is dealing with here?"

"I don't know."

"It's something he just didn't feel comfortable about, what with this new investigation and the lawsuit and all."

Again, I say nothing.

"He's already taking some heat from his own party for reducing Payne's sentence."

"But if he did something for Payne. That's what I don't get."

"It ain't fair, is it?"

"No, sir. It ain't."

"He did what he did for Payne before the lawsuit, you see. We didn't find out about the lawsuit until three days ago. And that sheriff up in Lebanon Church didn't call us about the Landon boy until yesterday."

"So if the governor had done something before then..."

"Well, I expect he'd have to live up to it."

"He's sticking to what he done for Payne?"

"That he is."

I smile. He looks at me, then he says, "As far as I know he is. I didn't actually ask him about that. But he complained about it enough."

"He did?"

"I expect he'll live up to it; go ahead and take the heat."

"It ain't fair. But I'm glad for Payne."

Buchanan shakes his head. "It's a damn shame is what it is."

I don't know what to say. Everything has gone out of me. My body feels like an empty sack. It seems odd that my eyes can see; the world is out there beyond the window, mocking me, and I don't feel a thing. I close my eyes slowly and think of death. Now they will come after me for this. I will never be able to make anyone believe me about the Landon boy.

Then the warden says, "I still want to reward you, John. Even if I have to do it myself."

"How?"

"You tell me where you want to work in the prison, and I'll okay it."

"You can do that?"

"I can."

"What will happen to me when the others realize what's happening?"

"Nothing."

"Sure," I say.

"The others ain't going to know about it."

"And nobody will notice."

"It doesn't matter what the others notice. You tell me where you want to work, and I'll see to it."

"If I said I didn't want to go on the road no more."

"I can arrange that."

"Not ever."

"I can make you a trustee, John. Then I can do any damned thing I please with you."

As he speaks, it hits me what I have to do. What I must do. He is talking to me, and I suddenly realize I have the exact way to get out of here. It's almost perfect. It all comes to me in a kind of flash, like a thing I've already done and I'm just remembering it. Being a trustee, with the freedom to move around the prison, is all I need. I feel like I'm coming back to life right before his eyes, and if I ain't careful he'll notice it. I shrug my shoulders. "Okay," I say. "I guess I'll take it."

"It's the least I can do," he says.

"Thank you."

"And I'm not giving up on the parole idea neither. I'll be here, in any case. And I'll put in a word for you. Maybe we can get a letter from the governor."

"Yeah," I say. "Maybe we can."

"So," he says. "Where you want to start out working?"

"I need to think about it."

"Sure," he says.

I get up to leave, then I turn back to him. I play this so that it seems I just thought of it, but I know what I want. It is the very beginning of what I'm planning. "Can I work on the janitorial staff first?"

He looks at me. "Really?"

"I think so."

"You can work anywhere," he says. "You don't have to be cleaning up after everybody. Why don't you think it over?"

"No, I think that's what I want."

"Why? You could work only in the machine shop—a cush job stacking license plates, if you want—or you could spend all your time in the dayroom or on the basketball courts. You can have a desk job in the mail room, or the..."

"No. I like the idea of working inside all the time. But in different parts of the place."

"Really?"

"Yeah," I say. "I won't have to stay in one place. Every day'll be different. And if I don't like it, I can change, right?"

"Sure." He shrugs his shoulders. "Okay, if that's what you want. I'll draw up the papers this afternoon."

"Thank you."

I pause at the door and look at him. He waits a moment, then he says, "I really am sorry, John."

"I know you are," I say.

"I did the best I could."

"Yeah, well."

"If I can help it, you won't be doing any hard time here, okay, John?"

"It's all hard time," I say. "But I thank you just the same."

He shakes his head, then sits down, starts turning papers on his desk.

I smile, almost without wanting to; I actually feel sorry for him, so when I open the door to go out, I stop and wait for him to look up at me.

"I *do* thank you," I say. "I know you ain't to blame."

PENNY

Sometimes late at night when the wind blows through the trees it sounds like a woman crying. Tory sleeps in my room, now. I don't let her out of my sight. Even with the new dead bolt on the door I still don't feel very safe.

The grave is gone. A circle of brown dirt and chopped grass remains there to remind me. Even the yellow tape is gone, now. The police and people in uniforms I didn't recognize spent most of two days digging up around the grave. They took out the old box, the sack with the drawstring. There wasn't nothing else in Terry Landon's grave, but a T-shirt, his blue jeans, tennis shoes, the yellow raincoat, and the bones.

I'll never forget the bones, so white they almost gleamed. Terry was a nigra, but his bones was as white as the moon, and small. So small.

Clare watched everything the police did, just sitting on the back porch, staring at them as they worked. When they was finishing up and cleaning the yard, I come out with a cup of coffee for her. She smiled at me when I give it to her, but it was a sad smile.

I sat down on the steps in front of her. It was quiet for a spell. One of the policemen come over and asked me if he could use the phone.

"Why don't you use your radio?" Clare says.

"It don't work this far up the mountain," he says.

"Sheriff Paxton uses his radio all the time," I said.

He shook his head, slightly, then walked off toward all the cars parked in the yard by the road.

"I wonder how much money there was?" Clare says.

"I don't care."

"It'd be nice to know. I'd like to know. And wouldn't you like to read them notes and scraps of paper?"

"What notes?"

"It wasn't just money. There was notepaper, too, with writing on it."

"I didn't see that."

"It was there." She sipped her coffee.

"I guess I'd like to see that myself," I said.

SHERIFF PAXTON and some fellow who says he's a detective spend most of a whole morning a few days later asking me questions about John. They come up early and knock on the door. I've just made breakfast, so I let them set at the kitchen table and wait for me while I take Tory to school. When I come back, Clare has served them coffee, so I sit down at the table with them. I can't remember very much about those days right before John went to court and got taken off to jail. I didn't see a lot of him during all the days and nights before the Landon boy disappeared, and then I did see a lot of him, because he helped in the search. The whole town—mostly all white people—set out to find Terry Landon. I remember thinking it was a downright good sign that white folks would spend so much time and energy looking for a nigra child. Not that they shouldn't, but I didn't think they would. Folks are funny about things like that up here.

John wanted so bad to find Terry. That's all I really remember about the whole thing. At least it's all I *want* to remember. How hard John worked to find him. He went out every night with the search party, until he could hardly stay awake. He'd work a whole day in the mill, then come home, eat some bacon and bread, then take his flashlight and rush out the door. And the whole time he was waiting to go on trial for manslaughter. He didn't have to do none of it. But he liked Terry Landon, and I know that. So he joined in the search. They combed every foot of this mountain, top to bottom, and found nothing at all.

I tell Sheriff Paxton and the detective all that.

"Well," the detective says. "How do you suppose the body of the little boy got buried in your backyard?"

I look at Paxton. His lips are slightly parted, and his eyebrows lift up a bit. I know he's already told the detective about the Gypsy Man.

"That ain't *in* my backyard."

"It's on Crawford land, not mine," Clare says.

I keep looking at the detective fella, and finally Paxton says, "This here's Mr. McKeldon. He's with the state police."

McKeldon says, "You know anything about how those bones got there?"

"No," I say.

He looks at Clare.

"I don't know neither."

"Doesn't it seem strange to you?"

"Yes, it does," Clare says.

"I wonder if you can remember anything at all unusual happening around that time—anything out of the ordinary that might have either distracted you or taken you away from here long enough for somebody to..." He stops.

"Yeah, something unusual happened," I say. "The Landon boy disappeared."

Paxton says, "How'd the body get there, Penny?"

"You already asked me that, and I already told you I don't know."

"You can't tell us anything about that time?" McKeldon says.

"No, I can't."

"And your aunt Clare don't remember nothing either," Paxton says. "Right?"

"That's right," she says.

"And yet, there's a body down yonder in your backyard."

"It's just off the property," I say.

"You don't remember the ground being tore up a bit?" McKeldon says. He sips his coffee, trying to be all friendlylike.

"No," I say.

"Was there always grass there?"

"Tall grass. Thick and high."

"Just grass?"

"Used to be poison ivy was always growing out there, too. John pulled all of it up one year."

"You remember when that was?" Paxton says.

"No. The poison ivy?"

"Right."

"It was a long time ago. I think that's when we first seen the stone."

"The gravestone?" Paxton says.

"We didn't know it was a gravestone. It was just a sliver of rock sticking out of the ground."

"I see," McKeldon says.

I look past them to the green yard outside.

"Well, you know," McKeldon says. "Even if he *was* just a nigra, it's a terrible thing to kill a child."

"I know that," I say.

"And I would like to get to the bottom of this if I can— you know—while I'm talking to you here."

"I been all the help I can be."

"Would either of you gentlemen like more coffee?" Clare says.

"For Lord's sake, Clare," I say.

She looks at me. "What?"

"Nothing," I say.

"You would have noticed if the ground was all tore up over yonder back when you was all looking for the Landon boy, right?" Paxton says.

"Even with the poison ivy gone, the grass still grew tall and wild over there. Don't you think I'd of seen a hole if there was one? I didn't notice nothing." I say the last part very slow.

"But did you notice the grass was still undisturbed out there?"

"I didn't notice nothing. None of us did. If we did, we would of told somebody."

Paxton says, "And what about you, Miss Clare?"

She shakes her head.

"Clare disappears on benders now and then," Paxton says. "But you was around here when all this was going on, right?"

McKeldon sets his cup in front of him. "Benders, you say?"

"I was here," Clare says. "I didn't notice nothing."

"Well, anyway, thank you kindly for the coffee," Paxton says. "It's better'n I did the last time I come up here for an interview."

"Ain't necessary for you to pretend you got any kind of manners," Clare says.

I don't even look at him. I hate it when he gets sarcastic.

"Clare, you have disappeared for a week or two or three—ain't that right, Penny?"

I still won't look at him. McKeldon's chair is turned around backwards, and he rests his chin on his arms folded across the top of it. He leans toward me like he can't really hear me when I speak.

"Penny, ain't that right? She disappears for days on end," Paxton says.

I say, "Ain't no call for that."

"Ain't no call for what?" McKeldon says.

Paxton stands up next to him, holding onto the back of his chair, and puts his boot up on the first rung of the chair. He leans forward with his elbow on his knee and his fist up under his jaw. Outside, the police have finished cleaning up the mess they've made. A few of them are kind enough to come back this morning and start putting the dirt back in the hole.

"Ain't that right, Penny?" Paxton says again. He's getting impatient. I'm wishing Clare would say something to defend herself.

"What difference does it make?" I say.

"I go away sometimes," Clare says.

McKeldon stares at his shoes for a minute. Then he says, "So you don't really know if your aunt Clare was around here back then or not, is that right?"

"I was here," Clare says.

"I don't remember much of anything about them days," I say. "But I know Clare was here."

"Was John in trouble yet, back then?" Paxton says.

"Yes. You know he was."

"I thought he was."

"It was just the trial and all."

He looks at McKeldon and says, "John's her husband."

"What kind of trouble?" McKeldon says.

"He killed a nigra girl," Paxton says. "Didn't he, Penny?"

McKeldon's face changes. He turns his head to look at Paxton. "An important piece of information, don't you think?"

"I told you about it."

"You said he was in jail for manslaughter, some accident."

"That's right."

"He killed a nigra girl?"

Paxton says nothing.

"That goes a long way toward solving this here little mystery," McKeldon says.

"No, it don't," I say. "It wasn't what you think. It really was an accident."

"It coulda been an accident," Paxton says.

"It *was* an accident," I say.

"Was he originally charged with murder?" McKeldon says.

"Originally?" Paxton says.

McKeldon seems impatient. He shifts himself in the chair a bit and says, "Did he plea down to manslaughter, or was that the original charge?"

"No, manslaughter, that's where it started," Paxton says. "But a lot of folks believed he done it on purpose."

It is quiet for a moment, while Paxton looks at me. Then he says, "I wasn't among them."

"You thought it was an accident, too?"

"Yes, I did," he says. "I still do. I know John. And he'd ..."

"He'd what?"

"It's a stretch to think he'd do that kind of thing."

I don't want to look at nobody just then. I remember John, the look of defiance in his eyes the last time I seen him, the way Paxton put his hand on the top of John's head and pushed him down so he wouldn't bump himself when he got in the police car.

"Why don't you tell Mr. McKeldon here about the Gypsy Man?" Paxton says.

"Why don't you?"

"I think you should."

I shake my head.

"Miss Bone," McKeldon says. "You might be of some help. I don't know anything about this Gypsy fellow, but I'd like to know about him."

"That's who took Terry Landon," I say.

"How do you know that?"

"That hole in the ground down yonder? Not Terry's grave but the real grave next to it?"

"What real grave?"

"It wasn't no grave," Paxton says.

"It had Wilbur's tombstone over it," I say. "It was some kind of grave."

"What about it?" McKeldon says.

"It was no body in it. There was a tombstone over it, with Wilbur Crawford's name on it. Wilbur Crawford is the Gypsy Man. And ain't no body in the grave."

"Well, there was *one* body down there," McKeldon says.

"It ain't Gypsy Crawford."

Both of them nod. Then McKeldon says, "We've pulled that box up out of there, Miss Bone."

"Mrs. Bone."

"Mrs. Bone. It wasn't no coffin. It was a pine box all right, but it was only four foot long. It might hold a child or a midget, but it wasn't really no casket."

"That's right," Paxton says. "Penny, why don't you tell us how you found that gravestone."

"When are you gonna give me my gun back?"

"When I'm good and ready."

"I want it back now."

"Leave it alone," he says.

"How long can he hold it?" I say to McKeldon.

"You ain't getting that gun back, Penny," Paxton says. "It's been officially confiscated."

Clare says, "It's been officially stolen."

Paxton looks at her, but he don't say nothing.

"Just tell us how you found the grave, and I'll see you get your gun back," McKeldon says. He touches my arm.

I say, "Well, like I said, when John cleared the poison ivy, he noticed it."

"So your husband found the tombstone then?" McKeldon says.

"No. It was just a stone. He wouldn't a said nothing except that it was so white. And for a while that was all you could see over there in the shade a that tree, like it was a little piece of the moon. Light glowed off it. But it was just a sliver of stone. That's all."

"Go on."

"It didn't take long for the grass to cover it up again."

He waits, just looking at me. Paxton puts his foot down, then keeps shifting his weight from one leg to the other, and every time he does, his leather boots creak. It sounds like he's sitting in a saddle.

"That was years ago," I say. "John wasn't in jail yet. I don't even think we was married yet. So it was at least seven years ago. Then just this past summer, Tory found lettering on it."

"Tory's..." McKeldon starts.

"My daughter." At the same time, Paxton says, "Her daughter." We look at each other. I say, "I can answer my own questions."

McKeldon sighs. "Go on."

"She plays in the shade of the tree. And she seen it one day and commenced to digging around it."

"I see."

"It was so white she wanted to see the whole thing. So she tried to dig it out of there, and that's when she found the lettering on it."

"And you never wondered about that stone until this summer?" McKeldon says.

"Not till Tory found the lettering on it," I say.

Paxton puts his foot back up on the rung of the chair, reaches into his shirt, and gets a pack of cigarettes and lights one. McKeldon says, "So you just left it alone until you found the lettering on it? That's all?"

"I didn't think about it. It's like it wasn't there."

"And that's all," McKeldon says.

"That's all," I say. "It was Gault's idea to dig it up."

McKeldon lowers his head and takes a deep breath. He sets there for a while, staring down between his feet, while Paxton puffs on his cigarette. I wait for one of them to say something else, but I ain't saying nothing. McKeldon looks at Paxton for a second and seems to shake his head. Then he leans back and almost whispers to him—like he ain't paying no mind to me at all, like I ain't even there no more. "We're not getting anywhere here. I'm not going to waste any more of my time on it either. It was just a nigger and he's been dead for six years."

"Terry Landon wasn't just a nigger to the folks around here," Paxton says.

"Well, let the folks around here figure out what happened to him." He gets up and hitches his pants up higher on his waist. His tie is twisted down the front and loose at the neck. He stands there for a minute, looking at me with eyes as gray as flagstone and his face as plain and pitiless as a hog's.

Sheriff Paxton says, "Well, it ain't like we have the—like we could just..." He doesn't finish what he started to say. Now he is only standing there with his mouth partly open and his head leaning over to the side a bit, like it's impossible to believe what he's just heard McKeldon say. He pushes his hat back on his head and then sets his hands on his hips. "I reckon," he says. "If you're done, you're done."

"Can you get me my gun back?" I ask McKeldon.

"Why are you so scared?" he says.

"I ain't scared," I say. "I just want my gun back. It belonged to my father. That's all."

There's a long pause, while Paxton looks hard at me. I can see he is considering something—his face turning sad, like he just found out he's lost his job or he's going to have to move to another country.

McKeldon says to Paxton, "If you didn't file charges or make an arrest, you can't keep the gun. You know that, don't you?"

"If I *do* give that gun back," Paxton says to me. His voice is suddenly very nice and like he wants to soothe me. "If I *do* give it back, you promise not to let that durn fool Morgan Tiller anywhere near it?"

"I don't want it for him," I say. Suddenly I realize I am fighting back tears. I don't want to cry in front of them. More than anything in the world, I do not want to cry. McKeldon's gray eyes cut through me, and Paxton lets this slow, warm smile cross his face, but he don't say nothing.

I sit there as mute and calm as I can be and let them look at me for a long time.

But there ain't no tears. When they go out, I'm smiling. I tell them, "Have a nice day."

They thank me for the coffee.

SHERIFF PAXTON

McKeldon didn't have to drive over to Josh Landon's place and tell him nothing; he didn't have to look into a still hopeful man's yellowing eyes and tell him about the brown clods of earth, the small collection of white bones, and little twists of hair—all that was left of his son, his little boy. No. He didn't have to do none of that.

He got in his car and drove on back to Roanoke. Gone and done with us.

I went ahead and give the gun back to Penny. She don't even thank me for it. I make a special trip, and all she done is take it out of my hand like I have germs or something, then she goes on back in her house and closes the door.

What would it cost her to say, Thank you kindly?

It don't shock me none, since I've been working with them mountain folk most of my life. What shocked me was finding the body of that little Landon boy right there just a few feet behind John Bone's property. That's really got me tied up in knots. All these years I been picturing him alive; figuring out in my mind what he might look like now. I just knew one day I'd find him, or find out what happened to him. I didn't never think I'd find out like that. I wasn't even looking for him, and there he was.

I didn't want to find him like that, neither. I wanted more than just the bones. I always half believed I'd find him alive. I'd take the boy back up to Landon's place and stand on that front porch with such pride Josh'd hear the beating of my heart before I ever touched my knuckles to the wood on the door.

Maybe I won't get a chance to do it, but somebody ought to ask Mr. Bone a few questions, and he better have some answers. If I can't get no one else to do it, I'm gonna see about doing it myself.

Terry Landon might of been just a nigra, like McKeldon says, but he still didn't deserve to die like that and end up in the ground under that tree up yonder. I ain't no saint but I know that.

I sure know that.

PENNY

"This fellow here is your granddaddy," Clare says. She points at a small picture on the page. Tory scrunches down and looks at it. They are sitting on the couch with a big photo album spread in front of them, most of it in Clare's lap, but it covers them both. Clare turns the pages slowly and carefully. The crisp old paper crackles, and when one of the snapshots falls off, she picks it up and puts the corners back in the little black holders glued to the page.

"And lookee here," Clare says. "Here's your momma when she was your age."

Tory laughs. "Look at you, Mommy," she says.

I am in the kitchen, heating a pan with oil in it, getting ready to make fried potatoes and cornmeal biscuits. I want to feel like I am safe, like time has moved far enough beyond the grave in the back that we can say life is going on. I have the gun again, and every now and then I go in my room, reach up under the mattress in there where I keep it, and take it out just to look at it. I want it to make me feel the way it did when I first found it. But I can't get those white bones out of my mind. A child's bones are small—fragile—like something made of soft white talcum.

The sound of the oil heating in the pan always made me kind of happy before, but now I am only impatient to get the dinner cooked so we can eat. With the stone gone, and weeks gone by without no trace of the Gypsy Man, nor no other trouble, I should at least feel safer. I went and put new locks and solid brass dead bolts on both doors, and I got a pistol in the house. But I don't feel safe.

Morgan come up here a few days ago and I fixed him a cup of tea. He was proud of the job he done on the doors. "These here doors won't open unless somebody turns them bolts," he says. "Anybody wants to come in this house now, he's got to break a window or find a way to smash a door in. Anyway, he's got to make a hell of a lot of noise."

I thanked him, and he smiled. "You still got to be careful," he says.

"I will."

"You never know," he says.

"You ain't seen no more signs?"

"Not since he burned down the back of my house."

I never told him the fellow in the truck was Clare's traveling boyfriend. I looked at him now and considered it, but I couldn't work out all I had to tell him about what Clare made me swear not to tell, so I didn't say nothing. He caught me looking at him, and I felt like he could tell I wasn't telling him something. I said, "Maybe he's come and gone."

"Maybe."

"How you doing on your house?"

"I'm getting it back to normal," he says. "It takes time."

"I know that."

"No, nothing since the fire," he says. "I told you about the pile I seen, didn't I?"

"Yes."

"Sticky and full of leaves and briars and whatnot?"

I nodded.

"Looked just like a man sitting there, looking at me."

"Did you just leave it there?"

"I think he was here, in Crawford," Morgan says. "You still got to be careful."

"I been careful," I said. I didn't tell him about the gun.

Now it's Sunday, and Tory is enjoying herself with Clare. They been looking at the pictures most of the day. Clare decided to leave the store closed, and I didn't have to go down to the Goodyear store. We just got back from church around midmorning, and we was going to let Tory do anything she wanted, as long as it was inside the house. And then when it come time to get settled for supper, Tory wanted to listen to the radio, but Clare says, "No radio today." She got out the photo albums and said to Tory, "You going to start learning about this family again tomorrow, so today we're going to start teaching."

"Teaching what?" I said.

She turned to me, holding the albums in a pile in front of her. "She's got a family tree project due this Tuesday in Mr. Gault's class."

"She sure does," I said. "I completely forgot."

"So I'm going to start her learning about this family."

"I already done that," Tory says. "I just got to make the tree."

"Well, we're going to do it again."

I smiled. I don't mind Clare when she wants to talk about family. I like the feeling it gives me. And she always tells me things about my father I never known. Or she talks about my mother and I get the feeling somehow my momma is with me, like a visit or a phone call from somebody I can't remember. It makes me feel like I remember, like I had the experience of knowing her and having her in my life. I was way too young when she died. Looking at the albums makes Clare happy, and Tory never minds it too much neither. She likes the stories as much as I do.

So they started in with the oldest albums—the ones with pictures of my great-grandparents, and with uncles and aunts I never heard of. There's pictures in there of men hunting and fishing; of people getting married; pictures of babies in carriages; and men and women all dressed up with umbrellas and canes and white shirts and collars. It's a different time, paralyzed on the page, but alive for both me and Tory anyway.

It is a warm day—like a summer day, except for the leaves have started to fall already. The hot sun feels unnatural what with all the gold- and red- and orange-colored trees everywhere. There ain't nothing on the earth prettier than the top of this mountain in the fall. Like God paints at night and you wake up in the morning and the colors so bright you don't want it to ever get dark again.

Tory never let on that she wanted to go outside and enjoy her last taste of a summer night on the front porch. I reckon that's what she wanted to do. It was early, though, and she probably thought she'd get some time out of me after dinner. Kids just don't remember from one year to the next how early it gets dark in October. The day seemed like a summer day to her, so she never thought about it.

It's getting near dinnertime, and I have just cut up the last potato when I see a figure coming up the walk. He has a big white hat on, and his head is down, so he can study the stones beneath him, but I know right away who it is.

"We got a visitor," I say.

Clare says, "Again? He was just up here."

"It ain't Morgan," I say.

I go to the front door and open it. When he gets to the bottom step he stops and looks up at me.

"You sober?" I say.

He is out of breath, so he half smiles, then shakes his head.

"How drunk are you?"

"I ain't drunk."

"Why'd you shake your head no."

He smiles again, only a definite smile this time. "Shall we say I was amused at the question?"

"Funny way to show amusement."

"And disgust, too."

"Disgust?"

"At myself, Penny. For having to endure such a query from one of the few people whose respect I'd hate to lose."

I say nothing.

"And at such an indelicate time."

"What's indelicate about it?"

"Well, I suspect it's dinnertime." He raises his head a bit, like a beagle hound picking up the scent of a rabbit. "Smells like fried garlic and onions."

"You don't have to flatter me none," I say. "Nor use them five-dollar words."

"I am aware that I have arrived unexpectedly," he says. "And that I may not be welcome."

I open the screen door. "You may as well come on in."

He comes up the stairs, almost hurriedly, then follows me in. He catches the screen door and lets it close gently. I go back to the stove and start putting potatoes in the hot oil. They sizzle, and he stands there watching me, his hat in his hands.

Clare closes the book of photos and says to Tory, "Say hey to your granddaddy, honey."

Tory gets off the couch and walks over to him. "You my granddaddy?" she says.

He seems ashamed, fumbling with his hat. "Yes, I am, sweetie pie."

She reaches up and touches the heel of his hand. He starts to take her hand, but she pulls it away.

"My, you've sure grown," he says.

She frowns, then looks at me.

"He's your daddy's father, honey," I say. "He just ain't been around in a long time."

"No, I haven't," he says.

It is quiet for a spell, then I say, "He ain't supposed to be coming around here."

"No, I ain't," he says.

"Why not?" Tory says.

"Your daddy wanted it that way," I say.

"I have news," he says.

"What?" I say. I feel my heart jump. "What's happened?"

"It's not bad," he says. "I don't mean to scare you."

I shake my head. Then I look at Clare. "Maybe you two should..." I stop. She nods that she understands. She gets up and takes Tory's hand. "Let's go on in your room and finish looking at these pictures," she says. She smiles at Mr. Bone, and he sort of raises the hat a bit towards her.

"How you been?" Clare says.

"Just fine."

"We'll get out of your way," she says.

I put the last potatoes in the oil and cut the flame down a bit so the oil don't spatter all over the stove. I get more wood, him standing there watching me the whole time. I stack the wood in a bucket next to the stove, and then he comes slowly into the kitchen and stands next to me, in front of the open window.

"You're blocking my light," I say. "And I need that air in here."

"I have news," he says.

I look at him. I am afraid of what he will say, and it must show, because he says, "It's good news."

"Good news."

"John's a hero."

I wait, staring at him.

"He's a genuine hero. What do you think of that?" Now he positions himself in front of me, waiting for me to say something.

"What'd he do?" I say.

"Nothing but save a man's life."

I can't speak. I am suddenly afraid of the words he might say. I gaze into his eyes, my heart beating like a bird's heart.

"And that ain't all," he says. "They may be letting him out early."

It's like them words burn into my soul. But I'm afraid, too. I can't believe how afraid I am. He just stands there looking at me, then I say, "John told you that?"

"He did."

"You seen him?"

"I visit him regular. The last time I was there—it was a few weeks ago. I told him I'd come see you right away, but then." He lets his head down, like he can't look at me no more.

"Then what?"

"It's been tough. I been planning to come down here and see you for a spell."

"You been drinking again," I say.

"He told me to let you know. He's up for a special parole."

My throat starts to burn and I know I might cry or laugh any second while he talks. I don't want to have that kind of hope right now. Not that kind of hope. Where you feel like your heart is swollen with tears and laughter all at once, and each minute of each day increases like a sheet billowing in the wind, and you think you will hear it, the voice of God, or some other miracle that will change the whole universe for you. And you can't sleep for the knowledge that it might not happen, for the grief you already feel in all of your heart for the bitter end of hope.

Mr. Bone goes on and tells me what John did, and about the newspaper articles calling him a hero, and how the warden is going to reward him somehow. The whole time he talks, I know he is waiting for me to show it, for me to jump for joy and thank him for the news, but all I want to do is rewind the clock somehow and get back to the time when he ain't come up here yet, so I can do something to stop it, so I can keep him from saying the words that open my heart to the possibility that John might come back, and I'll be finished with this exile forever. I don't want that kind of hope.

"John asked me to come up here and tell you," he says.

"Well, you done it," I say. "I thank you kindly."

He waits there. After a spell he says, "Seems like..."

I look at him.

"Seems like..."

"What?" I say.

"Ain't you glad?"

"I'd be happier if you said he *was* getting out early. That he was getting out tomorrow or the next day."

He seems to shrug, then he looks at the wall and down at the floor. When he meets my eyes again, I see such sadness in him I almost start crying right then. Finally I say, "I don't want nothing like this here *may*. He *may* be getting out early. He *may* be getting a special parole."

"I see what you mean."

"No, you don't," I say. "Ain't nobody I know ever felt this kind of pain from hope and belief. Nobody."

"Penny, when my wife was sick—I think I know what you're feeling."

"I'm sorry," I say. "Maybe you do."

"I do. You ain't the only one."

"You done what he asked," I say.

He nods, still looking at me with those forlorn eyes. Then he glances at the shelves and around the room.

"Hell," I say. "You want to sit down and have supper with us?"

He pulls at the collar of his white shirt, still eyeing the shelves in the kitchen.

"If you're looking for a bottle, Clare's got one."

He seems ashamed. He slumps a little, but keeps his sad eyes on me. "I probably deserved that," he says. "I just wanted to be sure you had enough."

"I got enough."

"To eat," he adds, just as I speak.

"I got enough to eat for all of us," I say.

He steps toward the window and puts his hat on the chair there. Then he turns around and looks at me again. In the sunlight, his skin looks pale and leathery. He ain't clean shaved, so his chin is iron gray. He has his hands hitched in his white pants behind where the suspenders attach, but he don't look confident the way he's standing. He looks like he's helping the suspenders keep his pants up. He put a lot of cologne on before he come up here, and just now a breeze from the window brings me the scent of it, and I am reminded of my father. The smell of Old Spice, tinged slightly with brandy, brings back so many early mornings when my father come to my room and kissed me good-bye, I find a part of me longing to be that little girl again. I loved it when I didn't know about loss—but then I realize I've always known about it. My mother died when I was too small to remember.

"You can sit down," I say.

He puts the hat on the back of the chair and takes a chair at the head of the table. After a while, he says, "You seeing anybody, Penny?"

I stir the potatoes. "You know I ain't."

"John said I should find out."

I wait, still flipping the sizzling potatoes in the pan.

"You ever—you know. Go out or anything?"

I look at him.

"You know. Like John told you to do?"

I throw the spatula on the counter and get another iron pan from the cupboard. I put the biscuits in the pan with a little oil, put the pan in the oven, then add wood to the firebox. The whole time he watches me, as if he expects I am thinking and I might answer him.

Then he says, "I didn't think so."

I pick up the spatula and stir the potatoes again.

"Anyway, he said maybe he'd like to see you."

"What?" I say.

"I think he'd like to see you."

"We swore on the Bible," I say. Just when I think I may not have to worry so much about the Gypsy Man, here comes Mr. Bone with another terror for me. "I declare," I say. "The world don't give a body a single minute's peace."

"No, I guess it don't."

"Why does John want to see me now?"

"He didn't say."

The sun is starting to dip behind the mountain, so the light seems softer now. In the shadows, with the weakening sun behind him, Mr. Bone looks a little like John. I see the sparkle in his blue eyes, and again I have to fight off tears for a second. I imagine myself sobbing and wailing. Sometimes I do that and it helps. I see myself caterwauling like an old widow and that helps me resist it. I won't do it. Not in front of him or no one. It don't matter how sad or terrified I get.

"I'm just telling you what John told me."

I stir the potatoes some more, move them off the burner for a spell, until the sizzling calms down.

"Oh, he also said you shouldn't trust no strangers," Mr. Bone says.

"Really?"

"That's what he said. Anyway, I aim to keep a close eye on you from now on," he says.

"You do?"

"John asked me to . . ."

"I don't need you to take care of, too," I say.

He seems to take in a deep breath, but he stops talking. He sits there looking at me. I can see he is figuring something in his head. Both he and his son show it when they are thinking. You just watch them a bit and you know it.

"What?" I say.

He speaks softly, but I believe he might be fighting off tears himself. He says, "I'm only doing what John wanted. But I understand you."

"You do?"

"I know what you mean. I understand," he says, losing strength in his voice.

"I don't know what it is you think you understand," I say. I flip the potatoes again. They sizzle in the pan, start to smoke. I put the pan down on the counter and cover the burner. "Potatoes are done," I say. He sits there looking at me. "I just . . ." I don't finish.

He comes over to me and puts his hand on my shoulder, then turns me around so I am facing him. I don't look him in the face. He takes me in his arms. I'm not crying, but I let him hold me. I shake with fear, afraid of all my wishes and hopes, afraid of the terror of having to accept the loss a second time. He pats the back of my head, smoothes the hair down, as if he understands all that. After a while, he stands back, holds me at arm's length. I don't want to look into his eyes, but he stands there until I do. Then he says, "I know what you went through with me."

"That ain't it," I say.

"I understand. I owe you. I am grateful."

I nod.

"I'm sober now. But I know you took care of me when nobody else cared."

I must have a hurt look on my face, because he puts up his

hand as if to stop me from objecting. "I know John was away in the army and couldn't. I know that."

"You don't owe me nothing," I say.

"I just want you to know you won't have to take care of me. Not ever again."

I put my head down. I don't want to look into those serious, sincere eyes, and listen to another perfect lie.

"I'm going to take care of you," he says. "You just wait."

"You going to move in here? Is that it?"

He lets out a brief, sincere laugh, pulls me close to him again. "Not on your life. Is that what you thought?"

I nod against his shoulder.

"You sweet thing," he says. "You sweet little thing. I feel— I feel just like you're my own daughter."

"It ain't like we don't have the room," I say. "I been sleeping on the couch anyways."

"I don't think I have to move in here. I got my own house to take care of. I can check in from time to time. I'll call you every day."

"You can move in for a spell if you want," I say, but I don't really mean it. Or at least I don't mean it exactly. I probably think it might be safer, or at least feel safer, to have a man around. But I don't need somebody else to take care of.

"Why don't we talk about it over supper?" He lets go of me and goes back to the chair by the window. "It's enough that you know I'm here for you. I won't let nothing happen to you."

It's quiet for a while. I can hear Clare and Tory laughing in the other room. Then Mr. Bone says, "Maybe you and Clare and the little one can come up and stay with me for a week or two."

"I don't see how," I say. "Not with Tory in school and all."

"Well, we'll talk about it at dinner," he says.

Then I remember what he said about John telling him to come see me. "You ever swore anything on a Bible?" I ask.

"Sure."

"What happens when you go against it?"

"What do you mean?"

"You swear on a Bible not to do something, then you go and do it."

"Some things ain't worth swearing on," he says. "What you and John promised was just a fool thing. I don't think the Lord expects that fool things should go on just because you swore them on a Bible."

"What'd you swear on?"

"When I married John's mother," he says. He speaks softly, not really looking at me. It is like he's praying.

"You listening to me?" I say.

He looks at me. "Yes."

"You want a drink, don't you?"

"Maybe just a taste," he says.

I shake my head.

"With supper."

"Sure," I say.

I put a little salt and pepper on the potatoes. "Why don't you set the table," I say.

"Sure." He gets up, and I show him where the plates and knives and forks are. He sets four places at the table. The late sun glistens off the plates and silverware and makes me feel like I'm home, like I'm just home and taking care of my home.

"I swore on the Bible," I say. "And John swore. But now he wants to go against it."

"What do you mean?" Mr. Bone says. He's sitting at the table now.

"He swore. No contact. Then he sends you up here."

"I see what you mean."

"I don't expect I got to live up to my end, now that he's broken his," I say.

"No, I guess you don't."

"So I want to go see him," I say.

"We can do that."

"That's what I want to do. As soon as possible."

"I go the end of the month—third Thursday, as usual. You come along with me why don't you."

"Why so long?"

"That's when I go see him. Third Thursday every month."

"I want to go see him tomorrow."

"Maybe you'd want to fix your hair a bit, and . . ." He stops. I look hard at him. "I don't mean you don't look wonderful now, but . . ."

"I got to see him as soon as possible," I say.

"I'll take you to him. But you got to wait."

"Why?"

"That's what we agreed to when John first went to jail. You got to set your visiting hours in advance. You can miss them, but you can't add to them or come early. You got to visit when you signed up for. That's the third . . ."

"Thursday every month," I finish the sentence with him. "It's stupid," I say. "I don't want to wait that long." I take the potatoes and dish them out, a little on each plate. Then I open the oven and take out the biscuits. When I have everything on the table I look at him. "Did you know about the Landon child?"

He lowers his head. "I heard."

"What'd you hear?"

"That they found him up the old Crawford place."

"They found him right over there," I say, pointing out the back window. "Down yonder by that tree." I can see he didn't know it.

"Gault found it. Him and a nigra from Lebanon Church."

"What were they doing up here?"

I told him about the stone and all. The writing on it and Tory digging there.

"I thought—I didn't know..."

"And a police detective come up here asking all kind of fool questions about John, and when he went down to the prison and all."

His face changes. He is doing the figuring himself.

"They think John may of had something to do with it," I say, and I feel my throat aching because of the tears I ain't going to let out. "So, you tell me how he's going to be coming back here a hero."

"I swear, Penny, I didn't know."

"I got to talk to John," I say. "As soon as possible."

He steps back a bit, seems to shrug. Then he says, "There really ain't nothing I can do. But it's only two weeks away. A little under two weeks."

"That's a long time," I say. "But I can do it if I have to."

"I'll see if I can make arrangements," he says. "Maybe they'll listen to me."

"You do that."

He sits down at the table again. I start dishing out the potatoes.

"They sure smell good," he says.

"Go tell Tory and Clare to wash up," I say.

"I'll take you down there myself," he says. He gets up and comes over to stand next to me. "It'll be like I'm bringing him a wonderful gift."

"Maybe it will," I say. "Maybe it won't."

He puts his hands on my shoulders and looks deep into my eyes. "He had nothing to do with that little Landon boy. You know that."

"Of course, I know it," I say. "But that state police fella don't know it."

He smiles, waits a spell, then he says, "We'll sort it out, honey."

"Knock on her door and tell Clare to come on to dinner," I say.

"Sure," he says. He goes to the door and taps on it. "Dinner," he says. I hear Clare say, "Be right there." Then she and Tory come out and go to the pump to wash. Mr. Bone is leaning on the side of the stove looking at me.

"Ain't that too hot?" I say.

"Good and warm," he says.

"Suit yourself." I wrap the biscuits in a towel and put them in a basket on the table. I go to the icebox and get a pitcher of cold milk. I am aware he's watching me.

Finally, when I meet his gaze he says, "Did you say your aunt Clare had some whiskey in the house?"

JOHN BONE

In my first week as a trustee, I work in every corner of the prison—sweeping with a broom, scrubbing with brushes, and wiping with rags. I am very patient. I know I can't do anything until I get what I want out of the laundry, and I have to have the vacuum cleaner for that. The prison has only one: a Hoover upright with a soft sort of bladder on the back of it that holds a thin paper bag to catch the dust and dirt. To replace the paper bag, you unzip the bladder and pull the bag off the intake pipe at the base of the machine. Then you have to slip a clean bag on the same pipe, position the bag inside the bladder, and zip it up. Most of the time, one of the guards uses the Hoover. It isn't prison policy or anything, it just turns out that prisoners can't go in the lobby or the warden's office without an escort, and you don't go to the infirmary unless you're sick. The Hoover is only used in those three locations in Bland, so even as a trustee, I have no chance to use it unless I request it for some other purpose.

So I tell Daigle one day. I decide to be completely honest about having to have it in the laundry with me.

At first, he doesn't hesitate. "We can get it, if you want."

But when we get to the utility closet and he's about to unlock the door, he stops and looks at me, frowning. "What you need it in the laundry for? Ain't no rugs in there."

"It'll just make my job easier."

"How?" His long face is always darkened by the shadow of a beard, and his eyes seem enormous, dark and lazy looking under thick, black eyebrows. The hair by his temples has just started to turn gray, but he can't be more than thirty years old. He always looks like he's half asleep because of the large eyes and the lazy droop of his eyelids.

"You never used a vacuum cleaner on a stone floor?" I say.

"No. Not one of them uprights. Those are for the lobby and the warden's office."

"Ain't nothing picks up lint and laundry soap scum like a upright vacuum," I say.

"Really?" He's interested.

"Lots of folks use them that way. You didn't know?"

"Well, hell," he says. "You want to lug that thing up there and waste your time, it ain't no skin off my back. I ain't going to do it."

SO I GET MY hands on the vacuum cleaner and take it with me to the laundry. I have such a feeling of triumph, I'm afraid Daigle can see it on my face. He seems reluctant to leave me alone. He walks along with me, making conversation. To keep calm, I tell him the Hoover is a commercial model. "Probably the top of the line," I say. "This baby will really do the job."

He just shakes his head. He wants to ask me if I've ever been much of a drinker. If I've ever been the kind of guy who ordered mixed drinks.

"All I drink is beer," he says. "I don't even know the names of most of them drinks folks order in bars. And in the movies, well..."

The Hoover has a high-capacity bag and even a light on the front of it. Not that I'll need the light. I'm more interested in the bladder where the dust bag goes.

I work in the laundry all day, biding my time. Daigle is in there with me watching everything I do and talking. He never shuts up. I scrub the inside of the washing machines, which takes the better part of an hour, then I lift the Hoover up onto the top of the dryers, over the vents, and turn it on. It works as I said it would, except the lint piles up and blocks the intake. But I pull the lint off, then feed it back in, slowly, while Daigle watches. He doesn't try to talk over the roar of the Hoover. I glance at him once, and he seems to smile. He looks like he might drift into sleep any second; as if it's an effort to hold his heavy eyes open. Then he says something I don't hear. I turn off the machine, and he says, "Looks like the damn thing's eating that lint."

I say, "Yes, it does."

I turn the machine back on and work at it awhile longer. Finally, I stop and stare at him.

"What?" he says.

"Nothing."

He shrugs.

"You got to stand there over me wherever I go?" I say.

He seems hurt. "Well, no. I guess I don't."

"I'm a trustee," I say. "Don't you trust me?"

"It ain't nothing like that," he says.

"Yeah, well." I go over to a big sink in the corner and wet a towel. He leans against the wall now, still watching me. I squeeze out the excess water and go back to the clothing bins.

He says, "You almost finished?"

"Almost." I'm beginning to worry how I'll do what I have to do if he never stops watching me, but then he says, "I'll be back in a minute."

"Suit yourself," I say.

He unlocks the metal door and goes out, closing it behind him. The echo of his shoes in the outside hall is the most exquisite sound I've heard in a long time.

As soon as he's gone, I move to the pile of laundry in front of the machines. I know what I'm looking for, and in all the yellow uniforms and gray sheets it isn't hard to find. It's pure white: a shirt and a pair of pants. I even take a pair of white socks. I roll them up in the smallest roll I can make, then stuff them into the bladder, behind the paper bag on the vacuum cleaner. By the time I hear Daigle coming back, I'm running the vacuum cleaner in the corners and just about finishing up. I turn the machine off when he comes in.

"I'm done," I say.

I am halfway home.

THE NEXT DAY, in the mess hall, I put one of the plastic salt shakers in my pocket. Nobody sees me. At lunch, I steal another one. They're small and easy to hide. And so many of them clutter the tables in that place, nobody will miss one or two of them. That night at dinner, I slip another one in my pocket. Just to be sure.

I start pouring salt in my water. I never drink water without putting salt in it. I don't care how it tastes, or how it eventually starts to make me feel. And I got to admit, it makes me feel really bad. Like something inside me is slipping down and coming loose under the skin, like my bones are starting to grow and swell. I go beyond thirst to a kind of mental dreamland. Horrific visions start to invade my whole mind—like a sudden fainting spell.

Finally one day I stand up, just for the evidence that I am a single consciousness, a body, a soul. I look around and realize I was screaming. There is Parchman staring at me, his eyes glittering with fear.

"What's wrong with you?" he says.

I look at him. I don't say anything, but I ain't screaming now.

"Why you making that noise?" he says.

"What noise?"

He shakes his head. "You got to see the doctor."

I know I'm getting pretty sick. I realize the next day that my stomach has started to swell, and I can't piss anymore. When the doctor finally comes to see me he doesn't like what he sees.

"John," he says. "You may have hepatitis."

"Really?" I say.

He touches my stomach where it bulges, and I recoil from it. "That hurt?"

"It don't feel good," I say.

"What's hepatitis?" Parchman says.

The doctor ignores him. "I'm afraid I'm going to have to put you in the infirmary for a while. And you're going to have to be quarantined until I can do some blood work."

Parchman says, "Quarantined? He got something I can catch?"

"We'll keep an eye on you," the doctor says.

"I got a trial for murder coming," Parchman says. He's almost whining. "A murder I didn't have nothing to do with, and I don't wanna be sick on top of everything else."

"You won't be."

"I'm owed at least that much," he says.

The doctor turns to him. "I'll take some blood from you, too. But that's why we're taking John to the infirmary, so he doesn't give this—whatever this is—to you."

"I don't want to go to no infirmary," I tell him. "I just want to keep working, doing what I'm doing. It helps pass the time."

"Do you even know who I am right now?" Doc says.

"Sure, you're the doc."

"Doctor Miles," he says.

"Glad to make your acquaintance," I say. His expression doesn't change. Parchman smiles, but he's quiet. Doctor Miles looks into my eyes with a little flashlight. "Hold still." He puts his hand on my brow, raises one of my eyelids with his thumb, and shines the light into my eye. Then he does the same thing to the other one.

"Having any strange dreams?"

"Sometimes."

"They ever come on you when you're awake?"

I don't answer him.

"You've got a slight case of jaundice," he says.

"I know what that is."

"You do."

"Yeah. It means I look yellow."

"Your eyes," he says. "Not so much the rest of you, but your eyes. And this swelling here," he touches me again. "I don't like that."

I shrug. "I guess it don't matter what a fella wants in here."

He smiles. "It won't be permanent. You want to treat this, don't you? Let's run a few tests and find out what's wrong."

"Okay," I say.

"Anything I can do for you now?"

"Yes, sir," I say. "Could you get me a drink of water? I'm mighty thirsty."

"What's the matter with the water in here?" he says.

"I don't like it much," I say. "It ain't so cold."

By now, I am so thirsty I would gladly die for just a small glass of cold water. And I know it is time to start flushing myself out, getting healthy again, and ready.

PENNY

Morgan comes in the store just before noon.

"Where's Clare?" he says.

"She took the Studebaker down to Lebanon Church to get some fresh bread."

"Day-old bread," he says.

I'm sitting behind the counter, counting one-dollar bills to put in the cash drawer. So far I've arranged everything neatly on the shelves, dusted all the plants, wiped off and neatly stacked all the old bags of potato chips, pretzels, and sticky buns. I've swept the floor and washed the front windows. I'm doing whatever it takes to spend time. That's what I want to do: spend time. This Thursday I'll go to Richard Bland and see John. The world isn't big enough to hold the hope in my heart when I think about it. And time's just froze. I've already decided what I will wear: a navy blue skirt and blue-and-white plaid shirt. I'll wear my black sling-back sandals. I got gold earrings that don't look too fancy. I already know how I'm going to wear my hair. I've tried several things with my hair. Two long braids looked silly. I tied it to the side and didn't like that neither. Clare has promised she will curl it for me, so I can just wear it down and let it hang naturally.

"Well," I say, "it's bread. Folks don't mind how old it is as long as they don't have to drive all the way down to Lebanon Church to get it."

"I'm glad the store's open finally."

"We been open a couple of times since—since..."

He looks at me.

"Since Clare got better," I say.

"Who's that setting up there on the porch?"

"Mr. Bone."

"Well, I'll be." He walks over to the front window and looks out. It is quiet for a spell, while he stands there, his back to me, hands on his hips. Mr. Bone don't even rock in the chair. He just sits with his legs crossed, staring out across the town to the valley below.

I close the cash drawer. Outside the air is almost cold, but the sun is full up and clear as any day. This morning, small clouds scattered every which way, low on the horizon, but now, up high where the sun has climbed, it's nothing but open, blue space.

Morgan comes up to the counter and leans against it. "What kind of tobacco you got?"

"Same old stuff," I say.

He looks through the glass at the McBaren's, the Sir Walter Raleigh, Half and Half, and Middleton's. "The old man drunk, as usual?"

"He ain't been bad," I say. "Leastways, during the day. He's feeling pretty poorly right now though."

He nods. "I know the feeling."

"He don't get so drunk you could tell it," I say. "He don't get loud or laugh too much; he ain't too nice or too mean. He just gets quiet and misty-eyed, thinking of his wife, I guess. Then he wanders off to bed. Or maybe I reckon he staggers. He makes us leave the light on until he's asleep, but it don't take long."

Morgan seems almost to laugh. It's a smile that crosses his face at the same instant he takes in air, so it looks like that. Then he says, "Well. It ain't nothing but a kind of discouragement."

"I guess."

"What's he hanging around for?"

I smile. "Just to be safe."

"You don't say."

"He's watching over me and Tory."

"That's right kindly of him."

"And drinking most of Clare's whiskey."

He laughs. "Between the two of them, that's a lot of whiskey."

I don't say nothing. He can see he's hurt my feelings, but I don't want to let on.

"I'm sorry," he says. "I was just..."

"Forget it." To make him feel better, I say, "They'll drink up most of my inheritance if I let them."

"You know I don't mean nothing by it," he says. "I respect Clare."

I sit down on the stool behind the counter. He studies the tobaccos a little while, then he says, "Lemme have a can of the Half and Half and the Sir Walter Raleigh."

I get them for him.

"I like to mix them. Makes a nice blend."

I ring them up on the register, and he pays me with a twenty-dollar bill. I give him his change and close the drawer. The ringing bells on the register make me think of money in a way I don't want to. I thought once, when I was a little girl, that the sound of the bells on that cash register would ruin me for any kind of bell the rest of my life. Even Christmas bells reminded me of cash.

"I ain't seen no other signs of the Gypsy Man," Morgan says. "Not since..."

"I've been almost too busy to think about him," I say. "But I'm beholden to you for the new locks and dead bolts and all."

"Well, maybe it's over."

"You think so?"

"Looks like all he wanted to do was burn my house down and he failed at that."

"And maybe he wanted us to find that Landon boy."

He shrugs. "Maybe."

I don't know what to think or what to worry about. I have been taking care of Tory, Clare, and Mr. Bone. I know I'm gonna see John soon. I go out to check the place where the stone was, but the weeds are starting to cover it, and aside from insects in it every now and then, it's behaving like any other patch of new weeds. I don't want to think about what we found, or how it got there. Police have been here, and they took everything they found away with them. There ain't no bones or no tombstone nor any other thing to remind me. I get better sleep, and Clare and I gone back to opening the store and keeping house and getting ready for Thanksgiving and Christmas. I am saving money for the trip down to Richard Bland, and for a long time now, that's all I can think of at night. When it's all settled in the house and I'm getting ready for bed, I'll suddenly hear John's voice in my head. I'll see him smiling that bright gleaming smile and I almost want to laugh, but I'm near tears, too. Then I lay on the bed and watch the stars or the moon and think about him; I try to remember all the times with him, all the things I've heard him say or seen him do. It's like a movie I try to remember—like a great picture show I just come back from with music that made tears ache in my throat and gave me the gift of distracted days and easy nights drifting into sleep remembering.

"You know, I tried to keep an eye on you, too," Morgan says.

"I know that."

"The Gypsy Man's come and gone. I do think so."

I say, "But I still got to keep an eye out."

"Nothing wrong with that."

I put his tobacco cans in a bag and hand it to him. "You want something else?"

He seems to think for a spell. Then he says, "If'n you need anything..." He stops. He wants to say something, but then he swallows whatever it was. It's like he is watching me and waiting for something.

"What?" I say.

"Nothing."

It's quiet for a spell, then he says, "Just..."

"Just what?"

"Come see an old man once in a while," he says.

"I work at the Goodyear store on Saturdays," I say. "But Sunday I might bring Tory down and see how you're doing."

He nods, suddenly a little more animated and alert. "That'd be great."

"They finished fixing the porch yet?"

"No, they're working on it. Making a hell of a racket, too."

I smile, waiting for him to leave. He has the bag in his hands. His knuckles look swollen and bent. It don't seem like he's between me and danger no more, so now I realize I feel right sorry for him. He's so alone.

"A hell of a racket," he says.

"I expect so," I say.

"You know that damn fire department down in Lebanon Church says it was hit by lightning?"

"Yeah, I heard that."

"Lightning. But I seen him go by in the truck. And I know he was a-setting out in front for a while before I seen him go by. I know it wasn't no lightning. I know that."

"I guess so," I say. I wish I could tell him who that was in the blue truck. But I can't. So I just look at him, and then he seems to read something in my gaze.

"Now you don't believe it neither?" he says.

"No, I do," I say. "Just, seems like a horrible thing finding that Landon boy back there."

"Yes, it does."

"You don't think the Gypsy Man put him there, do you?"

He shakes his head, slowly. "Sometimes," he says. "But most times, no, I don't."

"He don't work that way, right?"

"Not that I've ever seen," he says. "Truly."

"I was wondering," I say. "Maybe the Gypsy Man is just..."

He don't say nothing, but the way he's looking at me, I know he's listening.

"Maybe we got a little of him in ourselves," I say.

"What do you mean?"

"I mean, maybe—ain't it possible that we carry a little of him around with us? Like he don't need to be here, we bring him back anyway..."

"That may be." He almost smiles. It's like I've guessed something right, and he's pleased. But then he gets this serious look on his face and says, "You ain't suggesting the Gypsy Man don't really exist, are you?"

"Well, that's what I mean," I say. "Maybe we bring him back."

"But he ain't real?"

"No, of course he's real. Don't you see?"

"We ain't talking about Santa Claus," he says, almost smiling again. His eyes are bright now, and his face is gentle—the usual look of kindness that always makes me feel warm and safe.

"I was just thinking about what I'd say to Tory about all this," I say. "I know it wasn't no Gypsy Man that put the Landon boy in the ground up yonder."

"No, I don't guess it was," he says.

"So what was it then?"

He shrugs. "We may never know."

"Sheriff Paxton ever tell you what was in them papers? Or how much money it was?"

"I heard it was thousands of dollars. And that the notes was pages from a kind of personal diary."

"Sheriff Paxton told you that?"

"No. But I heard it. Some folks was talking down to the barbershop."

"It ain't none of my business, but I'd like to know."

He puts the bag up under his arm, cradles it there like a football. "Well," he says. "The body just happened to be there next to that box. It had nothing to do with it."

"No," I say. "I expect it didn't."

"That's another thing altogether." He just stood there, looking at me with sad eyes.

"I guess it is," I say.

"Probably Wilbur buried the money there. Ain't no safer place to bury money than under a gravestone. Even treasure hunters think twice about digging up a grave." He scrunches the bag up tight under his arm and seems as if he's going to leave. I go to the sink behind the counter and empty the coffeepot. I rinse it out, filling it with water and dumping it several times, then I refill it and return it to the coffee machine. He is still waiting there behind me without saying nothing. When I finish I pretend to be surprised to find him behind me.

"Thought you'd gone," I say.

"You know," he says, "they're going to be asking John a few questions."

"I know it."

"I wouldn't fret it none."

"They'll blame him," I say. "I expect it."

He lowers his head and seems to look for something at his feet, then he says, "That won't happen, Penny." He looks up at me. "You hear? It won't happen."

I don't say nothing. He's just trying to make me feel better and all, but I feel sorry for him again. I don't want to feel that way—like he needs me instead of the other way around. He has always been the one thing between me and disaster for so long, it feels terrible to recognize that he is helpless, that he offers his promises from somewhere beyond all his powers, and it is just empty talk from an old man. I hate feeling like this.

After a long quiet spell, I say, "Me and Tory'll come down on Sunday."

"That'd be just fine," he says.

At the door he turns around. He has his hand on the knob, but he's looking at me. "You got John's father here, does that mean...?"

When I know he ain't going to finish the sentence I say, "Does that mean what?"

He grins. "I just thought you might of heard from John."

"I declare," I say. "A person's business is everybody's business up here."

"I was just wondering," he says. "Most folks know about the promise on the Bible."

"Well, then you can ask most folks."

He lowers his head, seems disappointed. When he opens the door to go out, I say, "I'm going down there to see him." I realize I'm smiling to beat all, like it's something I'm giving to Morgan.

He stops and turns back, still holding the door open. "Get out," he says. "Really?"

"This Thursday."

"Well, that's just fine and dandy, hon." He is still smiling, standing there in the doorway. "I'm very happy to hear it." He's quiet a second looking at me. Then he says again, "So very happy to hear it." It takes him awhile, but when he realizes I ain't going to say no more, he nods briefly, seems to recover himself a bit, then goes on out and lets the door slam behind him. I watch him walk a ways up the hill until he has Mr. Bone's attention. At least he must think he does. He waves, his

349

arm fully extended, his hand open and bent upwards a bit at the wrist. It's a fragile-looking, bony white hand, tipping a bit back and forth as the arm waves. Mr. Bone just sits motionless in the chair, staring at him, or into space or out over the valley. I can't really tell what he's looking at, but he don't move and he don't ever seem to notice Morgan waving at him. Then Morgan turns and makes his way carefully back down the hill. I don't even know if Mr. Bone knows he was there.

It saddens me to watch the old man walking down the road, carrying the bag of tobacco under his arm. It's a beautiful day, like I said. The sun is bright and cool and almost tender, and Morgan is on his way home where he's by himself except for the noisy, strange young men who are rebuilding his back porch. It seems like when Morgan waved and Mr. Bone didn't pay no attention to him it was an awful lot like the world; like the way the world don't pay no attention to what one person wants or needs; like how the world don't give a damn about nothing a man or woman tries to save, or give, or create, or sacrifice, or offer. All our screams and sorrows, chatter and laughter ain't for nothing but ourselves. Ain't nobody else going to hear it. Same with all our offerings of love or sweetness or help for pain. I don't know. It's hard to say, but watching Morgan trying to offer a bit of friendliness to Mr. Bone, seeing him struggle halfway up that hill just to offer a good morning, and failing at it—coming back down the hill defeated—makes me feel so empty and desolate I almost start crying. Like I've seen God ignoring a needful prayer.

I rush outside and call out, "Morgan?"

He turns around, still moving forward a bit, until he sees it was me that called him. Then he stops. "You okay?" he says.

"I really am coming down on Sunday," I say.

"Good." Now he waves at me.

"I'll come for supper if you like."

"You cooking? Or me?"

"I'll cook if you want."

He smiles, nodding his head. He don't have the air to holler no more. He waves again, then turns and walks on down the hill toward town.

AMBROSE

I see that white woman Clare come down from Crawford. She stop fo' gas right here drivin' that old Studebaker her brother lef her when he killed in the war. And a man with a baseball cap walk up from the road with a ax handle in his hand. I don't know where he come from. He say, "Can I git some help?" like that to the white lady. She comin' back to the car from the sto'e and I be puttin' gas in the tank fo' her. The white lady don't look at him just right away, and the man with the ax handle say, "I's talking to you, honey," like that, and she turn 'round and smile.

"Well, look at you," she say. She don't expect him, like. Like she don't know what to do with him and then he stand there leanin' on the ax handle. "I come back," he say.

I don't know the man with the ax handle. His face be round and dirty, and his eyes be pale and dull like two small clots of phlegm. He look at me. I say, "You gots car trouble, suh?" And he don't say nothin' to me fo' a second. He take that ax handle, hold it up in front a his face, lookin' at me, and he say, "Boy, you say something to me?" and I say, "No, suh, I jes' thought you needed somethin' is all." And he say, "You mine your own business," and I say, "Yes, suh."

He turn 'round and see the white lady lookin' at his face real close, like she can't fine somethin' she be lookin' fer. He say, "What you doin'?"

"Is you painted up?" she say.

"What you talkin' 'bout," he say.

She don't look so happy to see him, but then he start laughin'. And she smile and then she be laughin', too. She laugh harder and louder than he do. "How you get yo' face so dirty?" she say.

Then he aks her, "Does I scare you?" Pokin' at her now with the ax handle.

"Don't," she say. "Don't do that."

He don't say nothin'. He set the ax handle back against his leg and stand there lookin' in her face. She 'most tall as him, and she stop laughin'.

"I come to fine out what I can fine out," the man say.

"Look at you," she say. "You got dirt from head to toe."

He laugh. "I been runnin' around."

She just lookin' at him, her eyes like spiders that curl up when you start tearin' at the web. Like she don't know what, but she be ready fo' it when the time come.

Meantime, he be laughin'. "Come on, honey," he say. "Let's go have a little fun?"

"It just be trouble," she say. "Now go wash yo' dirty face."

"I ain't gonna be washing nothin' right here," he say. He real calm, like he might fall asleep if she don't keep talkin' to him. His voice real high, like a woman's voice.

She stand there watching me put gas in the car. But she keep checking him, too. He lean on the ax handle, jes' lookin' at her. Then he say, "Promise you won't take another shot at me?"

"I ain't the one shot at you," she say.

"Who done it, then?"

"Morgan Tiller. A old man. He thought you was the Gypsy Man."

He laugh. Then he say, "I don't take it kindly." This time his voice sound real low, like he in the bottom of a well. "He put a hole in a water hose on my engine."

She don't believe it.

"Went right through the seat, under the dash, and into the motor," he say. He ain't laughin'.

"He thought you was the Gypsy Man," she say again.

"Well," he say. "I don't like to be shot at."

When the car full a gas they gets in and drives away. I see the lady lookin' kine a scared an' maybe excited, too. You can tell she feelin' somethin' but not like he do. He ain't smilin' or laughin'. He jus' look at her. She get in the car and they drive away. But she be feelin' strong with him. Like she fine what she be lookin' fer, and don't know if it be a thing that feel good or hurt. You know? It don't worry me. It ain't none a my business. It be white business.

I don't get in no business if it white business.

Then the sheriff, he come by. He pull in the same afternoon, tell me to fill her up. I know him. He the one lookin' fo' the Landon boy an' he always come around here act like he somethin' special 'cause he look so long fo' the Landon boy. And tell me he fine that boy someday. Like I just might be happy 'bout that. Like it be the best news fo me just 'cause I knows the Landon folks.

And then when he do fine him, when he uncover the very bones, what he do? He yell at everybody like we put them bones in the dirt.

"Why you yellin' at me?" I say. "Why you tellin' me all that 'bout the law and diggin' up graves? I already knows it. It ain't nothin' to me, noway. I never see the boy's daddy no more. His momma be gone a long time. So why you yellin' at me?"

He always comin' 'round here 'fore he fine the boy an' tellin' me how he still lookin'.

"Why you tellin' me that?" I say.

He say, "I thought you like to know."

I like to know somethin' all right.

What I like to know, how come what happen up the mountain so hard to fine out. That what I like to know. What

353

I say. I say all you got to do's go down an aks the poelice if the Landon boy be white what they be doin' 'bout it. You fine out. They be doin' somethin' 'bout it if he white. Oh, they all show up when he get lost; they all be talkin' 'bout finein' him. They put on a show. The whites. They always put on a show fo' the black folks. Even when they shows up with sheets over they head and crosses burnin'. It be a show.

I's a old man. I be workin' right here fo' 'most thirty years. Befo'e that, I been drivin' up and down the roads and in and out of the towns and cities all around. I been to Georgia and Oklahoma and Louisiana and Missouri. I 'most went to Califo'nia once. Made it far as Phoenix, Arizona. Been to France, too. Fightin' in the war. But I sees how it is. I knows what most white folks be carin' 'bout. And it ain't got nothin' to do with democracy. No, sir. It got to do with everythin' but. It got to do with who be on top a who and who be down below. You knows it, too.

When they wants somethin', they be talkin' like you important, like you matter. You don't matter. You be colored, you don't matter. But it ain't just color. It don't be nothin' like just color. They like a black man don't look black. Black woman don't look black. It don't matter how dark you be. They let you alone, you look white. You got black skin, and you be lookin' white? Okay. That be fine. You got white skin and you be lookin' like a black man? You a nigger. Don't matter the color skin. You a nigger. You look like a nigger, you a nigger. You look like a white man, you be welcome and they even treats you like a white man, if you lets them. A second-class white man. But a white man, just the same. Hell, they be proud to call you they fren'. They be tellin' folks, "Oh, one a my best fren's be a Negro." Until you be makin' trouble. Until you do somethin' that remind them you a black man. Until somethin' goes missin' in they house. You a nigger when that happen.

You see what I say?

I hear them talkin' 'bout a Gypsy Man. What is the Gypsy Man do? I don't know if he do nothin' bad. I ain't heard nothin' 'cept 'bout dis Landon boy. The Landon boy a Negro. He go to the white school. Then he be gone.

The white folks say it be a Gypsy Man.

I spit them words out my mouth 'fore I say 'em out loud.

You know why the Gypsy Man ain't black? That make sense to you? Seem like he be black if he bad. If he evil. Ain't nothin' bad that ain't black to white folks. So how come the Gypsy Man ain't black?

I knows why. The Gypsy Man ain't black 'cause they seen him. They be seein' him all the time.

That how come I know he real. I know he real 'cause he ain't black.

The man with the ax handle ain't no Gypsy Man, but he believe it, too. He know it, too.

The white woman be working real hard not to show no fear. I say that fo' her. She get in the car and drive off like it was nothin', like she be takin' a fren' fo' a ride. But I see she scared a little bit anyway. Any man know that who see it. She ain't jus' excited. No, suh.

The man in the baseball cap start to rub the side a her face and then pattin' her hair on the back a her head. Like he was pettin' a horse. But the white lady, she don't even look at him. She just hold onto the wheel and check back fo' cars on the road, and then she drive on off.

PEACH

If it don't beat all. I walk along the highway, find a ax handle laying right there. Brand new. I think it must of dropped off a truck. Somebody hit a bump and it fell. Probably.

I wonder if a planet's turning makes the wind and all. When you ride with the window down you feel the wind. If you had a strong wind blowing—a hurricane wind blowing at your back at say a hundred miles an hour, and you was driving at say, a hundred miles an hour, would you feel any wind at all? What if you was driving sixty, and the wind at your back was at a hundred, would the wind on your arm make you think you was going backwards at forty miles an hour?

I was watching the TV, and they said something about how if a spaceship got going real fast in the air, the air would heat up and burn the thing. But when I first get in my car, and the heat's made the metal real hot, it only takes a little moving air to cool it down. So that don't make sense. Air either cools a thing off or heats it up. It can't do both. I know that.

Don't anybody know it? Do they think we're stupid?

I got the ax handle, walking down the road. I don't know what I'll do with it. Use it for a cane. Or I could smash a man's head in with it. Yes, sir. Smash it real good. Ain't nobody better cross me while I got this in my hand.

I run into Clare again. She's still pretty as a painted picture. Glad to see me, too. I show her the ax handle. When I get in her car, she says, "Where to?"

"Whatever," I say. I don't give a damn, long as we're moving. I like the wind on my arm. I tell her to slow down though. Don't want no cops noticing us. Even with the ax handle. Someday, I'd like to learn how to make tattoos. It don't look so hard.

CLARE

What's the hurry?" Peach says.

"I ain't in no hurry. I just like to drive fast."

He holds an ax handle between his knees. In spite of the

chill in the air, he wears a short-sleeved shirt. The tattoos on his arms look like a kind of armor. I like being the one with the car this time, the one doing the driving. When I first seen him I got a little scared. He had that ax handle, and when he touched me with it, it hurt. He probably didn't mean it, but he pushed on it, and I felt it. Then he had this look in his eye I never seen before. Like something alive had gone. Like his eyes wasn't no window into the soul, but just openings that let light into a huge darkness, a thing truly empty.

But when we got into the car he didn't say nothing. I started it up and pulled out of the station, and he just smiled at me. Then his eyes seemed to come back to life a bit. I don't know how to explain it. He says, "Where we going?" And I think how good it is that he don't tell me to do nothing; he wants to know where "we" are going. I like the sound of it, and I like it that I'm the one that decides this time.

I drive on down to Lebanon Church and get the bread I want. He stays in the car, even when I open the trunk and fill it with loaves of bread. When I get back in the car, I say, "Thanks for the help." I feel glad and free to say that to him.

He's slumped down in the seat, his hat over his eyes, sleeping. He says, "Bread ain't heavy."

"Well, I could of used help loading it."

"It ain't heavy."

I start the car and get going again. He plays with the ax handle.

"What's that for?" I say.

"What, this?"

"Yeah, that," I say, still watching the road.

"Slow down a bit, and I'll tell you."

I let up on the accelerator.

"Just do the speed limit," he says.

I slow down some more. It's quiet for a little while, then I say, "Well?"

357

He holds it up. "I use this to make all the walking I done easier."

"You done a lot of walking?"

"After the truck give out. I had to."

"And you use that like a cane?"

He gives a short laugh. "I could use it that way. Both in walking and getting what I want, you know what I mean?"

I look at him, and he grips the base of the ax handle like a baseball bat.

"This here thing packs a wallop," he says.

"A weapon," I say.

He smiles. "I probably don't need one, but if I did, this here's just what the doctor ordered."

I drive on up to Route 13 and then into Crawford. I'm free and young, that's all. A lot of folks are older than me. I got the window down, and the rush of wind in my hair makes me feel giddy and like I should be laughing. Peach tries to light a cigarette. "Shut the fucking window will you?" he says.

I put my head back, breathe the cool air deep. "Don't you love this?" I say.

"I'm trying to light a cigarette," he says.

I roll the window up a bit, and he leans over against the other door and lights his cigarette. Then he takes another out of the pack and lights it for me. "Where we going, lady?" he says.

I take the cigarette from him and roll the window down again.

"Where we going?" he says again.

"It's almost time to pick up my niece," I say. "At school."

He says nothing. I take a deep drag off the cigarette. It tastes like youth—like when I was a girl, driving my daddy's car late at night, before I had a driver's license. It feels reckless and bad, and I know suddenly that for the minute I don't care about nothing. Then the grown woman in me says, "We should unload this here bread, first."

"Whatever you say," he says.

"Tory's not really my niece," I say, puffing on the cigarette. I turn the car in the middle of town and head up the hill to the store. "She's my niece's daughter."

I park by the back door behind the store. This time he gets out of the car and helps me unload the bread. We get it done in just two trips. Penny ain't in the store, and I don't see nobody up at the house. When I go around front, I see a sign Penny put up, GONE TO FETCH TORY.

I take the sign down and open the door. Peach is standing in the door frame at the back. "We don't have to pick up my niece after all," I say.

"What you want to do?" he says, flipping his cigarette into the grass outside the door.

"Let's stack this here bread on the shelves," I say.

He steps all the way into the store, walking slow. I still have some of my cigarette left, and the smoke, spinning in the sunlight through the windows, makes him look mysterious and eerie as he comes toward me.

"I don't want to stack no bread now," he says.

JOHN BONE

I can't believe how different everything looks. The trees seem thicker and larger, but I know that can't be. Not in just six years. I got a ride up here with a trucker, who didn't notice how tight these jeans are or how short. At least these old shoes fit me. He dropped me off a mile or so east of Lebanon Church. I walk for miles, up past several switchbacks and hollers. I stay away from cars. When I hear them coming I duck down into the weeds. In these hills, with so many sharp turns, it ain't likely that somebody would see me before I see them.

Near Crawford, I start feeling the whole thing in my stomach. All the fear and excitement and worry. I can't wait to see Penny. Sometimes I'll be working my way up an incline and I'll realize that I can't catch my breath, and then it hits me that I've actually been running, or trying to, with these brogans on my feet and the jeans digging into my belly. I am unbelievably hungry and still thirsty. I don't think I'll ever quench my thirst again.

I don't feel free yet. But I am not in captivity. That's how I feel. Not in captivity.

I WAS QUARANTINED for four days. On the fifth day, early, Doctor Miles came in. "Well," he said. "You don't have hepatitis."

I nodded.

"You should be glad of that." He was almost smiling. His hair was trimmed high over his ears and it was turning gray there, so he looked older than he probably was. He wore one of the white jackets, and he constantly clicked a ballpoint pen in his hand as he talked. "I don't think you need to be quarantined anymore."

"What do I have?"

He looked into my eyes again with the small light. I could hear him breathing. "Jaundice is almost cleared up as well."

I said nothing.

"You had some kind of sepsis, in your kidneys I think. But the antibiotics seem to have cleared it up. You're doing much better."

"You don't know, do you?"

Now, he did smile. "Nope. Nobody does. The lab report said your blood had unusual levels of sodium."

"What's that a sign of?"

"You were about to become a ham." He laughed briefly, looking at me, watching for a response. He took my wrist in his fingers and then studied his watch. "Your urine was more than three percent salt. That doesn't mean anything to you, but what it means to me is you were about to die from dehydration."

"Really?"

"It's no wonder you were having mad dreams. Your kidneys were getting ready to shut down."

"What causes that?"

"Drinking salt water for one." He was still studying his watch. I think my pulse must have increased when he said that. But then he went on. "Or an infection in your kidneys—if they don't do their job, odd things begin to accumulate in the body. Then your liver overworks, and you get jaundice."

He let go of my hand, then placed his stethoscope against my chest and listened. He moved it around, a look of serious concentration on his face. "But you seem to be doing quite well, now," he said. "Take a few deep breaths."

When he was finished he straightened up. "I was worried about the swelling in your liver and the fluid in your lungs. But it's all clear now."

"Can I get out of here?"

"I can put you in with the regular population in the infirmary, but it will only be for a day or so. Then I think you can go back to your cell."

"Back home," I said.

He didn't smile. "Yes, back home."

When he was gone, I stood in the door frame and waited for one of the guards to come for me. It wasn't Daigle. It was a fellow named Harper, who never had anything to say to any of the inmates. He was young and very tall, with long thin legs. He walked me down the hall to the main infirmary. He waited for me to empty my footlocker and carry all my belongings to the new room. I carried everything with my head down. I didn't want anybody in the infirmary to look me in the face. The guard left me sitting on a bed in a long room with more than twenty beds, most of them occupied by sleeping inmates. A few of the men were sitting up a bit, reading a book or a magazine. One just stared into space, his hair piled on his head like it was blown by the wind. Before he left, Harper looked around us, leaned toward me, and whispered, "I hear you saved Mac's life."

I nodded.

"I want to thank you."

I looked at him. He was not smiling. It cost him something to speak to me.

I said, "Don't mention it."

"Did you know about your friend?"

"What friend?"

"Parchman."

"No."

"You know he was charged with murder. An old man and woman. Up Charlottesville way, in the mountains."

I didn't say anything.

"When he and the rest of them escaped." He stood there, looking at me. "Did you know that?"

"I knew he was worried about it. But he never talked to me."

"Well, they found the car that belonged to them folks— over in Tennessee. And it had the knife in it. Right there on the floorboard."

I waited for him to finish, but he seemed to realize suddenly that he was talking—that he had actually been saying things to an inmate. He looked around, then almost whispering again, he said, "It was Peach. Just what Parchman said. Peach done it. They got his fingerprints on the knife."

"Did they catch him?" I said.

"No. He ain't caught. But he done it. Parchman said he'd be a witness."

I shook my head slowly, but I didn't say anything. He was waiting there, standing very still, watching me. Then he seemed to discover himself again, realize where he was. "Well," he said, "that's that."

"Good."

He turned and walked out.

I stood for a while at the door watching the doctors and nurses—mostly males—going through their daily routines. They changed shifts at six in the evening and six in the morning. A part-time shift came in from ten at night until three in the morning.

I waited for my chance. Monday went by, then Tuesday. Still, no activity. I was afraid the doctor would put me back in my cell before I had my chance. Whenever a nurse or another doctor approached the room, I laid in the bed and pulled the covers up over my shoulder and pretended to be sleeping. Sometimes the doc brought me more medication. I started thinking about how sick I'd have to be to get back in here, and just as I was about to lose faith in my plan, I heard the guard down the hall. He was vacuuming his way toward me.

I got out of bed and opened the footlocker at the foot of it. I took out a bottle of talcum powder, removed the top, and dumped it on the floor at the foot of my bed. I kicked it around a bit, then put the top back on the container and set it back in my footlocker.

The noise from the Hoover got louder and louder.

Finally the guard worked his way to the carpet in front of the door. I got up and watched him. It was Harper. He looked at me—but he said nothing. In spite of his youth, I realized he looked like a man who'd suffered more than most. Something about the depth of his eyes and the lines there. He had clearly lost faith in something. He looked sloppy, and like he'd given up a lot to end up here. In some ways, the guards were prisoners, too.

When he finished the room, he turned off the Hoover and started rolling up the cord.

"Can I borrow that thing?" I said.

He seemed surprised to see me there. "What?"

"Can I borrow that vacuum cleaner for just a second?"

"What for?"

I pointed to the talc on the floor. "That stuff is slippery."

"How'd it get there?"

"I don't know. It was here when I got here."

"No, it wasn't."

"I don't know how it got there," I said.

He seemed annoyed, but he unwrapped the cord again and went to plug it back in. I took the Hoover into the room with me. "I'll get it," I said.

He stood by the plug.

I knelt down, opened the bladder on the back, and reached behind the bag. The white clothes were still there. I pulled them out, lifted the mattress on the cot, and stuffed them under it. As I was zipping up the bag, the guard came around the corner.

"What are you doing?"

"Nothing. I thought the bag might be full."

He came over and unzipped it again. He felt around the bag, then looked at me. "It ain't even half full."

I shrugged. I could not believe my luck.

He stood up. "Well?"

I turned the Hoover on and ran it over the powder. When I turned it off, I said, "This thing does a good job."

He said nothing. He went out, pushing the vacuum cleaner

in front of him. I sat down on the cot, feeling immortal. Everything worked exactly as I thought it would. And I was stronger now, perfectly able to finish what I had started.

Now, I come to a turn in the road that I know will take me to Route 13, and up the hill to Crawford. I smell the pines running down their sap, and the leaves of the oaks and maples and sycamores turning in the breezes seem to welcome me home. The sunlight is so filtered, it sparkles at me, sends long, soft beams of light through the trees. As I'm crossing the road, looking down the hill toward Lebanon Church, I hear a car coming from the other way. I get myself into the ditch by the road, but not before a Chevy comes around the bend, going way too fast. I realize, as he passes, that it is Brad Crowly. I don't know if he saw me or not.

PENNY

Every now and then a breeze kicks up and sends leaves flying at us while we walk. Tory tries to catch them, jumping up and laughing when she gets one. "Stop that for a minute, honey," I say. We're walking up the hill toward the store.

"Why?"

"Because I'd just rather talk."

"Okay."

Mrs. Gault put a green ribbon in Tory's hair and tied it in a neat bow. The curls that fall by her face can't be more perfect if she'd a gone down to Lebanon Church to the beauty shop there. And they are natural curls. The green bow looks sweet and feminine in her hair and I tell her so.

"Thank you," she says. She walks along, watching the leaves.

"How'd you do on your family tree project?" I say.

"He ain't give it back yet."

Another gust of wind blows by.

"It's gonna get mighty cold soon," I say.

"Where's wind come from, Mommy?"

"The weather," I say.

"How does it come from the weather?"

"It just blows, I guess. The earth is moving, honey."

"Oh."

"I'm going away this Thursday, did Clare tell you?"

She looks up at me. The expression on her face is almost sad, and it pains me to see it. "Not forever," I say. "Just one day."

"Where you going?"

"Well, that's what I want to talk to you about."

She swats at a leaf flying in front of her. Then she looks at me, the straight line of her lips almost tilted toward a smile. She's such a quiet little girl when she wants to be, when she's thinking.

"I'm going down to Richard Bland to see your daddy."

She stops walking. I let go her hand and she sort of moves back a little, like she sees something behind me.

I hold my hand out. "Come on."

"Why?" she says.

"Why what?"

"Why you going to see Daddy?"

"Because I want to." I reach for her, and she lets me take her hand. "Come on," I say.

"Can I go?"

"Not this time."

We walk for a while. It's already getting cooler. I can almost smell it. Soon we'll all have to walk a lot faster under the naked trees. But now, it's kind of balmy, even with the blustery wind. I watch Tory's face, the curls in her hair, and let what I've told her sink in. I know she is thinking all kinds of things. I can see it in her face. She inherited that sort of active mind from her daddy. Finally she says, "You swore on the Bible."

My eyes start to water, and I think to tell her it's because of the wind. It's mostly from the wind and dust and even small fragments of the leaves, but I also know it may be the first part of remembering all I have missed in six years. I used to love the way John simply blinked or turned his head when he talked. I might of had that if he didn't insist on our promise. I wipe tears away from the corners of my eyes. My face feels cold when the wind hits it. I don't want Tory to think I am crying. "Something's happened, honey," I say. "Something important."

"Ain't you supposed to stick to it when you swear on a Bible?"

"Yes, you are," I say. "But your daddy sent his daddy up here to talk to us, and I think he needs to see me."

"Who needs you?"

"I think Daddy does."

We get to the broken steps at the front of the yard. Right then, I don't want to climb the hill to the cabin. I see Clare's Studebaker in the parking lot behind the store. I sit down on the steps and let Tory come up between my knees. I put my arms around her and hold her for a second. The smooth, soft, cool skin on her face smells of fall, of the outdoors and leaves and wood smoke. I kiss her. "I love this time of year," I say. "Or I used to."

Tory plays with the ends of my collar, not really looking at me. She's almost pouting. "Why can't I go with you to see Daddy?"

"I'll go the first time," I say. "And even if it's just this one time—even if your daddy never wants to see me again, I promise I'll take you down there at least one time..." I stop. I think I can make a promise to her and we'll swear on the Bible, but then I remember the promise I am breaking. I want a difference between promising *not* to do a thing you really want to do, and promising to do something you really *don't*. Soon as I try to see which promise I am breaking, and which one I'm about to make, I can't do it. I want to see John. Since the day they took him away I have wanted to see him. I want to take Tory down to Richard Bland, too. I want to see the look on John's face the first time he sees her. I hope I'll get to see him lift her and put her on his knee. That sight, by itself, is enough to make me throw out the Bible altogether. I can't figure out how to promise her I'll take her to see him, without her insisting that we swear on the Bible, and without her realizing what I have come to know: that I am fixing to quit paying attention to the Bible. I will have to make up my mind. That's all. If I make up my mind, it don't seem to matter one way or the other whether I swore on a Bible or not.

I wrap my arms around her again, smell her cheeks. "I promise I'll take you to see him next time. Okay?"

She's still playing with the tips of my collar. "Okay," she says.

"I'll keep my promise," I say. "Bible or no Bible."

She puts her hands on my shoulders and smiles. "Will Daddy know who I am?"

"Sure, he will." I pat the top of her head. I am about to go on up to the house when Clare comes out of the store with a man. He is broad and fairly tall. He has a belly that hangs a little over the front of his jeans, and he's carrying a ax handle. His hair is wiry and uncombed. He comes across the road and up the hill, walking next to Clare. Clare is saying, "Penny, honey, wait up. Wait for us, dear."

"I ain't going nowhere," I say.

She's a bit out of breath from the climb. Or maybe she was out of breath when she begun the climb. Her hair is a mess, and I see her jeans and blouse ain't too neatly arranged neither. "This here's . . . ," she starts, but he interrupts her.

"I'm Gordon," he says, holding out his hand.

I take the tips of his rough fingers in my hand, then let go. His skin feels like the back of a turtle.

"Gordon?" Clare says.

"That's right. Gordon P.J. Middleton. Folks just call me P.J."

"I been calling you Peach all this time," Clare says.

"So this here's Peach," I say.

"P.J.," he says. "People used to say Peej for short, and that got turned all around."

He leans on the ax handle and holds out his other hand toward Tory. "Well, missy, what's your name?"

"I'm Penny Bone," I say. "This here's Tory."

He moves forward slightly, like it causes him pain to move. He puts his hand on top of Tory's head. "Howdy do, little girl?" he says.

"Isn't she cute as a button?" Clare says. She stands real close to him, the wind blowing her mussed hair. Her jeans buttoned down the front, and the very bottom button is open. Suddenly I feel sorry for her. She wants to look and be so much younger than she is. I smell cigarette smoke on her. The skin on her white arms has started to dangle from the bone. She *was* beautiful once. I seen the pictures.

P.J. kneels down in front of Tory. "I said howdy do, little girl. Don't you hear so good?"

"She heard you," I say. "She don't take to strangers."

He looks up at me, then at her again. "Why, that's probably a good thing. Well, let me introduce myself. I'm P.J." He holds his hand out to her.

Tory touches it, then smiles.

"There," he says. "Ain't she cute?"

Clare says, "Just adorable."

"Looks just like her daddy," he says.

Clare and I both look at each other. I say, "You know John?"

"Yes, sir," he says, still looking at Tory. "I know John. Not too well but I know him." Then he puts the ax handle down and picks Tory up and sets her up on his shoulders. He has his hands on her knees, holding her there. Tory wraps her arms around his neck. She don't look frightened. She just stares at the top of his head. He smiles at me. "Where you want her?"

"Put her down," I say.

He starts up the walk. "We going up this a way, ain't we?" He's still smiling.

"Where you know John from?" I say, following him. Tory bounces on his shoulders, holding on, but she don't make a sound. I can't tell if she's scared or what. Clare gets up beside him and puts her hand on Tory's leg. "You okay, honey?" she says.

"I'm okay," she says. "I'm taller than you."

"Yes, you are," Clare says.

"Where you know John from?" I say.

"From prison," P.J. says. "I know John from prison."

Clare turns back toward me, a look of shock on her face. She mouths the words, "I didn't know," to me.

He looks at her. "What you saying to her?" he asks. He stops walking.

"Nothing," she says.

"You said something," he says. "I seen it."

"I want to get down now," Tory says.

He reaches up and grabs her arms, then gently hoists her up over his head. He sets her down in front of him. "You enjoy the ride?" he says.

"Yes. Thank you." Tory almost curtsies in front of him.

"Well, I'll ride you again sometime. She's a perfect lady," he says to me.

"You was in prison with John?" I say.

"Just for a little while." He smiles, and I see that one of the lower teeth on the left side is broken. It makes his smile look almost sinister. "I used to live around here. Spent the better part of more than a few summers digging up the grounds up there at the old Crawford place."

"Really?" I say.

"Looking for buried treasure."

"John never fell for them stories," I say.

Clare says, "Oh, I always believed there was money to be had up there. And come to find out, there was."

"There was?" P.J. says.

"Sure was. Thousands and thousands of dollars, buried right over yonder," Clare says.

"No fooling?" P.J. says.

I say, "It was just found. It ain't there no more."

"Well, hell," P.J. says. "That was one of the reasons I come up here in the first place."

"How long did you know John?" I say.

"Who found it?"

Clare says, "The damn sheriff got it. He was there when we found it, so now it ain't nobody's money, I guess."

"Well, I'll be," P.J. says.

"How long did you know John?" I say.

He looks at me. "Not long."

"He didn't send you up here?"

"No, ma'am. I did that on my own. And I almost got shot in the ass for doing it."

I forgot about Morgan's shooting spree. I don't know what to say. P.J. must of noticed the shock of memory on my face.

"How about that?" he says. "Was it you that taken a pot-shot at me?"

"No, sir," I say. "But if'n I had the gun, it would a been me. We thought you was the Gypsy Man."

He laughs a little, and this time the wide smile on his face don't look so bad. He just has the appearance of a ignorant hick with a big appetite and a loud voice. Except his voice is kind of high—high and soft, like a young preacher or even a woman. It don't go with the body it comes from.

"Let's go on inside," he says. "I'm hungry. And I want to hear all about the buried treasure and all."

"I can tell you all about it," Clare says. Then she turns to me. "Would you go on down and mind the store, honey, until we finish lunch here?"

"We ain't going to be long here," P.J. says. "We've got places to go."

"Where are you going?" I say.

"Got to help me get my truck back on the road, don't you honey?" he says. He puts his arm around Clare's neck and she looks at me, a sad smile on her face. She is begging me with it, telling me not to ruin this.

"You ain't going to be gone too long, are you?" I say.

"I don't think so," Clare says.

"We'll get back when we get back," P.J. says. "It won't be no longer than a couple days maybe."

"Last time it was almost a month," I say.

Clare frowns. But P.J. just turns and raises his arm up high behind her, then lets it fall by his side. "Did I keep this girl all that long?" he says. He shakes his head. "Shame on me."

"We won't be long," Clare says.

P.J. gets real close to her and says, "What was you saying to that'un there before?" He points at me.

"What?" Clare leans back a bit. His hands hang by his sides, but he is so close to her, if she leans back any further, they might both fall down with him on top of her.

"Before," he says. "When I was toting the little one, you whispered something to that'un there." He points again.

"I did?"

"You mouthed it. I seen you do it."

"You couldn't tell?" Clare tries to act lighthearted about it, but I can see she is starting to get flustered.

He looks at me. Now his face is as empty as a jack-o'-lantern and expressionless, too. Slowly, he turns his pitiless gaze back to Clare.

"I just said I didn't know you'd been in prison," Clare says. "That's all."

"I don't take it kindly," he says.

"What?"

"I don't like it when you talk behind my back like that."

"I don't..." She starts to say something, but he moves his arm up and places it again on her shoulder. He has his face right next to hers, staring in her eyes, leaning into her, and she stops.

"I don't take it kindly, sweetheart," he says, too loud in her ear. "You see what I'm about here?"

"Yes, I do."

"Let go of her," I say.

He raises his hand, and Clare glares at me. She wants me to keep my mouth shut.

"It's a rude thing. Ain't it?" P.J. says.

"Yes, it is," Clare says.

"So, I won't have it. You understand. I won't abide it."

"I'm sorry," she says.

Then he steps back and smiles. "Let's go on in and eat something, what do you say?" He pats his stomach with both hands. "I could eat a damn ox, fur and all."

He struts up the steps with Clare and Tory behind him. He reaches in his pocket, takes out a key, and tries it in the lock. When it don't work, he turns and looks at me.

"I had them locks changed," I say.

"Well, I'll be. A smart thing," he says. Clare moves by him and with her key opens the door. He goes by her, holding the other key up so she can see it. "Guess I don't need this no more."

I get to the top step and Clare turns back to me and says, "Where's Mr. Bone?"

"Back home," I say. "He went back this morning."

"You think he left me any whiskey?"

"I don't know," I say. "What do you think?"

"Hey," P.J. says from inside the house. "You coming?"

Tory clings to Clare's legs. "Honey," I say. "Why don't you come on down and set with me in the store for a while?"

She don't like it, but she takes my hand and we go back down the steps.

"We'll open a bag of potato chips," I say. "How about that?"

"Clare," P.J. hollers. "Get on in here."

"I'm coming," she says. "Hold your horses." She looks at me. "Men," she says, rolling her eyes. It makes her so happy to have a man call her like that. She goes on in and closes the door.

Tory and I start down the hill toward the store. "You know what, Tory, honey?" I say.

"What?"

"You're going with me this Thursday, I think."

"I am?"

"You can stay out of school. I'm taking you with me."

She takes my hand in both of hers and leans into me while we make our way down the hill.

Maybe P.J. or Peej or Peach, or whatever his name is, didn't beat up Clare, and maybe he was the one that brought her back and put her on the couch and covered her up so she'd be comfortable. I seen that he was capable of being very gentle. I seen kindness in the way he lifted and carried Tory. He taken her hands in his so carefully when he put her down, too. But then just like that he turned, and from what I could see, he was just as likely to beat up on Clare as he was to be tender. He is the type of man, you never can tell what he is gonna do, from one minute to the next, and you can't tell what his mood will be neither. His face just looks kind of uninterested most of the time, as blank as an old photograph.

And then, just like that, his face can change, and he looks like a statue that somebody made when they was angry.

SHERIFF PAXTON

I keep going over in my mind what must have happened to Terry Landon. What his last hours must have been like, his legs broken and crushed, his ribs smashed. The bones was in terrible condition, even forgetting they'd been buried in yellow plastic for six years. It must have been a horrible death. And who can do such a thing to a child? What kind of monster can do such a thing to a little, bright-eyed boy?

It was a grocery list we found in the sack with the money. And on the back of that, a list of the bills: Seventy-five one-dollar bills, forty-six five-dollar bills, sixteen hundreds, and six five-hundred-dollar bills. That was the inventory.

"That's a lot of money," Gault said when I told him. He dropped by the next day, acting like he was interested in helping me tell Josh Landon what we found. Like he really thought I'd wait a day to do that.

"No, it ain't a lot of money," I said. "It's $4,905."

"I'd like to have that much in a lump sum."

"It ain't no treasure."

"Who's it belong to?"

I opened my desk drawer and took out the piece of paper. I turned the desk lamp on, then handed the paper to him. "Have a look at this."

He looked at it. Scribbled on the top of it, in black ink, was the word *Take* and under that the words, *in the fullness of time.* Under that, in a scrawl that was definitely written by a shaky hand, *Gypys Man.* Then a list of various canned goods, meat, and bread. Cigarettes and matches. All written out in the same awkward hand.

"What's it mean?" he says.

"I don't know. That's what the bills was wrapped in."

He looked at it again.

"What do *you* think it means?" I said.

"Maybe Wilbur *believed* he was the Gypsy Man. Maybe he wrote this, and he really believed he'd be digging up that box one day."

"He misspelled *Gypsy,*" I said.

He looked at it again. "Oh, yeah. *G-y-p-y-s.* Maybe he just didn't know how to spell," he says.

"It's the craziest damn thing," I said. "You never know about them people up there."

He turned his head a bit, seemed to look at something out the window. Then he said, "I live up there."

"No offense, your honor," I said.

He frowned.

I leaned back in my chair, waiting for him to go on. I was beginning to wonder what he was doing there.

"Is this the actual sheet it was written on?" he said, finally.

"That's it," I said.

He turned it over and studied the list of bills written on the back. "Well, the buried treasure really existed after all." He handed it back to me.

"It ain't no treasure. But it was buried, true enough."

"Know what I think?" he said. "I think John Bone might know something about what happened to Terry Landon. That's what I think."

"You think so, do you?" I said.

"That's right."

"He was around when this happened," I said.

"I hope, for Penny's sake, that he didn't," Gault said.

"I know you do."

"It would be a terrible thing for her and the child."

"Yes, it would."

He sat there, looking at the things on my desk. A long time seemed to pass, then he said, "So who will the treasure go to?"

"You got me."

"Shouldn't it be Penny's?"

"It was found on Crawford property. I expect we'll look for a living Crawford first."

He seemed satisfied with that. He got up, brushed his pants a bit—like he'd just finished eating. "You need anything," he said. "Let me know."

"Of course, I will," I said.

"No, I mean it."

"I know you do, your honor," I said.

He stood there a minute, an odd look on his face—almost like he was frustrated, and confused at the same time. Then he nodded my way and went out the door.

THIS IS WHAT bothers me. John Bone was nothing but trouble, anyway, when you come right down to it. Even when he was just a kid, he had a mouth on him. Didn't take to authority, folks said, because of what happened to his mother and all. He didn't ever give a damn about nothing. And I caught him drinking when he was only twelve or thirteen years old. It's the truth. Carrying a jug toward the river down below the lookout where folks go to fish. He was supposed to be in school. I pulled the car up to the edge of the road above the lookout there, where he was walking, and rolled the window down. I asked him what he thought he was doing.

"Going fishing," he says, still walking, still carrying the jug under his arm.

So I said, "Where's your fishing pole?"

He says, "I keep it down there."

Now I *known* that was a lie. I rode alongside him for a while, and he kept walking, his eyes straight ahead like I wasn't even there.

"What's in the jug?" I said.

And he says, "Whiskey." Just like that, he says, "Whiskey."

I liked that boy. I *still* like him. But I can't escape the look on old man Landon's face when I told him I found his little boy's bones. The memory of it keeps covering everything I can see. Like a cloth over my skull. I can't see nothing else.

You can't imagine it.

I asked John where he got the whiskey and he said, "It ain't none of your business." Now this was just sass, you know? John would say what he meant and he always meant what he said. I'll give him that. But I didn't like it none.

I stopped the car and got out. But he kept on walking. I hollered at him to stop, but he just went on. So I caught up to him.

"You ain't old enough to be drinking this here," I said. I grabbed it out of his hand. He wasn't ready for that.

"Give it back," he says.

I took the cork out of that jug, and with my finger in the ring on the side of it, hoisted it up on my arm. I smelled the whiskey on the cork, but to be sure I put the jug to my lips and took a sip. It was durn good sour mash whiskey.

"Now I want to know where you got this."

He looked at me and then set his jaw. I mean it looked like he bit down on a dry piece of hard leather the way the muscles in his jaw started working. But he wouldn't answer me.

You see what I'm getting at? Maybe you don't see it, but

when the real trouble started, and he claimed he was pretending to drink that beer so he wouldn't embarrass himself, and that's why it was a full bottle when he tossed it out the window and hit little Denise Walton—well, I known better. He'd been a whiskey drinker when he was twelve. Why would the beer make him nervous? Does it make sense to you?

He ain't no kid. I don't think John was ever really a kid. Not at least after his momma died.

I was there when they took him off to Richard Bland. I seen them put the cuffs on him and take him off. I put my hand on his head to keep him from bumping it when he got in the squad car, and I told him I was sorry about all of it. I told him I'd keep an eye out on his family. And do you know what he said? His wife was standing right there, holding a baby in her arms, and he says, "I ain't got no family." Just like that. Can you believe it? "I ain't got no family."

I been to war, and I seen a lot of things, and I don't scare easy, but that boy's eyes like to froze my heart. He looked like he could not only commit murder, but like he'd already done it, you know what I mean? Like he'd already seen the life go out of a person while he stood over them with the weapon in his hand.

I'm going to talk to him about the Landon boy.

I had to go to Josh Landon and tell him I found his son's bones. I had to say them words to a man who's spent the better part of every year just looking for the boy—like the activity of looking nurtured his hope somehow. If anybody'd told me before I become sheriff that I'd have to do a thing like that—in this little town—I would not be wearing this badge.

Hell, the state's got no interest in it. Landon was a nigra. And this is Virginia. So that's it.

But I ain't going to just let this sit. No sir. I ain't going to do that.

MYRA

I wish he just wanted to watch the World Series. If he were a Chicago White Sox fan, he'd have something to distract him, and that's what I think he needs. Once he knew what happened to the Landon child, he seemed to wither somehow—as if the loss of the child was a bereavement of his own, a family loss. I can't get him to talk to me about it. He goes to classes all day, hears one or two traffic cases in the court in the later afternoon, then he sits in his study reading. I come in to see if he wants company, but he doesn't speak. It's as if I am a servant. He takes from me whatever I bring him, but asks for nothing. I bring him tea and he drinks it, or not. He lets it sit sometimes. It is almost as if he agrees to whatever social interaction I want to impose as long as he does not have to speak. He even pretends to listen when I talk to him, but he only nods his head, and continues turning the pages of whatever book he has picked up or the newspaper.

He came home the day they found the body looking as if someone had beaten him.

"What happened to you?" I asked him.

"Something awful, Myra."

When he told me what happened, I couldn't believe it. I cannot say I was overcome with grief, but then I had had six years to get used to the idea, and I had long since given up hoping for the best. At all events, even if they found Terry Landon alive after all that time, it wouldn't really have been the same little boy who disappeared. Still, the news did shock me.

Henry just stood there in the hallway, sweat running down the side of his face and out of his hair. "How can you bear it, Myra?" He almost whispered it.

"Oh, honey," I said. "Poor Josh Landon. What will this do to him? I'm so sorry." I reached for him, but he didn't want to be touched. He brushed my hand away, walked by me, and went upstairs. I heard him running a shower. I followed him up and took his dirty clothes off the bed. "Good Lord," I said. "I can see who did most of the digging." But he didn't hear me because of the shower. I stood outside the door and listened for a moment. I heard him in there, talking to himself, whispering to himself, but I couldn't hear it clearly. I put his pants in the hamper and went back down the stairs. I thought I might make him a cup of tea. I didn't know if he would want to eat.

I waited for him a long time. When he came out of the shower, and I heard him pacing upstairs, walking back and forth across the creaking beams in the ceiling overhead, it was almost completely dark outside and I simply couldn't bear it. I got up and turned the foyer chandelier on, then went to the bottom of the stairs and called to him. "Henry! You going to just walk around up there all night?"

It got quiet.

"Henry," I said. "You want to eat something?"

He didn't answer. The pacing had stopped though, and after a short time, he came down and sat on the couch in the living room. I turned on one of the standing lamps next to the fireplace, then settled in the chair next to the couch and looked at him, but he was silent. He sat still, not really paying attention to much of anything, just thinking I guess. I saw his eyes blink a few times.

"Well, honey," I said. "You want to talk about it?"

With a sudden flash of what appeared to be anger and scorn, he turned to me and said, "No. I don't. Not ever."

I sat back. "Okay. I'm sorry I brought it up."

"Don't ever bring it up again."

"I won't," I said.

"You hear me, Myra?" His eyes were so wide it looked as if he was staring at something that terrified him. "I don't ever want to talk about it."

"You're scaring me, Henry," I said.

He was quiet for a long time. I didn't know what to say. I waited as long as I could, then I said, "Would you at least like some tea?"

He got up, quickly, as though something in the couch had stung him. Then he stood there, staring at the paintings on the far wall, the vases with flowers in them on the mantel. He might have been looking for some object he'd placed there. "It's just too much," he said.

"I know," I said.

"You don't know."

"I think I do."

"You don't." He was not looking at me now.

"Have I done something to anger you, dear?"

"I'm not angry. I'm not..." I thought he might start pacing again. He started searching the floor all around where he was standing. He was like a person standing on a rock that would soon be underwater in a quickly rising tide, and he needed to find another one to stand on right away. "Jesus," he said. "Jesus Christ."

"What?" I stood up and took his arm. "What?"

Suddenly he was crying. He put his head on my shoulder and I held him, while he sobbed.

"Don't," I said. "Don't, darling."

He didn't seem able to stop it. I kept saying, "It's all right, hon. It's all right," while I held him. He did not put his arms around me or do much of anything but stand there with his face in the crook of my neck and cry. I kept caressing the back of his head and the side of his face, hoping he'd respond, but he didn't. He never even looked at me. Once he got control of it and started to settle down, he turned away and walked back to the foyer. He stood under the great light in there and stared up at it—as if he were seeing the face of heaven. Then he shook his head and started up the stairs. "I can't believe it," he murmured as he ascended, gazing down at his feet, taking one step at a time, slowly, as though he were mounting a gallows.

I know he is terribly bothered by everything that happened, and that he probably blames himself a little for it, but I never dreamed he'd take the news of the Landon boy's death so acutely. I must be more of a fatalist than Henry, because I didn't think it would end any other way.

Tonight he wakes up soaking wet, moaning so loud, for a second in my own troubled sleep, I think he is screaming.

"Henry," I say. "Wake up. You're dreaming." When I touch him I realize he is soaking wet. He mumbles something about the school, and I say, "Henry, wake up."

He turns over and looks at me. In the moonlight, his eyes shine like gemstones. "Goodness, honey," I say. "You're soaking wet."

He sits up. I get out of bed and bring him some dry pajamas and a towel. He sits on the edge of the bed, his head in his hands.

"Go on in and clean up," I say. "Take a shower. I've got to change these sheets."

He stands up and starts for the bathroom, but then he stops and turns to me. He is wide-awake, now. "I was trying to scream. Did you hear me?"

"You weren't screaming. You were moaning. I thought you were sick."

He shakes his head, runs his fingers through his hair. He holds the towel over his shoulders. Just as he opens the bathroom door, I say, "You mumbled something about school, hon."

"What?"

"I couldn't understand it."

He rubs the top of his head with both hands, then his face. He takes the edge of the towel and pushes back his hair with it, wiping his brow. "Shit," he says. "I guess I'm still dreaming."

"Are you all right?"

"Just trying to remember the dream," he sighs.

"Maybe you were dreaming about Terry," I say, feeling for the first time in a long time, really, like I might break into tears. I feel so sorry for Terry's father and mother.

"No," he says. "It wasn't about Terry. I don't think it was about Terry." He touches the door frame, almost as if he is about to caress it. "It's such a horrible thing, isn't it, honey?"

"Come back to bed when you're done in there," I say.

He doesn't look at me. He seems to study his hand resting on the door frame, then he turns, goes into the bathroom, and closes the door. I know he feels responsible because he brought the boy to our school.

I don't know if we'll ever be the same again.

MORGAN

I've just got out of bed, and I'm crossing from the living room to the kitchen when I notice a shadow to my left and there, staring at me through the screen door on the back porch, is John Bone.

"What the fuck are you doing here?" I say.

"Let me in."

"You scared the living shit out of me."

"Don't just stand there."

I unwrap the thin wire holding the back screen door against the new frame. "There's gonna be a couple of carpenters here pretty soon," I say.

He goes past me and on into the house. It is just before dawn, and the woods smell of fresh pine and hickory. There's no wind, nor much air movement at all, but it is very cool, and the falling leaves do their dance anyways. I look all around to be sure nobody seen him on my back porch steps, then follow him into the house. He stands by the front door, looking out on the road.

He turns and looks at me, a kind of smile on his face. He is dressed in blue jeans, a red cotton shirt, and gray suspenders. Both the pants and shirt are clearly two sizes too small for him. He has on black brogans, with no socks. His face is long and played out—like he's been fighting a long time. He has a shadow of a beard, and his eyes are two small black, dull stones. One of the straps on his suspenders is busted, so it hangs down in front of him. He notices me looking at it. "I stole these off a clothesline," he says. "You got anything I can borrow?"

"Well, John," I say. "How'd you get out?"

"I need some clothes that fit me."

He smells like clay, like earth. "How'd you get out?" I say again.

"It's a long story."

"I'll make us some coffee. You're safe here."

He looks out the window again. "I got to see Penny."

I go into the kitchen and put on some hot water. I hear him moving around in the living room. He sets a chair by the window, then gets a fire going in the fireplace. When I come back in with the coffee he is setting by the window, puffing on a cigarette, watching the road out front. His hands are shaking, and I realize it's still cold in the house, even with the fire. He pulls the curtain all the way back, so he can see up the hill toward the store and Penny's place.

"Here," I say. I put the cup on the round table next to the window, then set down myself. "That fire will warm things up a bit pretty soon, I expect."

"You got anything to eat?" he says. "I'm starving."

"Sure." I push the cup closer to him. "Sip some coffee for now and tell me what's going on."

"Ain't nothing going on," he says.

"Really?" I sip my coffee.

He picks up his cup and takes a small taste, then makes a face.

"Cream and sugar?" I say.

"I ain't had real coffee in a long time," he says. "Sugar would be good though."

I get the sugar bowl out of the kitchen. While he stirs two teaspoons of sugar into his coffee, I say, "You're gonna have to explain some things to me."

He looks up, the cigarette dangling from his lips, squinting his eyes against the smoke.

"I ain't going to be much help unless you tell me some things," I say.

"You want to know how I got out?"

"For starters."

He takes a long drag off the cigarette, then as he lets the smoke drift out of his mouth he says, "I walked out of that place dressed like an intern. I got on a bus with twenty or thirty other employees at the infirmary, during a shift change." He blows the rest of the smoke out then takes another long drag. He blows a smoke ring, or tries to. Then he says, "I rode out of Bland in style, in daylight, without a single alarm, or nothing, just because I was dressed in white."

"You really did ride out of there on a bus?"

He almost laughs. "I did. Someday I'll tell you what I went through to get the uniform."

"Damn. That's about the best trick you ever pulled."

He drags off the cigarette again, but I see it's getting pretty worn down. I get him an ashtray, and he snuffs it out. The fire in the hearth is starting to warm things up. He seems more relaxed, and he's no longer trembling. He takes out another cigarette and fixes to light it, but then he looks at me. "You want one?"

"No, thanks," I say. "I don't even smoke my pipe this early."

"It ain't early for me," he says. "I been up all night. It's just late."

I watch him light the cigarette. It don't seem possible that little John Bone—that kid that run all over this mountain when he was a youngster—is now a fugitive in my living room, blowing smoke out of his nose. He keeps looking out the window, as if he is waiting for somebody.

"I guess that cigarette tastes pretty good, don't it?" I say, trying to make conversation. I don't know what to tell him.

"I need some new clothes," he says. "And food."

"What are you going to do?"

He shrugs. "When?"

"Now. Tomorrow—whatever. Don't you got a problem here?"

"I don't know what I'm gonna do, tomorrow or any other time."

"You ain't got no plans?"

"I got to see Penny and Tory. Maybe they can go with me."

"Running," I say. "You can't run for long."

"No," he says, his eyes suddenly flashing the old defiance. "Hiding. We can do that for a long time."

"Maybe," I say.

He sips his coffee, puffs on the cigarette. At one point he thinks of something that causes him to fidget in the seat. He runs his hand through his hair. I can see he is tired.

"How long you been running?" I say.

"Just a few days. I hitched a ride up here."

"I'll see what I got to eat." I get up and go back in the kitchen. I'm a little afraid for him, and definitely I worry about Penny and Tory. I know he'll take them with him, and I'll never see either one of them again. I don't want to think about that too much, but when I am fixing him some flapjacks and syrup, it keeps forcing its way in on me, like something burning, simmering in my memory. It will be an ending—a permanent finish to a feature of my own life I never knew meant so much to me. I'll be alone when it is all done. I know it. And yet, I am prepared to help him do whatever he's fixing to do.

He comes in the kitchen and sits down, his hands resting in front of him on the table. He's not quite able to sit still, but he watches me, trying to be patient.

"How long's it been since you ate?" I ask.

"I ain't had nothing but field potatoes and a few raw carrots since I escaped," he says. "And the other night, I ate a pumpkin." He smiles at this. "Can you believe it?"

"Should of made a pie." I put a plate in front of him, get him a knife and fork.

"It was awful. The damn thing was slimy."

"Where you think you and Penny can go to?" I say.

"I don't know."

I put the syrup on to heat up. He is quiet for a long time. I make him a pile of flapjacks, and when he is done eating, he pushes the plate away, sits back, and lights another cigarette. I don't eat nothing, I just watch him. I can see prison has actually softened him a bit—put more fat, not meat on his bones, but he is still fairly trim and he might be stronger than I remember. Perhaps jail has toughened him, but I don't think so. He does not seem nearly so full of mischief as he used to be, and when he looks at me, he can't keep from lowering his eyes, almost like he is ashamed of something he done to me. He ain't no boy no more, that's for sure.

"How come you didn't go to your daddy's place?" I ask.

"I did. He wasn't there."

"You don't say."

He looks at me directly now. "I thought I'd find him there, drunk or something. But the place was empty and locked up."

I get up and pour myself some more coffee. "Want some?"

He nods and holds out his cup. As I pour it, he says, "I'll

pay you for whatever help you can give me. I know my daddy will gladly..." But he stops. He seen me frowning at him.

I put the pot back on the stove and come back and sit down. He averts his eyes again. Then he says, "The truth is, this is the first house I come to that I knew somebody inside wouldn't call the police when they seen me. I ain't been home yet."

"Probably a good thing," I say.

"I'm not even sure my daddy'll be there."

"You ain't?"

"That's the first place they'll look, right? Or if I go up to see Penny, I expect they'll be waiting for me up there."

"Who knows?" I say. "Maybe they ain't looking for you as hard as you think."

"They're looking."

"Well," I say. "If they was, I'd of heard something about it by now. Somebody in this town would of talked about it, don't you think?"

He nods slowly, sipping his coffee, but I can see he don't really believe me. Then he says, "It's good to be warm. To eat again."

"I expect it is."

"Thank you," he says. And then his eyes sort of shrink a bit, and I see that he might actually start to cry. He seems to cringe almost, then he shakes his head and kind of shudders. "It's good to be warm again, goddamn." He is nearly whispering, and I think I see him struggling to maintain himself; he ain't scared, but he ain't himself neither. Then I see him get it back—the look of defiance and unruffled calm, of pure, root-tangled tenacity—and he sets the coffee cup down in front of him. "I do appreciate any help you can give me," he says. "I trust you. But if you can't help me, I'll just be on my way."

"I'm happy you feel you can trust me," I say.

He touches the button at the open sleeve of his shirt, the cigarette in his hand sending up curling smoke. His forearms jut a good six inches out of the sleeve and he could not of buttoned it up if he wanted to.

"You steal them clothes from a midget?" I say.

"No," he sort of laughs. "I didn't have time to try nothing on. These here was wet when I put them on."

"I guess I got something you can wear that'll fit better'n that."

He goes back to the living room and sits by the window again. "What day is it?" he asks, gazing out the window again.

"I believe it's Thursday," I say.

He gets this pained expression on his face.

"What?"

"Nothing."

"Tell me."

"What if Penny's not there? Can I stay here for a while?"

"What makes you think she won't be there?"

"It's visiting day. She might of gone down to the prison with . . ."

"Your daddy?"

"That's another reason why I didn't go home," he says. "I wasn't sure, but I figured he might be on his way down to the prison."

"Penny told me she was going with him," I tell him.

"I hope she don't hate me for this."

"She don't hate you," I say.

He slowly shakes his head, watching out the window. "When did you say them carpenters would get here?"

"Any minute. But they won't come in here."

"You better get me them clothes."

I get him a new shirt and some pants. I give him a coat I used to wear years ago. It's a bit long in the sleeve but it will fit him. "It's gonna get mighty cold, before long," I say.

"Penny will have most of my things," he says. "I guess."

"You think so?"

"I better take this," he says, holding the coat across his arm.

"You can have it."

"Can I rest here today?"

"Sure," I say.

"I don't think I should go outside except at night."

BOOK V

PENNY

The country all the way down to the prison is gold and red and bright orange, with wildflowers and bluegrass everywhere. The fall is complete here, not a leaf has dropped, and everything is still, hanging in the thin, cool air like something painted on a board.

The long drive takes more time than I thought it would. Mr. Bone stops and gets out of the car every twenty miles or so and checks a bad sound he keeps hearing in the "undercarriage," as he calls it. "I swear," he says, "I'm afraid it's the differential, or the brakes. You don't hear that?"

I hear nothing. Tory sits next to me, her head under my arm, resting on my hip. She has been asleep most of the way.

Each time Mr. Bone gets out to check on the noise, he opens the trunk. I know he has a bottle there, hidden under the spare tire. When he gets back in the car, he smells like he's been inside the bottle, swimming in it.

Finally, I say, "You don't have to stop the car and get out every time you want a sip out of that thing."

"What thing?"

"I know what you got back there, Mr. Bone. And if you keep drinking out of it, I'm gonna have to drive."

"Penny," he says. "Please don't call me Mr. Bone."

"I ain't calling you Pa."

"Well, call me Dad then. That's what John always called me."

"You ain't my dad, neither."

"Nobody in my family should be calling me Mr. Bone."

I don't say nothing. He drives along, staring at the road. He's wearing a checkered shirt, a white sports coat, and brown pants and shoes. At one point he tells me he shouldn't have wore a short-sleeved shirt. "I'm cold." He puts the heat on in the car. We are in his Buick Skylark. It's a small car, and the heat vents blow hot air in my face. Tory shifts a bit and lets her head fall down to my lap.

"It's getting hot in here," I say.

"I'm sorry." He turns the fan down a little. Then he says, "I do think I'm hearing that noise again."

I sigh. "Just get the bottle," I say. "Please."

He pulls over again. When he comes back this time, he throws his jacket over the seat, and puts the bottle on the seat next to him. It is Wild Turkey, and it's half full. When he gets in I notice sweat running down the side of his face. "It's actually kind of hot in that sun," he says.

"You just put the heat on in the car because you was cold," I say.

"I mean when you're standing in the direct sun."

"It's cold out there," I say. "Maybe you should lay off the bottle for a while."

He pulls back onto the highway. I know I will have to drive soon enough, but I don't want to wake Tory. She stayed awake almost all night last night; she was so excited about seeing her daddy. She kept coming in my room, whispering, "Mommy, is it time yet?" She woke me so many times, I don't feel as if I slept neither.

I watch the side of Mr. Bone's face, trying to reassure myself that he is fit to drive. He looks sad to me—like he is beginning to find the ending of things, all things including his own self. And that bottle leaning on the seat next to him, like it loves him. The top of it rests on his lap in the same way Tory rests on mine.

"Pa," I say.

He looks at me, smiling.

"You okay to drive?"

"I'm fine," he says. "Really."

"Please don't stop the next time you want a pull on that." I point to the bottle.

The smile leaves his face.

"I want to get there," I say. "Okay?"

He drives silently for a while, then he says, "I guess you should do some of the driving."

"I guess I should," I say.

I can't explain how I am feeling. Almost nervous—but excited, too. Like I am going to see John for the first time, like nothing has ever happened between us, and I only dreamed of this moment, longed for it with all my heart, and now here it is. I think my hair looks good, but it ain't perfect. I'm afraid I should have wore a dress, instead of the navy blue skirt and white blouse. I feel like a schoolteacher or a librarian.

I *have* dreamed of this. I dreamed of it every night when he was first taken from me. I was going to do what he said I should do, but I never went to bed without wishing I could see him the next day, the next minute. I wanted him to cancel our agreement as fervently as any girl who wishes a man would ask her out on a date. That's how I thought of it. Even after six years and getting used to the idea of not having him around, I still dreamed of him saying forget the Bible, come see me. So this is like he has finally noticed me, finally decided to ask to see me. Only more important than just the first attention, the first attraction. Maybe it's like he has come back to life? Like I was forced to bury him—as all of us are forced to bury our dead—and now he's come back to life. I wonder what he will look like. When I find myself trying to imagine it, I realize I have tears brimming in my eyes. Tory has waked up, and she wants to know what's the matter.

"I'm fine, honey," I say. I don't want my makeup to smear.

She sits up straight and reaches up to touch my cheek. "You're crying," she says. "Are you sad?"

"No," I say. "I think I'm happy."

Mr. Bone looks at me briefly, smiling. "You want to drive, hon?"

"How much further is it?" I ask.

"Another hour, maybe."

"Sure," I say.

He pulls off the road, raising a blue cloud of dust in the gravel. He takes the bottle and gets out, I slide over to the driver's side, lifting Tory to my lap and putting her next to me on the seat. Mr. Bone gets in the other side, smelling once again of the whiskey.

"You couldn't wait until you was in the car?" I say.

"What?" He looks at me. He is ashamed, and I feel bad for calling attention to it.

"Nothing," I say. I pull back onto the highway. We are still high in the mountains, but the road is descending all the time. We won't be in flatlands, but we won't be in the high mountains no more neither. We are, right now, farther away from home than I have ever been since my father brought me to Crawford.

From the minute I realized I was going to come see John, I forgot about everything: Clare, what was buried under the stone in the yard, the Gypsy Man. Only Tory stayed in my mind, but even then, it was just me and Tory with John. When I thought of Tory at all, I remembered her with John: him holding her on his knee, laughing with her, telling her stories. Tory is the same age as I was when my mother died and my father carried me up the mountain to live with his sister. I barely remember my mother. She is a presence in my mind—like a big sky I once seen or a statue I stood in awe at the feet of. You know what I mean? Now I think of John, a big presence like that in Tory's mind, and she's going to see him. He's going to smile down on her. I imagine him touching the folds of a great blanket, moving it back so he can see her pink cheeks. I remember everything I seen him do with her. He barely had time to see her, much less hoist her on his shoulders and play with her. But that's how I think of her now: with him, making noise in the house.

I don't think we'll ever get to Richard Bland, but finally we pull into the parking lot in front of it. Mr. Bone is asleep on the other side of the car, leaning against the window. Tory is standing up on the seat, almost jumping up and down. Her eyes are so bright it makes me hurt a little when I think of what she will feel at the end of this day. I park as close to the entrance of the prison as I can.

"We're here," I say. I throw the keys in my purse. Mr. Bone is still snoring against the window. "Mr. Bone," I say.

Tory shakes him. "Wake up, Granpa," she says.

He is startled at first, but then he looks at her and smiles. "Well," he says, stretching. "We made it."

"Show me where to go," I say.

"Damn." He rubs his eyes, seems to sink further in the seat.

Part of me does not want him to wake up. As long as he is asleep, I can stay here in the car. I don't have to find out how John will look at me. I pull the rearview mirror down and try to see my hair. I put on a little more lipstick, smooth my hair back, and clip it more tightly in the barrette.

"You look fine," Mr. Bone says, sitting up straight, stretching again. "Really."

"Then why you feel you got to reassure me?" I ask.

"You're utterly beautiful," he says. "As always." Then he looks at Tory. "You too, honey."

I put back the green ribbons that Mrs. Gault tied in her hair. I dressed her in a lavender dress with white pockets on the front. She does look pretty.

"Show me where to go," I say again.

Mr. Bone blinks his eyes, waking up. He rubs his hands over his face and points to the entrance. "Right through there," he says.

I take Tory by the hand and we get out of the car. He remains there for a spell, and I realize he is taking another swig out of the bottle. When he gets out he locks the car and we walk through an archway to two large double doors.

"This way," Mr. Bone says.

He opens one of the doors and we follow him through a blue gate to another set of glass doors.

Inside a guard stops us.

"We're here for visiting hours," I say.

"Who you coming to see?"

"John Bone."

Mr. Bone says, "Hello, Jack."

The guard says, "Mr. Bone." Then he looks at me. "You Mrs. Bone?"

I nod. His uniform is blue with darker blue patches on the shoulders and the pockets. He wears black boots, polished to perfection, and a small black tie. On the perfectly creased right front pocket of his shirt is a silver name tag that says DAIGLE. The other pocket is almost covered by a large, silver, crest-shaped badge. His face seems to sag, with dark shadows on it, and great black, pitiless eyes. They look like a shark's eyes.

"Why don't you two wait over there," he says to me, "and me and Mr. Bone will be right back."

"I come to see John," I say. "I got his daughter with me."

Tory says, "Hi." A soft, single note of sweet music that stops Daigle.

He leans down and takes her hand. "Hello, little darling," he says.

"We'd like to see John," I say.

He looks at me, still holding Tory's hand. "Just as you like," he says. "I'll just be a minute."

He walks behind a long counter to an open office, then through a pair of gray metal doors in the back of it.

I look at Mr. Bone. "Well?"

He seems mystified. "Usually they just take me back there. I don't know what's going on."

We go over to a long brown couch with metal arms. It's under a big, clean window that looks out on the fields and hills below the prison. Across from us is a bulletin board, and pinned to the top is the story of John's heroic act. Mr. Bone points it out. I get up and walk over to look at it. It's a big headline: TWO INMATES SAVE GUARD'S LIFE. The story isn't too long, and it never mentions John's name except once, but it is enough to make me proud. I read it out loud to Tory, and she smiles and kisses me. "Daddy's a hero." She wishes they put a picture of him in the article so she can see what he looks like, and I realize I'm wishing the same thing. I haven't seen him for six years.

"I wish I could get a copy of this article," I say.

"I can get you one," Mr. Bone says. He stands next to me, looking at the board. It is taking a long time, and I am beginning to wonder what happened to Officer Daigle, when he comes back out and approaches us.

"Would you mind coming with me?" he says.

We follow him into the office area and through the gray metal doors at the back of it. This empties out into a hallway, but we don't go the way Mr. Bone expected us to go. We're walking down this long corridor, and Mr. Bone touches me on the shoulder. I turn and he gives me this look, like he don't know what's going on.

"What?" I say.

He says to Daigle, "Ain't the visiting room back that way?"

Daigle just keeps walking.

"Sir," I say.

He stops in front of another set of doors, turns to us, and smiles. "The warden would like to see you," he says.

"Really?" says Mr. Bone.

"I just want to see John," I say.

"This way," Daigle says. He opens the door on the right and then another glass door to the right of that one. He leads us into a huge office with chairs along the walls. A woman is sitting at a big desk, typing. Behind her is a bank of high windows that look out on the prison. "Have a seat," the woman says. "Mr. Buchanan will be right with you."

The door behind her opens and a tall red-haired man comes out. "Well," he says. "Mr. Bone. And I take it this is Mrs. Bone and..." He looks at Tory.

"This here's Tory," I say.

"And Tory," he says. "Hello."

Tory says, "Hi."

"Y'all come on in," he says. He's wearing a white suit and a yellow tie. His hair is short, close to his head. He has pockmarks on his jaw, next to his ears, and down his neck. He leans toward me and extends his hand. "Take a seat," he says. His eyes are bright green and kind. He offers us three chairs in front of the desk. In one of the chairs he places two telephone books. He says it's so he can see Tory's face if she sits in the chair. I put her on top of the books, then sit down in the chair next to her.

Behind the warden is another large window that looks out on the mountains beyond the prison entrance. He sits down at the desk and leans back in his chair, staring at us. Looking at me really. I turn my eyes away. I look around the office, then at Mr. Bone. Nobody says nothing for the longest time, then Tory says, "Where's my daddy?"

The warden says, "Well, well. She gets right to the point."

"What's the problem?" Mr. Bone asks.

"I come to see John," I say almost at the same time.

"You want to see John," he says, smiling. He puts his hands up behind his head. "Well, that's not going to be possible."

"Why not?" Both me and Mr. Bone speak at once. A little frantic, I say, "Has something happened to him?"

"He ain't here," Buchanan says.

"What?" I say.

"He ain't here. He took off."

I feel something small and cold blossom in my heart.

"What do you mean he took off?" Mr. Bone says. He asks the question almost like he's insulted by what Buchanan said.

"He escaped."

I don't know what to look at. I feel my face starting to burn. It is like the warden has told us John is dead. I can't make myself say nothing. Buchanan just sits there, looking at me. Finally I say, "But how? How could he do it?"

"We haven't figured out yet how he did it, but he's gone. Not a trace of him anywhere inside these walls."

"You've searched . . ." Mr. Bone stops. He looks at me, then back to Buchanan. "You know he's not on the grounds?"

Tory starts to cry. "Mommy, what's happened?"

"Quiet, hon," I say.

"The day before yesterday," Buchanan says. "We counted him in the morning. He was in the infirmary. That same evening, when we counted people before lights out, he was gone. His bed was empty."

"Was he sick?" I say.

"For a while. But he was almost completely cured. Had some kind of infection. We were getting ready to send him back to his cell."

"You don't know how he got out?" I say.

"Nope. Nobody does." He seems proud of it, but he is also setting himself against anger. He is like a man who has been humiliated in some way, publicly, but refuses to show it. He is pretending like it don't bother him. "It seems our boy's a pretty clever fellow."

You'd think I might be proud, but I ain't. Not yet, anyway. I'm just scared. And sad. I won't see him now. If he tries to see me any time in the future, they'll catch him. And I'll be without him again anyway. Also, it is just beginning to dawn on me that he won't get out early now. Not now.

"I thought he was going to get out," Mr. Bone says. "I thought maybe they was going to reward him for..."

Buchanan leans forward in his chair. He puts both elbows on the desk, folding his arms in front of him. "Well, that didn't work out." He lets out a long sort of mournful sigh, like it pains him to go on. Then, he says, "The governor wouldn't budge on it."

"The governor," I say.

"He's a reasonable man, usually," Buchanan says. "But he wouldn't go with me on this one."

"Son of a bitch," Mr. Bone says.

Buchanan don't look at him. He shrugs, his eyes focused on the papers in front of him. "When I told John about it, I guess it did something to him."

"I guess it did," Mr. Bone says.

Tory starts to cry. "Where's my daddy?"

I take her out of the chair and hold her in my lap. "Try not to cry now, hon," I say.

"Just last month, he was real glad about what you and the governor was going to do for him," Mr. Bone says.

"The governor don't take long," Buchanan says.

"No, I guess he don't," says Mr. Bone. At the same time, Buchanan says, "At least we found out right away."

I say, "Why'd the governor refuse? Wasn't it a good thing John done? Don't he want other prisoners to..."

Buchanan interrupts me. "It was a problem about the

car—you know he hijacked a car to save Mac's life." He looks at me. I think his eyes are sad now, but I can't be sure. He don't let much happen to his face when he talks. "Then," he goes on. "There's this business about a body they found up your way?"

"Really?" Mr. Bone says.

"But John was a hero," I say, helplessly. I hold Tory against me, but she ain't crying. She's sniffing and trying to listen.

"John was commended," Buchanan says.

I shake my head.

"The governor commended him and promised to put in a word at his first parole hearing."

"When's that going to be?" Mr. Bone says.

The warden looks down at the desk again, fiddles with some papers there. Then he says, "That's hard to say, now. Five years?"

"Fuck," I say.

Mr. Bone seems to sink into his chair.

"Some talk for a young lady," Buchanan says.

"Ain't it?" I say.

He blinks. "And in front of the little one."

Mr. Bone puts his hand on my arm, but I pull it away. I put Tory on the floor in front of me and brush the hair out of her face. "We're going, hon," I say.

Buchanan stands up, too. He leans forward and puts the tips of his fingers on the desk, supporting himself. "If you see John, and you probably will, I'm certain you won't feel obliged to tell us about it."

"Right," I say.

Mr. Bone slowly rises to his feet. "Let's go," he says. He looks like a person waking from death, like he's lost everything and this is his last defeat. It stops me when I see the look on his face.

The warden says, "Still, if you *do* see John, tell him for me it will go a lot better for him if he turns himself in."

"Sure," I say. "I'll tell him soon's I see him."

"I don't think you understand me, Mrs. Bone," he says. "If you'll just listen for a moment—"

"I understand you," I say.

"No, you don't."

"I understand perf—"

"No. You don't!" He says this very loud and it stops me. Tory stands back, too, leaning against my thighs holding my hand.

"I'm trying to do you a favor here," Buchanan says.

Mr. Bone is at the door already. "Let's go, Penny," he says, opening the door.

"Do *me* a favor?" I say.

"And John, too."

I don't say nothing. I just look at him, waiting. But he ain't got nothing more to say neither. A long time seems to pass. Then I say, "You doing me and John a favor."

"He'll come to you."

I don't say nothing.

"He won't go nowhere else. You know it and I know it."

"So?"

"I ain't told nobody he's gone yet," Buchanan says, not speaking so loud now. "You understand me? I don't have the whole state out looking for him, right now."

I got my arms around Tory, and I'm looking in his eyes. Mr. Bone don't say nothing, but he closes the door.

"You understand, Mrs. Bone? I could go to jail myself for this. But I haven't spread any kind of alarm yet."

"You ain't?"

"I'm willing to forget all about it. But John has to come back here."

"And if he does?"

He straightens up and spreads his arms. "No harm done."

"You mean that?"

"He'll go to you," Buchanan says, letting his hands fall to his sides. "When he does, you bring him on back here."

"And you're just going to forget about it."

"I mean everything I say." He looks at me again—right into my eyes. "You get him to come back here. If you don't..." He pauses for a second. "Well, it's enough that you know I'll do what I have to do."

"I'll try," I say.

"You got a week," he says. "I can't wait longer than that."

"There's this other thing," I say. "The Landon boy and all."

He shakes his head. "I don't know nothing about that. Whatever happens with that will happen, and I won't have a thing to say about it. But you got to get him to come back here."

Mr. Bone says, "A week's not a very long time."

"You got a week. I'm doing this for Mac." He stops, looks out the window a second. He shakes his head, like he's remembering something rueful. "And for me, too. I don't like the idea that anyone put one over on me."

I don't say nothing.

He looks at me. "Until this year I had a perfect record in this place, so I'm not just doing you and John a favor."

"I see."

"I was going to offer the same deal to Mr. Bone there. I didn't know you were coming."

"I'm glad you made the offer to me."

"I'm telling you all this so you'll believe me."

"I'm sorry," I say. "I'm sorry for cursing and..."

"I understand," he says. "I understand how you feel completely."

"I'll bring him back if'n I can."

"I know you will." He sits back down now. He is almost smiling, like he is pleased with me, but don't want to let on about it. "You just bring him back here."

"And you won't do nothing bad to him."

407

"I want to know how he got out of here."

"You won't do nothing bad."

"No, I won't. I promise not to do anything at all, as long as you get him back in here before the week's over."

Mr. Bone opens the door again. I start to leave, then I stop. When I face Buchanan again, he is staring off out the window, his chair turned away and his back to me. "Mr. Buchanan," I say. He swings the chair back around again.

"You a man of his word?" I say.

Now he does smile. "You want it in writing?" he says, amused by the idea. "That would get us both in trouble."

"I expect you'll keep up your end then?"

"I can wait a week. Much more than that, and I'm aiding and abetting. You know what that is?"

"I know what it is."

"Don't neither one of us want to be accused of that, now do we?"

"I'll do what I can," I say.

He don't say nothing. I look at him for a second, then I say, "Thank you."

He smiles and turns his chair back around so he can look out the window.

CLARE

In the kitchen of a house trailer in Quincy, sitting at a small round table, I ask Peach about John. "How do you know him?"

"I was down there for a spell," he says.

"At Richard Bland?"

"Right indeedy," he says. He sets on the edge of his chair,

looking at a newspaper, reading the comics. He smiles while he talks.

I always liked a man who is good with children. I think all women do a bit. It was just perfect the way he lifted Tory up and put her on his shoulders, yesterday. She really took to him, and he was so gentle with her. It surprised me, because I had the impression that he is mostly a pretty rough sort. I know he loses patience pretty easy, but don't most high-spirited men?

He has rented this trailer from the pastor of a Baptist church in Quincy. He's been staying here since I run with him several weeks ago. He looks at me and says, "And don't this place beat Richard Bland?"

I smile. "I ain't never been there."

He says, "Hell, when you was running with me, I should a took you down there. We could of stayed out of West Virginia altogether."

It must show on my face that he has reminded me of the fight, but he don't say nothing more about it. I take this for a sign that he's pretty sensitive when he has to be.

"What'd you do to get into Richard Bland?" I ask.

"You know," he says. "That there little girl Tory looks just like her daddy."

"She's on her way down to see him today, too."

"She is?" He puts the newspaper down and looks at me.

"She and her momma. That's where they was going early this morning."

"Well, I'll be."

After a while, I offer him another sandwich, but he don't want one. "I'm plain wore out, though," he says.

"You want to lay down for a while?" I say. "I'll clean up this here mess."

He comes over to me and kisses me on the cheek. "You are the sweetest thing."

"Just lay down in your room on the bed in there," I say. "Maybe I'll join you a little later."

"That would be just fine." He slaps his thigh and laughs. I watch him go on in and close the door. I hear him putting the change in his pockets on the dresser. It is so good to be with a man again. I know it's foolish of me to feel this way, and it won't be long before I'll complain about his sloppiness, his disorderly way of doing things. But just now, it seems like a thing I have missed—the hard scrapple stomp of boots on a wood floor, the smell of tobacco and whiskey and Old Spice.

I know, I know. I'm just so happy he decided to come back. I never thought he'd come back.

WHEN ME and P.J. left, I stopped by the store and said good-bye to Penny and Tory. She smiled while I kissed and hugged Tory, then she told Tory to mind the store and she come out-side with me. P.J. was waiting in the car. Penny put her arms around me and held on for a second.

"You be careful," she said.

"I won't be long away," I said. "If you keep the store open today, and maybe just tomorrow, I'll be back the next day, or the day after that. It's okay if you want to leave it closed after tomorrow."

"I'm going down to see John," she said. "Early. If'n I make it back in time, I'll open tomorrow."

I'd forgotten she was going to do that, and it made me sad that she could see I had. "I'm sorry, honey." I put my hands on her arms and then took her again in my embrace. "I forgot, didn't I?"

"I guess you got your own kind of thing going on," she said.

"I do." I smiled. She stepped back, and I seen tears in her eyes.

"You tell John you ain't never going to leave him," I said. "And make him to know you mean it."

She nodded, but she wasn't looking at me directly.

"The Bible don't mean you can't change your mind, hon. You swear on it so you won't betray yourself."

"What do you mean?"

"So you won't give up on yourself. That's why you swear on a Bible."

"I don't know what you mean."

P.J. honked the horn on the Studebaker, then he stuck his head out the window. "You coming or not?"

"I'll be there in just a second," I said.

"Well, come on then," he said.

"I got to go," I said.

Penny said, "What do you mean about the Bible?"

"Honey, do you always do what you want?"

"What?"

"Do you always do what you want? What you intend?"

"Yes."

"No," I said. "Think about it. How many times have you felt bad because you didn't do something you intended?"

She puzzled for a minute. Then I said, "Remember those times when John's father swore he wasn't going to drink ever again?"

"Yes."

"Well, he meant it. Don't you think he meant it?"

"Yes."

"But he never did keep any of them promises, did he?"

"No." She still looked puzzled.

"Honey," I said. "We swear on the Bible to keep to a thing we've promised ourselves. When we don't want that promise no more, why should we keep to it?"

"It would a helped a lot if Mr. Bone kept just one of them promises."

"Okay," I said. "Maybe that's a bad example. The point is . . ."

The horn on the car honked again.

"If you make a good promise and don't keep it, you've betrayed yourself."

She nodded.

"And if you make a bad promise, and you don't keep it you ain't betrayed nobody."

"I ain't?"

"You only betray yourself if you *keep* a bad promise. That's what swearing on the Bible is for. To find out which is a bad and which is a good promise."

P.J. hollered from the car, "I'm gonna drive this thing off myself if'n you don't git down here now."

"I'm coming." I started down the steps. When I got to the walk, I turned and looked back at Penny. "If you swore on a Bible to put Tory up for adoption, you wouldn't want to keep that promise, right?"

"I'd never make a promise like that."

"Well, if you did."

She just stared at me.

"You shouldn't of made that promise about John, neither," I said.

"I'm going down to see him," she said.

"Good." I waved one more time and then went to the car, and when I went to get in I seen that P.J. had put himself behind the wheel.

"I want to drive," I said.

"Get in the other side," he said.

"But . . ." I started to object, but his face got real serious, and his eyes narrowed—like he was squinting in the sun.

"Do you know where I parked my truck?"

"No."

"Well, get in. I'll drive us there."

I went around the other side. When I was seated next to him, he smiled. "I don't like giving directions when I'm going somewhere and I know where I'm going."

"Okay," I said.

WHEN I FINISH cleaning up in the trailer, I go into the room and lay on the bed next to him. He really is sleeping, and I start to feel my eyes getting droopy and lazy myself. I don't know how long I drift off, but then he's there waking me. "Come on," he says. "We got to get to work on my truck."

"What time is it?" I say.

"I think it's pretty late."

I wash my face and hands, then put on a fresh skirt. When I come out he's already sitting in my car with the engine running. When I get in, he don't say nothing. He drives down the mountain to a hardware store parking lot in Lebanon Church. His truck is parked in the back. The back window has a small hole in it and the cracks around it look like a spider's web. Locked in the truck is a white bag with a small, curved hose, and two metal clamps. He has a toolbox behind the seat.

The air is cold and it promises to get colder. The sun is a small, dull light behind white clouds. He opens the hood of the truck, then points to a place near the back of the engine, way down. "See that hose right there?"

I lean over the fender and try to see what he's talking about. Way down, on the back side of the motor, is a small, curved black hose with a silver clamp on it.

"Yeah," I say. "I see it."

"That's what's got to be fixed."

"Why don't you have a mechanic do it?"

He don't answer me. He gets down on the ground and crawls under the truck. I think he wants me to do more than watch. "What do you need me for?" I say.

413

"Okay," he says. "Hand me the tools when I ask for them."

"I don't know about any of these things."

"Just give me the toolbox."

I set it on the ground next to him. It is very heavy. When I open it, a few of the tools come out on the pavement. The sun tries to emerge from the clouds, and I can see the outline of it, but it don't heat very much. I'm starting to shiver.

"I should of wore a sweater," I say.

He feels around until he has a screwdriver. "I could of got you that," I say. "I know what a screwdriver is."

He makes a sound. I think it is a short laugh, but I'm not sure. He starts working on the clamp at the back end of the hose. I watch what he is doing from above, leaning over the fender with my head under the hood. Once he looks at me and laughs. "Well, look at you."

It takes a long time, but he finally gets the old hose off. He shows me the bullet hole. It really is a round hole in the hose.

"All the water in my engine leaked out," he says.

"I didn't think he hit anything," I say.

"Who?"

"Morgan, when he fired the gun."

"He almost killed me," P.J. says.

I don't know what to say. I feel so bad about it. "I tried to stop him," I say.

"Well, I know where he lives," he says.

"You do?"

"Sure."

"I didn't know."

"I used to live right up yonder—on the other side of the mountain."

I tell him I wish I'd known it.

"You don't remember me, do you?" he says.

"No."

414

"I remember you." He ain't smiling. His hands are almost black from the work he's done, and he still has to put the new hose on the truck.

"You remember me?"

"I danced with you once, down at the old Ranchero."

"You did?"

"You remember the old Ranchero?"

"Wasn't much different than the new one," I say.

He smiles then. "Well, we danced there once."

He's lying and I know it, but I let him go ahead. We never danced at no Ranchero. "And you know Morgan Tiller?" I say.

"I knew him." He flips the old hose up and catches it. "I worked one whole summer for him, hauling wood."

"I declare," I say. He may be telling the truth about that. Years ago, when he was younger, Morgan Tiller always had men working for him.

He walks back around the front of the truck, then gets down and crawls back under it. He has the new hose, and he asks me to hold it in place so he can tighten the clamp on it. I lean way over, try to reach it but I can't. "I can't reach it, honey," I say.

His face is in the dark there, under the car, but I see it change. He looks like something cut him the way his eyes scrunch up. Then he says, "Well, get down under here then."

"I can't do that."

"Why?"

I'm still leaning over the fender, staring down at him. "Because I'm wearing a clean skirt, silly," I say.

I smell the grease under the hood, the baked dust on the motor. He moves away, so I can't see him no more, then I feel his hand on my ankle.

"Get down here," he says. He pulls my foot off the ground and my shin slams into the car.

"Ow!" I say. "That hurt!"

He holds my ankle tightly so that my shin is still against the wheel well of the car.

"You're hurting me."

"Lay down and get under here," he says.

I get down next to him and he lets go. He looks at me, his face dark and dirty—his white eyes back under the car in the dark look like something evil.

"You hurt me," I say.

"Come on," he says.

"You son of a bitch. That hurt."

"I'm sorry," he says.

"Goddamn it."

"You done?"

"Done what?"

"Cursing me."

I rub my shin. "I know it's going to bruise."

"I'll make it up to you. Will you just scoot down here and help me? It's getting mighty cold."

I lay down and try to slide myself up next to him. "Lay on your back," he says.

I try to turn over, but my blouse catches on something under the car. "I tore my blouse," I say. "Now goddamn it." I start to pull myself out of there, but he grabs me by the hair.

"Wait a minute, little lady," he says.

Now I am frightened. I lay still. "Don't hurt me," I say.

"Get yourself up here and hold onto this here hose," he says. "I can't tighten the thing unless somebody holds it."

I move up next to him, not thinking no more about my blouse or how dirty I'm getting.

"Jesus Christ," he says. "Don't make such a production."

I don't like this. I feel my heart beating. I don't say nothing more. He shows me where the hose is, and I reach up and hold onto it, and he forces it in where it goes, then tightens the clamp on it. It takes a long time, and he never looks at me. He concentrates on getting the hose on right, and on tightening the clamp. I hold on until the clamp is in position and he's got it on pretty tight. He says, "That's good. You can let go of it now." I crawl out from under there and get to my feet. I brush my skirt off. In the sideview mirror of the truck, I see my hair is all over the place and I've got something black in it. Black smudges cover my right cheek and my forehead. The right shoulder of my blouse is ripped open.

I watch him moving from under the car. He puts his tools back in the box. I stand there, shivering, watching him. I don't want to be with him no more. My leg is throbbing. I pat my hair down, take a Kleenex out of my purse, and try to wipe my face with it. The grease and dirt won't come off.

"Come on," he says. "I got something will take that right off." He stands next to me, smiling. "Let's go back home."

I don't say nothing. I get in the car and wait for him. But he comes around to the driver's side and flips the keys in on the seat. "I'm driving the truck," he says. "You drive this piece of junk."

"It's a Studebaker," I say. I take the keys and move over to the driver's side. As I'm starting the engine, he reaches in and pats me on the shoulder where my blouse is ripped. "I'm sorry, did I cause this rip here?"

I don't answer him. I stare out at the road. I've made up my mind I ain't taking no shit off him, or any man. It ain't worth what you have to go through to be with the goddamned children who call themselves men in this world. And that's what a man is, plain and simple. A big, hairy, brutish child.

"I'll sew that right up," he says.

"I'm going home."

"I'll follow you."

"You go back to your trailer," I say. "I'm going home."

"Now you're mad." He plays a bit with the torn fabric, gently, his dirty fingers leaving their mark I'm sure.

417

"Don't," I say, shrugging my shoulder away from him. "Your hands are dirty."

He leans down and looks at me. "Where you think you're going?"

"I'm going home."

He takes his hands and puts them around my neck. He does this very carefully, and with no pressure, but he positions his fingers, moving them around a bit, gently. He looks off as he does this. I freeze. I watch his face, and he's adjusting his fingers and looking all around, up and down, like he's making sure nobody's watching him, and the whole time he's saying, "Home is where the heart is. Home is where you want to be. And that's where I'm going to be. Where you going to be? Huh?" He is whispering now. "Where's your heart? You can tell me."

"Let go of me," I say.

"Now, now." He starts to squeeze. It's not hard, but I know it's there, like a tight collar. His hands are huge and dirty and black. In the rearview mirror, I see his fingernails white and lined black like burned pearls.

"Please," I say.

"Where we going, little lady?"

"Home," I say.

He whispers in gasps of air now, like he's trying to lift something heavy while he talks. "And where's home?"

He grips me tightly now. I can barely get air.

I try to pull his hands away, but each time I do, he squeezes harder. I feel my head turning red, my eyes beginning to bulge.

"Where's home?" he says again.

Now I can't get any air. "Okay," I choke. "Okay, okay, okay." I can't be sure he understands me.

He lets go and pats the hair down on the back of my head. His choking turns instantly to a kind of caress. "See," he says. "See how easy that was?"

I say nothing. I am trying to breathe. I have the dirt from his hands all over me.

He stands up, his hands now just touching the side of the car. He is smiling down at me. "I'll follow you, okay?"

I nod, still gasping for air. I have never been so afraid.

He smiles at me. "Let's go on home, okay?"

SHERIFF PAXTON

There ain't nobody at Clare's place, and the store is closed again. I look around the cabin, just moseying, but I don't find nothing. It's right chilly now, but the wind ain't so bad. I walk back to where the body was. The ground is covered, and weeds are already claiming it back again.

I wonder where Penny is.

Back in my car, I radio the office, see if anything's happening. My secretary, Mrs. Sue Ann Barnes, says, "Guess what?"

"I ain't guessing on the radio, Sue Ann," I say.

"Old man Crowly's boy Brad was in here this morning, looking for you."

"What for?"

"Said he seen him walking up Route 13."

"Seen who?"

"Well, you got to guess."

"Seen who, Sue Ann? I ain't gonna guess."

There's a long silence. I listen to the static in the radio for a while.

"Sue Ann," I say.

"Yes, sir?"

I wait. Then she says, dejectedly, "It was John Bone."

I start the car. "Where is Crowly now?" I say.

"I guess he went on back home."

I thank Mrs. Barnes and then cruise down the hill and up the other side by the lookout to Crowly's place. When I get out of the car, the old man opens the front door and comes out on the porch.

"Brad seen him," he says. "It was John Bone."

I walk up to the front porch steps and he opens the screen door there. His eyes are red, and his face looks almost sunburned up against the white beard. "Come on in," he says. Then he coughs, a deep and long, kind of breath-stealing cough. He raises his hand, as if asking me to wait.

I step up on the porch, let the door close behind me. The place smells like boiling cabbage. Maybe a baked ham in there, too. "Want a cup of coffee?" Crowly says, when the coughing subsides.

"Thank you kindly."

He goes back in the house, and I sit down in a chair that sets in front of a big old white trunk. I hear the old man coughing again in the house. He comes back out with the coffee. He's wearing coveralls, with the suspenders drooping around his hips. A T-shirt that's so big it shows the gray hair on his chest and under his arms. When he sits down next to me, he grunts, then coughs again. "Got this here damned cold," he says. I can tell he ain't getting any air through his nose.

"Could be allergies," I say. "This time of year."

"Ain't never had something like this regular."

I don't say nothing.

"It's a cold. Bradwell's got it, too."

"Is he here?"

He hollers, "Bradwell! You, Bradwell!" Then he starts coughing again.

Bradwell comes out on the porch. He's wearing only a T-shirt and jeans, and he's carrying a box of Kleenex. He sits down in the chair next to the trunk.

"Tell me where you seen John," I say.

"I was coming down from up the store way..."

"From Miss Clare's place?"

"Yes, sir. Thought I might could get some bread. But she closed the damn place again."

"I know. I was just up there."

"Well, sir, I was coming down from there, and I seen this fellow in jeans—black brogans, too, with no damn socks, a-walking up the road. I was coming at him from behind, so he didn't notice me at first."

"Where was he?"

"Just up the road from the lookout. Looked like he was headed for old man Tiller's place."

The coffee is black and bitter. I drink a bit of it anyway. It ain't none too hot neither, but I don't bother to tell the old man about it. "You're sure it was John?" I say to Bradwell. "You ain't seen him in six years."

"It was John. When I went by him, he turned and looked right in at me."

"Did he recognize you?"

"I mean, it was like he was scared who I'd be or something, the way he stopped and..."

"Did he see you?"

"I don't know. Once I seen his face, I drove on off."

"You're certain it was John?"

He looks at my cup of coffee, which I'm holding up in front of my face, like I might take another sip of it. Then he looks me in the eye. "What'd I just say?"

"Well, but you see, I ain't had no report of it or nothing."

"So?"

"The state prison would of released a bulletin—I'd of got a bulletin if he escaped."

"What if they let him go?"

"I'd of gotten something about a parole, too."

"It was John. That's all I'm saying."

I put my coffee cup down on the trunk. "Well," I say. "I guess I'll take a ride over to Morgan Tiller's place and have a talk with him."

GAULT

I lie in bed at night and go over all of it in my dark mind. I think of sleep as something I used to be able to do. When I close my eyes, searching for sleep, I enter those minutes when we found the body and I am there for hours and hours. It doesn't seem possible that those few minutes can take so long in my mind. The sheriff's voice says, "Likely this here's the little Landon boy," over and over, even when I open my eyes and surrender to wakefulness. Myra sleeps next to me, her quiet, easy breathing an affront to all my nerves. I sit up, go to the window, and stare at the pale, unalterable moon.

I can't keep from going back to that night when we found the body. I search everything I remember. What did I say to Myra? When the sheriff had finished with us, and the police were there carefully picking out the bones, I went right home. I remember I had trouble getting my breath. I felt as if I had run a long way. Myra was sitting on the porch waiting for me.

"Where's the little one?" I said.

"She got tired."

I stood at the bottom of the porch steps.

"I made her lie down for a while. She didn't like it, but she's being a good girl."

The trees seemed to whisper. I looked into Myra's eyes and felt a sadness so strong it momentarily took my breath away.

"What's wrong with you?" she asked.

I didn't know if I could say it. "Honey..."

"What?"

"We found—Sheriff Paxton found Terry Landon."

For a brief instant, her face brightened, but then she realized what I meant. She didn't say anything, but I watched a look of horror come to her face, and then she, too, was unable to speak. I told her the whole story, how the body was wrapped in its yellow raincoat and nothing but bones remained. I didn't tell her how white those bones looked against the reddish-brown dirt, the green saw grass and weeds, the yellow raincoat.

"Well," Myra said, finally. "It's what I expected."

"But a *child*, Myra. A child like that."

"Who could have done such a thing?"

I shook my head.

"He was such a good boy," she said.

I went into the house and up to our room. Myra stayed downstairs for a while. I took a shower. I remember hearing her voice, but not fully understanding what she said. When I came out of the shower, I found myself pacing the room. Myra called to me, told me to come downstairs and eat something.

The whole night is a blur. I remember going downstairs for a while, but I couldn't stand to have Myra there, watching me, waiting for something. She wanted to talk about it, and I didn't want to be conscious of anything. I think I must have run up the stairs to get away from her.

Since then, it's been a nightmare, just trying to fall asleep. I drift off only briefly, then my stomach turns and I feel utterly sick—as if my life is curling up in my stomach and will soon swirl out of me. It is a cold, empty sort of feeling that makes it impossible for me to sit still.

This morning, Myra said she was going to buy me some sleeping pills. "You've got to start sleeping again."

"You sleep like a baby," I said. "So how do you know I'm not sleeping?"

"Because you're drinking too much, and you look awful," she said.

Now, she stands out in front of the house, watering her roses. I don't want to go near that garden or any garden. I sit on the front porch. School has closed for the day.

Myra comes up the walk, smiling at me. "You feeling a little better now?" she asks.

"I'm all right."

"You going to take a nap?"

"Yeah, I guess."

I go into the house and get a bottle of gin out of the cabinet by the sink. I take a small glass and pour it full. Myra comes in behind me. I know she is still watching me, to see how I am taking it, but I don't want to talk to her or anyone.

"Was Tory in your classes today?" she asks.

"You know she wasn't. Was she in yours?"

"I can't wait to give her back the family tree project. She did so well on it."

"I think I want some music," I say.

"What?"

"Put some music on. Something bright, and..." I don't finish the sentence. I realize how foolish it is to strive against how I am feeling with the brass sound of some youthful band.

Myra moves next to me and puts her hand on my shoulder. "Honey," she says.

I take a big gulp of the gin, nearly emptying the glass. It burns my throat and tastes like stainless steel. I put the glass down on the table and pour it full again.

"Don't," Myra says.

I look at her. Her eyes are moist and sad, and when she puts her head on my shoulder, I reach up and pat the hair over her ears. "It's nothing," I say. "I just want to be a bit numb for a while."

She doesn't answer.

"If I was serious about this," I say, holding the glass up again, "I'd drink whiskey."

"Has anyone told Mr. Landon yet?"

"I don't know," I say, emptying the glass again. "I'm sure Sheriff Paxton talked to him."

"The poor man."

I reach for the bottle again, but Myra puts her hand over mine. "It won't change anything, darling."

"What?"

"The gin."

"It'll change my state of mind," I say.

"Henry."

"He would still be alive," I say.

"Don't." She holds my hand.

We stay like that for a while, then I say, "He would still be alive, Myra."

"Yes, I know."

"If he hadn't gone to our little school."

"Don't, darling. Don't torture yourself."

I take another long pull of gin. "When I parked the bus it was empty—I'm almost sure of that. I *said* I was sure of that to the police, but how sure can you be of something you do routinely every day? I know I walked up and down the aisles of that bus, but I can't really remember looking behind every single seat or under each one. You go along doing what you always do. You're not conscious of each and every feature of your daily routine, right?"

"Of course not."

"Think about it. I checked to see the bus was empty and walked away from it thinking it was. He wasn't outside the bus, or anywhere around it I could see."

"So you can't be blamed," she says.

But what she does not know, cannot know—what I've never told her or anyone—is I was in a hurry. I was in such a hurry...

I look into Myra's eyes. She is perfectly sad, as much for me as the Landon child, and I know she loves me. That is where all of her beauty resides—in her pure and generous heart. How can I ever return her love so that it matches for her what it has always produced in me?

Feeling stronger, I say, "I distinctly remember picking him up though."

"Yes," she says.

"I know I picked him up, because it was raining, and he was wearing that yellow raincoat—the one we found him in."

Myra puts her hand up to my face now and touches me gently. "Let's try to forget about this, now."

"I will," I say, almost shaking my head as if to clear it. The gin has started to work behind my eyes.

"Let's have a normal day," Myra says.

"Okay."

There's a slight pause, while we look at each other. Then she lets her hands fall to her sides and steps back a little. "It's getting late in the day. Do you want something to eat?" she asks. She's always believed in me so.

I smile. "You're a lovely girl."

She says, "Tell me what you're thinking."

"I'm thinking I'd like something to eat, yes."

She turns and starts for the kitchen, then she stops and turns back to me. "I suppose the whole town will blame this on the Gypsy Man."

"Oh, certainly," I say.

She shakes her head, her voice stronger and striving to sound sensible, but her eyes are still moist. "Well, I declare," she says. "What next?" She goes on into the kitchen, starts rattling pots and pans in there. She will busy herself, and eventually she will not have to think about Terry Landon.

I pour another glass of the gin and drink it.

PENNY

All the way back to Crawford, Mr. Bone talks. He tells me everything he remembers about John, about his wife, and their lives together. The Wild Turkey is almost gone, but he is not sleepy now. It's like the news about John has shocked him into awareness. He talks fast. I do all the driving. For the entire one hundred twenty miles, he sits well away from me, leaning against the door talking so fast sometimes I can't understand him. As we're pulling into Lebanon Church, he says, "You want to get something to eat?"

"I want to get home," I say.

Tory says, "I'm hungry, Mommy."

"We got to get back," I say. "John may be coming."

"John and me used to fish together every day," he says.

"I know," I say.

"Did I tell you I let him play hooky with me at least twice a year?"

"You did?"

"All through school. I mean, I wanted him to take school seriously..."

"I'm hungry, Mommy."

"We'll eat," I say.

"But I didn't want him playing hooky on his own. So I figured if I just let him skip school with me once in a while, and maybe go fishing or hunting, perhaps the urge wouldn't strike him so much at other times." He opens the bottle and drinks the last of the Wild Turkey. I don't know how full the bottle was this morning, but it was more than half full when he first brung it out and set it on the seat, and now it's empty.

"I swear," I say.

He looks at me, still holding the bottle in front of his lips. "What?"

"You never will lick that, will you?"

He looks down, then puts the cap on the bottle and sets it down on the seat next to him. He says nothing, but I can see I've hurt him. He is such an accomplished liar, he can even convince himself most of the time. He never really tells a hateful or bad lie, because whenever he tells me or John he's going to quit, he really does mean it. Then when he lies to us about what he's been doing, it's to protect us from the knowledge that he slipped again. It's his way of doing us a favor and protecting our sensibilities. So it never seems malicious to him, and whenever we accuse him of any sort of lie that might be considered a bad or selfish lie, he pouts. He really feels wrongfully accused. Of course, all of his lies are bad and selfish. They are meant to conceal the fact that he is just a helpless drunk and worth nothing to nobody when he's drinking. The fact that he is so good at lying to himself don't excuse him none from the lying.

"Mommy," Tory says, and her voice is starting to sound like a whine.

"I said we'd eat, now hush," I say. She is in the backseat, laying down. I thought she'd sleep on the long drive, but she's been awake the whole time, listening to Mr. Bone.

At one point she says, "My daddy's a jail breaker, ain't he?"

I watch the road, but Mr. Bone actually laughs a little. "I guess he is," he says. "A regular bona fide jail buster."

In Lebanon Church we stop at a diner. I yank on the emergency brake, open the door, and get out. I see Sheriff Paxton's cruiser go by. He looks up and spots me, speeds the car up a bit, makes a U-turn at the end of the street, then comes back and pulls into the parking lot. He comes right up next to us and parks. When I get out of the car, he sort of waves to me.

Tory jumps out of the backseat. Mr. Bone is still leaning against the window on the other side. I don't know if he's going to get out of the car or not. It's almost dark again, and the moon has started to climb. The bright lights of the diner sort of weaken the moon's light, so it only seems to sparkle a bit just above the black trees.

Sheriff Paxton gets out of his car, walks around the front of it, and stands there with his arms folded. He don't approach me though. He's in my path, leaning against a Buick, just a few feet away, waiting for me. He knows I can't get to the diner unless I walk past him. I could walk around behind his car and get to the diner by going on the other side of him, but I don't. I take a few steps until I'm right next to him, then I say, "Sheriff."

"I was just on my way up to see you," he says.

"Oh?"

"You ain't carrying that pistol, are you?"

Tory comes up next to me and wraps her arms around my thigh. With my blue skirt on, this don't look so good, so I take her hands and move her back a bit. "Just a minute, honey," I say.

Mr. Bone finally finds the energy to get out of the car. He slams the door and then walks a bit unsteadily over to where I'm standing. "Let's go on in," he says.

I look at him.

"Although," he says. "I must confess, I'm not really that hungry no more." His head bobs back a little and he notices Sheriff Paxton. "Good evn'n Sherf," he says.

"Penny," Sheriff Paxton says. "I need to talk to you alone."

"Well," Mr. Bone says. "Suit yerself." He puts his chin down on his chest and tries to burp, then says, "Come on, li'l one," to Tory. He takes her hand.

"Help Mr. Bone up the steps," I say to Tory.

"I don' need no help," he says.

When he and Tory are inside the diner, Paxton looks at me with very sad eyes and in a very matter-of-fact voice, says, "Penny, I've got John."

My heart sinks.

"He's in the jail. I arrested him early this afternoon."

In spite of every ounce of strength I possess, I realize I am crying. He puts his arms around me, but I recoil from it.

"Don't," I say. "I don't want that."

"Did you know he escaped?"

I shake my head yes. "The warden wasn't going to report it."

He just looks at me.

"He told me if I could talk John into going back, he'd forget all about it."

Paxton crosses his arms and tilts his head a bit, studying me.

"All I had to do was talk him into going back." I'm getting control of it, but not enough that I don't need a tissue or something. I start back toward the car, but he stops me.

"Here," he says.

I take a handkerchief from him and wipe my eyes. I know mascara is running down my cheeks. I see it on the handkerchief. "I just had to talk him into going back."

Paxton shakes his head.

"Maybe," I say. "If you could . . ."

"I've got him now."

"But if you'd let him go . . . let me . . ."

"Penny . . . ," he says.

I give him back the handkerchief. "The warden said he'd forget all about the escape. And John's a hero, did you know that?"

"He ain't no hero," Paxton says.

"Yes, he is. I'll show you a copy of the article."

"Penny, he killed the little Landon boy."

I feel the breath go out of me. "What?" I step back. I only see his shadow in the light of the diner. I don't feel the air or smell the food. I can't hear nothing. For a second, I'm only light, myself, like a beam of light. Then, I understand what he said, and everything comes back—the loud, brute world and Sheriff Paxton with his gleaming badge and those words in his mouth.

"That's a lie," I say.

"Well, you may think so. But I believe it's true."

"Why?"

"John told me as much not more than an hour ago."

CLARE

I don't want to stay here no more he thinks he can just do anything he wants with me I hate his hands on me his sour whiskey breath in my ear his face twisted next to me I want to get out of here but I'm afraid he'll kill me

we all die he says *we all die*

don't hurt me I beg him don't hurt me no more

that hurts

you think that hurts we all die give me that come here you think I don't know what you're up to girl you think that take that off and just by god stand there until I tell you to move

dear lord if you will forgive me and let me *easy to die*

dear lord oh my god I am heartily sorry for I have offended thee and give us this day our holy bread hail mary full of grace

how's that one there tell me how's that that un's just gonna be a beauty when I finish it hold still

don't touch me his weight on me his breath

I'll do more than touch you come here no *come here I said goddamn it* hail mary full of grace the lord is with thee please our father who art in heaven *we all die*

sing that song I like to hear the one about franky and johnny
he says I can't sing it I said no please don't make me please
don't *sing it sing it* he says *make it loud make it real loud*

He says *I'm going out back and I'll be a sawing wood for that
there stove and I want to hear it then you understand I want it to
be loud enough that I can hear it or you and me will have another
lesson in how to make a tattoo* no please no *where you want it
this time*

no no no

it don't hurt

oh my god I am heartily sorry for having offended thee
and I detest all my sins because I dread the loss of heaven and
the pains of hell but most of all because I have offended thee
my god who art all good I can't stand his snarling in my ear

that don't hurt now shut up

no no no no

and deserving of all my love deserving of all my love

*we're going down the mountain a little further to get some
money* we get in his truck and drive for miles

and then he goes inside a small store at the gas station
alongside the road and when he comes out he's got money and
I say you rob those people and he says *I borrowed it* where'd you
get this truck I say and he says *picked it up in tennessee* and I say
this is stolen too ain't it and he says *it ain't none of your business*

hell he says *ain't everything we get in life stolen in some way*
no it ain't

*sure it is you stealing life every time you take a breath because
the world wants you dead ain't nothing in the world that don't
want you dead you just living in spite of all of it* I want to go
home I want to go home please no more I want to go home

so do I

no please he hands me a bottle *drink some more of this*
I can't

sure you can have another cigarette

don't touch me oh dear god please I can't stand his weight his breath

we all die we all die we all die

PENNY

When I first see John, it's like only his eyes and mine are in the room. Like the inside of me sees the inside of him. It stops me. Sheriff Paxton takes me right to him. He tells Tory to wait with him in the outer office of the jail. "Some things, a little girl her age ought not to see," he says.

"I want her to see her daddy," I say.

"Maybe in a little while. You go see him first. Talk to him about all this."

"He didn't do this thing," I say.

"Talk to him," Sheriff Paxton says. "Find out."

So he leads me back there, and John is sitting on the cot in the cell, just sort of looking into space until he sees me. Like I said, it stops me for a second. Paxton says, "I'll leave you two alone."

"Thank you," I say.

"You can't put your hands through the bars nor nothing."

"I won't."

"It's okay, if he wants to—he can hold your hand or something, if he wants."

"You're so kind," I say.

"Suit yourself. I ain't paid to be kind. I just want you to know I understand a thing or two."

I am still just looking at John. The expression on his face has not changed since I walked in. It is a look of wonder, like he's seeing something for the first time that he only imagined was possible. I don't think he has changed much since the last time I seen him. He looks the same to me, except maybe a little more wiry than I remember. The thing I always pictured in my mind about him was the way the hair by his temples sort of makes a perfect point, then sweeps back toward his sideburns, where it thins out and becomes very fine. I used to like to kiss him there.

"Penny," Paxton says.

"What?"

"I want you to talk to him about this."

"I know it."

"This is more serious than maybe you know."

"I know what you think he done."

He opens the door and goes out. I walk slowly toward John's cell. It ain't nobody else in the jail. There are six cells, three on either side, each one with a bare lightbulb behind a cage in the center of the ceiling. John's cell is the last one on the left side, back in the corner. When I get to it, he stands up and puts his hands on the bars.

I don't know what I should say. He smiles, and I think my heart might break. I feel my knees go weak.

"You know what?" he says.

"What?"

"This is the same cell they slapped me in back when I stole all those batteries."

I laugh, which startles me. Then I say, "John," and start crying. He reaches out and I take his hands and put them against my cheek. Just the smell of his skin, the fine black hair on his knuckles, is enough to bring everything back. "I've missed you," he says. "Oh, Penny, how I've missed you."

The whole world turned on us. For the past six years, we lost everything most people take for granted, and only fools never hope for. We was stolen from each other out of sheer accident, the luck of the draw. It wasn't nothing either one of us could help or avoid. And when he says those words to me, I welcome the ache in my heart and want once again the treasure of our loving. Nothing and no one will ever talk me into giving it up again. I know at once and finally that I will love this man, all the rest of my days. It no longer matters how, or from how far, or what barrier might be between us. So long as he is alive, and I am alive.

"John," I say. "I want you to tell me the truth."

I'm still holding the back of his hand against my cheek, but I look into his eyes. He waits, not saying nothing.

"Did you do this?"

"I didn't kill him," he says. "But I buried him there."

I let go of his hand. "How? Why?"

He puts his hands up on the bars again. "What difference does it make?" he says. "I don't want to talk about it now. I ain't seen you in six years and . . ."

"We have to talk about it."

"I want to see Tory. Did you bring her with you?"

"Tell me what happened."

"You just want to do what Paxton wants? Is that it?"

"I want to know for myself," I say, a little too loud.

He shakes his head.

"Do you know who killed him?"

"No. I just know everybody will think I did."

"Why?"

"I found him. It was right after Denise Walton. I hadn't even appeared in court yet, and . . ."

"Where'd you find him?"

"You remember when everybody was looking for him? You remember that?"

"Yes. Of course, I do."

"Well, everybody knew about Denise Walton then."

"So?"

435

"The sheriff looked at me on one of those nights—when I was helping to look—and he said, 'If it turns out you had anything to do with this at all, you're a goner, you know that?' And I said, 'I didn't,' and he said, 'I hope so,' like that. And when I found Terry..."

"Where'd you find him?"

"I was just sitting there with him in my lap. I was looking into his wide-open eyes." He lets his hands drop to his side. He is still very close to the bars, and I get close, too. "Go on," I say. "Tell me."

"It was near dark," he says. "You were working at the Goodyear store and Clare was feeding the baby. I was sad and feeling kind of temporary. They'd called off the search, and I had nothing to do but wait for court and what would happen to me. So I went down below the lookout to fish..." His eyes are glistening now, and I wish I could take him in my arms. "I just wanted to get away from all of it, be like I was before everything happened..."

"Before you—before the accident?"

"Before everything. My mother, my dad and the booze. I wanted to be a boy again, I guess, or at least to remember it."

"So, you went fishing..."

"And I caught something. I thought it was a big catfish, except the line didn't move a lot. But it was heavy, and it seemed to come with me when I reeled it. After a while, I just thought I was reeling in a big branch or something. The water was muddy, and I couldn't see what it was."

The idea of it makes me sick, but I don't say nothing. He looks at me, and I'm afraid he won't go on, so I tell him to finish it.

"I moved downstream with it on my line, letting the current bring it toward me, and down at the bottom of the lookout—where the stream bends, I pulled it up out of the water.

It was…" It's quiet for a moment. He reaches up and grabs one of the bars again, and I put my hand over his. "You know what it was."

I can't think of nothing to say at first.

"There it is," he says.

"Why didn't you just leave him there and call the sheriff?"

"I might've done that, but you know what this place was like back then. Folks talking about killing Negroes, and me already in trouble with the accident and all. Tory'd just been born, Penny. We hadn't been married but a few months. I was afraid it would be thrown my way. I'd get blamed for it. I was already in enough trouble."

I just watched him, shaking my head. It stops him. It's like he can see what I'm thinking.

"I know," he says. "I'm not that dumb."

"No, you ain't."

"Maybe I am. I just didn't think. It was almost automatic. I waited till dark, then carried him up to the only place I knew I could dig a hole deep enough to bury him."

"Under the white stone," I say.

"What?"

"Under the gravestone."

"I figured nobody'd ever dig there. And if it was a grave there, I could dig it deep enough."

"You never told me it was a gravestone."

He smiles a little. "I didn't want you worrying about a grave so close to the house."

"So then you made it a real grave."

He don't say nothing.

"Why didn't you tell me?"

He looks at me with them dark eyes. "I couldn't tell you, honey."

"Why?"

"What would you have done?"

"I don't know."

"His skull was crushed..." He starts to go on, but then he's almost crying. "It wasn't in the water long..."

"Don't," I say.

"I think his legs were broken, too. Or at least one of them was."

"The poor little boy," I say, remembering his bright black eyes and trusting face.

"He had a blue chord tied around him, and a couple of rocks tied to him to keep him on the bottom, but the current was too strong. He had so much mud on him, I think he was dragged a long way in the water before I..."

The door opens and Paxton says, "You ready for Miss Tory now? I can't seem to contain her."

"Sure," I say.

John seems to get taller. He strains to see, and Tory comes in, walking slowly, almost as if she is in a procession or something. She holds onto a plastic rose that Paxton must've give her, and she peeks into every cell as she comes down the center aisle. "Over here," I say.

She stands in front of the cell, her feet together, two hands holding the flower.

"John Bone," I say. "Meet Tory. Your daughter."

She gives me the rose and makes a little curtsy. "How do you do?"

"Look at you," John says, his voice seeming to weaken. "Hello, Miss Tory."

She steps up and touches the bars. "Can I come in?"

He kneels down so he is eye to eye with her. "You are just the most beautiful thing to me," he says.

She smiles, then looks at me. "Can I..." She starts to say something, but she turns back to John. "You're my father?"

"Yes," he says.

She reaches through the bars and touches his face. He puts his hand up and covers her hand with his.

"Darling," he says.

She studies his face for the longest time. I watch both of them, and I can see them thinking. He says, "You were just a little frog the last time I saw you."

"I'm big now," she says.

"Yes, you are."

"Are you going to come home?"

John closes his eyes and lowers his head. She withdraws her hand and stands back. "I'd like to come home," he says. "I wish I could come home."

I start to cry again, and he looks at me. "Ain't nothing for it, honey," he says. "Not a damn thing."

"There's one thing," I say.

"What?"

"There's the truth," I say. "You can always tell the truth."

"I'm in the same predicament I would've been back then. Who's gonna believe me?"

"I'll believe you, Daddy," Tory says.

MYRA

I can't get any more molasses because Clare's store is always closed now. I planned to bake a loaf of dark bread, but I guess I'll just make do without it. I don't bake often enough to use that much molasses, but from time to time I like to have it on hand. And you know, sometimes it's been sitting so long in the cupboard, I think it just gets up and walks away, like a cat after a nap.

Clare's gone off on another one of her benders, and Penny is too busy spending all her time at the jail and then taking care of Tory. So the store just seems to be permanently locked up.

I had to go all the way down to Lebanon Church to buy things for Thanksgiving dinner. I tried to get Penny to bring Tory over for the celebration, but she wouldn't hear of it. "I'll make my own dinner," she said. She's a proud woman, and I understand why she thinks she needs to be strong and independent. But she could surely use a little break from her steadfastness. We all could.

Henry is much better, now that he has decided to defend John. He spends all his time on that, and I've sort of taken over in the classroom. We've combined a few classes, and I'm using his lesson plans, but when I run into difficulty, he's always ready to stop what he's doing and help.

I know Penny is grateful to him. He even gave her a few dollars to buy Tory some Christmas presents. "Just tell her they're from Santa," he says.

I was surprised that Penny took the money, but she did. She said, "I'm much obliged," and folded it up and put it in her jeans. I feel so sorry for her. She is such a pretty girl, and she's headed for the same kind of life as her aunt Clare. I can see it.

Nobody knows where Clare is. She's been gone almost five weeks now. Ever since John was arrested. And wouldn't you know the man harboring an escaped convict and suspected murderer was none other than Morgan Tiller. I think he should go to jail, too. He was in jail for a while, right after Sheriff Paxton caught John. Found him at Morgan's place. The sheriff told Henry he drove up to Morgan's place, and just as he was about to knock on the door, he saw John going out the back, heading for the well carrying a bucket. He was wearing a sleeveless undershirt, and had shaving cream all over his face. The sheriff said he climbed down off the porch and walked around back of the house and just went right up to him. John drew the water, looking at the sheriff the whole time, then he said, "Can I at least finish shaving?"

"Go right ahead."

John smiled that winning smile of his, and before the day was over he and Morgan Tiller were in the Lebanon Church Jail.

THIS MORNING, Henry comes down early for his coffee.

"It's not ready yet," I say.

"I've got to go now," he says. "I'm meeting with John again."

"Have you decided..."

"It isn't my decision, Myra."

"I know."

He gets his cup and stands by the percolator. He is all nervous energy now, tapping his fingers, rattling the cup on the counter.

"A watched pot never boils," I say.

He doesn't answer me. I get myself a cup and saucer. "Come on," I say. "Sit over here while you wait."

He comes to the kitchen table and sits across from me. I swear now that he's gotten involved in this case he is younger looking. I think he's trimmer, and his hair has darkened a bit, though I know that can't be true.

"Do you think John's innocent?" I say.

"I can't talk about it. You know that."

"You can tell me what you think."

He shakes his head. "I think he's going to confess, that's what I think."

"Didn't he confess to Sheriff Paxton?"

"He said he buried the body there. He claims he didn't kill the boy."

The pot on the stove begins to percolate. The sound is almost soothing, and I smell the coffee beginning to brew. I look around my kitchen, at the lights, the cookbooks and jars, the angle of the early sun's light through the windows, and I am inexpressibly happy. "Maybe he's telling the truth," I say.

He looks askance at me. "Really?"

"I admit, it sounds fishy."

"He says he found the body, and was afraid people would blame him for it, since it was right after the Denise Walton thing."

"Makes sense."

"He's smarter than that, isn't he? Don't you think John's smarter than that?"

"Maybe it's *because* he's so smart that he buried the body up there on the Crawford place."

"What do you mean?"

"Well, he didn't just protect himself. He protected this whole mountain."

"What?" Henry says, incredulous. "You must be kidding."

"Well, he protected us," I say, and I realize that I am becoming aware of these things as I say them. "We benefited from people thinking it was the Gypsy Man, didn't we?"

"What do you mean?"

"Folks didn't blame the school, or race, or anything like that."

He doesn't answer me. After a while I go to the stove and turn off the fire under the percolator. I pour two cups of coffee and bring them back to the table. Henry lights a cigarette, sets an ashtray next to his coffee.

"I don't know how you can do that so early in the morning," I say.

He drinks some of the coffee. The smoke curls above his shoulders and twists toward the light.

"It was very smart of him to put that stone there," I say.

"He didn't put it there. It was always there."

"It was?"

"Whoever buried that money up there used the stone to mark where he left it. It was probably Wilbur himself."

"Really?"

"Sheriff Paxton said all of the bills were dated before 1917."

"So it was just dumb luck that the stone was there?" I say.

"Dumb luck."

I shake my head, slowly. I can't believe it. Then Henry says, "Dumb John Bone luck."

"I guess," I say.

"He accidentally kills Denise Walton just trying to throw a beer bottle out the window..."

"Even if that bottle hadn't been full it might have killed her," I say.

"Then..." He shrugs. "Can you believe it? What kind of luck is that?"

"Like you said. Dumb John Bone luck."

"You know, don't you, it will go easier on him if he simply confesses to the killing."

I place both hands around my coffee cup. I watch the steam rising out of it. "You don't have to talk about it," I say. "I know you're not supposed to."

"You just don't repeat anything I say."

"I won't."

"If he gets in front of a jury and denies it, and they find him guilty, he might go to jail for life. Hell, he might even get the death penalty."

I'm just listening. He is not looking at me. He's watching the smoke rise from his mouth and nose, then he looks at the cigarette, turns it in his fingers, and takes another puff off it.

"If he confesses to manslaughter," he goes on. "An accident. Well, I can get the prosecution to agree to another ten years on his sentence."

"But if he really didn't..."

"It will save his life, Myra," he says.

"Well, is that what he's going to do?"

"I think he is. I'm working on him."

"Does he know who really killed the Landon boy?"

He sets the cigarette down on the edge of the ashtray, rolls it around to touch the ashes off it, studying it as he does this. I wait, watching his face.

"It doesn't matter who really killed the Landon boy," he says, trying not to show impatience. "That's not the issue right now."

"I guess I'll never understand the law."

"The issue right now is to save John's life. Everything else is . . . well, it's ancillary, but it's not crucial. See what I mean?"

"I guess," I say. "I'd sure like to know how *he* did it though."

"What do you mean?"

"You said you picked him up that day. You said you saw him on the bus."

He shakes his head and douses the cigarette. "I've got to get going," he says.

"How did John get anywhere near him? You see what I mean?"

"Forget it," he says. "Just let it be."

"I don't know why you have to be impatient."

He gets up and stands in front of me. The cigarette he put out in the ashtray is still smoldering. I think he is going to say something awful to me, judging by the look on his face, but then he reaches out and touches me on the shoulder.

"It's not important," he says. "We're just trying to save John's life."

"I know you are," I say.

He takes my hand, pulls me gently to my feet, and wraps his arms around me. I let him hold me, and I caress the back of his neck and then just put my arms around him. We stay like that for a little while, and I know he is thinking again of how little time we have on this earth to love each other, how small an embrace really is in the face of time and movement and change. You can never hold a person long enough, it seems— you never really have enough of it, even when you have to just let go and go on with your day. He loosens his grip first, and I start to stand back, but then he grabs me again and whispers in my ear, "Myra, no matter what happens, I'm going to remember all my life how much I love you right now."

"I love you, too," I say, and I feel kind of sad. All of the eventual future weighs on me when I feel this way. All the lost time in the world.

He does let go now and stands back, smiling. "I should be going," he says.

I reach up and touch his chin with just the tips of my fingers. He takes my hand and squeezes it, kisses my fingers in a bunch, then lets go. "Maybe I can make it home for lunch," he says, turning for the door.

"I'll ring the bell at the school at 12:30, like always."

He goes out the door, not looking back.

I stay there by the table for a second, watching the way the cold windows turn hazy with the warmth from the stove and feel, once again, that I am the luckiest woman alive.

PENNY

I ain't sure I'm ever gonna be able to forgive Clare. She's been gone again, more than a month now. Thanksgiving come and went, and she ain't even called nor nothing. I know who she's with this time, and I can guess what she's up to, so I ain't worried about her. I'm just so frustrated and mad at her. It just seems like sometimes she don't care about me or Tory or the store, or nothing. And she don't know what's happened here. I want to tell her about John.

I guess, to be honest, I wish she was here so I could have a little help. That's crossed my mind more than a few times. Every weekday now, I take Tory to school, then I go down to Lebanon Church to see John. When school lets out I go get her. I bring her home and cook dinner, with John's daddy sitting right there in the kitchen pretending he don't want no more to do with whiskey. "I'm through with it," he says. And he looks at me like I should do something for him, like I should drop everything and launch a big parade and hang banners all over the house.

"That's nice," I say.

"I know you don't believe it. But it's true."

"I know you think it's true," I say.

After dinner, if I ain't going to the jail to see John, I go down and open the store for a few hours in the evening.

I get some help from Morgan, sometimes. He'll stay in the store for a while or watch Tory. I won't leave her alone with Mr. Bone because of the drinking. He's good with her, don't get me wrong. I'm worried about carelessness, not meanness. And I guess I don't want Tory to see him like that when she's by herself. It might upset her.

Morgan come by this morning. I'd just taken Tory to school and decided to open the store for a while. As I was opening the door, there he was. I was glad to see him, but it bothered me a little that I knew he was probably trying to find out the latest gossip; the whole town of Crawford was talking about me and John, and the Landon child, and I suppose they was letting Clare in for some of it, too.

So now, he sits in one of the folding chairs that we got for sale, and I'm sitting behind the counter. He's smoking his pipe, leaning back in the chair like he thinks it might rock if he just presses on the back of it enough. He's wearing the same blue coveralls and a red flannel shirt with long sleeves. He come in with a blue navy peacoat on, with the collar pulled up behind his head, and I said, "It ain't that cold."

"Wait 'til you're my age," he says.

"If I'm anything like Aunt Clare, I think I'm only gonna be hot. She complains in the freezing cold."

"She ain't my age."

He takes a puff on his pipe now, tamping it down with a little silver tool he carries around. I have just told him everything that John told me, and he seems to be thinking about it.

"That's everything John said," he says.

"That's it."

"Hard to believe."

"What?"

"That John would do such a thing."

"He was so . . . I can't find the word for it. But the Denise Walton thing changed him for a while."

He nods, working the pipe from one side of his mouth to the other.

"He was ruined. That's the word. The exact word."

"Well, John's still John," he says.

"But he was ruined."

"Maybe."

"I knew it when he made me swear on the Bible."

"That was strange all right, but you know? I think I can understand his thinking."

"I could, too. I wouldn't have swore on it if I didn't."

"Twenty years is a long time to young folks."

"He didn't want me to wait ten years, much less twenty."

He tamps the tobacco down in the pipe again, then relights it. Blue smoke curls and billows around him. It's almost the same color as the thin wisps of hair on his head.

"Hard to believe that was more than six years ago," I say.

"Well, if you was going to wait until his first parole hearing, that's probably only three or four years away, right?"

"I don't know."

I tell him about John saving the guard's life and the trip down to see him. I tell him how I felt when I thought John might get out early because of it. That seemed so long ago, too—that hope and belief.

"I'd like to talk to John," Morgan says.

"He goes to court this weekend so they can decide what sort of trial he's gonna have."

"Really?"

"That's what Mr. Gault explained to me. It's called an arraignment."

"Yeah, I know about those."

"That's when John has to decide what he's gonna do."

"You think you can get me in to talk to him?"

"Probably. Why? I ain't left out nothing."

"You may've forgot something."

I shake my head.

"You ever think," he says, gently tamping his pipe now with his finger. "Maybe it was the Gypsy Man that left the Landon boy in that river?"

"No, I never did."

"Think about it."

It is true that I ain't even thought of the Gypsy Man since I went down to Richard Bland. "Ain't it a bit different from what we know about him?"

"How so?"

"I never heard nothing about bodies in the river."

"Maybe that's how those who was taken disappeared."

"Don't seem likely."

"Why?"

"We'd a heard something, right?"

"I don't know now," he says. He puts the pipe in his shirt pocket and stares out the front door. A car comes to the front of the store, slows, then goes on. "It just seems strange. I found another sign the other day."

"You did?"

"Same thing. No fire nor nothing, but a pattern."

"Shaped like a man?"

He nods. "So I want to talk to John, if you'll help me get in there."

"You can go with me tonight if you want," I say.

He stands up, takes his peacoat off the back of the chair. "Fine and dandy," he says.

I watch him go out. I realize that I never went down to his place with Tory that Sunday. By then, I'd found out about John, and I just forgot everything for a while. I spent every day I could in the jail just talking to John, or sometimes, when there wasn't nothing to say, just looking at him. I watched him sleep for a half an hour once. I longed to lay down on the cot next to him and just hold him; just smell his hair and listen to him breathing, and drift off into long, peaceful dreams.

I hated the cold metal on them gray bars.

GAULT

Well," I say. "How you holding up?"

"I'm okay," John says. He sits upright at the table, proud as ever. "I been talking to Penny."

"I'm glad."

"She comes here a lot. Brings Tory, too."

"Your daddy been down here?"

He looks away. "Once."

I lay my briefcase flat on the table, open it up, and take out my legal pad and a pen. "I've made some notes about your situation here, John."

"I guess you have," he says, looking at the pages I lay in front of him. I clear my throat. "Of course we've talked about most of this."

He shrugs, looks at the pad.

"You mind if I smoke?" I say.

"Give me one," he says.

I light a cigarette, then hand the pack to him and he lights one. I set a big blue ashtray between us. "Now, let me explain what's going to happen tomorrow."

"I know about it. I been there."

"Well, I want to be sure. It's not exactly like what went on with Denise Walton."

"It ain't?"

"It's not," I say. He puffs on the cigarette, his arms folded in front of him on the table. From the way his fogged eyes stare at me, I don't think he's slept very well. "Last time, you sort of told everybody it was you from the start."

He nods.

"And so far, it's been our strategy not to make any statement to the police beyond what you've already said. So tomorrow the court's going to want one."

"I know."

"I think I made it plain what we're going to do, but I want to go over it."

"I should say I done it."

"Right—but see how I've got it written down here. You should say it just like..."

"Even though I didn't."

"If you want to go to trial and plead not guilty, I'll fight like the dickens for you, John. But you know what is likely to happen..."

He puts his hand up to stop me. "Yeah, I know."

"It is *very* likely, John."

His eyes sort of clear up when I say that—almost as if they get darker. "I ain't stupid," he says.

"I know you aren't," I say. "You were one of the best students in the school and I always..."

"What are the chances again?"

"I wish I could say fifty-fifty, but I can't. I don't think a jury will believe you—especially a jury from around here— one that knows you. We won't be able to mention it at trial, but everybody knows about Denise Walton. I don't think I can get a change in venue..."

There's a brief convulsion around the corner of his mouth, like he might break out into a smile, but I could be wrong. He takes a long drag on his cigarette, waiting for me to continue.

"In all likelihood, a jury would find you guilty, and then you could easily get life in prison."

"Or the death penalty."

"Or that, yes. That's possible, too. The only thing in your favor is this was a Negro child. A white jury might not give you the death penalty for that."

"Why can't I just tell the truth?"

"You can. I never said you couldn't. But I want you to be aware of the consequences."

He shakes his head, staring down at the burning tip of his cigarette. His hair is in his face, and he hasn't shaved today, so he really does look like he is right where he belongs. If Myra could see him like this, perhaps she wouldn't feel so concerned about his welfare. It seems that lately she's been rather more interested in John's case than she should be. She doesn't know him like I do.

"Look," I say to him. "I'm just trying to give you the best legal advice I can, under the circumstances here. If you want another attorney..."

"Penny says I should just tell the truth."

"You can have the court appoint a lawyer for you."

He sits himself back, extending his arms so that his hands still rest on the edge of the table. The cigarette dangles out of his mouth now. "I don't know."

I start putting my papers back in the briefcase. "Well, you let me know what you decide. But it'll have to be soon. I'm filing these papers with the court at the arraignment, unless you tell me not to."

"I think I want to tell the truth."

"John," I say. "It would be a mistake."

"I don't know. What Penny wants me to do feels right to me."

"Does she know what might happen? Did you tell her that?"

He snuffs the cigarette out in the ashtray as he talks. "I told her," he says.

"Did you remind her what happened when you told the truth about Denise Walton?"

He has no answer for that. I snuff out my own cigarette and rise from the table. I stand over it, locking the straps on my briefcase, waiting for him, but he doesn't say anything.

"We go to court in the morning," I say. "I hope you come to your senses by then."

"Can you keep me out of court tomorrow? So I have more time to think?"

In spite of myself, I find that I am smiling. I realize I do like this young man, and that in spite of everything, I hope he will be spared the worst that can happen to him. "John," I say. "If I could give you more time—if I could get that for you, I'd be a happy man, and that's the truth."

He waits there looking at me.

"Tomorrow, son. That's how much time you got."

"Okay," he says.

"In the meantime, think about a life sentence. Think about

being taken from this place and your wife and daughter until..."

He turns away, running his hand through his hair.

"I can guarantee you get no more than fifteen to twenty if you plead guilty," I say. "Maybe out on parole in ten years."

Sweat beads on his forehead. Under the lightbulb in the ceiling he looks pale and almost sinister.

"You got another cigarette?" he says.

"Sure," I say. "I'll leave you the pack."

CLARE

The sun cuts through the blinds and runs across the ceiling. When I open my eyes, I don't know at first where I am. Then I recognize the padded squares in the ceiling of the trailer. The light makes little curves and twists and dips in and out of the squares so it looks like a landscape. A valley full of farms. I can't feel nothing yet. My hair is in my face, but when I push it back I realize it ain't hair at all. It's part of a green blanket. I can't hear nothing except birds singing outside. I know it's morning. I ain't dead. I'm afraid to move. I listen hard, trying to figure out where P.J. is, if he's still here or maybe he's gone. Then my bones start to smolder and twist inside the muscle, and I remember pain. I'm laying with my legs folded under me, curled up like a child. My arms are sore and there's blood on the sheets. Everywhere he has tattooed me, it hurts. I've got a picture of a knife with blood dripping off it on my shoulder, a small heart on my arm. He tried to put a tattoo of a lightning bolt on the back of my left hand, but it bled too much. Now it looks black, and I can't move my fingers without stretching the skin. It feels like fire when I do, and the skin cracks again and bleeds. On my back, he says, is a picture of a

453

turtledove, and below it the words IN LOVE FOREVER. He held me in front of the glass and forced me to look at it, but I couldn't see nothing. I was crying too much. *Ain't that the most prettiest thing you ever seen*

I move my head slightly. Still no sound. I'm afraid he's right there in the bed next to me. The room smells of candle wax and urine and sour milk. I can't make out what it reminds me of. Like a burned barn maybe. And it's too warm. I'm sweating. Suddenly, I realize I am hearing my own heartbeat in my ear. Against the pillow it sounds like a tree smashing against a wall. I turn my head, very slowly. I don't want anything to sense that I have moved. The green blanket is bunched up too high next to me. I can't see if anyone is there. I listen for the sound of breathing, but all I hear is my own.

I try to hold my breath, but instantly my back seems to freeze and the sting of the tattoo sores is replaced by a spasm that takes my breath away. I feel tears running out of my eyes.

It is quiet. Even the birds seem to fall silent.

I have to go to the bathroom. I move as slowly as I can—I imitate a clock—turning myself so that I can see what is next to me. The pile of green blanket seems to move, and I don't know if it is because of me or not. *Oh please oh my god I am heartily sorry for having offended you*

No shadows move in the room. It is so cramped in here, even with the blinds down and the sun sliced into thin, weak rays, it is unbearably hot. I can't get air.

I smell him.

oh my god I am heartily sorry for having offended thee for thou art all good

hail mary full of grace

I move a little more, this time taking my leg and letting it slide toward the edge of the bed. I am on my side, with the top leg now very near the edge. I start moving the bottom leg, trying to get both legs off the bed, so I can swing them down to the floor and only have the top half of my body on the bed. Then with my knees on the floor, I can straighten up and I'll be out of the bed. I can do this without waking him. I can do this without waking him.

If he's there. I'm still not sure he's there. I'm afraid to move the blankets. This bed is so small, I tell myself. He must be gone. I'd know it if he was here.

But I smell him.

I get both legs in position now.

Then suddenly I hear him take a deep breath. I know he is there. Sleeping without sound. Like he's dead. It's the most frightening thing about him, now. That he don't seem to be living when he sleeps.

Now the tears ain't just from the early morning sleepiness. I realize I'm crying again. If he hears me I'm finished. I think he really will kill me this time. Last night, he started the tattoo on my hand. He poured whiskey down my throat—whiskey I didn't want and never want again. *my god I swear it I swear it*

Last night he said, *I gotta fuck penny just once. See how you compare. I'm gonna fuck her good and you can watch us*

Now, he turns slightly, and the green blanket falls down some. I see the hair by his ears.

The birds outside have gone. Something crosses in front of the sun and the valley of farms disappears for a moment. Then it comes back.

"Goddamn," he says, moving his lips and seeming to be chewing on something. "What time is it?"

I stay completely still. I don't say nothing. He is still laying with his head tilted slightly away from me. I can see his beefy hand now, the knuckles I hate, with black hair on them, tufts of black hair, like an ape's. I am constantly haunted by a vision of him as a little boy. I see him a child, with big, innocent eyes and no hair. Somebody holding him in their arms. It must be that somebody at sometime cradled this animal. How is that possible? I can't stop thinking about it, and when I do I fall so deeply into the dark I can't come back up. I want to die. There ain't no hope for the whole world. And I didn't see it in him. I cry when I think that I hoped he would come back, that I wanted him to come for me. Why couldn't I see it in him, if I can see that little boy all the time? It don't make sense. I hate it that it don't make sense.

He moves slightly. Then he turns over on his side—away from me. He raises his head up and hits it back down on the pillow. He moans.

The sound he makes goes right through me. All my bones vibrate with fear and hatred.

I got my knees on the floor now. I've slipped from under the covers. Just the top half of my body is on the bed now, and I'm looking at him. I feel my heart hammering against the mattress. The hand is resting on his hip now, and I see the blanket wrapped around him rising slightly every time he breathes.

The door is on his side. I have to walk around the end of the bed and go right by him to get out. I can't tell if he's really sleeping.

My head throbs, and I'm feeling the tattoos again. He bruised my upper arm last night when he threw me on the bed, and now it aches almost as bad as my head. I have to move now. I need to figure out if he is sleeping again.

I don't know what to do. If only he made some noise when he slept.

I move further away from him, put my hands on the edge of the bed now. I can stand up if I want, but I don't. I push off the edge of the bed and kneel there, looking at him. My head is spinning. I watch him spin by me in a panic, but then it all settles down. I think I might crawl around the foot of the bed and then try to run by him. I let myself down to the floor, breathing as quietly as I can. My heart is pounding so loud, he must be able to hear it. How long can it beat like that? I'm too old for my heart to beat like that. *oh my god I am heartily sorry for having offended thee*

I have to go to the bathroom. I'm afraid I will pee on myself and then he will want to punish me for it. He's punished me for peeing myself twice. I can't help it. He wants to have complete control over me.

what you got to do
I got to go to the bathroom
no which one you got though front or back
front
I'll tell you when you can go little lady

He makes me hold it, and when I can't any longer, he tells me I have to be disciplined. *I've got to housebreak you goddamn*

He laughs and laughs. He punishes me. *goddamn after you I'm opening a tattoo parlor*

hey school
don't
that's what I'm gonna call you from now on you're my ever loving school
hey school how 'bout another lesson
you better not scream like that again you hear me school
we all die

I realize now that I am not crying no more. I'm too frightened. I back up, on all fours, toward the foot of the bed.

"What the fuck time is it?" he asks. He moves. He is moving on the bed. He is turning over, looking for me.

I stand up. "I fell out of the bed," I say.

He looks at me, his eyes small and yellow. "What the fuck?"

He is not fully awake. I walk toward the door. Just as I get next to him he reaches out and grabs my leg.

"Where you going?"

"I have to go," I say.

"Front or back?"

457

"Back."

The grip of his hand on my leg tightens. He can get his whole hand wrapped around my shinbone. I think he can crush it if he wants.

"Maybe I'll let you go," he says. "Where's the keys to the cars?"

"Over there on the table," I say. "You can see them."

"What the fuck you all teary-eyed about? Didn't you sleep well?"

"Don't. Please don't."

"Don't what?"

"I've got to go."

"Was you telling me the truth last night?"

I can barely hold it any longer. I don't have no more tears, though. I have only hate and rage and fear. I don't know what he is talking about.

"Was you?"

"Please."

"I ain't letting go until you tell me."

"Tell you what?"

"Was that the truth last night? About the treasure."

Now, it comes back to me. I told him we lied to him about the treasure on the old Crawford place. I wanted him to believe we still had it, hidden at the house. "The sheriff didn't really take it," I said. "We got it." I acted like I didn't want to tell him. I made him force me to tell him.

"Yes," I say now. "I was telling the truth."

"How much was it?"

"Too much to count," I say. "We was going to count it all up one time, but we never got around to it. It would of taken us too long."

He lets go of me. "Well, I'll be."

I start for the door again, but he says, "When you get back we'll plan our day."

I stop. "What do you mean?"

"I told you I wanted to give Penny a try. We'll go on up there and maybe I'll get lucky and hit two jackpots." He laughs, whoops really loud. "Two jackpots. You hear that?" He sits up in the bed and rubs his hands through his hair while he laughs. "I'll be goddamned."

I just want to get him up there in the same house with that gun Penny has. That's all. I'll worry about what to do once I get him up there.

deliver us from evil oh lord
for thou art all good

PENNY

I let Morgan go in to talk to John alone. I wait in the lobby outside Sheriff Paxton's office. I'm wearing blue jeans, a red scarf around my neck, and a thick navy blue jacket. In my lap is a wool cap and a pair of leather gloves. I got on black boots, and my hair is pulled back in a ribbon at the back. I want to look good for John. Everybody in this office stares at me, so I hold my head up and pay no attention to them.

Sitting across from me, at a big mahogany desk, is a woman in a red-and-white-striped dress, typing very fast as she reads a letter attached to her typewriter.

Sheriff Paxton is on the phone in his office, and I've been told to "Hang on a minute."

I said, "I ain't here to see you," but he didn't hear me. He'd already picked up the phone and was talking into it. So he thinks I'm waiting here to see him.

"Miss Penny," the lady in the red-striped dress says.

I look at her.

"You here to see your husband?"

459

"Somebody already took Morgan Tiller back to see him," I say.

She nods, turns back away.

I say, "Is it okay if'n I sit here for a while?"

"No, it's fine. But you don't have to sit here. You can wait outside the visiting room if you'd rather."

I unzip my jacket and stretch my legs out. It's quiet for a long time. I can't think of nothing to say, but I feel bad just sitting here watching her work and listening to Sheriff Paxton on the phone.

THE DOOR OPENS next to Paxton's office, and a deputy escorts Morgan in. His old muddy boots creak as he walks. He wears blue coveralls, bulged and wrinkled at the knee, and they hang down off him as though they are two or three sizes too big. He's holding an old brown Stetson hat all scrunched up in his hands. He walks with a decided limp, and the top half of his body is slightly curved so that it looks as if it would cause him measurable pain to straighten up. He turns to the deputy and thanks him, then he moves toward me as though he's in a hurry. I sit forward a bit and look up at him.

"You done talking already? What happened?" I say.

"It ain't no Gypsy Man who done it," he whispers. "But I think I know who it was."

"You do?"

"You bet I do, by Christ."

He puts the hat on his head and then turns to the woman in the striped dress. "We got to talk to the sheriff," he says.

The sheriff, I can see, is still on the phone.

Morgan says, "Wait right here," to me, then before the woman behind the desk can stop him, he goes into Paxton's office and closes the door.

I get up and stand there watching the door. The woman says, "What's this all about?"

"I don't know," I say.

I don't know how much time passes, but then the door opens and both of them come out.

"This better be good," Paxton says.

Morgan don't say nothing, he's just waiting there with his hat in his hands again. Paxton turns to me and says, "What about you, little lady? Where you think you're going?"

"She's with me," Morgan says.

"No, she ain't."

"I got to pick Tory up, anyway," I say.

Paxton frowns and looks at his watch. "You got to pick her up this early in the day?"

"It's only half-a-day school," I say. "On account of Mr. Gault's got the arraignment this afternoon."

"Well, I expect this ought to work out right nicely," he says.

"What you mean?"

"Mr. Tiller here thinks he's solved the whole thing. Maybe we can gather all the evidence we need and cart it on down to the courthouse and see what the judge thinks of it." He is putting on black gloves as he talks, with a satisfied kind of smile on his face.

"You won't need no cart," Morgan says.

"Come on," Paxton says. "Let's see what you got."

They move to the door. Morgan pats me on the arm as he goes by and says, "See you at the court trial."

"It ain't no trial," Paxton says, not turning around. He swings the door open and waits for Morgan. When the old man goes by, Paxton looks at me and tips his hat. I follow them through the door.

Outside the wind sweeps everything clean, blowing leaves up high and twisting herds of them into broad circles and swirls. The sun moves like a cat behind enormous white clouds that seem to grow upwards and out across a sky that is the darkest and purest blue I ever seen. Only the wind is cold. I watch them get into the squad car and drive off. I am not thinking of anything. Not praying. I'm not praying on purpose. I'm just going to go through this day without my mind and heart if I can. Just this one day. I don't want to hope, and I don't know what to hope for.

I drive to Gault's house. Going up his front walk, I keep my collar up high, and the red scarf wrapped tight across my mouth. I got my hat down real low, so only my eyes feel the wind. The cold makes them water, and I feel cold tears on my face when I pick up Tory at the school. Mrs. Gault says, "She did very well today," and hands me a small white bag with homemade cookies in it. She looks at Tory. "You make sure you do your math problems tonight."

"I will."

"Thank you for these," I say.

"You're welcome, honey." She has a sad look on her face. I start to turn away, but she makes this movement towards me, raises her hand a bit as if she might touch my face. Then she says, "Good luck today, honey."

"Thank you," I say, surprised that real tears start to fill my eyes. I feel an ache in my throat and can't say no more.

"I'll be praying for you," Mrs. Gault says.

"Thank you kindly," I say.

"What's the matter, Mommy?" Tory says, when we're down at the end of the walk.

"It's this wind," I say. "It makes my eyes water."

WHEN WE GET to the house, I see Clare's Studebaker in the parking lot of the store. "You go on up to the house," I say to Tory. "I'll be right up."

462

Tory scrambles up the hill, staying on the grass. I walk to the store ready to say some hard things to my aunt Clare, but when I get to the door it's locked and I realize the store is closed. I turn and cross the road and start up the hill myself. I call to Tory, "Wait up. Wait for me." But she don't hear me or don't want to hear me. She steps up onto the porch and strides to the door, and I see it open for her. "Clare," I yell. "You, Clare." Tory disappears into the house, just as I'm crossing the yard and walking under the clothesline. "Goddamn it," I say. I don't want Tory to hear what I'm going to say to Clare, and I'm thinking of the problem as I approach the porch, when the door opens again and P.J. steps out.

"Well, look at you," he says.

"Where's Clare?" I say, still coming on. I walk up the steps and start to walk past him but he puts his hand out and sort of grabs my shoulder to stop me.

"Don't," I say.

He reaches up and pushes back my wool hat.

"Stop it." I back away.

"You shouldn't cover up such fine black hair," he says.

I move to go around him, but he steps in front of me.

"Clare," I holler.

"Why, you know, I'd describe your hair as—what's the word for it? I heard it on the TV just the other day." He thinks, looking up at the sky, his hand around his mouth. "What was that durn word? I know. Luxurious. How's that sound?"

I pull my hat back up over the top of my head.

"What do you think?" he says. He's smiling, and the broken tooth seems to sneer at me. I smell whiskey on him.

"You're drunk," I say.

"No, I ain't." His eyes are dark and small. "No, I ain't had nary a drop." He's wearing a red-and-black sort of plaid flannel jacket, Levi's, and dirty, black boots. On his head, tilted a little toward his brow, he wears a red-and-white knit hat. His hands are bare, and fat, with broken and gnarled knuckles. His round, dirty, indifferent face and the choirboy sound of his voice makes me shudder. "Nope," he says. "I'm sober enough to appreciate your blinding beauty..."

"Clare," I yell again. I can't understand what she is doing.

"Let me ask you a question," he says. Now, there's a glint in his eye—like he might break into laughter.

"Will you let me pass?"

"Did you ever buck a fuzzard behind a fox of bodder?"

"What?"

He laughs, a short kind of snort, without smiling. "Did you, huh?"

I move to go around him and he puts both hands on my shoulders and turns me so that I'm directly facing him. I can't believe how strong he is.

"What're you in such a all-fired hurry for?"

"Where's Clare?"

"She's in there." He jerks his head a little toward the house. "Why are you so antisocial? To your very own kin."

"You ain't no kin of mine," I say.

"Why, I'm your ever-loving uncle."

I was pulling slightly against his hands, not exactly struggling to get away from him, and when he says that I stop. He notices the shock on my face and now he's really laughing.

"Me and Clare got hitched," he says. "Ain't you happy for us?"

I don't know what to say. I'm afraid, and I have to get him to let go of me. He stands there, holding me in place, smiling that dirty smile. After a while, I say, "You and Clare is married?"

"Ain't we now?" he says. "So why don't you give your uncle P.J. a big kiss."

He leans toward me, and I struggle against it, but he kisses me. At first it's just on the cheek, but then he brings his slobbering mouth around to my lips and I turn away. "Don't."

"There," he says and pushes me away. It's like he's finished constructing something and he's done with it.

I can't help it. I reach up with a gloved hand and wipe my mouth. He watches me, not saying nothing. His expression is empty now and dead looking. Whatever light moved in his eyes seems to have clouded over—so now the white of each eye looks like the back of a cut worm.

I move around him, cautiously, trying to get to the door. I push it open, with him still standing there watching me. As I start to go in, he sort of pats me on the rear and moves me forward into the house, with him right behind me. "Why don't you set over there in the green chair and we'll just talk for a while," he says. He goes to the stove and adds wood to the fire in there, then he takes a poker and stokes it. Sparks fly in the dark cavern of the stove.

I move to the green chair, but I don't sit down. I can see back into Clare's room, just the end of her bed, and I see her feet sticking out of the covers there. She's laying on her back, and she must be sleeping. I want to make noise and wake her, but I'm afraid to call to her again. I don't want to upset him.

"Tory," I yell. "Tory?"

The feet don't move.

"Tory, honey."

He looks at me, then closes the door on the stove.

Tory comes out of her room, and I see she has let her hair down and put her coat away. She's wearing slippers with a little pink puff on the front of them. "I'm hungry, Mommy," she says.

I start for the kitchen, but P.J. says, "Set there," pointing at the chair. He turns to Tory. "What would you like, little one?"

She pays him no mind. I watch her walk to the kitchen and sit at the table. She takes a napkin from the top of the counter before she does this, and when she is seated, she places it in front of her like a place mat.

P.J. walks over and stands over her, patting her on the head. "Tell your uncle P.J. what you'd like," he says. His voice is soft, almost sweet. My heart is beating so fast I can feel it under my blouse. I'm standing in front of the green chair, waiting. I don't know what to do, but I know I don't want no trouble with Tory in the room. I think if I stay where I am, he won't hurt her.

She points to a bowl of apples and pears on the counter. "Can I have one a them apples?"

"Why you sure can."

He takes an apple out of the bowl. He starts opening cupboards and cabinets, and I say, "What are you looking for?"

"Little bitty plates—you know." He stops to consider. "What do they call them things?"

"A saucer."

"Yeah, that's it."

"That cupboard right yonder," I say, pointing to the one in the corner by the window.

He gets the saucer, then takes a penknife out of his pocket, opens it up, and slices the apple and places it on the saucer. He hums to himself as he does this, and Tory watches him, smiling.

"What song is that?" she says.

"Why, that's a Christmas carol," he says. "You recollect which one?"

"Nope," she says.

He whistles it, and Tory starts singing, "Silent night. Holy night. All is calm, all is bright..."

"That's it," he says. "Very good." He places the saucer in front of her, and she starts eating the slices.

"That taste good?" he says.

"Yum," she says. She studies the other slices while she eats, starts arranging them a little better on the plate.

He goes to the couch and sits down. I let myself down slowly in the chair. He looks at me, then he sits forward and takes off the flannel jacket. Underneath it he's wearing only a long-sleeved undershirt, with tan suspenders. When he sits back I see his white belly, with dark twisted curls of hair, and I look away.

"That stove puts out the heat," he says.

Still Clare doesn't move. I lean over to see further into the room, but I can't make nothing else out. She's under a pile of covers in there. P.J. leans forward, lets his arms dangle between his legs, his elbows on his knees. He stares into space, not looking at me or Tory.

"Me and Clare got home about a hour ago," he says, still staring off into space. It's like he's reciting something he memorized. "We just been a-setting here wondering where everybody was."

Tory says, "Can I have another one, Uncle P.J.?"

He sits back and rubs his belly. "Hell," he says. "I just did set down here."

"I'll make it," I say, starting to get up.

"Well, what do you think?" he says, putting his hands on his knees and struggling to his feet. "You think I'm a lazy bastard?" When he says the word bastard he puts his hand up with just his fingers over his mouth, gets this shocked expression on his face, and looks at Tory, then back to me and then at Tory again. "Goodness," he says. "I cursed."

"What's Clare doing?" I say.

He goes to the kitchen and gets another apple. I watch him slice it, waiting for him to answer. When he sets the saucer down in front of Tory, he looks at me. "This girl is a big eater."

Tory looks back over her head, smiling at him. Then she starts eating the apple slices. I watch her fine little white hands and feel like my heart might break. I know this is terrible. This is what I know. I am frozen in the chair, watching P.J. pet her again, his hands just barely touching the top of her head.

"What's Clare doing?" I say again and get up. I think to

467

walk to her room and just go in there, but then P.J. comes around the kitchen table and approaches me, very fast. I stop.

He don't say nothing. He sort of moves me back to the chair and places me in it. Then he says, "You don't want to wake her now. She's been drinking a bit."

"She has?"

"You know how it is."

"Yes, I do."

He stands over me. Outside the sun climbs out of the clouds momentarily and an eerie shadow crosses the room. Tory says, "Can I have some milk?"

"Why sure you can, honey," P.J. says. "But why don't you take your milk in your room, where you can read a nice book."

"No," I say, too loud.

Tory looks at me, her eyes suddenly wide open. "What's the matter, Mommy?"

"Sure, she can," he says. "You go right on in there, little one."

Tory is looking at me, waiting.

He turns and looks down at me, points at Tory, and whispers, "You set still and shut up or I'll cut that'n there just like a apple."

My heart turns cold. It's like it beats in little murmurs under ice water. "Nothing, sweetie," I say. " You can go in your room if you want."

P.J. whispers to me, "I mean it, missy. You stay right there till I come back."

I can't say nothing. I just stare at him, only half believing this is happening. He takes out the pocketknife, opens it, and runs his finger along the blade. He's smiling again, the gap in his teeth looking black. "You understand what I'll do," he says.

I nod.

"Well," he folds the knife back up. "It's enough that you know what I'll do."

Tory gets down off her chair and starts across the kitchen.

"You going to bring my milk?" she says.

"Yes, indeedy," P.J. says.

SHERIFF PAXTON

Morgan sits next to me, giving me directions. He tells me to drive all the way up to Crawford. He don't tell me that until we're on Route 13 for quite a spell, and I tell him I ain't going no further unless he reveals our destination.

"Crawford?" I say.

"It ain't that far."

"If this don't excite me none, you're gonna pay the county for this here gas," I say.

When we get there, at the intersection near the lookout, he says, "Turn left."

"Left," I say. "I thought we was going up to the old Crawford place. Up to Penny's house or Clare's store."

"No, we ain't. Go left."

"What for?"

"What we're looking for is right down yonder underneath them boards."

I pull the squad car down the hill toward the old gazebo. I park in the weeds just off the road, and Morgan opens the door and struggles out of the car. He has to walk carefully because of his legs—which wobble like they might give out any second. "It's down here," he says.

I follow him. It's not easy stepping down the hill under the lookout. It's covered with leaves and little bitty pine trees and sticker brush, so it's hard to move. The crunch of dead leaves and branches makes a racket that would scare every wild thing for miles and miles. For the first fifty feet or so we have small, gnarled dogwood trees to hold onto as we move, but then it opens up pretty quickly and there ain't nothing but the hill and the clutter of leaves and underbrush and baby pine trees. Under the white grass is black dirt from a thousand years of rotted leaves. I have to make sure of the placement of each foot as I move down the hill, and in front of me Morgan is almost down on his haunches, letting each foot move ever so slowly in front of him. He leans back toward me, afraid of what a tumble forward will do to his bones, not to mention the fact that at this time of year, the river below us is moving durn swiftly. It's full of brown water and I can see leaves and sticks floating by pretty fast.

"Take it easy, old man," I say. He almost falls and reaches out to grab my arm. "Don't try to go so fast."

"Jesus, look at the river," he says. "I always forget how close it is here."

"Folks can jump from the lookout up there and hit nothing but water if it wasn't for them there dogwoods," I say.

A gust of wind blows the leaves up around us. It looks like a little explosion—like a few hundred souls have escaped the earth and are wandering up into the air towards heaven. Just at the base of the tall six-by-six timbers that support the old lookout and gazebo, Morgan makes a sharp left and starts clambering up the hill, into the shadow under the boards.

"I wouldn't go up under there," I say.

He stops and looks at me.

"In this wind, ain't no telling if these old timbers'll hold this thing up." I point to the long deck and gazebo above us.

"It ain't going nowhere. It's been windier than this up here." He turns and keeps scrambling up the hill in the dark now. I can barely see him. The ground is far less overgrown under there, because the sun don't ever see it, except through a few cracks in the boards.

I follow him, out of breath now. Finally, I stop and wait. He goes all the way up to where the boards meet the earth, and he struggles with something up there. I'm afraid the old man is having a heart attack, but he turns and starts back down towards me.

"What's that you got?" I say.

He is sitting on his butt now, scrunching down the hill toward me. I watch him come. He's holding something in his lap. When he gets to me, I see it's two oddly shaped stones. They're covered with black dirt, and they're tied together with a blue rope that's started to rot pretty good.

"What the hell's that?" I say.

"I'll show you," Morgan says. "Just help me carry these up the hill and back to the car."

"What the hell is this all about?" I ask.

"Just let me show you."

"Show me what?"

"This here is what John said was tied to the body. These stones and this rope."

"How'd you know it was there?"

"John told me. He told me the whole story."

"I know about how he found the body, and all . . ."

"Right down yonder in the river," Morgan says.

I ain't buying any of this and I say so.

"I know this don't prove nothing," Morgan says. "But I want to show you something anyway."

"It better be good," I say. "I'm pissed off just a little bit because I got to climb back up that dad-burned hill."

He hands one of the stones to me. Then he starts to hand me the other.

"I ain't carrying that damned thing." I turn and start back up the hill. I hear him say, "They ain't that heavy."

He comes up the hill behind me. When I get to the car I can

barely get enough air to remain upright. My legs feel like they're full of some kind of porridge, and I'm actually sweating—even though the wind is damn near spiteful it's so ice cold. I stand by the car, gradually catching my breath and watch him coming up through the dogwoods, stopping every few feet. I feel sorry for him, so I let myself back down a ways and take the other stone away from him. "Can you at least carry the dad-burned rope?" I say. He nods, gasping for air. He clings to one tree after another, breathing so loud I can hear him when I get back up to the car. I watch his white hair blown high off his head by the wind, and suddenly I admire him. He's old and you'd think he'd be finished with the world a little bit. He ain't got no kin; not a soul on this earth gives a damn about him, really. He done all he was gonna do, and some of it was worth remembering. He fought in the war and pretty damn good if you believe all the stories. He got decorated, not only by his own country, but by the French, too. I seen the medals. And here he is, risking his life if you think about it just a little bit, just trying to help out a young friend. It's got to inspire you, I think. I don't feel sorry for him no more. I just admire him.

When he gets back to the car, I say, "Where we going now?"

"We could walk there," Morgan says, just barely able to get it out between breaths. "Or . . . you could drive."

"Let's drive," I say. "Put them stones in here." I open the trunk on the squad car and lay the stones in on the black rubber mat in there. I take the rope from Morgan and throw it in.

I drive up the hill now, toward Clare's place and the old Crawford farm. At the intersection though, Morgan says, "Turn right."

This time I don't say nothing. I'm curious now. I make a right onto Route 13 and we head east. When we get to the front of Mr. Gault's school, Morgan says, "Stop."

I pull over and he gets out of the car—a little sprightlier now. He goes around behind the car and waits for me.

I open the trunk, and Morgan reaches in and grabs the two stones. He carries them over to the rose garden at the end of Gault's long front yard and there, at the end of it where the stones disappear into the green bank, he places first one then the other stone in the odd-shaped cement. It's like putting teeth into a perfectly shaped gum, right where they belong.

"I'll be goddamned," I say.

"What do you make of that?" Morgan says.

"How'd you know they would fit there?" I say.

"I been trying to get Mrs. Gault to let me repair this here wall for a long time," he says. "When John told me what was wrapped around the body when he drug it out—I figured it was worth a look."

"And how'd you know where to find them?"

"John hid them there, the same day he found the body."

I said, "What the hell'd he do that for?"

He don't look me in the eye, and he talks like he's ashamed. "That's where he hid the body right after he found it. He was going to leave it there."

"Why didn't he?"

He shakes his head. "He said he couldn't stand the idea of the boy laying there like that." He looks at me. "And he was afraid somebody'd find him there. That, too."

Nobody says nothing for a spell. I go over and pick both stones out of the cement, and put them back in the trunk. "This still don't prove nothing," I say.

"Well," Morgan says. "It sure makes what John said a little more believable, don't you think?"

"I ain't sure what I think," I say. "But I'm sure gonna have a talk with Mr. Gault."

MYRA

Today I make a light breakfast of coffee, toast, and orange slices. Henry says very little, then retreats to the living room to read his newspaper. Earlier this morning I made our first fire of the season, and it crackles in the fireplace. I go in to add some wood and stoke it a bit, and while I'm doing that, Henry comes in and stands behind me.

"You know what I want?" he says.

"What dear?"

"I want to sit in here and relax in front of the fire for a few hours."

"Don't you have to be in court?"

"Not till one-thirty," he says. "I've got a few hours."

His voice sounds so sad, I get up and place myself in front of him. I try to look in his eyes. "Are you worried about today?" I ask him.

"No," he sighs. "Well—I guess. It doesn't seem fair."

"What doesn't seem fair?"

"A person makes one mistake. An accident really, and—well..."

"I know. And I feel so sorry for that young girl."

He looks at me as if he cannot fathom what I am talking about. Then his face lightens a bit and he says, "Oh. Yes."

"Are you quite all right, dear?" I say.

"I just want to sit and relax in front of the fire. I've missed doing that. It's one of my favorite things this time of year."

So he sits down to read his paper. I start to go back into the kitchen, but he stops me. "Sit in here with me a while, will you?"

"I've got to clean up the breakfast dishes," I say.

"No. Leave it. Sit in here with me. Just a while. I love that, too."

I sit across from him and watch the fire. He reads the paper, turning the pages in front of him. Every now and then he puts the paper down and looks at me. "It's a nice fire, hon," he says.

Later, I ask him if he wants a cup of tea and he smiles. "Just now," he says. "I'd like nothing better."

When I bring the tea to him, he isn't sitting by the fire anymore. He is in the dining room looking out the window.

"What are you doing?" I say.

And he says, "I heard a car door slam."

I set the tea on the end table next to where he was sitting and he says, "No, bring it in here."

He holds the curtain back. Down the hill, all the way down at the end of our walk, Sheriff Paxton has parked his car. I look over Henry's shoulder, and see that he's got another fellow with him—though they're too far away for me to make him out clearly.

"Henry," I say.

He says nothing. He's holding a part of the newspaper in one hand, and when I hand him the cup of tea, he places it on the sideboard next to the window.

"Come on," I say. "Let's go back in by the fire."

He reaches back, touches me gently on the hip, but he's still peering out the window.

"What's he getting out of his trunk?" he says.

"Who?"

"Paxton. Paxton. Who do you think?"

I just watch out the window with him. I know he is on edge, and I don't want to provoke him. I go to the other window in the dining room and pull the curtain all the way back.

"Is that Morgan Tiller?" Henry says.

"I can't tell."

"I think it is."

"What would he be doing down there with Sheriff Paxton?"

"I don't know."

I watch them doing something near my rose garden. One

475

of them sets something down in it, and then both of them stand there and look at it.

"What are they doing, Henry?" I say.

He doesn't answer me. I look at him and I see him leaning toward the window, steam beginning to form on the glass. Very slowly he folds the newspaper and sets it next to the cup of tea. He never takes his eyes from the window and what's going on down the hill. I've never seen him so intent—his eyes so frozen in place.

"Henry?" I say.

He seems to wince at what he sees, and when I turn to look, they are taking whatever they put in my garden back out of it. They carry it over to the trunk of Paxton's squad car and put it back in there.

"What is that?" I say.

Henry seems to sag, his head dropping, his hand letting go of the curtain. He turns to me and I see such sadness in his face it alarms me.

"What?" I say.

"It isn't fair," he says, and tears begin to fill his eyes.

I go to him, take him in my arms. "What? What is it?"

He doesn't say any more. He just holds me—breathing warm and steady on my cheek—and I remember once again how much I love and admire him. He has never been inaccessible to me, never closed himself off, and I know this sadness will come to light when he feels that he can talk about it. My husband feels the world's pain much more deeply than other folks, and it costs him. It's what makes him such a great teacher, and it's why he continues to do it. I whisper in his ear that I love him, and he looks into my eyes and smiles. "I love you, too. More than I ever thought possible." He steps back, folds the newspaper under his arm, picks up the cup of tea, and moves back into the living room to sit by the fire again.

As I close the curtain back over the window I see Sheriff Paxton's car pulling off. I wonder what in the world they were up to, and I have a pale, empty sort of nervous feeling in the pit of my stomach when it hits me that whatever they were doing, Henry knows about it, and it upset him.

I know he will tell me, but right now, I'm afraid to know. I don't want to know.

PENNY

It's quiet except for my heart. I can't hear nothing in the other room. The wind outside don't seem to move, and then I hear it push against the windowpanes and the wood seems to crack. P.J. is in Tory's room. He just carried her a big glass of milk, smiling at me as he went past. I wait for him to come out, to hear some sound from Tory. I can't sit here no longer. I get up and start toward the hallway. I don't want to make no noise, and I'm still listening. I hear Tory talking, and it calms me a little. I get to Clare's room, and push the door back. It makes a slight creaking sound and I stop, holding my breath. I'm in the hall outside Clare's room and right next to Tory's bedroom door. Tory says something I can't understand, and then P.J. says, "You never know," and he laughs.

In Clare's room, as I approach the bed I realize she will make noise if I disturb her sleep. I don't hear her breathing. I know she has been drinking. When she passes out she don't make a sound. I turn to leave, and then I see her left hand, dangling over the edge of the bed. Blood drips from it to the floor. My heart stops.

I can't move. I wait, almost counting in my mind.

There ain't no window in her room, so I can't see her face.

I lean down and slowly pull the covers down off her. She is naked. I see dark places on her stomach and high on her shoulder. The room smells like stale beer and whiskey.

I hear whistling.

"Silent night," Tory sings. "Holy night. All is calm."

"That ain't it," P.J. says, laughing. "You guessed wrong."

"It was, too," Tory says.

"Try again."

The whistling starts again.

Tory says, "You're such a good whistler."

He laughs again. I hate the deep, cornered scuffle of his laugh. Like a man in a fight thinking of something funny.

Next to Clare's bed, my shadow crosses over her face. She don't move. I am absolutely terrified that she will say something, but she lays completely still. I move over to her, lean close as I can. I take one of the sheets to cover her, and she turns to face me. In a deep, lost kind of desperate breath of air she says, "Get the gun." Then all the air seems to rush out of her.

I look in her eyes, then the words hit me. Of course. *I have the gun.* I didn't think of it until she said the word. *the gun I got the gun I can get the gun and we'll be safe*

She lays there staring at me. It don't hit me yet that she's dead. I can't get my mind around nothing like that, now. I cover her with the sheet, carefully, like I might later come in here and take her back from death. Then I go back out into the kitchen. It's suddenly quiet in the house. Now I'm not afraid. My heart is still racing, but fear ain't what it feels like no more.

P.J. is still in there. I can't hear him or Tory. There ain't no more laughter. Tory ain't saying nothing. It gets dark in the windows for a second, then the sun breaks through and lights the room like somebody turned on a switch. I don't know how many minutes have passed. Still no sound.

The gun is in my room, under the mattress. It's all I can think about. I don't hear Tory no more. It's quiet in there. I walk soundlessly to my room, pull the quilt back, lift the mattress, and feel the gun. It is cold. I take it in my hand, then move out into the hall again. I listen a moment at the door, then push it open.

P.J.'s sitting in a chair by the window, looking out. Tory is on the bed, lying facedown.

I point the gun at him. "What'd you do?"

He looks at me, his eyes blinking, lazily. "She got it wrong," he says. "That's all."

"Tory!" I say. "Tory!"

She don't move.

He gets up and comes toward me. "What you gonna do with that?" he says.

"I'm gonna use it, you son of a bitch."

"No you ain't."

"What'd you do to her?"

"Give me that." He steps toward me.

I point the gun at his crotch and pull the trigger.

The blast almost knocks me down. It's like the gun explodes and leaps back at me. P.J. sits down on the floor almost instantly as soon as the gun goes off. He goes down so fast, I hear his bones hit the floor. The sound of the gun is still ringing in my ears and he says something to me. There's something else, a high-pitched screech of a sound that I don't recognize at first. P.J.'s got his hands in his lap, and he looks down at himself, a look of embarrassment and humiliation on his face. He snorts a little, then laughs. "I'll be goddamned," he says.

I step toward him.

Then Tory moves on the bed, and I realize the high-pitched sound is her screaming. She pushes herself up onto her knees and then sits up, her hands covering her face.

"Tory," I say. I go to her and put my arms around her. I've still got the hot gun in my hand. It smells like fireworks and sulfur and death.

Tory screams in my ear, tries to get away from me.

"You scared the little one," P.J. says. "For god's damn sake."

She settles in my arms, still screaming. I feel her hot face on my cheek.

Something moves behind me, and I pull Tory off the bed, roughly and stand back against the door. P.J. is still sitting there, looking down at himself. Tory screams even louder. I'm not sure what she is saying, then I realize she is calling my name, "Penny, Penny, Penny."

"It's me," I say. I kneel down next to her. "Tory, calm down. It's me." She wraps her arms around my neck and squeezes me tight. I don't know if she's seen P.J. yet. I watch him begin to scoot himself back towards the wall. He pushes the chair out of the way, and it crashes over on its side next to the bed. Tory jumps, but I hold her. "Don't, honey," I say. "It's all right."

"What is it? Mommy, what is it?"

"It's okay now, hon. Hold onto me. It's okay."

"It's okay, honey," P.J. says. Then he laughs. "That's easy for you to say." He laughs again, only this time it stops. I hear something liquid in his throat.

He leans his back against the wall. Blood streaks the floor where he has dragged himself. I can't tell where the bullet hit him. I hear him breathing, when Tory stops screaming. She snuffles against me, her head on my shoulder, and I'm kneeling down next to her.

"Shit," P.J. says.

Now, I look at him. He's still holding onto himself, his hands in his lap. I see blood all over his stomach. The bullet hit him in the upper thigh, just at the hip. His head is down and I think he may have passed out, but then his head moves, back and forth, and I realize he is looking at himself, concentrating on it like a man fixing something intricate and very small. "Ah, shit," he says, and looks up at me.

Before I can think of a thing, I say, "I'm sorry."

He gives a smirk and shakes his head.

"I thought you had..." I can't say the words. I think I may start crying.

"I was whistling to her and then she said she was gonna be a old log, that's all," he says. "For Christ's sake. I thought she was asleep."

I don't say nothing.

"Hell. I was about to fall asleep myself."

"You shouldn'a hurt Clare like you done."

He looks up at the ceiling, then out the window at the cathedral clouds. "I ain't hurt no child," he says.

"You told me you'd cut her." I won't let him off the hook, and when I say this he looks at me scornfully.

"Well," he says, breathlessly. "I say a lot of things."

I watch him. In the bright light under the windows, the blood on the floor in front of him almost gleams.

"Truth is," he says. "Half the time, I never knowed what I'd do..." Then his head drops and something odd happens to his eyes. They ain't seeing me no more. It only takes a few minutes and I realize his eyes are fixed in place, like Clare's eyes, seeing nothing at all ever again.

SHERIFF PAXTON

Snow covers the mountain now, and I can't get up to Crawford even if I want to. Not today anyway. If I could I'd go up there just to see the funeral. I know those folks don't take it kindly when outsiders barge in on something like that, but I'd like to say something kind to Mrs. Gault. Ain't none of this her fault.

She was just blind to a lot of things, like most people are who think they've found happiness. Not that I think anything's wrong with that. I'm pretty happy myself, and I admit, I'm probably as blind as the next feller about certain things.

I knew a man once—a long time ago—who said he could tempt his own future, the fates, even death, just by standing in the face of a cold wind and demanding his own demise. When there wasn't no wind, he'd get on his motorcycle and ride it as fast as he could.

"That's what I do," he says to me. "Whenever I'm feeling mortal, I get on my motorcycle and ride up the mountain, up and down and around them curves, and let the wind blow in my face. Then I say out loud, 'Go ahead. Kill me.' And you know what? I'm as invincible as Superman when I do that."

He believed it. You could say it was how he kept the bank account of his happiness in the black, if you take my meaning.

Course, one night, in the rain, he rode that damn machine off the edge of Elizabeth Furnace ridge and fell so far and bounced so much, by the time they found him most of the bones in his body was powder.

I guess he was happy while he was living though. I had to give him that.

How do you explain something like Mr. Henry Gault? He done everything that was ever expected of him, at least until six years ago. He graduated high school, went to college, then the army, and fought in the most terrible god-awful war human beings ever had. Come back a hero and went to law school. Become a lawyer in the state of Virginia—a state that was forged and founded by the greatest lawyers in God's history—and then he comes home. He returns to the place that birthed and raised him and becomes a lawyer, a judge, and, most important, for my money, a teacher. He founds his own school and builds on the young people at the top of that mountain. Ain't nobody ever give a damn about them until he opened that school, you understand.

A century ago, most of those folks up there would a been coal miners.

And he tries to be what he preaches every day. That's the part that really makes you wonder. He strives every day to be just what he says a man ought to be. And he tells those children they ought to do the same. Ain't no chance another white man in these hills would a thought of bringing in a black student to the school. No way in hell. And he done it before the government *told* everybody they had to do it.

You take a man like that, in church every Sunday with his wife. He kids about being forced to go, and how he don't really credit too much of what he hears, but there he is. Every Sunday. And once or twice a year, he invites the Reverend Sloan up for supper, treats him to a fine meal and a quiet evening of sipping wine, or brandy, enjoying the good life, the small-town life.

And then, one day—one lousy minute out of the countless hundreds in a day—he makes the mistake that will by Christ destroy him, and everybody close to him, no matter what he does, really. Suppose he had just reported what happened? He'd a lost the school, for sure. The right to practice law in Virginia, most probably. Certainly he ain't going to be no judge in a state that finds him guilty of negligent homicide or manslaughter. What chance did he have? Could he take the chance that nobody'd care? It's a measure of the man that he assumed the death, in those mountains, of a small Negro child would a counted for so much. Because it counted for so much to him. That was as bad as *any* death to him. In some ways, maybe it was worse *because* Terry was a Negro, the only Negro in the school. What would folks make of that?

AT THE ARRAIGNMENT Gault was setting outside the courtroom, and I approached him thinking to tell him about the stones and see what he had to say. But he seen me coming, and he put some papers back in his briefcase and stood up to face me.

"I know what you want," he says.

"You do?"

He nodded. I never seen a face so beaten and desperate in my life—not even during the Great Depression. "It wasn't John," he says.

"John said he fished that boy out of the river," I said.

"That's right. He's telling the truth. I put the body there myself."

I folded my arms across my chest and looked him in the eye. I didn't know if I should arrest him right there or not. He had to go in the courtroom in a minute and represent John Bone. But at the time, before I had the wherewithal and inclination to think about it, I was pretty well pissed off.

"Did you tell John that?" I said.

"Not yet."

"I want you to write it all down for me."

"It was an accident," he says, and then his face changed. He was struggling not to cry. "I was in a hurry, trying to park the bus. I backed it up and Terry was..."

"So that's why the bones was crushed."

"I don't understand why he didn't just go right on into the school. Why he waited there for me. He never made a sound. I didn't see him until I had backed the bus all the way up." He wiped his face with a white handkerchief he took out of his breast pocket. "If you had seen that small, still bundle lying in the dark mud. I'll never get that yellow raincoat out of my mind. I thought I'd die from grief."

He told me how he thought of what would happen. How his school would probably be closed, and his work—his life work—ended. He couldn't think of no other thing. So he strapped the two stones to the body, drove it all the way up beyond Crawford—all the way over the other side of the mountain, to a place where he used to fish as a young man and where a promontory of land jutted out over the deepest part of the river, and he dropped the body down off that.

"It disappeared in the current," he says. "I didn't expect it would ever turn up."

"No, I guess you didn't."

Then he told me something I'm still turning over in my mind.

"I couldn't have everybody thinking the Crowlys or some other family had anything to do with Terry's disappearance." He sat back down on the bench, and I felt like I could sit next to him. I figured he wasn't going nowhere.

"Go on," I said.

"I just hated the idea of people blaming each other . . ."

I waited. People was scurrying around us, rushing to get in the courtroom, but I wanted him to finish. He looked up, started to move, but I grabbed his arm. "Finish it," I said.

He looked at me. "I'm ashamed of this, too."

"What?"

"I sort of encouraged the talk about the Gypsy Man. I left signs for Morgan to find whenever folks started talking again about what happened to Terry Landon."

I shook my head. "Well," I said. "If anything, you were thorough."

He stood up. "I'll tell John, and then we can get him out of here. I don't think there's going to be much to pay for what he done."

"He broke the law, too," I said. "And he is a fugitive."

"You going to take him back?"

"If I can. I'd like to be the one. I caught him."

He shrugged. "I suspect pity won't be on anybody's agenda, officially anyway."

"What do you mean?"

"Nothing," he says. Then he turned and went back into the courtroom.

That was the last time I seen him alive.

I DID TAKE John back to Richard Bland. The judge give him ninety additional days for not reporting a crime, and then tacked on three years for escaping from prison. He was just really lucky that the prosecutor didn't want to pursue charges of accessory after the fact, or aiding and abetting. But John never really done them things anyway. He didn't know who done it, he only knew he didn't want folks to think it was him. He wasn't no different than Gault, if you think about it. He seen what might happen to his own chances, and to protect himself and what good he might do for his family, he made a big mistake. One he will live with for the rest of his life.

And now, he's got more years tacked onto his sentence.

Penny Bone got a small reward for killing P.J. Middleton. Of course it was self-defense, plain and simple. She shot him in the hip, but the bullet must have bounced off the bone there and traveled down a ways, because it severed an artery. That's what the autopsy said. She saved her little girl's life. We was sitting in my office, shortly after the arraignment, and she was just finishing her statement. I asked her to sign it and date it. Then I told her, "Maybe your luck is changing."

She looked at me kind of funny. "What date is it?"

"December eighth."

Then while she's writing the date, she says, "What do you mean?"

"It was a kind of luck. It was luck I give you back that dad-burned pistol. And it was even better luck he didn't hurt Tory."

She wouldn't look at me, and I realized what she was thinking. "It wasn't no trade-off," I said.

486

"What?"

"You didn't choose between your aunt Clare and Tory. He already done what he was gonna do to Clare."

"Even if I had to choose..." she said.

"I know," I said.

"I just wish..."

"Clare made her own trouble," I said.

"In a way, she saved me," Penny said.

"Really?"

"I don't think I'd of remembered the gun."

"As much as you hounded me about that thing?"

"I was so afraid," she said.

I got up and put my hand on her shoulder. "I'm sorry about all of this. I wish I had caught that feller before he caused such things."

She picked up her coat and scarf and got ready to leave.

"You going to keep the store open?" I said.

She wasn't looking at me. Her head was down and she was tying the scarf under her chin. "I don't know what I'm gonna do about the store," she said.

"We'll all miss your aunt Clare," I said. "She was a hell of a woman."

Penny looked me in the eye and smiled. "Thank you," she said. Then she went on out the door.

SO HERE I AM, sitting in my office, watching snow pile up outside. The jail is empty, and there ain't nobody moving in Lebanon Church at all. Everything's white and silent. I lean back in my chair, watching out the window, and I'm thinking of getting one more cup of coffee, when danged if I don't notice a black-clad feller coming up the sidewalk on the other side. He's alone, slumped over in the white, driving snow. He don't move so good.

I sit forward so I can see him better. There ain't no sun, and the gray sky is whitened by snarls of snow.

I put my cup on the desk and walk over to the window. He's moving to the corner, and out of habit, he looks both ways—as if there might be silent, snow-laden traffic, immune to ice and slippery roads—then he crosses the street and heads right for the front door. Just as he looks up and sees me in the window, I realize it's old man Stooch. Goddamn. Wouldn't you know it. He's coming to see me and there ain't no place to hide.

I walk around the desk and go out into the lobby. Ain't nobody here but me, so I open the door for him.

His face is whiter than the snow, and the hair over his eyes is so thick it has collected enough ice to form little icicles over his eyes.

"Come on in and warm up," I say.

He struggles to step up over the threshold. I take his arm and help him move to a long bench on one side of the room. It's next to a radiator and very warm there. Steam rises from the old man's coat and off his hat. He sits down, looking at me with drawn eyes, a stretched mouth. He looks like a man who is falling upside down from a great height and he's trying to see what he's going to hit.

"You shouldn't be out in this weather," I say.

He removes a pair of thick black gloves, and then with bony fingers takes out a pad of paper and a pen. The ink in the pen is frozen, though, and he can't get it to write. I go into my secretary's desk and get another pen and offer it to him.

He shakes his head, finally closing his toothless mouth. He puts his own pen under his shirt, then up under his arm. There ain't enough fat there to warm up a penny and I tell him so.

"Just use this one," I say.

He sits there, trembling. The icicles over his eyes start to melt and water starts to look like tears running down his face. The mouth lolls open again. I have this sudden, deranged impulse to believe he is death, come for me. It makes me stand up and back away from him a bit.

"Damn, Stooch," I say. "What do you want?"

Finally he takes the pen out of his shirt and starts to write. I watch him, struggling with it and start praying he don't have a lot to tell me. But he don't want to tell me nothing. He wants to ask me a question. He hands me the note. It says, *on December 17 1959 henry Galt hang self up deth?*

"That's right," I say. "Henry Gault hanged himself."

He waits for more.

"He hung himself in that shed where he kept the school bus." I realize I'm talking like he is hard of hearing, and of course he does, too, because he puts his hand up and leans back a bit.

In a more normal voice, I say, "You remember when he bought that old school bus?"

He smiles.

"It took him a slap year to get it on the road, but it run like a top ever since." Now both of us are smiling. "You know, I bet he would a made a great mechanic, too. There just didn't seem to be nothing Henry Gault couldn't do."

Stooch writes on the pad, *Myra?*

"He left a note for her, telling her he loved her. Course, if you love a person, you don't bail out on them like that. That's what I say. I think it was a damn cowardly thing to do. A rotten thing to do, really. But he left her everything, of course."

He seemed like he wanted to smile.

"She was helpless with grief," I said. "You know that. She loved him a lot."

He nods his head. Then he takes the pad back and starts writing again. But it don't take long. He gives it back to me. *funral to-day? December 20 1959. please*

"Yes. Or at least it was supposed to be. Who knows, with all this snow."

He reaches for the pad again. *you have ride to funral today please?*

"Ain't no way up that mountain in this kind of snow," I say.

He looks down at his pad, shakes his head.

"Why you want to go all the way up there for his funeral?"

He bends over and starts writing.

"Why don't you just go on home and have a merry Christmas," I say.

It takes him a long time and I regret asking him why he wants to go to the funeral. I wait, thinking it ain't going to be fun trying to get him back to his room. Am I going to escort him to the door and just let him go back out in this? Or am I going to go with him, help him walk in it—it ain't but a few blocks up the street. Or am I going to have to dig out the squad car and drive him up there?

Then he hands me the pad.

galt was a good man who always help me. out. On june 21 1950 he got me settlement from govoerment that give me income every year til I die. I remebme him when he was alitle boy. he threw snowball at me and I laugh and he laugh. I liked him.

I put the pad back in his lap and say nothing. He's right, of course. Most times, Gault *was* a good man.

PENNY

No one goes into what we now call Tory's old room. It's all cleaned up and all, but I can't stand the sight of just the windows in there, letting light in. The house is half empty all the time because Clare is gone. I know I lived there so many days when she was off running with somebody, but it don't seem the same now. It's like the house lost rooms and space. Memories crowd my mind when I just want to hold Tory and listen to her voice, answer her questions.

And sometimes, late at night, I will miss her so much I'll start crying. I don't let Tory see me, but I do. I cry myself to sleep, missing her. She really was a kind of mom sometimes. And a good friend. That was what she was mostly. A good friend.

I go from day to day, living toward my plan. What I will do after Christmas. I don't think about Peach or P.J. or whatever his name was, at all. John told me all that he done, and when I seen what happened to Clare, I felt like what I did was, just maybe, a good thing. It was a mistake—I really don't think I'd a shot him if I didn't think he'd hurt Tory. It's hard to even think the words, but I thought he'd killed her. When I hold her against me now, I can hear her voice still, screaming in my ear, "Penny, Penny, Penny." She was so frightened she didn't even call me Mommy. It was somehow, deep down, a kind of elemental fear that come out of her, and she was just one person hollering in terror for another. It breaks my heart now to think of it.

Outside, the snow has settled all over the mountain, and it's already begun to melt off the roof and drip down outside the windows like a drizzling rain. The sun is so bright it hurts your eyes to be near a window, much less outside. But it is still pretty cold.

Three days ago, I walked down the hill in drifting snow, and a blowing wind and hitched a ride on Morgan Tiller's tractor up to the church for Gault's wake. Just about everybody was there, including the Crowlys. Mr. Henderson, who was my boss at the Goodyear store, and his wife was there. Reverend Sloan give a good talk—he listed all the good things Mr. Gault had done over the years. Mrs. Gault had no one to sit with, so I went over and put my hand on her arm, and she smiled at me. I sat down and she leaned against me. I felt so sorry for her—she never done nothing but treat me like a woman, like I was a human being and deserved to be paid attention to. She taught me math and geography and how to fix Tory's hair in a French braid. She never deserved this.

Maybe Mr. Gault didn't deserve what happened to him neither.

Or Clare.

I know John was innocent.

Mrs. Gault held her head high all through the ceremony, and when it was over, she pulled her boots on, put on a heavy white coat with a brown fur collar, and walked out to the grave site like a queen. They had cleared a pathway from the church to the graveyard, but by the time we tried to walk it, it was almost buried in snow again. The wind had drifted some across it, and she had to step over high, twisted heaps of snow. If she had cried, her tears would have frozen on her face.

When it was over, she got into a black car and it drove off, wheels spinning on the ice even with chains on the wheels, up toward her place. I waved, but I don't think she seen me.

I didn't take Tory with me to the wake. I left her with Mr. Bone. When I got back, I had to set at the table and tell them all about it. "Mrs. Gault was a lady," I said. "She behaved just like a royal kind of lady."

Mr. Bone was wearing a white shirt with the sleeves rolled up. He ain't had a drink since we buried Aunt Clare, but every now and then he looks at me and I know he is trying to find a way to have just one drink. One final, small drink. He don't say nothing about it, but I see him struggling with it, sweat beaded on his forehead, running down the side of his face.

Whenever Morgan comes to visit, he makes me tell him again how I shot Peach. He is proud of me, but it makes me uncomfortable. I feel like something solid has been stolen from my bones, and if I tell the story too much, or start to feel good about it, my whole skeleton will collapse. I really don't want to even think about it. In spite of what everybody says, I felt sorry for Peach when he looked down at himself, seen all the blood and where the hole was, and come to know he was gonna die; when he come to see this was his death. You just don't know until you look into a person's eyes who knows it's the end of the world. You just don't know.

I would of thought, for what he done to Clare, I'd feel differently about it. But I really don't. Not at all. I don't let on about it, but some nights, I can't sleep for remembering it.

One night, not long ago, when I tried to tell him what I was feeling, Morgan says, "You're a kind of hero, don't you see?"

"I don't feel like one."

"You ain't got nothing to fear from no Gypsy Man, I'll tell you that."

"If I ever did."

He nodded his head. "It was just molasses, in all them leaves. You know? He made all them signs just to get me going."

"I know."

"I feel like a damn tool or a machine. He just pushed a button and I was off and running."

I shrugged. We was sitting at the kitchen table drinking tea. He sipped a little brandy that he kept in a small bottle in his pocket. He didn't want to have it on the table because he was afraid it would tempt Mr. Bone.

"I used to hear Myra complaining about running out of molasses, but I never thought..." I didn't finish. He looked at me, his eyes kind of sad. I said, "Well, I didn't see it neither. He fooled me just like he did you."

"I'm older. I should be wiser."

I didn't know what to say to that. I finished my tea, and he didn't say no more until he was done. Then he said, "I'm going to miss you, Penny."

"Mr. Bone'll be here. I'll come for visits and all."

He looked in his cup. It was getting late, but he didn't say nothing about that. He studied the bottom of the cup for a spell, then he says, "You dreamed about him yet?"

"Who?"

"Peach."

"No."

"You will."

"I will?"

"Yes, you will. I know. I don't want it to bother you. I killed men in the war. They *all* come back to see me. Every last one of them."

I didn't want to think about it. I turned my head away, tried to imagine John and me sitting in a boat, floating lazily down a blue stream.

"Just be ready for it," he says. "And don't let it bother you."

"I won't."

"It ain't real. It just seems real."

When he got up to leave he put his arms around me. "In a way, I feel like you're my own daughter."

"Me, too," I said. Then we both laughed. "I mean..."

"I know what you mean."

"You're my friend, too. Don't forget that," I said.

"I won't."

When he left, struggling a little in the snow, I felt empty and kind of sad, not for him, but because I knew I'd miss him.

But I wasn't gonna swerve from my plan. I ain't gonna keep the store or the house. I am moving down the mountain to a place called Leonardtown—which ain't but five miles from Richard Bland. I'm gonna rent a place down there and put Tory in the public school.

And Mr. Henderson at the Goodyear store? He says there's another store just like it down there, on the highway that leads into the town, and he thinks he can get me a job there. "They do a lot of business," he says. "I'm sure I can get you fixed up."

If'n he can't, it don't matter. I got my trust fund from my daddy's insurance and I think I'll have more money when I sell the house and the store. Mr. Bone says he'll help me pay my rent until I find a job of some kind or until I get things worked out. The important thing about my plan is, I ain't waiting 'til I have a job to go down there. I'm packing our bags and we're going as soon as the snow melts and folks put away their plastic Santas and take down their Christmas trees and put away all the lights and decorations.

And once we're in Leonardtown? Two days a week, three days a week—whatever Mr. Buchanan will allow—me and Tory will go see John.

She will know her father, and he will know her. And John and me will love each other, and be with each other, and listen and talk and laugh and cry and just look in each other's eyes a wondering. Plain as day.

And we will live our lives that way, just as long as we have to.